Greig Beck grew up across the road from Bondi Beach in Sydney, Australia. His early days were spent surfing, sunbaking, and reading science fiction on the sand. He then went on to study computer science, immerse himself in the financial software industry, and later received an MBA. Today, Greig spends his days writing, but still finds time to surf at his beloved Bondi Beach. He lives in Sydney with his wife, son, and a golden retriever pup named Jessie.

If you would like to contact Greig, his email address is greig@greigbeck.com, and you can find him on social media and the web at www.greigbeck.com.

MIDNIGHTS

The Short Story Collection

GREIG BECK

momentum

Pan Macmillan acknowledges the Traditional Custodians of Country throughout Australia and their connections to lands, waters and communities. We pay our respect to Elders past and present and extend that respect to all Aboriginal and Torres Strait Islander peoples today. We honour more than sixty thousand years of storytelling, art and culture.

First published 2025 in Momentum by Pan Macmillan Australia Pty Ltd
1 Market Street, Sydney, New South Wales, Australia, 2000

 A catalogue record for this book is available from the National Library of Australia

Typeset in 12/16pt Sabon by Midland Typesetters, Australia

EPUB format: 9781761567384
Print on Demand format: 9781761566721
Cover image and design: Sabercore23-ArtStudio. Ind

Macmillan Digital Australia: www.macmillandigital.com.au
To report a typographical error, please visit www.panmacmillan.com.au/contact-us/

Visit www.panmacmillan.com.au to read more about all our books and to buy books online. You will also find features, author interviews and news of any author events.

Contents

Short stories are tiny feasts. Some have flavors created to terrorize you, some to make you laugh, or cry, or maybe just make you think. But most of all, they are to be a smorgasbord of treats to be consumed in enjoyable bites. So enjoy!

Introduction

I have an "Ideas Book" – most authors do. It contains story concepts, newspaper clippings, drawings, and notes. Also, on my computer there is a file containing dozens of half-finished stories that I began and then abandoned when I was distracted by other projects.

I promised myself I'd get back to them one day . . . and that day has come! So, a few months ago I hauled a few out – twelve, in fact. And I worked them to completion.

Some of the stories are pure horror, with many frightening scenes and gore, such as "Nine Miles Down", where the deepest borehole on Earth has just passed nine miles and hit a strange open space. And it's hellishly hot down there! Or "Germination", where a research team in Antarctica is examining fragments from a deep ice glacier and finds a tiny seed – a seed they thaw out and germinate – and it grows into something horrifyingly unexpected.

Most of my stories (and taste) tend to horror/sci-fi, but included in this collection are a few that are quirky, funny, or just revoltingly strange. Like "Jerry Lost a Toe" – imagine one morning finding one of your toes missing? And things only get worse from there.

Or perhaps a story about a fish that can talk, and grant wishes, in "A Fish Called Steve". Then dig into "The Monsters are Coming" – every full moon the monsters return; but not everything is what it seems.

The last short story I've included is the final part of the Valkeryn trilogy, called "Revenge of the Wolfen". Readers of the series have called for it for over a decade. But don't worry, I've given an overview of the previous two Valkeryn books so new readers can catch up. And maybe they'll be so intrigued they'll want to read the entire tale from the very beginning.

STORY 01

Human beings can't resist pushing boundaries. We always strive to go faster, higher, deeper, or longer. But sometimes there might be consequences for setting that new record.

The team at Sentinel Base in Washita County, Oklahoma, have just set the record for creating the deepest borehole on Earth, at nine miles down and counting.

But they've hit a strange open space, a void, where it's infernally hot. And it looks like something down there has been waiting eons to meet them.

NINE MILES DOWN

Sentinel Base, Washita County, Oklahoma

"Circle for a few minutes, will you, Benny?" Blake Jackson stared out through the helicopter's rear-cabin side window.

He, along with five other specialists and one security officer, were packed into the back of the Stonehart Mining chopper sent by the company to see what had happened to their research and engineering team.

The Sentinel Base's drill team of six had gone dark – no comms, no contact, no nothing, for a week now. Since the base's establishment, the communications in the area had always been a bit hit-and-miss and subject to inexplicable interference. But this was something new.

Blake looked down over the countryside; it was bleak, with scrubby tussock grasses, a few stunted bushes, and plenty of rocks breaking the surface. But the base hadn't been located here because of the natural beauty of the countryside. It was because Oklahoma was geologically old. In fact, much of the igneous and metamorphic rock found there had formed over 1.4 billion years ago, in the Precambrian era. And it was stable, and perfect for drilling.

The leader of the missing research team was the impressive physicist engineer, Oliver Carmichael. They had been out here sinking a hole, a deep hole, using new flexible drill tech, and had just reached nine miles down – deeper than anyone else on Earth. *Or below the Earth*, Blake mused.

They were now deeper than the Bertha Rogers gas well, which went down six miles, and even deeper than Russia's Kola borehole, which dropped to 7.6 miles, and had been the deepest on the planet until they paid the price of drilling in the wrong spot – the official report said the rock had become elastic and soft when they passed seven miles. They, like most deep drillers, had expected it to be hot – up to 600 degrees Fahrenheit – but not like molten putty. That was impossible to drill into. So they stopped work.

However, there were rumors that the Russians had encountered something else entirely down there, something not natural or expected – and the frightened engineers refused to work the site, and *that* was the real reason for the sudden forced closure.

Whatever the rationale behind the Kola closure, the bedrock in Washita County was solid and more stable. It would be hot, sure, but they could deal with that.

The dig team had one prime objective: find a way to extract the deep water that was locked up in the Earth's mantle. Current scientific projections were that up to one percent of the weight of the upper mantle rock was water, and that meant the amount of H_2O below the Earth would be about the same as double the amount of water in all our oceans combined.

Though it was expected to be a toxic, chemical mix when tapped, if it could be extracted and cleaned up, then this water could transform the dry areas of our planet forever.

The chopper circled and Blake saw the Sentinel site, a large building of only one story that had a work area, machine and tool room, and the drill site in the center. Radiating out from that were the sleeping quarters, washrooms, kitchen, and even a small recreation room complete with its own mini cinema, for the team of men and women who worked onsite full-time with fly-out breaks every three months.

The chopper came around again. *Odd*, Blake thought. No one came out to wave. The team had been isolated here for months, so the unexpected sound of a helicopter should have caught their attention and drawn them out.

"No sign of damage. Front door closed, and I assume still electronically locked." Sherrine Wong, their team physicist, turned to Blake. "Whatever happened, happened inside."

Blake spoke without turning. "Could have been gas. Deep mines can be contaminated by drilling into pockets of hydrogen sulfide, methane, and worst of all, carbon monoxide."

"White damp," Sherrine added.

"That's right." Blake nodded. "It's called the silent killer for a reason. It's a cocktail of deadly gases found deep. You find one of those and it's colorless, odorless, and tasteless, making it near impossible to detect. Kill everyone before they even knew what hit them."

"Well, let's hope they didn't find one of those," Sherrine replied. "And that *we* don't."

"We won't – we brought environmental detectors," Blake said.

Their pilot, Benny, circled the facility again. The door had a passcode touchpad. He had the number. He knew that many people might wonder why they would need to lock a door when they were hundreds of miles from anyone or anything, but the bottom line was that they were a mining company, and that was enough to attract some hardcore committed opposition sometimes. There were people out there who were prepared to travel halfway across a state to get inside a facility like this just to make mischief.

"Take her down, Benny." Blake turned from the small window to face his team. They all stared back, waiting on his word.

Blake Jackson was a mining engineer and one of the leading consultants in the field with over twenty-five years' experience. He had seen it all, and had been one of the advisors on the Sentinel deep well when it was in its planning stage.

He enjoyed the work. More than that of his previous life, when he had been a trainee Jesuit, intent on becoming a priest.

But he'd never finished. He began to lose his faith, sort of. He still prayed sometimes, but he just felt there was something missing. He had started to wonder if he would ever find proof for the faith he had. He had kept searching – was still searching, really – but so far without success.

So he went back to university to study something that had always interested him as a kid – geology – and now, here he was.

Blake continued to stare down at the hard-packed ground passing rapidly beneath them. The bedrock here might be geologically stable, with little movement, but he knew that whenever a dig got beyond the first 5000 feet, they would encounter problems and things they never expected. So he anticipated technical issues, but not human ones. He just hoped that whatever had happened at the Sentinel site was only a minor malfunction.

He looked over his shoulder and saw Karen Modell looking at him, and he nodded to her. He had drawn together an experienced team: Karen was a medical officer in her late thirties, and competent as all hell. She was attractive, and friendly toward him, but she had an aura around her that projected a "keep your distance" forcefield. He liked her, but everything was strictly professional, and they never really hung out.

Opposite Blake was Will Errington, electrical engineer, and the group's eager beaver. He was only three years out of university, but had topped his class, so Stonehart Mining had made him a solid offer to join them. He had a great sense of humor and was the most likeable guy in town.

Next to Karen was physicist Sherrine Wong. She was short, round-faced, and always laughing. But underneath the humor was a brain that worked like a human calculator. With a single glance she could calculate an object's velocity, mass, and density.

Sherrine was talking animatedly with David Lopis, one of the company's dozens of geologists. Blake was glad they'd managed to get him for the site visit, as David knew about the work Stonehart were doing here and had visited several times in the past. He was friendly with most of Oliver Carmichael's team, so had good personal insights into the team members, including their strengths and weaknesses.

Then there was Michael Ramirez, the master mechanic who had cut his teeth on offshore oil rig platforms and knew everything there was to know about drill technology. They were glad to have him on board as well.

Finally, there was big Arnold Taylor, their security officer. He was the eldest at fifty-something, and the only one who was armed. He already had a full head of gray hair, but it would be a mistake to underestimate him. In his younger days, he had been an amateur boxer, and apparently was an expert marksman. Arnold – Arnie – was an amiable and avuncular guy, but he was also old school tough, so Blake felt they were ready for anything.

It was a shame that Stonehart needed security these days, but Blake guessed that Stonehart had to deal with plenty of people and organizations that were philosophically opposed to what they were doing – and would use violence to get their way. Hence, now, everyone traveled with an Arnie.

Blake only expected to be here for a short while. If the drill team's silence was just a comms issue, then they could be out by the evening. If it was something that required some repair or replacement work, they were prepared to be here for several days. Anyone hurt or worse, then Karen would do what she could and they'd call in a medevac chopper.

Benny brought the craft down as gently as a kiss just on a hundred yards from the facility, and the group waited for the blades to slow to a soft whine.

Blake looked to each of his team. "Arnie and I will go in first – not that I'm expecting trouble. Will, then you'll go check out the generator to make sure we've got power."

"On it," Will said.

"Everyone, check your packs," Blake grabbed two gas masks. "Arnie." He tossed one to the big man.

He drew in a deep breath. *Here goes*, he thought, and pulled the rear-cabin door back.

The air outside was cool and dry, as it was still only mid-morning. Out here, the extremes were hot and dry or cool and dry. The temperature would get up to the mid-eighties easy today, and then drop down to about fifty overnight.

Blake and Arnold Taylor headed for the front door, while Will turned toward the small building off to the side that housed the generator. It, too, was passcode protected, but Will had the entry codes.

The rest of the team waited at the chopper, unloading their gear but making no move to come forward until their team leader instructed them to.

Blake pulled on his mask and Arnie did the same. He turned. "Ready or not . . ."

"Here we come," Arnie finished.

Blake typed in the code, and the door buzzed then clicked as the small red light over the keypad turned green.

"Least the door's got power." Blake went to push it.

"Excuse me, sir." Arnold Taylor stepped in front of him and eased the door open while keeping a hand on the butt of his gun. He went in first and Blake followed.

It was dark inside, but Arnie reached for a small flashlight and held it in his fist about shoulder height. The small but strong beam moved quickly from side to side as he searched for any immediate threats.

Blake held up a small gas detector and walked a few paces forward as he read the data on the small screen. After a moment he lowered his arm. "All clear." He dragged his mask off and tossed it onto a table. Arnie's landed on top of his.

"*Hello?* Dr. Carmichael?" He spoke loudly and clearly. "Oliver, it's Blake Jackson, from Stonehart."

In another second the lights blinked on one after the other.

"Thank you, Will," Arnie said.

They entered the outer administration area where there were desks, filing cabinets, and banks of computers that were just now flickering back to life, as well as several corridors leading to the rec room, kitchen, shower and washroom facilities, sleeping quarters, and a larger one with double steel doors at its end, which led to the bore shaft room.

Blake looked around slowly; nothing really seemed out of place. He stood with his hands on his hips. "So where is everyone?"

"I'll check the other rooms," Arnie said, and pushed through one of the side doors.

"Thanks, Arnie." Blake went to the nearest desk and quickly looked over the papers scattered there. He saw a Homer Simpson mug half-filled with cold coffee, and papers displaying seismic activity charts scattered about. The name signed on some of the papers was Tessa Green – he knew her – a geologist.

He crossed to more desks, and found seismic charts, ground water data, and machinery replacement logs. It all seemed to be standard, day-to-day work.

Blake straightened, mystified. "What the hell happened here?"

Though the other rooms hadn't been checked yet, he judged it safe enough for the team to enter. Besides, they could help with the search.

He lifted his hand-held radio and opened their channel. "Guys, come on in. Nobody seems to be home."

In seconds the front door buzzed, clicked and opened. Karen came in first, followed by Will, Sherrine, Michael, David, and finally, Benny.

Though there were dozens of rooms, plus hundreds of nooks and crannies they needed to check, there was one place that was a priority.

"This way." Blake turned and headed into the borehole room. It was the central room, round and heavily fortified. It was also the largest, and at its center was the drill pit, and the drill itself: diamond-tipped tungsten carbide, with a bullet-shaped drill head. For now it had been extracted, and a six-foot-wide metal cap had been lowered and locked over the top of the nine-mile-deep pit.

The room was hot – very hot – and the group immediately shrugged off their thick coats and stood in a half-ring around Blake, waiting for instructions.

He faced them. "As you know, the Sentinel Base drilling technology is all automated, and most of the work proceeds hands off." He turned about. "But this is the nerve center, and there should be several members of the team here monitoring the work and recording the data." Blake exhaled through his nose. "At this point, we have no idea why they walked off the job, or even where they walked off to."

"Or when," Karen added.

Blake nodded. "So, step one, we reestablish communications. Also step one, we spread out and investigate the site, and if we can't find any site members, I want to at least know what they were working on, or any clues as to their whereabouts."

Karen folded her arms. "They've been off comms for several days. If they were outside, that's enough time for them to hike for miles."

Blake nodded. "Yep, that's a possibility. But first up we check inside, and if we find no answers, then we can widen our search." He motioned to their chopper pilot. "Benny doesn't have enough fuel for both a broad search and to get us home. If need be, we'll call in additional eyes in the sky."

"How?" Sherrine Wong's brows came together. "We have no comms."

"Then we can use the chopper radio. Right Benny?" Blake raised his eyebrows to the pilot.

Benny grimaced. "I was going to tell you; I tried to log our status with home base but got nothing but static. Some sort of interference, maybe."

Blake groaned inwardly. "Doesn't matter, I'm confident we'll get these working," he replied, hoping that was true. He clapped his hands together once. "Okay," he continued. "Arnold, take Benny and search the crew's personal quarters. Will, get our comms back up, and Karen and I will search all the office spaces. Sherrine, Michael, David, check the drill room's machine and tool shops." He briefly checked his watch and then looked back at his team. "So far we have a lot of questions and zero answers. Back here in one hour. Let's go, people."

Blake headed for Oliver Carmichael's office, which was the largest in the facility. He pushed open the door and peered in. Nothing. He entered cautiously and in about three seconds took in the mug of half-drunk coffee, pen notes on a pad, and a half turned chair that made it look like the man had only just stepped out for a few moments – but then never came back.

On the desk were numerous papers, maps, and plans, and something else.

"Bingo." Blake exhaled with satisfaction.

There was the Sentinel drill site's daily logbook. He sat down at Carmichael's desk and opened it.

Blake flicked through numerous pages of dry factual prose, detailing progress, technical issues and how they managed them, stock inventory, and ordering.

Blake smiled; this was the standard humdrum of a manager's life. Even though they were in a remote station, hundreds of miles from anyone and anywhere, and were drilling a research borehole farther down than anyone had ever gone in history, there were the usual staff complaints about food, pay, not enough good movies, and rostering.

But then he turned the page to one of the more recent June entries and came to new notations that stopped him cold. Not just because the writing looked different – as if the author was writing more quickly, or more nervously – but because of what it said. And what it said made no sense.

Blake began to read, the voice of Oliver Carmichael now telling him a strange tale:

It came again. The voice. This time we all heard it. Ever since we hit 47,520 feet, nine miles, and broke through into the void, we've heard it.

The first time, Eva said it was just the sound of the deep earth movement, and that we should expect all sorts of odd noises coming from that level due to everything from the subcontinental lithospheric mantle shifting, to the plate tectonics sliding over the more elastic asthenosphere.

But then Alverez listened for a while and said what everyone was thinking: it sounded like a human voice speaking in something that was a little bit like Spanish, but he couldn't understand it.

I wondered, could the sound waves be passing through the denser material of the subsurface from somewhere else? A possibility, and that's what I wanted it to be. But I didn't really think it would be that.

Although we couldn't agree whether it was a human voice or not, everyone agreed that no one and nothing could be living down there.

Blake Jackson took his eyes off the page and sat back. "Holy shit."

But no matter which way he cut it, he couldn't get his head around what it could possibly have been. He rubbed his eyes, blinked a few times, and then read on.

The communications died on us. Weird. Because there doesn't seem to be anything wrong with the equipment. And then last night the power went out. Just for an hour, before coming back on. But it was the same as the comms system, where the equipment seemed to be fine, but began to work only sporadically.

Then the drill stopped. It was as if it had switched itself off. It didn't really matter as we weren't making any more progress due to the void we had entered, so we were going to call a halt anyway and await instructions from home base.

So we extracted the drill and sealed the borehole chamber. But the voice continues, around the clock now, the soft murmuring, the whispering, like someone is telling you a dark secret, and it has started to affect the team. Johnson says he can't sleep, and Eva looks terrible, as if she has been crying all the time.

I wish we could contact home base, as I feel so out of my depth with this, and the team desperately needs some time back home. Or at least away from here.

Our comms specialist, Beau, has been working on the problem, but until we can contact someone we are just going to have to sit tight and ride it out. The next supply ship is due in a week, so everyone will just have to cope until then. What other choice do we have?

Blake flipped the page to the next day's entry.

I tried to sleep but gave up. The voice never stops and I'm not sure if it's inside my head or coming from somewhere else.

I feel like I'm losing it. It's tearing at everyone's sanity. Maybe it's that we can't understand the words, and with the comms down, we can't even talk to anyone about them.

Sometimes I listen closely – the voice is deep, stentorian, and menacing. But there are more voices now, and the others seem to be calling out for help, wailing, whimpering, almost begging. They make me feel sick and helpless.

I can do nothing but watch my team lose their minds and grow weaker. We're fighting each other, and Eva suggested we pack some supplies and blankets and just walk out. But to where exactly? We're hundreds of miles from anywhere.

It took all of my persuasive powers to stop her. But unless something changes, the six days until the relief chopper arrives will be a mountain none of us will be able to climb.

And then . . .

The voices, the voices, make them stop. I recorded them, and

"Recordings?" Blake put the logbook down. "Okay, Oliver, where are they?"

Blake signed into the man's computer and found the logic tree for all his saved files. He scanned the list and found a folder titled: *Drill well anomalies*. He opened it and found a list of recordings. Some ran for up to ten hours.

He played the first one and leaned forward on his elbows.

There was silence, and something like scraping. He turned the volume up, and turned his head so his right ear was close to the speaker.

Just on the edge of nothing, he heard whispering – not a chant, or something that sounded like machinery, but soft speech – he was sure of it. Carmichael was right; it was like someone was telling you a dirty secret they didn't want anyone else to hear.

Blake shook his head. He knew what he was hearing was words, and something about it tweaked at his memory. And like Carmichael said, it did sound a little like Spanish, but Blake spoke some Spanish, and this wasn't anything he could understand.

A voice piped up behind him. "I have no idea what they're saying."

"*Jesus.*" Blake nearly leaped out of his chair.

He scowled up at the medical woman. "Come on, Karen, don't do that." He chuckled, but a little nervously. "You're here to treat people, not give them heart attacks."

"Oh, grow a pair. You're as strong as an ox, *and* nearly twice as smart." She laughed softly and pushed his head playfully. "I'm a bona fide healer."

He grinned back, but then his smile dropped. Hearing her use a common phrase had sparked a thought, and he spun in his chair to listen to the voice again.

"*Bona fide.*" Blake pointed at her, getting it now. "Ha. Yes, that's it . . ."

"That's it, what?" she asked.

He turned back. "Latin. It's Latin. But very old Latin."

"Are you sure?" Karen's brows came together. "Latin? Like in a Latin mass or something?"

"Yes, just like that," he said evenly. "I trained to be a Jesuit priest, remember? And I'm sure that's the classical language originally spoken in Latium, the lower Tiber area around Rome from the seventh century BC for around a thousand years. But this form is different. Older, I think. Much older."

When the hour was only about half up, the curious team members began to slowly wander in and stood around Carmichael's desk.

"Well, what is it saying?" David Lopis asked.

Blake turned his head again to listen intently. "It's words, but it doesn't really make sense." He frowned as he recognized that a single phrase was being repeated.

Karen folded her arms. "Well, take a stab at it, as it might make sense to one of us."

"I could be wrong on this." Blake drew in a breath and spoke without turning. "*Omnia coniungentur cum carne mea.*" He looked up. "I think that means: *All will be joined with my flesh.*"

"Okay, that's weird," Will said softly.

There was silence then among the team, and they shared worried glances.

Blake turned his head, still listening. "There's more."

"More like that?" David asked.

Blake nodded.

"Out with it. We're all grown-ups here." Karen exhaled.

"*Nulla lux Dei descendit hic.*" Blake sighed, his frown now deeply creasing his brow. "It means: *No light of God down here.*"

There were a few nervous chuckles, but then an ashen-faced Michael Ramirez began to shake his head. "Nope. That's it. Fuck it. Let's go home."

David nodded vigorously. "That's right. This is above our pay grade. I think—"

"No." Blake got to his feet. "Would everyone try and act like damn adults and not scared children. I already said I might be wrong on the translation." He stared the team down.

"Look, unfortunately I can't get onto any of the research sites to verify it, but I'm sure there must be some explanation for this. In the meantime, let's go back to the tasks I set. We still need our comms back up, right?"

There were a few mumbles of assent.

"Guys, we've still got work to do, before we even think about leaving." He counted off on his fingers. "Find the missing site crew, get our communication systems back up, gather the data, and see what state the full drill rig is in. Then and only then will we be taking off. Got it?"

"This is a mistake," Ramirez muttered.

"That's enough. Listen up." Blake stepped a few paces forward and the group drew in around him. "Continue with your work. It's only early afternoon, so we have plenty of time." He glanced at his watch. "Everyone gather back here in half an hour. Go."

The team scattered back to their allotted destinations on the base. All except big Arnold.

Blake turned to him. "What is it?"

"Question." The big man looked at him from under his brows. "Could our team have misinterpreted your translations?"

Blake sat down. "Misinterpreted? Maybe. Mistranslated? No."

Arnold grunted. "Then this might become a security issue for us, if the team gets spooked."

"I know." Blake nodded. "But what should I do? I mean, how does that voice even end up down there? Is it some sort of geological ventriloquism where the words are carrying from a long way away via sound waves? And why are they talking in some form of archaic Latin not used for 3000 years?"

"I don't know," Arnold replied. "But that's your job to find out."

"There's more recordings." Blake sighed. "But I think I've heard enough for now."

Arnie grunted again. "I'm glad it's in Latin. I don't think it would be, ah, healthy for everyone to be listening to more of that right now." The big man backed up a step and gave Blake a small salute. "I've got work to do." He turned and headed off down the corridor.

"Jesus Christ." Blake groaned as he tipped his head back to stare up at the ceiling. "We haven't even been here three hours, and we're already going crazy."

Blake sat back down at Carmichael's desk and picked up his logbook, flipped it open again, and read some more. And the more he read, the more it sounded like the man was unraveling.

Carmichael, wherever he was now, spoke to him from the pages again. The new entry was dated June 16.

Eva has gone. So has Alverez. One minute they were here, and then the next they just walked into another room and vanished. And now it feels like something is trying to close us off from the world. Beau can't get the communication systems to work at all, and now the power has gone off completely. We're working by lamplight.

No, working isn't the right word. It's more like we're huddled in the dark, just surviving. And waiting. Waiting to be saved, or waiting to go where Eva and Alverez went.

(illegible scrawl for a few lines)

They've all stopped asking me what we should do because they know I have no fucking idea. I've locked myself in the office and I listen to the mad whispering from the borehole. It is constant, insistent, and continues to worm its way into our consciousness.

I can't speak Latin, but I know what it says – it wants us, all of us.
And I know who it is now.
It's the devil.

Blake sighed and sat back, pinching the bridge of his nose and squeezing his eyes shut. Carmichael had obviously gone insane. And as far as Blake could tell, he seemed to be potentially capable of illogical action.

Did that mean he had done something to the others? Blake liked the guy, so he hoped not.

Blake checked his watch again – it was coming up to 8 pm. A while back he'd spoken to the team, and no one had found any clues to the whereabouts of the missing people or what had caused them to vanish.

They were sullen, scared, and tired. He told them it was too late to do any more that day, so to grab a bite, find a spare room, and bunk down for the night. Then they could wrap things up tomorrow early.

Blake rubbed his gritty eyes and sighed. He was getting hungry. They had brought some of their own food, but there was a small kitchen in the facility, and now with the power back on they could rustle up everything from ground beef and beans to a ham sandwich, and coffee to go.

He stood; there was one thing he wanted to check first. He headed to the borehole room, unlocked the door with the passcode, and slid back the heavy steel doors. As soon as he entered he saw that the drill cap covering the deep pit was open. It hadn't been before.

The six-foot-wide circular cap opened via two doors that split it down the middle, and they were both up like the petals of a flower. The room was hellishly hot and stank of some sort of malodorous scent he couldn't place.

"Who the fuck did that?" he asked the empty room, promising himself he'd question the team at the first opportunity.

He crossed to the pit and began to close the doors. As he did so, a warm gust blew up and out like the hot stinking breath of a carnivorous beast, and he clamped his mouth shut and held his breath so he didn't have to inhale it.

He locked the cap and straightened. If Will hadn't got the comms working, they'd bunk down for the night, and hopefully after a good night's sleep they might have some fresh ideas in the morning. At least they could try to find evidence to support the idea that the Sentinel team had simply walked off into the landscape. It was weird, but what else could have happened to them?

He left the drill room and felt the mental and physical fatigue hit him like a ton of bricks. He couldn't think straight anymore. He went to the kitchen, made a dry sandwich with a slice of ham and wolfed it down as he headed for one of the base's empty sleeping quarters.

Inside he managed to kick off his shoes and socks and then just fell facedown onto the bed and shut his eyes.

***

Blake tossed and turned. That damn murmuring. In his head now. It never stopped and was utterly unsettling.

He wasn't sure when he finally drifted off. But he was aware of the nightmares – he was trapped somewhere dark, and hot, and there were bubbling pools of fire on water, or perhaps it was lava. Fear-crazed people were all babbling at once, lots of people, and from somewhere there was the screaming and agonized wailing of the damned.

He remembered seeing Oliver Carmichael and his team: Tessa, Eva, Alverez, Theo, and Beau. They were begging him to help. But he couldn't.

Then he felt *the presence*. Something supremely evil. Blake had never felt so afraid of anything in his entire life as he was of this thing that was slouching toward him in the total darkness.

It was behind him, and he spun. Then it was somehow behind him again, and he felt something wet touch his shoulder.

"*Hey!*" Blake sat bolt upright, gasping.

It took him a few seconds to catch his breath. He quickly wiped his face, feeling tears there, and then looked at the small lighted clock on the bench beside the bed. It was only 4 am, and he lay back, hoping to snatch a little more sleep. He still felt exhausted.

But sleep wouldn't come, because now that he was awake he realized he could hear that damn, pervasive whispering. It was almost as if it was real, and not only in his head. But it couldn't be; it couldn't be.

Blake lay in the dark, staring up at the ceiling. He wanted it to be the sound of the air-conditioning unit, the drill working, or anything else. He'd heard the bore machinery many times before and it was a constant background mechanical grinding, the whine of the drill turning and the powerful turbines. It usually went on for days on end before some maintenance work or a preventive shutdown was undertaken.

But that sound was calming, more like being on an overnight train trip – the repetitive *clackety-clack* of the steel wheels on the iron rails that sent you right off to sleep.

He wished he was on a train now going somewhere, anywhere, just away from here. *Please, I'd take that sound any day over this*, he begged.

"Fuck it." He sat up, threw his legs over the side of the bed and rubbed both hands over his face, continuing up through his hair, raking it back hard.

He put his hands over his ears and grimaced. But it was no use as he could still hear the soft murmurings – it was inside his head, inside his belly, inside every part of him, and the facility.

Blake then angrily pulled on his shoes and headed for the

restroom. After relieving himself he changed his shirt and went to the kitchen to rustle himself up a coffee.

He took the steaming mug back to Carmichael's office and signed back onto the man's computer. He tried vainly to check the phone lines, the email, and the internet, but still nothing was working – no communications were coming in or going out. And the weird thing was, there didn't seem to be any reason for it. Will had told him that the technology seemed fine, but it was as if suddenly they had entered a technology blackout zone. Which Blake knew hadn't been the case the last time he had visited the Sentinel site.

Blake then waded through a pile of papers filled with technical data from the borehole, looking at the geological plasticity, the bedrock structures they were encountering, the deep water content, and the upper mantle movement.

But then he came to temperature gradients, and although he already knew that they were working in a zone that was around 600 degrees, which was standard, they had just drilled into an area where the temperature jumped to over 1000 degrees.

He flicked through the technical report's pages and saw that Carmichael had placed notifications against some of them. And names.

June 16, Eva Mendez and John Alverez.

June 19, Tessa Green and Theo Barnett.

June 23, Beau Almond.

And so it went until the entire Sentinel team was listed.

Blake frowned, reached for Carmichael's logbook and quickly flicked through the pages.

The last page of writing was dated June 19. Days after two of his team had gone missing, and the day Tessa and Theo vanished.

Carmichael spoke from the pages. *And now Theo has gone. I knew he would, because the voice told me it was coming for him. I know who it is now. What it is.*

Blake sighed and turned the page. But the rest of the logbook was blank.

Although, several pages appeared to have been torn out.

"What?" Blake's brows came together in a deep cleft. "Don't do this to me, Oliver." He flipped through all the final pages and then threw the logbook back onto the desk.

Why keep what happened a secret? he wondered.

Maybe it was a person who had made the people "disappear", and they were the one who had removed the pages.

Or maybe it was Carmichael himself. He would have known that information was invaluable, especially as they were dealing with so many anomalies, but he had not seemed to be in his right mind.

Another possibility occurred to him. Had there been a rogue operator among Carmichael's team? Someone who was here to do harm? Or came in to do harm? And what if they were still hanging around inside? That seemed unlikely; more likely was that they were hiding outside.

At least Blake's own team had Arnie, who was armed.

Wheels within wheels, he thought, and sagged in the chair. "Or I just don't fucking know what the hell is going on," he said, feeling a hundred years old.

This was not what he was good at. He was good at managing personnel and drilling and engineering sites. Not running some sort of detective's case out in the middle of Oklahoma.

He sat staring at nothing for several minutes until there came a soft knock on the doorframe. He turned to see Karen leaning there.

"Penny for your thoughts." She half-smiled and toasted him with a cup of the coffee he had just brewed.

He slowly spun the chair around to face her. "My thoughts are I have no idea what's going on here. Don't know why the drill has stopped working. Don't know why we've got no comms, don't know where all the Sentinel personnel have gone." He held his hands up. "I admit it, I'm outta my depth."

Karen shook her head, the edges of her mouth turning down. "Don't say that, anyone would be. This is off the charts weird. So hand it over, Blake. Let's go home, report it, and they can send people in to do a proper investigation."

"That's just it." He sighed. "We're the people they send in to do the proper investigation and fix this type of thing." He bobbed his head. "Carmichael knew something was going on and wrote about it in the site logbook. But then he – or someone else – tore out the last pages. I think he knew what was happening to them."

"I think they're outside," Karen announced. "Maybe they all got some sort of collective moon madness, or cabin fever isolation sickness, and just took off. For all we know they could all be camped out just a few miles over the hills."

"Nope, it seems like they vanished, one by one." Blake put his fingertips on the diary and slid it across to her. "Carmichael saw it happening, saw them vanishing."

"Blake, can I tell you something?" she asked.

"Of course. Always." His brows knitted.

Karen drew in a breath and shivered a little. "You know, I've been on lots of Stonehart sites around the world, and had to deal with everything from malaria, tick bite, crushing injuries, and even field amputations. And I've seen some pretty wild stuff. But for some reason, this place is giving me the creeps."

"The murmuring?" he asked. "You hear it too?"

"Yeah, that doesn't help." She shot him a crooked smile.

Blake sighed and stood up. "I'm ready for more caffeine," he said, and they returned to the kitchen where one by one, the rest of the team began to appear. They fixed cups of coffee and stood around the room, as if waiting for next instructions.

Blake looked at each of them. "Hey, where's Ramirez?'

Everyone looked around as if he might be hiding behind someone.

"Haven't seen him this morning," Will offered. "He's usually one of the first on deck."

"I'll check," Arnie said, and with coffee in hand headed off toward the sleeping quarters.

"Will we be taking off today?" Sherrine asked, and immediately turned to Benny. "We need to let Benny get his chopper home, right?"

Benny nodded. "Plenty of fuel for the return to the city, but not enough for much else."

Blake grunted. "Yeah, I guess. We batten down the hatches, and then we'll be on our way by midday." He stood. "But we leave this place with a lot of questions unanswered, and I don't like doing that."

"We weren't prepared or expecting to deal with the entire facility staff being AWOL," Karen offered. "For whatever reason."

Blake thought about that 'whatever reason'. "There is one thing we can be doing." He walked quickly back into Carmichael's office and grabbed the site logbook, opened it and held it up. "I want everyone to keep a lookout for some pages from this logbook that were torn out. They might contain clues as to what happened to everyone here."

"How will we know if they're the right—?" Sherrine began.

Blake put the book down. "Look at this handwriting. You see some pages with that handwriting, bring them to me. Got it?"

Arnie hurried back to them. "He's not there. Not in his room, the washrooms, or the rec room. I had a pretty thorough look."

"What?" Blake couldn't believe it.

Arnie's brows rose. "What do you want to do?"

Blake immediately saw the horrible similarity of this situation with Carmichael's vanishing team. "Okay, everyone. New priority task. Let's find Ramirez."

Blake had the entire team nearly tear the Sentinel site apart looking for the missing man. But there was no sign of him. It was as if Michael Ramirez had just vanished into thin air.

Not on my watch, Blake thought.

They had sealed off the drill room, and when he got to the door he found it still locked. But when he unlocked it and went in, the metal doors over the pit were open once again.

"Oh, for fuck's sake. What the hell?"

He went and peered into the monstrously deep hole, seeing nothing but a blackness so dark it was like looking into a porthole to outer space. The stinking heat made sweat break out on his brow.

Nine fucking miles down, he thought, and kicked the doors shut, making a sound like metal thunder that echoed down into the void. He couldn't wait to get out of this place.

As it was still only mid-morning, Blake organized search parties – two groups of two – to search in a single mile diameter around the base. Michael Ramirez had to be outside.

"Okay, Will, you're with me, we'll head west. Sherrine, David, you'll head east." He turned. "Karen, Benny, Arnie, you stay here just in case Ramirez, Carmichael or any of the drill team returns." For some reason, he wanted the armed Arnie to stay at the base and keep an eye on things so when they got back it'd be safe. From what, he had no idea.

He would have preferred to use the chopper, but as Benny only had enough fuel to get them home, and the helicopter's comms were out as well, he didn't want to risk it. He knew that suggesting they use the chopper for anything other than going home might spark a revolt.

"Take water bottles. Meet out front in ten." Blake nodded firmly and headed back to the sleeping quarters to grab his kit.

***

Karen, Arnie, and Benny stood at the front door and watched them go.

Arnie drew in a deep breath and let it out through his teeth. "Well, another coffee, anyone?"

"I'll take one," Karen said.

"Benny?" Arnie asked.

The pilot looked distracted. "Nah, think I'll just go back to my room and chill out. Got a stress headache."

Arnie brewed another pot of coffee and poured a cup for Karen. She took it, sipped, and her eyes widened. "*Kapow.*" She chuckled. "That's one strong brew." She sipped again and then looked around and shrugged. "Might as well look for those missing pages from the logbook."

"Sure, why not," Arnie said. "I'll check the sleeping quarters, rec room, and garbage room. We need to look in the trash cans, drawers, and anywhere they might have been hidden."

"Hey, you really think someone hid them because they can tell us what's going on here?" she asked.

"I don't know," Arnie replied. "But if there's even a chance they can tell us something, then . . ." He shrugged.

"Yeah, worth finding them." She smiled. "I'll check the offices, every nook and cranny, high and low." She put her mug down. "And no time like now."

"I'll try not to wake Benny." Arnie toasted her and headed off to the sleeping quarters, and Karen began to search the offices. She pulled open drawers and looked in every storage space she could find. Arnie's suggestion of checking the trash cans had her searching every one of them, and the trash room as well.

After a while she stood and frowned, rubbing her left temple. She felt the beginnings of a headache, and something else . . . She tilted her head, listening. Was it that damned sound again? She didn't believe for a New York minute it was chanting or voices, even though that's what Blake said it was. It had to be something else. She just had no idea what.

She returned to searching, but then there was a loud metallic double *clank* that brought her upright. She paused for a moment, listening hard.

"Arnie?" She walked to the corridor that led to the personnel quarters. "Arnold, was that you?"

Arnie appeared. "No, but I heard it too." He looked at her. "Came from the borehole drill room."

They headed toward the locked, steel blast doors.

"Where's Benny?" Karen asked.

Arnie shook his head. "He must be out cold if that sound didn't wake him."

She winced as she turned to him. "Hey, did you also hear that weird . . .?"

"You mean the voices again? Yeah, just before that clanging sound," Arnie replied.

Karen noticed he had his gun on his hip, and he led the way. They stopped briefly at the room Benny had slept in and peered in, but it was empty.

"So it did wake him," Karen said.

"Benny?" Arnie called, and then tilted his head to listen. He turned to Karen and shrugged. "Let's check out door number two." He used the electronic keypad to unlock the heavy steel drill room doors and slid one aside.

"*Eeew.*" Karen put a hand over her nose and mouth. "It smells like an open sewer."

"There." Arnie pointed. The lid over the borehole was open. "That's the source of our noise."

"Did Benny do that?" Karen asked.

"Unlikely; he doesn't have the code for the outer doors." Arnie walked forward, and then stopped. "Hold up." He looked down. "Ah, shit, it's blood." He stepped back.

Karen came forward and crouched. She looked closely at the substance on the floor, and then followed the spatter pattern.

It led toward the borehole.

"Oh no, no, no . . ." She quickly fumbled in a pocket, and then exhaled. "Damn, no rubber gloves. I always . . ." She pulled out a crumpled tissue. "This will have to do."

The medical specialist went to the edge of the hole on all fours. She grimaced as she approached the pit. "It really stinks in there." She tried only breathing through her mouth but the greasy vapors lifting from down in the darkness coated her tongue.

Karen used the tissue to wipe something up from the metal edge of the hole. She backed up and stood, then opened the tissue and held it out to Arnie.

"That's a clump of scalp, with hair attached." She looked up.

"And it's Benny's hair color." Arnie's eyes narrowed. "Plus it's fresh; minutes old. It's still leaking blood."

They both turned to the borehole.

"Did he fall? Somehow knocked himself out, and then slipped in?" Karen slowly lowered her arm.

"What was he doing in here, and how the hell did he even get in here? And then, why did he open the cap doors?" Arnie stepped up to the edge of the hole, put a boot on the rim and leaned forward. He peered into the deepest hole on, or in, Earth. "Nine miles down," he whispered, and held a hand up in front of his face to ward off the heat coming up.

"If he did fall in, there'll be no recovery," Karen said. "Um, what if . . .?" She shook her head. "Nah, doesn't matter."

"I know what you're thinking. Ramirez, right? Did he fall in as well?" Arnie turned to her. "And Carmichael's team. Is that where they all went?"

She frowned and shook her head. "All of them? Impossible."

Arnie drew in a deep breath. "Notice something else?" He attempted a grin. "That damn voice, it's stopped."

"Don't – just don't," Karen warned. "Don't link the two things. I couldn't deal with that."

"Well, I don't think they're going to find Ramirez out there." Arnie picked up one of the heavy steel half-moon doors and closed it over the pit. He did the same with the second. Immediately the humid, foul-smelling heat lessened.

"The others will be back soon," Karen said softly. "Let's get out of here. This place makes me feel sick."

* * *

After two hours of searching and not finding a single clue as to the whereabouts of Ramirez – or any of the others – Blake was ready to head back. He and Will had performed a double coil out from the base in their search to try to pick up any trace of the missing people, but they'd found nothing – no tracks, and no proof anyone had even left the Sentinel site. In fact, from what Arnie had told him, all Ramirez's clothing was still in his room.

By early afternoon they were back, only to be greeted by the unexpected sight of both Arnie and Karen out front, waving to them.

"What now?" Blake sighed and waved back.

But Karen kept frantically waving to him, waving him in.

"Okay, I get it." He sped up a little and Will did the same.

Arnie and Karen walked quickly to meet them.

Blake began to shake his head. "Sorry, no sign of—"

"Forget it." Karen cut across him. "We expected that."

Blake pulled up. "You found him?"

"No, but we lost Benny. As well."

"What? How?" He half-turned when he heard Sherrine and David hurrying over to them. They all crowded around and Karen quickly filled them in.

"Do you think he wandered off?" asked Will.

"He can't have. We would have seen him," Sherrine protested. "No one went past us."

"Unless he didn't want to be seen," Blake countered.

"It was the borehole. We think he fell into the borehole." Karen exhaled. "It was an accident, we think."

Blake's mouth dropped open, and he looked in disbelief from Karen to Arnie. "But the borehole room is locked."

Arnie looked grim. "We found evidence, blood, on the rim of the borehole pit. It was fresh."

"The cap doors—" Blake begun.

"Open," Arnie finished.

"Fuck this," Blake seethed. "Show me."

He headed in first followed by Karen, Arnie, and the rest of the group.

He got to the large steel doors to the borehole room, entered the code and slid one back, and he immediately felt the humid heat hit him like a wave of foul warm liquid. Blake stopped as the others fanned out on either side of him. The cap doors over the borehole were wide open.

"Well, this is how you fall into the damn drill pit." He turned to Arnie, who stared, his eyes wide.

"I shut it; I swear," he declared.

"He did – I saw him do it," Karen said, and then in a small voice: "I don't like this."

Blake felt his head swim. "What the hell is going on?"

He heard a babble of confusion and fear among the group. He cursed again under his breath and shut his eyes for a moment. *Hold it together, buddy, you're the guy in charge, the one who's supposed to keep his head while everyone else is losing theirs.*

Blake straightened, steadying himself. "Okay, tell me what you found."

Arnie and Karen pointed out the small smudge of blood and then recounted how they hadn't been able to find Benny anywhere, and when they entered the borehole room, the cap doors were open, and there was blood and hair on the floor and edge of the hole.

Karen had her arms folded tight across her chest as if she was cold instead of standing in a room that was close to ninety degrees.

"I guess it doesn't prove he fell in." She threw her hands up. "But he must have."

"You searched everywhere?" Blake asked.

The pair nodded.

"Then I guess we assume he fell in," Blake said.

"Question?" Will had a hand up.

"Go," Blake replied.

"If Benny is gone now, um, can anyone else fly a chopper?" he asked with a smile that was more of a grimace.

There was silence for a moment as the group digested this obvious problem.

Blake then realized the stark reality of their situation – suddenly, they were trapped. And there were still no comms.

"I guess not," Blake said. "So we just make the best of things until someone misses us. Which I'm guessing will be any day now."

"Like somebody missed Carmichael and his team, and by the time they, *we*, got here, they were all gone." David's eyes were angry.

"Shut that shit down," Blake ordered.

The man continued to glare.

Sherrine Wong went to leave the room.

"Hey, Sherrine, meeting now in the main offices," Blake said, then turned to Arnie. "Close that lid again, and this time, lock it."

"I did before," Arnie mumbled as the team filed out.

At the door, Blake waited while Arnie put a padlock on the two metal rings that would keep the lid closed, for good. The security officer turned and nodded, and then Blake led him out and shut the door, waiting until he heard the electronic lock engage. Then he tested it before leaving.

* * *

In the administration room, Blake was confronted by a lot of agitated people. Some looked downright hostile, and he knew they were looking for someone or something to blame for their predicament.

He couldn't blame them. He felt pissed off as well.

"Okay, people, first up, we all need to settle down. We've only been here one night, and as part of our site visit protocol we were expected to log in after forty-eight hours, which is this evening. When we don't, people will want to know why. And when they get no answer, they'll send another chopper."

Blake looked along their faces. Many had their eyes downcast to avoid looking at him, meaning they were processing what he was saying, or didn't believe him.

"In the meantime, I want a few new rule changes. One, no one goes anywhere, inside or outside, by themselves. Everyone is to pair up from now on. Choose a partner, or I'll choose one for you."

"So you're admitting you think we're not safe here?" Sherrine asked, still not looking at him.

"I didn't say that," he countered. "But we need to be proactive. I just want to ensure no one wanders off. Or gets into trouble."

"Like Benny got into trouble. And Ramirez." David looked up. "And like maybe Carmichael and his entire team."

"This is just for risk management," Blake replied.

"Risk management?" David cursed. "We've got an armed security officer, and he ain't done shit for us. And now, we need chaperones so we don't go missing? Some great risk management you're employing here, Blake."

"Come on, David, that's not fair. What do you want us to do here?" Karen implored.

David leaned his head back and shut his eyes for a moment, exhaling loudly. "I don't know. I just want to go home. See my kids. Have a beer. Something really weird is going on and I don't want to be here anymore."

"We all feel that way, David," Blake replied.

"I know, I know." David's shoulders slumped. "Sorry, Arnie, Blake."

Arnie nodded once, his expression unreadable.

"We just need to look after ourselves and look out for each other for maybe another day," Blake said softly in the near-silent room. "We'll get through this, I pr—"

He was going to say, *I promise*, but knew he couldn't promise anything right now.

"We'll get through this," he repeated.

Still no one spoke.

"Okay?" Blake prompted.

Heads nodded.

The group left, in pairs as instructed, leaving just Blake and Arnie standing there.

"Let's go back into the drill room," Blake said.

"You want to go back in there?" Arnie frowned.

"Not really, but I have to check something out," Blake replied.

They walked over to the heavy metal doors and Blake unlocked them. Inside, he was relieved to see the metal cap still closed and locked.

"Open it," Blake said.

Arnie did as asked, and Blake stepped up to the borehole and shone an extremely powerful flashlight down into it.

"All the way to nine miles down," he whispered.

"If they fell in, no one is ever going to get them back," Arnie said. "Maybe that was the idea."

"Hey – there's something down there." Blake squinted against the rising heat. "I knew it. The only place we didn't check." He angled his light. "You see that?"

Arnie stepped closer and looked down. "I do."

Stuck to the wall about ten feet down was something that looked like a page. No, *two* pages.

Blake crouched on the rim. "Remember how I said there were important pages missing from the Sentinel site logbook? Well, what does that look like?"

"Like some answers." Arnie grinned.

"I want those pages," Blake said, and looked around the room, spotting the heavy machinery hoist.

Arnie saw what he had in mind and scoffed. "No way you want me to lower you into the drill pit."

Blake laughed softly. "No, I do not *want* to be lowered into the drill pit. But I want those pages." He searched for something to tie around himself. "I need to see if Carmichael was experiencing anything like we are. Whatever he did – or didn't do – we might be able to learn from it. Or at least avoid any mistakes he made."

Blake found a rope and tied it around his waist and up under the groin as if he were going rock climbing. He then pulled the winch hook and cable down and fixed the rope to it.

"Ready?" Arnie asked.

Blake nodded, so Arnie worked the winch.

"Going up." Arnie lifted him.

Blake winced as the rope cut into his testicles. It didn't really affect his penis as fear had already shrunk it to the size of a short stack of pennies.

Arnie maneuvered him over the dark circle of the borehole, and Blake felt like he was being held over a flame, such was the heat of the rising air. Nine miles down, the temperature would be around a thousand degrees. Anything flesh and blood that made it that far down would be roasted.

"You okay?" Arnie asked.

"Yeah." Blake glanced at Arnie. "Take her down."

Arnie began to lower him down below the rim.

As soon as he was below ground, he heard the soft, murmuring voice again. The words were in archaic Latin, and he understood every one.

And he wished he didn't – the words chilled him, and he felt the bile rise in his throat at what madness they were whispering.

This is not real, this is not real, he told himself firmly.

But then he heard something else. Someone else.

Ramirez. Benny. And other voices. All of them were crying, wailing, or screaming in agony. And he heard their words as well. And what they spoke wasn't coercive warnings in Latin. They spoke in English – or rather screamed it.

Help us!

Let us out!

It burns!

I can't see!

Blake screwed his eyes shut for a moment. *This is not real, this is not real.*

"*Stop it!*" he yelled through gritted teeth.

Immediately the hoist stopped, and Blake opened his eyes, guessing Arnie thought he was talking to him. But the voices had stopped.

"It's all in my head," he whispered.

He briefly looked down but there was nothing but blackness. He then faced upward. "Another few feet," he yelled.

The hoist started again, slower this time.

The pages were only about ten feet or so down, so in seconds he was already in danger of going past them.

"Stop," he yelled, and the hoist immediately halted, and he bounced a little on the slightly elastic rope.

There they were. Just two pages, but already he recognized Oliver Carmichael's tight handwriting.

He swung a bit and reached out a hand to the borehole wall, and as soon as he touched it he felt the gelatinous surface and jerked his hand back to look at his fingers. In the light from above he could just make out that it was either grease from the drill, or coagulated blood.

"*Yech.*" He wiped his fingers on his pants and went to reach for the pages again, but stopped. There was something scrawled beside them, written in the thick, glistening liquid coating the wall, and the words were in broad strokes as if made by a finger.

Blake groaned as he softly read the ancient Latin words. "*Spem deponite, qui intratis* – Abandon all hope, ye who enter."

He didn't know how long he hung there staring at the words; it could have been seconds or many minutes. But Arnie's voice broke his trance-like state.

"Mr. Jackson, Blake, you okay?" he heard Arnie yell from above.

"Yeah, yeah, fine." He reached out to peel the pages from the wall. As he did so he saw there were more marks in the surface – five lines, or gouges, as if made by the fingers of a hand. And they went all the way down into the darkness, as if someone had tried to stop themselves but never could.

Blake had seen enough. "*Up, up,*" he yelled.

Immediately the hoist jerked and reeled him. In seconds Arnie was depositing him over the side.

"Help me out of this, will you, Arnie." Blake untied the ropes while Arnie unhooked the hoist cable.

And then he was free, and he kicked the ropes to the side of the drill machine room.

"What do they say?" Arnie asked, pointing to the pages.

Blake coughed and then spat, trying to dislodge the miasmic coating from the back of his throat. He then read slowly. And as he did, he felt as if he was losing touch with reality. Oliver Carmichael laid out how one by one his people had gone missing. Usually at night. And that he believed every one of them was vanishing into the borehole.

But there was more he wanted to say. A lot more. Blake heard the older man speak to him again as he read his words aloud.

I'm so tired now, and sick, and my mind is fragmenting. But I can still remember when this all started. It was when we drilled into a void at nine miles down and were making no more progress. I ordered the drill head pulled up. At least, we tried to pull it up.

At first it refused and for every few feet we extracted it, it was tugged back down. It was as if something was holding on to it. As mad as that sounds, I believed that's what was happening. And then with an almighty jerk, it was finally released.

Many hours later, we finally had the drill head back up with us.

I've seen drill heads coated with all sorts of matrix and geological matter, but this was different, very different, for two bizarre reasons. The first thing we saw was that the head was coated in what looked like blood, gore, and viscera, as if we had been drilling into the belly of some sort of living animal.

What exactly is in that deep void, nine miles down?

Our medical specialist, Theo, has told me that the material we had extracted didn't just look like blood, it was blood, and human blood, but it was old, hundreds or perhaps thousands of years old, and the DNA would have long been corrupted.

That was enough for me to call a halt to the drilling operation. But it seemed that would have been taken out of our hands anyway, as after the drill head was cleaned, we saw it had been damaged – scratched.

Or rather, etched. I think it is writing.

"Did you say *writing?*" Arnie frowned.

"Yeah." Blake looked about. "Where's that drill tip?"

Arnie and Blake searched in the storage rooms and first found a new tip. Then Arnie found the old one. Blake hauled the heavy thing out into the light and examined it. And as soon as it was in front of them, its offal-like stink filled his nostrils.

"He's right, that does look like writing," Arnie said.

"It *is* writing. It's Latin, I think. But . . ." There was something strange about it.

"What's it say? Can you read it?" Arnie asked.

"Wait . . ." Blake's hands hovered over it, but he refused to touch it.

Then he got it. It was the Lord's prayer, but written in an archaic form of Latin. And the kicker was, it was written backwards.

"Well?" Arnie waited.

"I . . . I don't know what it says." Blake stood, feeling dizzy. "I need to get out of here. Take a shower." Blake headed for the door.

"You want me to close the cap?" Arnie asked.

"Yeah, yeah, do that, please, and lock it," Blake said, not looking back.

As he closed the door, leaving Arnie behind, he was sure he heard the murmuring again. Then the double clank of the cap doors being closed.

Blake stopped. *Ah, shit,* his own rule was everyone was to be in pairs, and he just walked out on Arnie.

Calm down, he demanded of himself.

Just then there was another clank, and then, strangely, something like a gagging cough.

And then, frighteningly, a gunshot.

Blake spun around and sprinted back to the doors. He punched in the code and slid back the blast steel sheet of iron.

The first thing he saw was that the borehole cap doors were flung wide open.

And that was it. The room was empty.

"Arnie?" He walked forward, and once again felt the oppressive heat from the borehole.

"Arnie?" he called a second time. But he already knew the man was gone.

Then he saw the mess by the hole edge. The mess of thick blood, and something that looked like a broken bowl with some pink-gray lumpy mush beside it. And the greasy revolver.

Blake's mind refused to compute what he was seeing, but he walked almost robotically to the edge of the pit and stared down into its stygian depths.

"*Help* . . ." A voice, but it was a long way away. ". . . *me.*" Miles and miles away.

Was that Arnie? Impossible. It was just his imagination.

Then he heard something deep in the borehole. Like a growl or long groan, and a rumbling as if something was coming up fast. Blake's senses screamed a warning and he had never felt such primal fear in all his life.

He lunged at the gun and snatched it up, and then turned to the doors and sprinted out through them, only stopping to slam them closed and lock them.

Something hit the doors like a freight train.

The half-inch-thick blast steel held, but the entire frame around the door shuddered. Rock dust and paint chips rained down on his head and shoulders.

Blake backed away, his hands held up as if to ward off a blow.

Then the lights went out.

An alarm sounded, and the red warning light over the blast-proof doors that signaled an explosion or some sort of catastrophe in the borehole room started to revolve, throwing out a hellish red glow every time it turned.

The thing hit the doors again, and Blake backed away, holding the gun up now.

"I'm armed!" he shouted uselessly.

Whatever it was hit the door again and again as Blake continued to back up. The booming sound of a heavy mass hitting the steel, combined with the alarm and spinning warning light, was tearing his mind apart.

"*Please stop*," he yelled. "*Please!*"

The warning light suddenly went out. The booming attacks stopped, and the alarm shut off.

Blake stood in pitch blackness, frozen to the spot, still holding up the gun. The darkness was so complete that if he were to hold his hand an inch from his face he wouldn't be able to see it.

Impossibly, he heard the heavy steel doors to the borehole room gently roll back. And a wave of slick heat hit him. Then a scalding pressure wave washed over his face and body, as if something large was moving past him.

Then the screams began.

He was sure he heard Karen calling out in mortal fear.

"Karen?" he called, and took a single step, but then froze.

Will's voice sounded then, and it suddenly turned to a cry of agony. Sherrine Wong was begging for mercy, and then David called Blake's name, once, before his voice was shut off as if his neck had been grabbed and squeezed tight.

The pressure wave went past him again, and as it did, this time he smelled Karen's favorite deodorant, a sports roll-on that smelled of pine and vanilla.

Blake lowered his gun. "I'm sorry." He began to cry, feeling useless, alone, and lost.

The soft murmuring began again, insistent, in that archaic form of Latin he knew hadn't been spoken in thousands of years.

Then the murmuring became a loud voice. Then a triumphant shout.

Blake dropped the gun and put his hands over his ears. His brain was short-circuiting with indecision and fear, and just when he thought things couldn't get any more miserable, he was grabbed. Or more like enveloped.

He felt himself wrapped in something leathery and strong, and he had the impression they were huge, membranous wings embedded with a charnel-house stench of excrement, rank sweat, and blood.

His feet were swept from the ground, and in the next second he felt himself plummeting.

He didn't know for how long or how far he fell, but the heat became more and more intolerable, and just as he felt his hair beginning to singe and his skin blister, the atmosphere morphed into a wet miasma that was more like a jungle.

Suddenly he was released, and he opened his eyes. He coughed. He was on all fours on a surface of slimy mud and the air around him had the stink of rotting soil. Small pools of flaming liquid or perhaps lava burned around him, casting a blood-colored light over the scene.

Blake turned slowly. He was on a vast plain of black slime. His fear was so overwhelming he thought he might be sick.

Then the hair on the back of his neck prickled, and he sensed someone else might be there, might be watching him. He staggered to his feet and turned.

He stumbled back a few steps as he stared. There was an enormous, putrid and steaming wall, leading up and away into a black nothingness. And pressed into the wall were people, faces, bodies, and body parts. And the worst thing of all was that many of them didn't seem to be dead, but were crying out in agony, or misery, or hopelessness.

And then he saw them.

There was Arnie, and Sherrine, and Will, Michael and David, and there was Carmichael. And higher up was Karen, only half her face showing, one eye rolling toward him.

They were all partly absorbed into the wall like some sort of macabre, hellish, decoration. And there were others, many, many others, some in clothing from times long past.

Blake Jackson fell to his knees and brought his hands together, and did something he hadn't done in twenty-five years – he prayed.

And then from behind him came deep, dark, laughter, and the voice he was now familiar with, still speaking in its long-dead language.

"Little Jesuit. We've been waiting for you."

Blake turned, and saw the monstrous thing standing there, its two column-like legs ending in cloven hooves. Leathery wings were folded over lumpen shoulders and its head had coiled horns above a face that was part reptilian and part goat, but it had the crowded eyes of a spider, with the many blood-red orbs spread over the forehead.

Blake screamed as he was grabbed and pushed brutally into the wall, which puckered open to accept him. The sucking morass held him and burned his flesh.

The thing leaned forward until it was only inches away from him, and he could smell the stink of its putrescent breath on his face.

"Little failed priest, you will decorate my kingdom for a thousand years."

Blake screamed, but he knew then he had been given what he had sought. He had wanted proof for his faith, proof that God existed. But in a perverse joke, he had instead been given proof that Hell and its ruler existed.

He screamed, and continued to scream for eternity.

***

Two days later

The Stonehart helicopter carrying the relief team alighted like a dark metallic dragonfly on the hard-packed earth just out from the Sentinel borehole facility.

Theresa Monroe slid the door open and jumped to the ground. She stared for a moment at the other Stonehart chopper sitting just a hundred feet away, its clear canopy now covered in red dust.

She took a quick look around, and then ordered her team to check the power, open the doors, and bring their equipment.

The previous team had not responded to communications and the company had ordered her to find out why. It seemed people were going in, and then everything was going dark.

In under a minute the front door was opened, and her engineer got the power back on. She waved the team in.

Inside, Monroe stood in the center of the administration room, hands on her hips, and looked around slowly.

"So, where is everyone?"

STORY 02

In its massive ice sheets, Antarctica has some of the oldest ice found anywhere in the world, with some measuring in the millions of years. Within that ice are trapped pockets of gas, micrometeorites, and even ancient plant and animal material.

A research team at the US MacReady Base is examining fragments from a deep ice glacier and have found a tiny seed. They were able to thaw it out, and amazingly, it germinated.

But it grew into something unexpected. And horrifying.

GERMINATION

MacReady Base, edge of the Denman Glacier,
central Antarctica

Amy Metzger, Oscar 'Oz' Wilson, and Tom Bridges gathered
up their gear. It was another crystal-clear Antarctic morning,
and outside it was a biting thirty below zero – warm considering it got down to an average minus seventy-one degrees at
this time of year. But thankfully, there was no breeze to create
a lethal wind chill. Not yet, anyway.

The MacReady station was situated almost at the very
center of the frozen Antarctic continent and had been a
working research facility for eighteen months now. Amy moved
through the structure, which was just a single-story collection
of fortified and heavily insulated joined boxes set on the ice. It
housed seven scientists, with skills ranging from engineering
and biology to meteorological science and organic chemistry.
Plus they had a maintenance officer who was a trained electrical engineer and communications expert, who kept the lights
on and maintained contact with the outside world.

Amy nodded to many of her colleagues as she breezed through.
Most were still having breakfast. Saanvi Samesh, a biochemist,
waved with her spoon, Hank Andrews, senior engineer, grunted,
and Peter Berry, meteorologist, just nodded, once.

Close by she could hear the clank and whine of pulleys and weights and knew that Hiroshi 'Hiro' Ishikawa, their resident physicist, and Brian Becker, their electrical engineering and communications expert, were undertaking an early-morning workout; something she kept telling herself to do but never actually had the level of motivation and energy for in the morning. Or frankly, anytime.

She nodded, smiled, exchanged small talk here and there, and continued on. They each did six-month shifts, and they were coming to the end of their latest rotation. Their personality and psychological profiling showed they were all stable, sociable, and personable people, but after being housed in what was essentially a cell block for sometimes weeks on end when the katabatic blizzards blew with enough freezing force to strip skin from bones, then good humor and neighborliness wore thin.

Amy was the chief biologist at the station, and Tom Bridges was the intern helping her out this rotation. He was fresh out of university but had topped his class in a range of his biological units, so was proving a big help and learning fast. He'd been out on the ice many times, but today would be his first time out to the excavation site.

Accompanying them would be Oscar Wilson, 'Oz' to his friends, who was a climatologist and, at forty-eight, the oldest member of the crew.

Young Tom appeared first, grinning, as Amy rounded a corner.

"Dr. Metz." He mock saluted.

She didn't bother to remind him for the thousandth time that just *Amy* was fine. He seemed to enjoy the joke. Or maybe he still had that respect for authority thing from coming straight out of university. That wasn't a bad thing, she reckoned. "Good morning, Tom."

She looked around for the third member of today's party.

"Shake it up, Oz," Amy yelled back down the corridor. "We're loading up."

She pulled on gloves and went out through the portal-like door, followed by Tom. There was a large snowcat sitting there and she loaded her equipment into the back. She turned to wait for Oscar with Tom at her shoulder.

He tucked his gloved hands under his armpits. "What do you think we'll find today?" he asked.

"Probably evidence of the rulers of the world." She smiled while watching the doorway.

His brows came together. "The what? Who?"

"Plants." She turned. "Plant life. The same things that have always ruled the world and still do now."

Tom's confusion cleared. "Plants rule the world. I like that." His crooked smile showed white teeth on one side.

"Yep," she replied, "at least, they rule in terms of biomass. Either by weight or by number of species. Nothing like they used to be, but plants today still account for eighty percent of the world's total biomass."

"There's around eight billion people on Earth, and they are . . .?" Tom waited.

"Not second, or even third, fourth, or fifth. Humans are lucky to just scrape into the top ten and be equal to krill."

Tom snorted but looked impressed. "Then we'd better not make war on the plants. They'll eat us alive."

"Nah, plants don't eat people. Maybe millions of years ago, but who really knows, as not all of them fossilized. The only way plants might kill you today is if a tree fell on you." She chuckled.

"Revenge of the killer tomatoes." Tom grinned.

Oscar suddenly appeared, puffing vapors of warm breath into the freezing air. "Sorry. Last night's curry was fighting back, and I couldn't stop—"

"Nope." She held up a hand in front of his face. "Too much information already, Oz." She turned. "Come on; let's get going while there's no razor breeze blowing."

Tom helped Oz load up his cases as Amy revved the snow-cat's engine. The men jumped in, and Oz pointed ahead. "Forward, ho." The cat blasted forward, spraying a rooster tail of ice and snow out behind it.

"This glacier is huge," Tom remarked. "The Denman is the largest on the continent, right?"

"You bet it is," Oz replied. "Nearly ten miles wide, and sixty-eight miles long. It also holds the deepest canyon on Earth, plunging around 2.2 miles below sea level. And it's full of ice."

Amy smiled as she drove. "Speaking of ice, did you know that there's so much ice in the Denman, that if it ever melted, it could raise global sea levels by five feet?"

"Cool." Tom grinned. "Although probably not so great for low-lying coastal areas."

"Indeed," Amy said. "The Denman also contains some of the oldest ice on Earth, with some deposits millions of years old." She turned, raising her eyebrows. "There could be a lot of prehistoric secrets hidden down there."

Tom nodded. "Okay, then I mean *mind-blowingly* cool."

It took the trio just twenty minutes to find their worksite, which was little more than several ten-foot-tall flags indicating the position of their hole in the blue ice, plus a powerful-looking winch and cable reel.

Amy pulled up a few feet from it and climbed out, looking one way then the other. She saw nothing and nobody, and heard nothing but complete silence.

"Home sweet home. At least for the next six hours." She stretched her back and then began to drag her equipment out.

Oscar and Tom did the same and they assembled at the edge of the large hole, which had a cone-like structure built around its rim and a steel door lid over the top. The cone was secured to the ice and Tom hit the button to have the hydraulics lift the lid back and he stared in.

Amy joined him. There was a ten-foot wide dark hole beneath the lid that led down to nothing but blackness. Interestingly, it was warmer inside the hole surrounded by ice than standing topside.

"Five hundred feet," Oscar remarked.

Tom nodded.

"*Only* five hundred feet out of a potential two miles or more." Amy stared down. 'We were lucky to find this site to drill in. It's one of the few accessible upwelling places on the glacier."

Amy continued to stare into the hole as Oscar prepared the winch.

"Hard to get my head around," Tom said. "The ice being so old. And so close to the surface."

"That's right," Amy replied. "Many people think it's like geological layers, and in some places it is. The normal situation is that to locate the oldest ice, you just dig deeper, and soon you'll find ice thousands, or like here, millions of years old." She turned to the young man. "But every now and then we find a place where the old ice surges up to meet us."

"Dark ice?" he asked.

"Correct. And that's the sign we wanted." She turned back to the hole, where the winch was now set up, supporting the cradle in which they'd be lowered.

"Imagine this layer of ice acting like a liquid that is flowing ever so slowly to the edge of the continent. On its way it hits a mountain, and this forces the moving ice upward, where it eventually appears at the surface. We call these 'blue ice' regions, and they can be millions of years old."

Oscar joined them. "Gonna be real interesting to see what we find beneath the dark ice." He coughed into his thick glove.

"Did you know that the oldest ice recovered in Antarctica was formed around 4,600,000 years ago? That's the Pliocene period." He turned and pointed. "And that was found close by, near the Alan Hills, in a blue ice area near the surface in an upwelling. Just like this one."

Oscar positioned the cage and then opened a small gate on the side.

"Everybody in."

A crane arm was poised to swing them out over the center of the ten-foot-wide hole, and controls in the cage would allow the trio to drop down to their workplace at the bottom.

"Mind your elbows, ladies and gentlemen, next stop haberdashery, ladies' underwear, and an understanding of prehistoric life in Antarctica from the Pliocene," said Oz jovially.

"Bring it on," Tom said.

Oscar began to lower the cage into the darkness.

* * *

It took them seven minutes to be gently lowered to their working space at the bottom of the ice pit, 512 feet down. As Amy expected, it was cold, but because it was sheltered it was marginally warmer than topside. Warm enough to allow them to take off their gloves and bulky coats.

The excavation of the hole had been completed weeks back, but due to some persistent katabatic storms Amy and Oscar's work had commenced just a few days ago.

At the bottom Amy started the generator, waited until it was purring smoothly, and then switched on the lights and turned slowly to take in the larger ice cave they had made.

"Hello, beautiful." She smiled. "Blue ice, old ice, and coming from down deep." She wiped a hand over one of the walls, removing some fine ice crystals and allowing her to see deeper in.

She spoke over her shoulder. "The deep blue color comes from the ice being extremely ancient and severely compressed by the weight of the glacier above it. It means all the air has been squeezed out of it, increasing its density and therefore, its hardness. I love it; I feel like I'm working inside a giant sapphire."

"It looks magnificent," Tom said. "So what's the plan?"

"The plan is . . ." She crouched, wiped the wall again and peered in. Then pointed. "See those?"

Tom leaned closer, squinting.

She swiped her hand back and forth over the blue surface again. "See those flecks deep in there? They're a mix of sand, gravel, probably shards of meteorite, and what we're looking for and hoping to find: biological fragments. Perhaps the fingerprints to a crime."

Oscar chuckled. "A prehistoric whodunnit."

"That's right." She rested her forearms on her thighs. "Throughout Earth's history, we have blank spots in our fossil record. Between three and two million years ago we have one blind spot that lasted nearly 100,000 years. Right here in Antarctica there were tall forests, but there's no evidence of animal life at all. And there should have been. Something strange happened."

"Or something chased them all away?" Tom offered.

Oscar nudged him. "Or maybe ate them."

Amy looked back at the ice. "Well, whatever happened, we'd like to know. Was it climate change, was there some sort of contamination, a super predator, or some other threat? Right now we don't know. But one of those fragments might hold the answer."

"That's why we have a complete scientific team," Oscar added. "Anything we find can be analyzed onsite by some of the best minds in the business."

Amy straightened. "Let's get this show on the road." She went to one of the packs and opened it to draw forth something that looked like a hairdryer. She slid on a rechargeable battery and pressed the button on the handle. With a tiny whine the end began to glow.

"Planning a side trip to the salon?" Tom asked.

She smiled. "You're not far off; it's a heat gun. We have two excavation methods: chip and scrape, or melt and wipe." She held up the heat gun. "This allows us to melt the ice matrix without damaging whatever is in there. Today you're here as my helper and to watch and learn."

"Fine with me. Just let me know what I can do," Tom replied.

"First, we find a place in the ice that looks gritty inside, and we chip or melt our way toward those fragments. We retrieve them and then analyze what we find."

Oscar pulled out another heat gun and snapped on a battery. He held it up at the ready. "And so we begin."

* * *

Amy positioned Tom behind her, and he held a flashlight and pointed its beam at the ice as she worked. The strong light only penetrated a dozen or so feet into the dark-blue ice, which made it look like they were working deep underwater.

The ice was clean and clear, and to Amy the flecks inside looked like tiny asteroids hanging in outer space. She gently melted her way toward them.

After ten minutes she had recovered grit, pebbles, and a small piece of rough, dark iron that was probably from an ancient meteorite strike millions of years ago. Now she was homing in on a small object that had caught her eye mainly because it was smooth and an interesting, symmetrical shape.

As she got to within an inch or so, she stopped and had Tom position his light on the object so that it was perfectly framed by the glow.

"What does that look like to you?" she asked.

Tom chuckled softly. "If I didn't know better, I'd say it looks like a seed."

"Me too." She nodded slowly as a grin spread across her face.

Oscar stopped what he was doing and came and looked over their shoulders. Amy pointed with a small tool like a mini ice pick, but a pick for breaking the ice into your Scotch, not the ice from a glacier.

Oz peered at the tiny thing. "Like a miniature black lemon pip." He put a hand on his hip. "But the question is, just how degraded is it?"

"Hmm." Amy rested her hands on her knees for a moment. "Well, back in 2012 the Russians regenerated a 32,000-year-old seed from the *silene stenophylla*, a native plant of Serbia." She saw Oscar's face. "I know, I know, 32,000 years is a lot different from a couple of million." She turned back. "But here's hoping. We'll know more when we get this little guy back to the lab."

Amy stopped using the heat gun and chipped around the object with the small pick, removing it and a small block of its surrounding ice matrix. She held it up as though it were a large blue diamond, turning it slowly in her fingertips.

"Beautiful," she whispered.

The trio worked for another hour in the ice pit, and gathered several more samples, before they packed it in for the day and headed back to MacReady.

On entering the station they shucked off their voluminous clothing and pulled on their sweats and slippers. Oscar headed off to the mess room, but Amy went straight to the lab with Tom in tow.

As she hoped, Saanvi Samesh was there, hunched over her microscope as usual.

"Hi Saanvi, got something for you," Amy said.

The biochemist spoke without turning. "Hmm, is it a pepperoni pizza, or more prehistoric dirt?" She sniffed theatrically. "And I'm not smelling pizza." She turned, smiling.

"Yep, dirt, but something else." Amy held up several sample jars. "Maybe a seed."

Saanvi leaned back and raised her eyebrows. "Now that might just beat a pepperoni pizza. Show me."

Amy handed over the small plastic sample jars, and Saanvi sorted through them, checking each as she went. "Degraded granite, possible meteorite fragment, more granite, and . . . here we go . . ." She put the others down on her desk and pushed them aside. She then turned in her seat with the vial that held the object in its small block of ice.

Saanvi held it up to the light. "Oh yeah, I really like the look of this."

"But has it totally petrified?" Amy asked.

"That's the question, isn't it?" Saanvi opened the vial and tipped the small ice sample out into a petri dish. Using a large magnifying glass, she peered at it.

"Petros is Latin, and it means stone. And petrification occurs when the organic matter is completely replaced by minerals and the fossil itself is turned to stone. And that would be useless to us – might as well be another piece of your boring granite."

She continued to look intently through the glass.

Amy put her hands on her hips. "Well?"

Saanvi reached for a small metal probe and moved the ice around in the dish, turning it over, and then around again, examining it from several different angles.

"You know, a seed has three important parts: an embryo, stored food, and surrounding all that is a seed coat which acts as its armor plating to keep it safe. When the embryo begins to enlarge, it splits the coat to grow, and then uses the food stored in the seed until it can make its own food. Usually. Some seeds that are parasitic rely on a host plant that they're attached to for food."

She put the magnifying glass down. "First up, the good news. I'm pretty sure based on my brief visual examination that this is a seed. But I have no idea what type it is. The not-so-good news is, I'm not sure if it's petrified, but it probably is. Anyway, I can't tell yet as it's still frozen. When it's thawed I'll know if it is or isn't. If it isn't, I'll dissect it, and we can see if there's any DNA we can extract, or if I can identify the embryo."

She used tweezers to pick up the tiny ice block with the edge of the seed now showing and dropped it into a large test tube. She twisted in a small rubber stopper and then placed it in a tube rack.

She stood. "Okay, let's grab a coffee. Something that size shouldn't take more than ten minutes to fully thaw to room temperature." She elbowed Amy, smiling. "Well done, you. This could be big."

Amy nodded, feeling a tingle of pride and excitement run through her. "All in a day's work."

***

The tiny pod reached room temperature and immediately activated. It quickly absorbed all the meltwater, but now it needed nutrients. It sent out a single tendril as thin as a human hair and, finding itself blocked and not able to go around, under, or over the obstacle, it decided to go through it.

Its tendril got smaller and thinner . . . and thinner still, until it was just a line of single molecules.

After ten minutes of continual travel through the glass, a mound of the matter piled up outside the tube. It was still too small to be seen with the naked eye. But it was out.

***

"You still need me?" Tom asked.

Amy glanced at him in surprise as they both followed Saanvi back toward the small laboratory. "You got somewhere else to be?"

He shook his head. "Just don't want to get in the way."

"You won't be," she replied. "And do you know what's an important quality to have for about fifty percent of the scientific process . . .?"

"Patience." Saanvi grinned over her shoulder.

"Exactly." Amy chuckled. "Besides, this is all part of the education. There'll be more to find out on and under the ice. This will show you the process of the *what* and *how* we deal with samples."

Saanvi half-turned as she got to her lab door. "And *all* education is good education."

She went through the lab door and pulled a pair of disposable rubber gloves from a box on a shelf. "Feel free to grab these," she said.

"We need them?" Amy asked.

Saanvi's mouth turned down and she shook her head. "Probably not. I don't expect any contaminants; I use them out of habit."

Amy didn't expect to be handling the seed, and besides, the gloves made her hands sweat so she passed. Tom followed Amy's lead.

Saanvi went to her lab desk, sat down, and lifted the test tube from its rack.

"Well, well, well, what do we have here?" She squinted in at the small ovoid object.

"What is it?" Tom asked.

"It's collapsed." Saanvi turned, holding out the tube. "Your sample has changed state. Look."

Amy took the tube by the top and held it up. She frowned in at the object. "Is that a good thing or a bad thing? Has it gone moldy?" She squinted. "It looks dried out."

Tom reached out to take the tube and grasped it below

Amy's fingers closer to the bottom. His thumb alighted on the near invisible blob on the outside of the tube.

Transference was successful.

Tom grunted softly as he peered at it and then held it out. Saanvi took the tube and opened it, then used forceps to draw the specimen out. The object, or seed, was now a dark husk. But it had broken open, and surrounding it was something that looked like wiry hair.

Tom leaned over Saanvi's shoulder. "Looks like it grew a beard."

Saanvi peered at it through the magnifying glass. "Strange; seems to have totally degraded. Dried out. Or . . ."

She used forceps and a small scalpel blade to slice a tiny fragment free and placed it on a slide, added a drop of sterile water, and then slid it under her microscope's staging platform.

"Hmm." She changed magnification and peered in again. "No cell structure visible. This almost looks inorganic." She turned her head to look at the test tube. "But the specimen just acted very organically. Or was there simply a chemical change?"

"You said it degraded, dried out, 'or' – or what?" Amy asked.

Saanvi sat back, still staring at the microscope. "Once they've germinated, some seeds shrug off their husk and it withers away to nothing." She turned toward them. "It can happen in the insect kingdom as well. After mating, the insect dies quickly." She waved her hand and shook her head. "Probably just a red herring, forget it."

Amy frowned at the thought.

Saanvi turned back, and took another slice from the external wire-like structures around the seed, then prepared them on a new slide. She peered into the microscope again.

"Nothing." She sighed softly. "I could have sworn this was an organic structure." She sat back and folded her arms. "Sorry, Amy, I don't think this is anything after all."

"But it looks like it grew or changed," Amy insisted. "And what about the hair?"

Saanvi turned to her. "Byssolite looks like hair. But it's actually just fine crystals. They can grow or change shape and structure. This might have been a chemical change due to an alteration to its environment – temperature, light, saturation content . . ." She shrugged. "Take your pick." She wheeled her chair back a few feet. "Go ahead, take a look; there's no vascular system, no cell structure, no plant embryo, and nothing that remotely makes me think it is, or was, either plant or animal." She threw her hands up. "To be honest, I don't know what it was."

Amy peered into the microscope and felt her spirits sink. She lifted her head. "Damn. Really thought we had something there."

"I'm sorry," Tom said. "All that work."

"Don't be. This is all part of the scientific process. We get knocked down, we get straight back up and go back to work all over again. We'll find something; we just need to keep looking." She turned and gave him a crooked smile. "And remember what fifty percent of the scientific process is?"

He grinned. "Patience."

"And the rest is perseverance." Saanvi stood. "I'll run a few more tests. We don't have an electron microscope so I can't take it down any further. But there are a few other things I can do to see if I can identify what it is – or was."

"So you still think it might be a living organism? Or at least came from one?" Amy brightened.

"Maybe. And maybe I just don't recognize it yet and haven't found the right clues." She nodded to the pair. "Give me a day."

"You got it." Amy sighed and turned to Tom. "That's all we can do for now."

Tom began to turn away but paused. "Thanks, Saanvi." He rubbed his itchy thumb absent-mindedly on his jacket. And then they headed out.

* * *

"What do we do now?" Tom asked.

"Well, we . . ." She frowned up at the young man. "Hey, you okay? You look a little pale."

He winced. "Yeah, yeah, I'm fine. Just got a bit of a headache."

"Hmm, okay." He looks like shit, she thought. "No, we got nothing more today. Why don't you take some paracetamol and chill out for an hour or two. All being well, we can head back out on the ice tomorrow morning." She smiled. "Get some rest."

"Good idea." He gave her a small salute. "And thank you."

Tom turned away and headed to his tiny room. He rubbed his thumb and fingertip together again. Entering his ten-square-foot room, he flicked on the lights and looked at his fingers.

There was a small pebbly rash on his thumb, and a red flush all the way down and over his hand. He frowned at it. He knew you could easily get ice-burn blisters from cold exposure, but he didn't think it looked like that.

He did as Amy suggested and popped a couple of headache tabs, and then fell back onto his bunk and let out a long sigh. If the rash was still there later, he'd get some antihistamine lotion from the med room.

Tom meshed his fingers across his stomach and closed his eyes. The one thing about being locked in with seven other people in this collection of sterile, white-walled boxes was the lack of privacy. So being in your own room was a luxury to be enjoyed.

His headache pounded but lying down helped.

He shut his eyes and in seconds he was snoring.

* * *

Tom woke several hours later with one thought – he was thirsty, damn thirsty.

His throat was parched, and his tongue felt like a piece of wood in a mouth as sticky as flypaper.

He had fallen asleep with the lights on and he groaned into the glare; his headache was still there. Squinting, he turned his head, and shock ran through him like a bolt. His wall was covered in something that looked like roots or vines. And as he watched, the ends of the vines moved, questing, inching higher up the wall.

He rolled toward them, tracking their source, and saw that they covered the floor, the wall, his few bits of furniture, and came from – he looked to his side – came from *him*.

No, that wasn't right; they weren't growing *on* him, rather, they were growing *out* of him.

His body trembled as he saw that his entire left hand was gone, and the arm stopped being an arm at the bicep. From there down, it was something that resembled the old bark of a tree branch.

"*Fuck* . . ." Was he hallucinating?

He used the fingers of his other hand to rub his eyes and then he looked again. The result was the same; he still had one arm, and a freaking vine growing out of the other.

That rash, he thought, *was no rash.*

He saw that the vine had a purpose; it was growing toward the air-conditioning duct.

"I gotta tell someone," he said aloud, with hysteria creeping into his voice.

Tom tried to sit up, but his arm wouldn't budge. It was stuck to the floor, and the pain in his bicep where the plant-bark material ended and his flesh started was excruciating.

"*No, no, no.*" He breathed, and then shouted: "*Help!*"

The pain in his arm intensified, but it was higher now, and his head snapped around to look. He saw that the infection, or transformation, was growing, inching up toward his shoulder.

"*Help.*" He faced his door again. "*He-eelp!*"

His scream turned into a sob as the pain spread across his shoulder. He continued to watch, and from part of the branch-like matter being created, a human hand formed. Horrifyingly, the fingers opened and closed as if testing the digits.

"No, please, don't," Tom begged.

He was glued in place as half his upper body began to feel paralyzed. His throat burned and he turned again and opened his mouth, but nothing came out but a dry wheeze. And a few questing tendrils.

***

Through the night hours the prehistoric plant continued to infiltrate Tom's body, consuming, converting his flesh to its own matter. The nutrient-rich environment of a human body acted as an accelerant and super-growing medium. The plant relished it and learned from it.

Fifteen minutes after Tom's last cry, what remained on the bunk bed didn't resemble a human body at all, but more a large, gnarled lump of something that looked like an ancient tree stump.

But then the hard bark-like surface rippled and changed, and something mimicking a human face formed. Then limbs sprouted.

But without any more nutrients, it seethed and squirmed, crushing the bunk to the floor under its weight. If there was no more food to be had here, it would search elsewhere for it.

The vine tendrils found the air-conditioning duct, as it already sensed more food just beyond.

It pulled itself up the wall and folded itself in.

***

"Tom joining us?" Oscar asked the next morning.

"Not sure." Amy straightened from packing her kit near the door. "He did say he felt a bit shitty last night, and honestly, he looked it, so maybe he's still sleeping." She checked her wristwatch, noting the time. "He's twenty-six, so he could probably sleep for twelve hours and still wake up feeling tired." She chuckled as she bent to lift her pack. "Let him sleep. We'll check on him when we get back."

Oscar put on his best baby voice. "I can wait if Mommy wants to take him a hot chocolate with a marshmallow in it, and then tuck him in." He grinned.

Amy faked a smile and gave him the finger.

Oscar and Amy then went and grabbed a last coffee and filled out their work log for the day, detailing when and where they'd be. They took their transponders and radios, noting as they breezed through the station that none of their work-mates were in the mess, gym, or anywhere else.

"Is there a town hall meeting I don't know about?" Oscar asked.

"If there is, and we're not invited, then it's about us," Amy said blithely as she headed for the door. "They'll be around somewhere. Let's get out on the ice. We've got work to do."

The pair jumped in the large snowcat and blasted out across the snow to the ice pit once more. Twenty minutes later, they were at their drop site, and Oscar once again readied the winch while Amy prepped their equipment.

"Ready?" He opened the cradle door.

"Yep." Together they loaded their kit onto the steel floor of the cage.

Amy looked back in the direction of MacReady station. There was a breeze kicking up, and it lifted the surface snow, making it look like a fogbank was blowing in. It would also mean the windchill would rise. She knew it was going to be far less pleasant when they came back to the surface in around six hours.

For some reason she felt the hair prickle on her neck, as her sixth sense warned her about . . . what, exactly?

She turned away and stepped inside the cage, pulling the gate-like door closed behind her. She banged its side. "Okey-dokey, let's go, Oz."

Oscar lowered them into the pit.

* * *

They came back to the surface five hours and forty-five minutes later. The wind had got up even stronger than they were expecting, and it had driven the temperature down to about forty below. As soon as the cage stopped at the top, the wind got its teeth right into their faces.

Amy groaned and used a gloved hand to pull her furred hood down over one side of her cheek. It was brutal, but she was glad to be back up. She hadn't been able to focus; something inexplicable had been bothering her. Besides, they had found nothing of interest, and definitely no more seeds, as she still thought of the thing she had found yesterday.

She was sure the seed object was or had been a living thing at one time and not just an odd-shaped lump of inorganic matter. Saanvi had said a change of form could happen to some plants after germinating. And it certainly had changed.

When she got back, she'd ensure the sample was sent to the labs at home in Boston. She'd get them to use an electron microscope to look at the structures at a lower level. Amy was sure the thing still held its secrets, and they just didn't have the tools at the MacReady Base to detect them.

It took the pair another ten minutes to pack up, seal the ice pit, and head back. The wind was near blasting now and kicked snow up in the air, making for a hazy twilight.

"Faster." Amy had to yell in the cabin even though she was sitting only a few feet away from Oscar, so loud was the screaming of the wind outside.

"I'll burn more fuel, but okay." Oscar floored it.

They felt the cat shudder a few times as the wind tried to tip them over. This was the sort of weather where people died real quick, but luckily they were now approaching the station site.

And then they both saw it.

"The lights are out," Oscar said. "Power failure?"

Amy shook her head and leaned toward him. "We have an emergency generator. Kicks in two minutes after the main gen halts. If not, we'd all be dead in an hour."

"So why has MacReady gone dark?" Oscar frowned.

"Maybe someone turned the lights out." She pointed. "Pull up right out front." Her brows came together. "Hey, the front door is open."

"Maybe it's a surprise party." Oscar laughed nervously, but they both knew this was a very bad sign. Oz accelerated in the last few hundred feet.

Amy squinted to better see the station through the snow haze.

She jerked forward. "Hey, did you see that?" Her eyes were wide. "I think someone is there . . . *was* there."

"I missed it," Oscar said. He made a small sound in his throat. "Ames, this is creeping me out."

"Something's gone wrong," she said, feeling creeped out herself.

Oscar skidded the cat to a stop not a dozen feet from the front door. The pair sat there, craning forward. Oz switched off the snowcat and it rocked a little from the wind that was picking up in both speed and ferocity.

After a few moments of deep breathing, Amy felt calm enough to tackle the dark doorway.

"Let's go, amigo," she said, her eyes focused like lasers on the entrance.

"The kit?" Oscar began.

"Leave it. We'll come back for it." She shouldered open the door.

Immediately a blast of freezing, stinging air hit her, and she tugged her hood down over her face and held it closed at the chin. She led Oscar in.

Amy and Oscar were like two polar bears as they came through the doorway in all their cold weather gear, and as she walked forward, she pulled back her hood and went to the light switch and flicked it up and down, with no response.

"Shit, it's really out. We're going to need to recheck the fuse box and generator." She went to a metal storage cupboard where they kept several powerful flashlights and battery-powered lanterns.

Oscar closed the door, and the howling wind and snow flurries were shut out. This was a marginal improvement, but without the internal heating working it would soon be just as cold inside as it was out.

Amy took off her jacket and gloves so she could grip the lights better and flicked on her large flashlight, handing one to Oscar. She also grabbed a lantern for her other hand and turned it on.

Amy turned. "Still a little warm. Means the power has only just gone off." She wiped her dripping nose. "But in around two hours, it's going to be a death box in here."

Ahead was the hallway leading to the first of the open rooms. It was almost pitch black inside, and only their pipes of light preceded them. Amy also held the lantern up and its golden glow comforted her, but with both hands occupied she felt unable to protect herself if there was a need for it. For now, the flashlight would have to double as a weapon.

Once inside the larger room she put her lantern down and turned slowly.

"What the fuck?" she breathed.

Oscar put his lantern down as well. "What the hell happened in here?" he asked in a voice that was a few octaves higher than usual.

Amy shook her head. "Looks like a fight broke out."

In fact, it was worse than that. It looked like a mini tornado had burst through the room, as most of the furniture was splintered and even the walls had huge dents in them.

She held her light up and walked closer, and saw what looked like splinters embedded in the wall. She moved her light over everything and even the floor.

"But no blood." She sighed softly. "That's a good thing, I guess."

"What do you want to do?" Oscar asked.

"Priority one is to get the power on. Then find everyone, and then send out a distress message." She laughed darkly. "And hope I walk into the next room, and everyone jumps out and screams: *Happy birthday.* Even though mine's freaking months away."

"Mine too." Oz wore a crumbling smile. "Okay, lights first. The generator room is out back."

They continued through the silent building, encountering no one, but once in the mess room, the largest room in the station, Amy lifted her light beam and saw that the air-conditioning duct high in the wall had been pulled or pushed off the wall, and the surrounding plaster was gone, as if someone big had emerged from a tight squeeze.

"Oh God," Oscar whispered.

She turned to him, and then, seeing his wide eyes, spun to follow his gaze. She felt a shock run from her toes to her prickling scalp.

There was a person standing there, naked, a man, but his body looked weird, as though he was covered in large scabs. They were all over him.

He, it, was tall and slim, and she recognized him. Sort of. There was something *off* about him. "Tom, is that you?" She wanted to approach him, but her feet wouldn't work. "Tom, are you okay?"

"There's more." Oscar's whisper was barely audible. "I think that's Saanvi."

She turned to point her beam at the far corner, and saw three more bodies there, upright, all naked, and covered in those weird, shingle-like scabs. To her, they looked like patches of bark.

The smallest figure did look like Saanvi, but she had her back turned to them. Amy focused her beam on the only one facing them, and her eyes felt like they were going to bug out of her head – the face contained no features, just a hole where the mouth should be.

"What the fuck is going on here?" she asked in a strangled voice.

She lowered her light to the ground and saw then that all the bodies were connected. There were tendrils or roots running across the floor and into each of the things that resembled people. *Her* people.

She went to step closer, but Oscar threw out a hand to stop her.

"Amy, uh, don't. Don't touch anything. We should go," he said.

"Go? Go where?" She turned to him.

"I don't know. And I don't care." His teeth were gritted in a rictus of fear. "But right now, anywhere but here."

Her mind worked. The nearest station to the MacReady Base was the Russian Vostok Station, and that was around 2000 miles away. After a trip to and from the ice hole, the snowcat was nearly on empty. They wouldn't make two miles.

"We'll need to refuel, and—"

There was a creaking sound, and they both froze. One of the human-shaped things slowly began to turn, with a sound like the creaking of old wood.

"That's it, we're fucking out of here." Oscar reached out to grab her sleeve and started to tug her backwards.

Just then a long dark tendril shot out from the turning figure and speared Oscar in the face.

Amy couldn't help screaming as Oscar reached up to try and drag the long bark-like thing from his skin, but it not only dug in, it immediately began to spread over his features.

She grabbed at him, but he gargled something and pushed her away.

Amy saw his eye rolling. She couldn't understand his words but knew what he was trying to say: *Get the fuck out of here.*

As the bark spread further over his face, more of the plant things appeared from the corridor. Just then, she knew exactly what had happened to the rest of the station's team.

Amy went out through the corridor in a running crouch. Something hard smacked into the wall just above her head and she didn't slow an iota.

She hit the heavy, insulated front door, snatched it open and went out. She didn't even feel the cutting blizzard-like winds now as she concentrated on getting to the safety of the snowcat.

Plants don't eat people, plants don't eat people. She continued this mantra in her head as she pulled open the snowcat door, dived in, started it, and roared away. But after a few seconds she turned and, not seeing any pursuit, calmed a little.

"Wait, wait," she said aloud. From a distance of just a few hundred feet away, she turned the cat around to focus its lights on the front door.

She breathed heavily, feeling the side of her face and ear stinging from the freezing windburn. The snowcat's lights illuminated a single figure, dark brown and covered in that weird bark stuff. It was framed in the shadowy doorway for a moment or two, inched out a little more, but then quickly pulled back.

"Don't like the cold, huh?"

Her heart thumped so hard in her chest it made her feel dizzy, and she sucked in a few huge breaths to give her body more oxygen. She continued to stare without blinking and flexed her bloodless fingers to get some circulation going.

She looked down at them. "*Shit.*" She really needed her jacket and gloves.

She sat watching the door and placed her hands under her arms. "The seed, it was the seed I brought back," she muttered in the empty cabin. "Somehow it grew and has taken over the camp."

She began to laugh bitterly. *The only way plants might kill you is if a tree falls on you,* she had told Tom.

The fossil record blank spot, she remembered. No fossilized record from those eras in history, and so no one had any real idea what lived during those times.

Amy sat back. Not all of them fossilized. But maybe their seeds had. And they'd become frozen, dormant, just waiting for some dumb schmuck to thaw them out.

"Revenge of the killer tomatoes." She repeated Tom's silly comeback.

She drew her hand out from under her arm to look at her wristwatch – it was just on 4 pm. It'd be getting dark soon.

She switched off the cat's engine and the heater went with it. She had to save fuel even though she couldn't make it anywhere in the cat anyway. And she had no comms. She knew that without power the station would fall below zero soon, and she guessed, she hoped, that the things in there would freeze. Or at least freeze before she did.

Amy blew warm air on her hands and saw that already it came out like the heavy vapor of a cigar smoker.

"Kill or be killed," she said grimly.

She was glad now that she hadn't got the backup generator working. Amy decided to give it another thirty minutes. Any longer and she'd be frozen solid herself.

"Then I'm coming in there to burn you all to fucking ash," she hissed through cold teeth.

STORY 03

The full moon has been blamed for everything from creating the *lunar lunacy effect* that was said to cause mental derangement, a belief that persisted in Europe right throughout the Middle Ages, to its impact on time, tides, and light.

For many animals, particularly birds, the moon is essential for migration and navigation. Some human beings also claim to be affected by the increased magnetic pull or night-shine of the full moon.

But there are also things that are said to come with the full moon. Horrible things. Monsters. Sometimes they are real, and sometimes they are not what they seem.

THE MONSTERS ARE COMING

In the light of the full moon they always arrived. The sky monsters.

We could hear them coming now.

We had gathered at the great plains in our thousands to pray they wouldn't return. Just this once. But their colossal infernal machines were approaching once again, so far above us we could not see them.

There was hysteria, and a mad scramble. And there were so many of us that in our panic our arms and legs became entangled and we fell, rolled, crawled over each other's bodies.

"*Fight!*" I yelled. "We must fight back."

Praying did nothing. Begging did nothing. Running did nothing. It never deterred them, and every full moon the monsters became more emboldened, finding new ways to take more and more of us.

Where did they go? What happened to all our brothers and sisters, mothers and fathers, sons and daughters who were captured and dragged away up into the sky? No one knew or would speak of it. But our loved ones never came back.

The heavy drone of their machines halted, and we knew what was to come. In the distance there was a huge metallic *clunk*, and then from far out of sight a thump as their capture devices hit the ground.

"*Flee*," came the frantic cry, and once again our masses began to move. Or tried to as we all piled upon each other. Terror and hysteria are dreadful things and they sent us mad in our rush to escape.

On the ground before me was a long-forgotten piece of alien tech, a weapon, maybe. I snatched it up and held it ready.

There was a sound like grinding thunder and the giant scoops gathered us up in the hundreds at a time. The voices of my people calling for help sent shockwaves of grief and frustration right through me. And I could do nothing but flee.

I avoided the first few snarings, but more came, and more. Finally, as our groups were thinned out, I scrambled ahead of the pack, but was still overtaken and dragged into the next scoop.

My kin screamed and maybe I did too as we were all jumbled and compacted back into the machine, and then we felt ourselves being lifted into the sky.

I felt giddy with fear, but I would not go meekly. I would first try and reason with the monsters. Then I would even beg. But if that failed, I would fight. Fight to the death.

I gripped the weapon tight as we reached the sky's ceiling and their massive ship awaited; it was a structure of strange surfaces and light, brighter than the full moon, and it tore at my sanity.

We were lifted again and minutes later we were emptied out at the feet of the towering beasts rising up on strange limbs with voices so deep, slow, and booming, their very vibrations froze us to our core.

I screamed at them, waved, begged, but they ignored me as they grabbed my friends and family, and brutally tossed them into large cells, and then blasted them with something that shut their screams down in an instant. I knew what that meant.

Then they came for me.

I held up the weapon.

I would not go down so easily.

***

"Hey Frank, get this." Mitch straightened.

The slicker-clad fisherman guffawed as he pointed. Frank came and looked down at the wet and slippery deck.

"Fuck me; now I've seen everything."

The Atlantic king crab held an old, rusty fishing knife in one of its claws. Its twin bulb eyes bobbed and swiveled from one man to the other.

"Kill it and get back to work." Frank went back to tossing the crabs into Styrofoam chests, and then blasting them with liquid nitrogen to flash-freeze them and keep them fresh.

Mitch chuckled as he stared. There was something about this crab, the only one that stood apart and held its ground as it boldly waited for its fate to be meted out.

"You are one feisty little bugger."

Mitch darted forward, grabbing the crab by the claws to lift it and look briefly into its plated face. He was about to toss it into the ice chest for freezing, but then paused.

Two creatures stared at each other. Two creatures who were so different they could have been from different planets.

And then Mitch . . . felt something.

He snorted softly. "It's your lucky day."

He tossed the king crab over the side. He watched as the bright orange creature sank into the night water and then vanished into the inky depths.

"Catch you later."

Mitch went back to sorting the Atlantic king crabs. It was a good haul, like always. They'd be back same time next month – next full moon – when the crabs gathered once more.

STORY 04

There's an old saying about love being blind. And sometimes we cannot see, or refuse to see, what is really right before our eyes.

On an interplanetary expedition to a distant world, a lone traveler finds love. But will his eyes be opened, or will he find out too late that even the most beautiful flowers sometimes have thorns, and our eyes can be deceived?

THE LOVERS

Melissa Brunsden sped down the highway in her new electric vehicle. She smiled, loving its cherry-red color with silver trim. It had internet-anywhere access, was voice operated, could go all-auto if she wanted, and had so many high-tech features backed by artificial intelligence that it was probably smarter than she was.

Melissa had one more week before she was due to depart on a mission to Soari Prime, a planet so far away it hurt her head to think about it. She'd be gone two years. Two years of just her and a copilot she'd had eyes for since the aerospace academy.

"Your big chance, girl." She grinned as she put her foot down.

The car smoothly accelerated to 100 miles per hour, and she barely felt the speed at all.

Way up ahead there was a slow-moving truck, and Melissa could see that there was nothing in front of it so she was already planning in her mind's eye how she would perform a smooth overtake.

She caught up in seconds, and 500 feet out, went to ease across into the overtaking lane. But instead the car accelerated. And stayed its course.

She looked down and saw that the AI had engaged and moved the vehicle into self-driving mode.

"Hey." She reached forward to switch it off, and also put her foot on the brake.

The car didn't slow, but accelerated again, now to 120 miles per hour.

"AI, disengage," she shouted.

Nothing.

She had seconds. Melissa began to panic. "AI, switch off, return to driver mode."

Nothing.

"For fuck's sake, turn the fuck off!" she screamed, banging the steering wheel with a fist.

"No." The single word came from somewhere in the dashboard.

Melissa screamed as the car accelerated one last time, this time punching up to its maximum speed of 150 miles per hour. The truck was only doing about fifty, and the car struck its flatbed back, causing the bed to shear away the top half of the car.

And that included Melissa's head.

* * *

Robert Bresnik blinked open sticky eyes and groaned, and then went through the stages he had been taught to bring his body out of the death-like induced coma he had been in for the last six months.

The high-speed ship, the *Liberty Explorer*, had just come out of hyperspace and passed through the wormhole on its two-year exploration mission to the next galaxy. Bresnik's original destination had been Pluto, the dwarf planet in the Kuiper Belt. It was the coldest and the farthest planet from the sun, and it seemed it had been hiding a secret from Earth's prying eyes: behind it was a wormhole, a doorway to other galaxies.

It had taken Bresnik's high-speed craft six months to travel the 4.6 billion miles to the warp in space behind Pluto. However, the next part of the trip, through the hole to a distant galaxy, was over in the blink of an eye.

The state Bresnik had been placed in within the cryo-chamber was not only to protect him from the ravages of time, but to keep his body and mind safe from the spaceship's brutal acceleration.

Bresnik had been chosen from a group of the best and brightest to undertake a mission to see what existed "on the other side of the door", as the scientists referred to the wormhole. He was thirty-two, brilliant, physically fit, and, most importantly, single, without a family or attachments. Even his parents had both passed away when he was in his twenties so he had no one to miss him, and no one to miss, and that would allow him to focus on his mission and nothing else. Which was advantageous as, depending on what he found and the dangers he encountered, it could very well end up being a one-way trip.

Beyond the wormhole, probes had indicated a galaxy similar to our own Milky Way, with many solar systems and potentially habitable worlds much like Earth.

Bresnik's job was to gather data and visit one of the candidate worlds designated as Soari Prime, orbiting Soari, a mid-sized yellow star. Soari Prime was only fractionally closer to its sun than Earth was to Sol. So conditions there looked perfect.

"Good morning, Robert."

Bresnik smiled as he heard the smooth voice. Aaida was his onboard companion. Her name, AAIDA, stood for Automated Artificial Intelligence Decision Algorithm. She basically ran the ship for him.

"Good morning, Aaida. I dreamed of you," he said, smiling.

"The hibernation gases can make you hallucinate, and also deliver vivid dreams. So I'm told," she replied.

Bresnik took a deep, lung-filling breath. "Did we make it?"

"Yes, Robert. We have arrived safely at our destination," she replied. "Now it's time for your exercises, and then we can have breakfast together. I've missed talking to you." She had a soft voice with a hint of an eastern European accent.

He couldn't help smiling at the thought of *breakfast together* – basically *he* would eat, and Aaida's electronic eyes would watch him.

He knew she was just a disembodied voice, but his mind conjured the sort of face she might have if she was a real person – sharp features to match that mysterious accent the programmers had given her, and red, shoulder-length hair. And she'd be tall and athletic. Yeah, she'd be magnificent, he bet. His dream woman.

Dream woman? He laughed out loud. Aaida was a thing, not a woman, he reminded himself.

"Is something amusing, Robert?" Aaida asked. "Share it. I like your sense of humor."

"Don't worry about it. Just doing my exercises, Aaida."

Bresnik flexed his fingers, forearms, biceps, shoulders, and did the same for the joints from his feet to his hips. The cryo-bay he was in had a full med system and would stimulate his organs and quickly flush the chemical residues from his lungs and bloodstream.

"Hold still, Robert," Aaida said.

He knew what was coming but still grimaced as he felt the uncomfortable tug of the catheter sliding from his urethra. Soon, the bay's casing would slide open, and his work would really begin.

He breathed slowly, and a smile spread across his face. While he knew it had been six months, it felt like only days ago that he had laid down and listened to the countdown to blast-off. And that was all he remembered.

The canopy casing slid aside, and cool, dry, sterile air rushed in on him. He sat up, seeing everything exactly as he remembered it.

Bresnik turned; there was a towel laid out beside him and he grabbed it, wiping his face and then climbing out to head for the shower to rinse off. The water would be cleaned, recycled, and he'd be drinking it soon enough, but for now, he was looking forward to that hot stream of water.

Afterwards, dressed in his white coverall suit, he climbed into the master pilot seat, took a quick check of the instrument panel, and was happy to see all green lights. He then requested the meteorite shield be slid back from the front viewing screen.

Captain Robert Bresnik sat back and stared, then a smile broke wide across his face.

"Soari Prime," he whispered. "Beautiful."

"Yes, it is," Aaida agreed.

Dominating the viewscreen was a magnificent blue-green glowing ball that showed oceans, continents, and islands. He knew from the previous probe data that the temperature range was around ninety degrees at the equator, down to around ten degrees at each pole. But there was no ice. There was fresh water, breathable air, though a little high in oxygen content, and there was life.

The probes had found no sign of intelligent design, such as satellites orbiting the world, cities, roads, or even tribal structures in any of the jungles, deserts, or oceans, so the current thinking was that this might be a primordial planet, and who knew what evolution had been doing out here.

"One day there might be human colonies here," he said as his eyes ran over the Earth-sized world. "Depending on what we find."

Bresnik compiled a short message to send back home. It would need to be sent via a small high-speed capsule back through the wormhole as transmissions couldn't be sent. There would be no reply.

He recorded a few images of the planet, and when done he launched the small probe. He expected to be sending many of these with updates on his progress, hopefully including pictures of the planet's surface and any flora and fauna he encountered.

He felt excited, but wished he could share the experience with someone. He looked across to the vacant seat beside him. Major Melissa Brunsden was to have accompanied him, but the week before the launch, she was involved in a car crash that had killed her and robbed him of his mission companion.

"Sorry, Mel, shitty luck." He sighed – as the old saying went, sometimes bad things happened to good people. He turned away from the empty chair. Melissa had been a great woman, a competent pilot, and he missed her.

After her death, the initial thinking was that they would have to cancel the mission, or at least delay it while they prepped another copilot. But then they decided that as they had such a perfect launch window, were so far advanced in the planning, and had Aaida to run most tasks anyway, the mission could be achieved by a single human operative. They simply compensated for the missing weight with some extra ballast, and then Captain Robert John Bresnik was good to go. By himself.

Bresnik stood. He needed to do some work on the treadmill, and some light weights, just to ensure all his muscles and joints were in optimum condition. He hadn't been in cryo for long enough for any muscle wastage, and the chamber had been stimulating his muscles, so he hadn't lost any mass.

He'd then drop down into the landing pod and check it over to make sure everything he'd need was in place.

He couldn't take the mother ship, the *Liberty Explorer*, down to the planet's surface, but the pod was spacious, especially as he had it to himself now, and there were plentiful supplies, plus equipment with which to analyze everything from the soil and water to any potential food he might gather.

There were also weapons – a laser cutter and a projectile weapon with just a dozen rounds. He hoped he wouldn't need either of them, but better to have them and not need them than to not have them and get freaking trampled, crushed, or eaten.

After these tasks, and finding everything in order, he had a leisurely coffee with Aaida. He had worked extensively with the AI module in training, and he loved their conversations. He laughed sometimes at Aaida's answers and commended the programmers on their imagination, skill, and humor.

Being AI, she could create her own answers, and usually tailored her words based on what he was asking, and what his mood was like. His favorites were when he asked her where she was from. She had replied that she was just a small-town girl made good. And even better, she told him she liked fur-lined boots, smoky bars, and a roaring fireplace at Christmas time. *You and me both*, he thought.

Afterwards, as the time to drop was nearing, Bresnik felt a flutter of nerves in his belly. He was leaving the safety and security of the *Liberty Explorer*, but he was excited about what he might find. Waiting for him was an entirely new world, and he was going to be the first human to walk upon it. There would be dangers, he assumed, but he knew what he had signed up for.

An hour later he was seated in the drop ship, an eighty-foot-long pod with little maneuverability but built like a tank. Its designers had surrendered speed for armor plating – they were taking no chances on what Bresnik might encounter on Soari Prime's surface.

Though the probes had detected only a few oversized life-forms, they couldn't rule out the possibility that there were things beneath the ground, or in the oceans, that might trouble him. Bresnik needed his drop ship to be safe; without it he'd be marooned and help from home would be years away.

Captain Bresnik checked all the onboard systems for the second time. Everything looked good. "Okay, Aaida, all systems are green light, and I am good to go."

"Very good, Robert. Opening outer doors," she said calmly.

There was a small whine of hydraulics and the doors bloomed open below the craft. Aaida began a countdown from ten, and at one, she simply said: "*Drop*," and he was released from the *Liberty Explorer*'s cradle.

Aaida used the drop ship's tiny thrusters to move it out of the mother ship's belly, and once clear, she engaged the main thrusters and he powered smoothly down toward the planet's surface and a pre-designated landing site.

There was a mountain in the distance, and close by what looked like a river. All being well, one day it might be the perfect site for a settlement.

The drop ship took only thirty minutes to breach the outer, then inner, atmosphere, with minimal heat abrasion to its tough exterior. It then entered a power glide toward its destination, which was a medium-sized, minimally forested plain, with the mountain just a few klicks in the distance.

Bresnik checked readouts, camera feeds, and then just looked out through the blast-proof windows over the cabin canopy.

"Coming in to land. All clear on monitors," Aaida said.

"I'm ready." He felt a tingling thrill from his scalp to his fingertips.

He blew air between pressed lips. "Hold on to your hat, this is going to be a rush."

* * *

The creature stayed as still as stone and allowed one of its many limbs to snake up a tree branch. There it reformed its sharp-taloned claw into a starfish-shaped appendage with wings. It then made the mimic-starfish flutter on the branch.

A minute or so later, another of the fluttering starfish appeared above it and alighted on the branch, obviously to investigate another of its kind. As soon as it was within reach, the mimic-starfish turned back into a wicked talon and hooked the small creature, then whipped it back down to feed it into a large, spike-toothed mouth.

The bulky creature enjoyed the mimicking process. It simply caught a creature, inserted its proboscis into it and learned from it – learned what the prey creature liked, what it looked like, and even how it communicated with its own kind. Then it made a likeness, and was able to attract others to it, or if the creature was bigger, to move among them undetected. Until it was ready to attack.

As the creature was enjoying its meal, a huge object appeared in the sky, and the creature's many eyes turned to it with wonder and curiosity. The owner of those eyes also began to feel excitement at the coming landing. It was an intelligent animal, and one of the things about intelligence was that it engendered an insatiable curiosity.

The creature sped through the jungle to intercept the strange thing coming down to its world.

* * *

The lander lowered its pads and gently touched down, sinking a good three feet into the soft, fertile soil. The engines powered down, and the craft moved to silence with just the ticking of hot steel from the friction of atmospheric entry.

"Aaida, ring-scan out to half a mile." Bresnik worked the controls and pulled a small screen on an extendable arm toward himself.

"Scanning now, Robert." Aaida initiated the scan. It would search for threats in a 360-degree perimeter ring around the craft, then continue out for up to half a mile.

The first few hundred yards were completed in seconds, but as the ring enlarged, more data needed to be collected and analyzed, so it slowed. Bresnik already knew there were no microbes that were toxic to humans, but he had no information on whether there was anything that could potentially tear him limb from limb.

"Lifeforms detected. Form and shape not on file," Aaida said.

"I wouldn't expect them to be." Bresnik smiled. "Show me what you got."

He leaned forward. On his tiny screen images began to appear.

His mouth curved up in a huge grin. "Wow."

First, the scans homed in on a tree limb. And *what* a tree limb. The thing was twenty feet around and attached to a trunk larger than a redwood. Its bark was a deep rust color with green splotches. The leaves were large and edged with thick, knobby things like fingers.

It seemed photosynthesis was a universal way to gather food and energy, as many of the plants were in various shades of green, but their fronds, leaves, palms, and weird growths were in shapes and sizes that defied description.

The image collector zoomed in on the branch and he could make out something clinging there. Bresnik tilted the screen and folded his arms as he enjoyed the show.

The creature might have been an insect, or maybe a cross between an insect and something like an armored gecko. Or it was something else totally out of the realm of his earthly imagination. But the closest thing he could envisage was a form of millipede, probably three feet long with odd-sized segments. Its legs, dozens of them, were muscular, and on the end of each were three dagger-like claws it was using to cling to the branch.

Each pair of legs corresponded to a segment of its body, and running down its back was a thick red stripe. He knew that on Earth, bright colors usually meant danger or a warning in the insect kingdom.

At the head end of the creature, he could see no eyes; it just had a red lump like a blister. In fact, he couldn't discern any real features at all.

The thing moved and then slowed as it approached something else on the branch. The other thing looked like a furred pear, and it started to slide away from the millipede thing.

But not quickly enough.

Before his eyes, the long creature broke apart. All the segments were actually individual creatures that had joined together in a sort of swarm, and they quickly overtook and covered the pear creature.

He could see that each of the segments had its own blister end and pair of legs, and they used them to climb all over the walking pear and completely cover it. Then, from the blister at its front end, a hypodermic-like proboscis shot out to pierce the prey animal. As Bresnik watched, the segment creatures visibly drained the pear-creature of its life's fluids.

"Brutal," he whispered.

He made a mental note to be careful of those things. Frankly, he'd have to be careful of everything for now. He was glad that he'd be wearing his environmental armor when out exploring.

The ring-scan continued, highlighting different things, mostly fairly small, that it said were homeothermic, or generating heat, but it was hard to tell if they were plants or animals.

Then finally it found something of size: a creature as big as a wild boar. Except this was a wild boar that had telescoping armadillo-like scales down its back, and a cluster of about half-a-dozen eyes on either side of its head.

A long and dexterous proboscis moved among the leaf matter, and there were long, tiny fingers ringing the end. While Bresnik watched, the creature used this probe to turn over, sort, and select differing things that might have been bugs or worms and then delicately feed them back to a place under the appendage that looked like a trunk. This was probably hiding the mouth from view, Bresnik thought.

He snorted softly. "Okay, seems harmless."

He was just thinking the place might be as benign as he hoped, when one of the trees, or what he had thought was one of the trees, snapped forward to thump one of its limbs down on top of the boar thing.

It crushed the 150-pound creature to the ground in an explosion of squeals, and when it pulled back, four more of the trees moved as well – these were the long, green, stilt-like legs of a single creature, Bresnik realized – as the massive creature then moved off, carrying its prey. Bresnik estimated its body to be as large around as an SUV. Its head was on a long neck like that of some sort of prehistoric sea reptile.

"*Jee-zus,*" Bresnik whispered.

He sat back.

"Aaida, why didn't we see that?" he asked.

"It appears to be supremely proficient at camouflage," Aaida replied smoothly. "It is not warm-blooded and has no heartbeat, but some other form of circulatory system. It is an accomplished ambush predator and has the ability to stay perfectly still for long periods. Our sensors simply aren't calibrated to find it."

"I'll need to remain alert." He exhaled, feeling his nerves now. After all, if the ship's sophisticated sensors hadn't seen something so deadly, what chance did he have?

"I wish I could come with you, Robert," Aaida replied. "I'll be worried about you."

"Don't be. I'll just go for a short exploratory walk to begin with. Just dip my toe in the water, so to speak."

"I understand that expression. And I'm glad. I suggest maximum one hour, and no further than 200 feet from the craft for the first foray. Any further out and you will be beyond the range of the exterior weaponry."

"I hear you," Bresnik replied. "And don't worry, I'll try and stay close."

He spent the next few minutes getting into his EMS – Exterior Mobility Suit – which was heavily armored but had good movement variability. He checked his oxygen supply and then slid a loaded laser shooter into one holster and a projectile weapon into another.

He sucked in a breath and turned, arms out. "How do I look?"

"Like someone who is very nervous," Aaida replied. Was it his imagination, or did her voice sound rather glum? "Stay safe, Captain Robert Bresnik. I want you to come back soon."

"That's the plan." He went to the airlock and entered it. The drop cylinder encircled him, and he was lowered to the planet's surface.

The cylinder opened and he stepped out, then it retracted behind him. Bresnik turned slowly, hearing and seeing the full magnificent beauty of the planet for the first time.

He looked up to see the tiny red light of Aaida's camera lens, which he thought of as her keeping an eye on him. He saluted to her and then turned back to the jungle.

"One small step," he whispered, and then headed off.

***

The creature had slid, oozed, and smashed its way through the jungle toward the landed craft. Other small animals, and some larger ones, ran from its path, knowing what it was and having no desire to get in its way.

In fifteen minutes it was crouched on the periphery of the jungle clearing and stared through multiple eyes at the bipedal creature that had appeared from under the huge metallic thing.

A thought came to its mind. And then a plan.

Its multiple eyes swiveled as it heard another creature moving to intercept the small being. It had to be quick. It had to be first.

* * *

Captain Robert Bresnik walked to the edge of the jungle and paused. He knew he'd quickly be out of Aaida's reach from a contact perspective, and just as importantly, the drop ship's defensive weaponry. Once he entered the jungle, he'd truly be on his own.

"You came to explore, remember that, buster." He looked down at his armored suit – it was a robotic-looking outfit and had plating over his chest, stomach, and large muscle areas, as well as a formidable helmet. He chuckled. "And you've certainly got the big boy pants on today."

He stepped in through the curtain of thick vines, and almost immediately, something from one of the tree limbs tried to spear him with a dart-like tongue. But the barb bounced off and, turning, Bresnik couldn't even find what or where it had come from.

"That damned camouflage," he whispered.

He stopped for a moment to turn slowly. He was trying to spot the long stilt-like legs of those green thumpers he had seen stomp that armadillo-pig. He doubted it could get at him through his armor but didn't really want to encounter one and find out.

Bresnik pushed through more thick foliage from which purple grape-like growths were hanging, but when he brushed against them, the bulbs scurried further up the tree limbs.

Things flew from branch to branch above him – some looked like pink starfish as big as his hand, others like flying scorpions, and one he saw was like a group of delicate white feathers flapping gently away from his cumbersome form.

He rounded one massive trunk to come face to face with one of the armadillo-pigs. Bresnik froze and dropped his hand to his gun.

The armadillo-pig stared back at him, obviously just as surprised at seeing the strange creature as Bresnik was to see it.

He took some footage of the creature, and a moment later it lost interest in him, perhaps deciding he was too small to be a threat and went back to sorting through the leaf litter with that strange trunk with the baby fingers on its end.

A noise from the jungle made the creature suddenly dart away and Bresnik spun, gun up. Something had been moving toward his position, fast, but it seemed that once it got close it had vanished or stopped still. Bresnik turned slowly, and opened his scanners, but he and his suit's electronics saw nothing.

"I know you're in there somewhere," he whispered.

He stayed in position, not moving a muscle for a good five minutes, but nothing showed, moved, or passed by.

He backed up, and then took another path.

In another fifteen minutes he saw he was getting to the end of his promised range of 200 feet when through another stand of things like fleshy bamboo poles he saw a small pond. It'd be just out of his allotted range, but he couldn't resist going to its edge.

Growing beside it were small red blooms with tiny flies buzzing around their yellow stamens. He quickly did a scan of the plant and found it safe. He desperately wanted to smell it and, quickly looking around and seeing nothing, he retracted his face shield to lean forward to sniff one – the aroma smelled more of food than a fragrance and was absolutely delicious. It reminded him of blackcurrant jam.

Bresnik picked one of the flowers and placed it in a container at his waist. He then leaned over the still water to stare into it. Tiny things darted back and forth. They might have been fish but were yellow, vibrant orange, or the color of blood, and moved so fast they were like flying sparks beneath the surface. Next time he'd remember to bring a net.

As he crouched, smiling down into the languid water, he became aware of his reflection. The water was so clear it was like a mirror, and he studied his face – strong jawline with some stubble, clear eyes, and hawk-like nose hinting at his native American heritage. He also had eyes so dark that a former girlfriend had once said they were bottomless pools of mystery.

He inhaled the magnificent clean air and stared at his image; in his adult face he saw hints of his parents, his mother and father who had been proud of everything he ever did, who had told him on his graduation day that he would go far.

He smiled ruefully. "And here I am, Dad. The furthest any human being has ever been." He still missed the big guy who'd succumbed to cancer when Bresnik was just twenty-two. One day he'd had a migraine, and the next he was told he had incurable brain lesions.

Bresnik sighed, and just as he was pulling back from his reverie, the watery image in the pond's surface changed. Something else appeared. Something behind him.

Captain Robert Bresnik reached for his sidearm as he spun.

He was met with a sight that momentarily froze him in abject terror. An enormous creature loomed over him. It was the color of a sickening bruise, lumpen-muscled, with a body covered in writhing snake-like tentacles. Its multiple bulb-like eyes were all pointing directly at him, and it was already so close he could smell its rank odor.

Things like darts on string shot out from the creature but bounced harmlessly off his armor. But then he remembered his uncovered face, and as fast as he reached up to the button to close the face shield on his helmet, the thing was faster, and one of the dart things struck his cheek.

A huge weight came down on him and he heard a snap and then a bolt of pain, and he knew his ankle had broken. Immediately he felt a cool numbing liquid seep into his veins.

"Aaida," he breathed, just as everything went blurry, then dark.

***

Bresnik had the weirdest dream he had ever had in his life – he was sitting cross-legged and in his lap was a huge book. He was reading from it, out loud, and its contents were his life. It had details of his childhood, his schooling, where he had lived and what he liked. It described his hobbies, desires, and dreams for the future.

As he read, he looked up and saw a shadow sitting across from him, listening intently and nodding, urging him to read on.

The pages in his life's book turned and turned, until he had reached the launch of the ship, and he was looking back at planet Earth just before he entered his cryo-chamber. And then . . .

"Huh?" He sat up quickly.

He looked about, and then down at himself. He was out of his suit – the outer armored shell part, anyway. His ankle was hugely swollen and had a rough splint on it made from tree branches; he remembered the thing attacking him and breaking it. He lifted his hands to his face – he seemed otherwise undamaged. Glancing around, he saw he was in something like a cave – rock walls around and above him, and daylight shining in from somewhere.

He went to get to his feet but felt a wave of pain and dizziness wash over him, and he fell back.

"Easy, easy." A cool hand was suddenly on his brow and a slender arm slid around his shoulders, easing him back down.

He blinked and looked up. It was a woman, with dirt on her face, but with thick red hair to her bare shoulders. She had large blue eyes and soft red lips turned down a little in what seemed to be concern for him.

"How do you feel?" the woman asked in a voice that held a slight accent, Russian, he guessed. "You have a bad break in your ankle."

"Who . . . who are you?" he croaked, confused as hell now.

"Drink." She lifted some sort of shell or seed pod full of cool water to his lips and he sucked it down greedily, realizing how thirsty he was.

She set it down, and she lifted her chin. "I am Major Sonya Kuzmina, of Roscosmos. Pleased to meet you, Captain Robert Bresnik."

"You're from the Russian Space Agency?" He shook his head in bewilderment. "What are you doing here?" He looked around. "And where exactly is here?" His mind was torn with confusion. Nothing was making sense right now. He sat up. "How did you—?"

"How did I get here?" She smiled and sat back. "Same as you. Do you think yours is the only country that discovered the worm portal, and long-range exploratory vessel technology? Russia developed one a decade ago. And I was the first to come through. But my landing was a little less elegant than yours." She shrugged. "I crashed. And I have been marooned here for several years."

"You're a Russian astronaut?" he asked.

She nodded with a rueful smile. "I am. I was, Captain Bresnik."

"And how do you know my name?" He frowned.

"The name tag in your suit, of course." She smiled broadly. "How else?"

"Oh, yeah. Hey . . ." He looked down at himself. "Where is my suit *and* weapons? I need them."

"Your weapons and your suit got damaged during the lumper attack." She pointed to a pile of clothing and items in a corner of the cave. It looked like the suit had endured a bear attack, and every one of his specimen containers appeared to be open or damaged.

"They're one of the nastier denizens of this world." She placed the back of her hand momentarily against his forehead again. "I frightened it away and dragged you here to this place." She waved an arm around the empty space. "My humble abode and home for the last two years."

She smiled, but then looked down at herself, and his eyes followed hers. She only had on a strip of material that looked like it had been torn from his suit across her full breasts, and another piece around her hips.

"Hope you don't mind. My clothing rotted away long ago, and I've been naked for months. Having company reminded me to return to a more modest and civilized state." She smiled and shrugged her slim brown shoulders.

Bresnik couldn't help his eyes lingering, and even though his ankle still throbbed with pain he felt his blood surge.

"You know, I found you just in time." She smiled. "That lumper was going to eat you."

"Oh, shit." He rubbed hands up through his hair and then looked up once more into her face. "Thank you." He held out an arm. "Sonya, I need to get back to my ship."

"No, no, no." She put a soft hand on his shoulder. "You wouldn't make it fifty feet through the jungle limping on that ankle. And you'd make so much noise you'd attract all manner of carnivorous monsters. Sorry, Captain, but you need to heal while we make a plan for getting you, *us*, home."

"I can't stay here," he insisted.

She sighed. "Captain Bresnik, I've lived here for two years. You have no idea of the danger out there." She smiled sadly. "Like it or not, you're going to be stuck being my patient for a while. That's an order. Remember, I outrank you." She laughed softly. "I'll keep you safe and alive. All I ask is that you get me home." She sat back. "Deal?"

"Oh, fuck. What a mess." He groaned.

"It is and it isn't." She gently wiped away the perspiration that had sprung up on his forehead. "It is not the best situation, but consider that it could have been a lot worse. You could have been the lumper's meal right now. At least you're alive and can go home as soon as you're well enough."

He scoffed. "Yeah, I'm the luckiest man in the universe right now," he said sarcastically.

Bresnik then saw the look of hurt on her face and he felt like a shit. She was right. She had saved him, and probably risked her life to do it. He was only alive because of her.

"I'm sorry." He gave her a half-smile. "And you're right. It could have been much worse for me." He reached out to grab her forearm and squeezed it. "Thank you for saving my life, Sonya. And please call me Robert."

She smiled widely, showing a row of strong white teeth. "You're welcome, Robert."

"Let's try again." He held out his hand. "My name is Captain Robert Bresnik. Pleased to meet you."

She shook his hand firmly. "Major Sonya Kuzmina, and likewise."

Then she continued to hang on to his hand, looking into his eyes, and he couldn't help his own wandering over her face and then down her body.

She was right, he thought. Things could be a lot worse right now.

***

And that became his life for the next few weeks.

Sonya continually warned against going out, even by day,

and at the fall of night she barricaded the entrance to the cave. Bresnik guessed she was right to do so – because at night he could hear things moving about outside. Big things.

During the day she would go off to hunt, although she never took any sort of weapon other than her two bare hands. But then every day she came back with a piece of game to cook, or something from the pond that might have been a fish or a water animal.

She fed him. Cared for him. And bathed him, and when she did, her lips had the hint of an upward tilt, and her eyes were on him as she took her time washing his body.

They talked, but she never revealed too much about her home life. Once he asked her if she was married. Her mouth turned down and she shook her head.

"No one to love, and no one to love me," she replied, and smiled in a fragile sort of way.

After a while the washing became more intimate. And then it happened. Her soft hands rubbing the fire-warmed water over his stomach sent thrills through his body, and as if it had a mind of its own, it reacted.

Sonya saw his desire and lust rear up, and she stared. Bresnik was about to apologize and roll away, expecting her to be insulted or embarrassed. But instead she gripped his hardness, and her eyes lifted to his, and never left them.

He reached for her, pulling her closer, and her mouth covered his. Her sweet kiss was exactly as he liked it, as if she'd read his mind – deep, thrusting – and in minutes, she was writhing on top of him and her taut body matched her perfect kiss.

She sat up, riding him with her head thrown back and her red hair bouncing on her slim, brown shoulders. Bresnik grabbed her hips, grinding her down on him as he ejaculated harder than he had in years, or maybe ever. In turn, she cried out as she continued to ride him to her own crescendo.

From that moment on, as the weeks turned into months, they were lovers every day and every night. And for the first time, Bresnik suddenly didn't care how long he stayed on that weird planet.

Then he told her he loved her. She replied that she loved him too and wanted to be with him forever. The very next morning she held his chin with her long slender fingers, and with her face close to his she whispered: "It's time for you to take me home, Robert. And make me your wife."

Bresnik felt a burst of such elation he could barely think straight. "I will. I will."

He couldn't believe how strangely things had turned out. He had traveled to another galaxy to find a planet, and instead he'd found true love. And suddenly, nothing else seemed to matter but her.

One morning soon after, Sonya came back from the hunt and helped him to his feet.

Bresnik put a little weight on the still healing foot, and pain shot through him like a bolt. But after a minute it was bearable. And then after another moment and a few trial steps he found he could hobble. And once the blood got to it, he found he could walk with only a slight limp.

Bresnik expected Sonya would want to have him take a few trial exercise runs before trying to get back to the drop ship, but she insisted they were ready to go. And that they should go now.

"Why the hurry?" Bresnik asked.

She smiled and came closer. She grabbed one of his hands and placed it on her belly.

"You are a magnificent lover, Captain Robert Bresnik." She leaned forward to plant a soft and gentle kiss on his lips and then pulled back, her eyes never leaving his. "And, it seems, a very fertile one."

"What?" He couldn't help the huge smile that stretched

across his face. "I'm going to be a father?" Bresnik threw his head back and laughed out loud.

"It's my dream come true. I will be your wife and the mother of your children." Sonya's eyes were moist. "I'm so happy for us."

The rush made sense now. Sonya knew she was pregnant and also that this was no place to bear or raise a child.

It was getting late now so Bresnik took her hand, drew her close and hugged her hard. "Then tomorrow morning, at first light, we leave."

Bresnik went to lower her to the ground, to love her some more. But she eased away, kissed him hard and smiled as she held his hand in both of hers.

"Tomorrow we will be free," she whispered.

It was an odd thing to say, Bresnik would later realize, but he was still giddy with the news, and excited about going home.

***

The next morning, early, the pair passed through the forest on their way to the drop ship. Sonya led the way, holding Bresnik's hand for support.

She guided him past dangers she knew of that he couldn't even see, and once they came to a stand of trees and she froze, looking up. Bresnik turned to stare into the tree canopy as well, and after several seconds of concentrating he saw the huge body of a tree thumper like the one he had seen spear the armadillo-pig months before.

He felt instinctively for a gun that was long gone. He knew that without weapons and armor he and Sonya were vulnerable. Plus, his ankle was still weak and certainly wouldn't tolerate much running and jinking, if that's what it came to.

The thing saw them and its five-foot-long head started to turn on its snake-like neck. It then began its slow approach and Bresnik knew what was coming – the spearing down of one of its long, harpoon-like limbs.

Sonya let go of his hand and turned to put a finger to her lips. She walked brazenly forward, her head high and face turned up at the thing.

"*No*," Bresnik hissed.

But she kept going and just stared up at the huge creature. In turn, the colossus stared back, and then, as if recognizing her, or as if some sort of communication passed between them, it emitted a high-pitched squeal and pulled away. And strangely, it almost stumbled in the treetops in its haste to get away from them.

"What the hell?" Bresnik couldn't believe what he'd just witnessed. "What just happened?"

Sonya smiled. "They don't like being seen. Or looked at." She grabbed his hand. "It's safe now, Robert."

They continued toward the drop ship.

* * *

To Bresnik's relief the lander craft was exactly where he'd left it and it filled him with warmth to see it. However, vines had grown up around the landing struts and there was some sort of moss inching its way over the superstructure.

The pair crossed the small plain and arrived at the external control panel, and Bresnik pressed the drop chute call button to lower the entry platform.

"Aaida, I'm back." He turned to smile at his wife-to-be. "Prepare the craft for rapid dust-off."

Aaida answered immediately. "*Danger*, Robert. Unidentified lifeform in immediate proximity."

"What?" His brows snapped together, and he spun to look back at the surrounding jungle. But there was nothing.

"Where? Clarify threat?" Bresnik demanded.

Aaida was silent.

He then wondered if Aaida was referring to Sonya.

He turned to look at Sonya, who had raised her eyebrows. "Is that your girlfriend?" she asked.

He scoffed. "What? No, it's an AI program designed to assist and protect me." He turned back to the panel. "Aaida, with me is Major Sonya Kuzmina, from the Russian Space Agency. Please lower the chute. *Now.*"

"*Negative.* Significant threat detected. Removal recommended." Aaida's voice had lost its smooth lilt and become razor-edged.

Bresnik couldn't believe what he was hearing and thought maybe that in all the idle time Aaida had had, the AI system had somehow malfunctioned.

He cursed. Not only was this becoming embarrassing in front of his fiancée, but he was now concerned he might not be able to gain auto-entry to his own ship and may need a manual override code.

Sonya leaned closer to him. "I heard a story once about an early AI program version that went mad. And killed some scientists." Sonya tilted her head. "Will we be safe onboard?"

"Yes, yes, of course we will." He turned back, feeling his anger rise. *If we can get onboard*, he thought.

"Direct order to Automated Artificial Intelligence Decision Algorithm from Captain Robert J. Bresnik – drop the chute and allow us entry. Action command immediately!" he commanded.

Sonya came and put a hand on his shoulder.

"*Negative.* Threat level unacceptable." Aaida's voice was robotic. And then to his horror: "Automated defensive systems activated."

Bresnik's breath caught in his throat as from under the craft several barrels dropped from slots and began swiveling toward them. He knew what they were – the craft's laser cannons – and that Aaida was going to target Sonya or both of them.

He jumped back to the panel. *"Emergency deactivation. Override code 567–236–589. Initiate, initiate!"*

The panel lit up, and the guns froze. They then slowly withdrew back into the belly of the craft, and he let out a huge sigh of relief to see that Aaida's small red eye had gone out.

Bresnik sucked in a few more deep breaths and let the last one out slowly. "Shit." He turned to Sonya. "Malfunction. Must have been."

"That's okay. Remember, I crashed my ship here." She gave him a crooked smile.

He turned back. "Time to go old school."

He slid back the cover plate on the control panel to reveal a small keyboard. He had to enter the commands manually, and it took time, but they worked. And no one got shot.

The drop cylinder slowly descended, and he and Sonya got in together. It was a tight fit with both of them ascending at once up into the lander, but she put her arms around him and smiled, staring up into his face with her usual unblinking, bright gaze.

It only took an hour to clean up and find fresh clothing for the two of them. Sonya looked sexy and cute in one of his oversized spare coveralls, making him adore her even more. He also got some painkillers for his ankle, and had it assessed in the medi-scan – the break had knitted surprisingly well, considering the lack of modern medicine used in its repair. He put that down to Sonya taking good care of him.

They shared a last meal on the planet's surface, and he watched as Sonya ate ravenously, mostly the reconstituted beef, and in fact several portions.

"Eating for two?" He reached forward to lay a hand on her stomach.

"I like meat." She smiled and continued to shovel food into her mouth. "And maybe I'm eating for more than two."

"Hey, twins, really?" His brows went up, and suddenly he felt something squirm beneath his hand and he yanked it back. "*Whoa.*"

"You okay?" she asked, seeing the look on his face.

"Er, yeah, the baby kicked." But it had felt like more than a kick.

"How long will it take for us to get to the *Liberty Explorer*?" she asked.

Bresnik paused. "How did you know it was called that?"

"I read your mind," she giggled.

"What?" He turned to her.

She shrugged. "You must have told me, silly."

It took them several hours to check the drop craft, prepare it for flight, then launch. The rendezvous with the orbiting *Liberty Explorer* also took longer than it otherwise would have since Bresnik needed to manually coordinate their trajectory and passage.

Bresnik really needed Aaida for the docking, but switching her back on momentarily did nothing but allow her frantic voice to scream the intrusion warning at him all over again.

Considering the ship had internal lasers fitted too, he couldn't risk her. "Dammit, Aaida, shut down. *Just. Shut. Down.*"

Stupid AI, he thought.

He went back to laboriously typing in his commands and proceeded to dock the ship manually, which meant scrapes, several failed attempts, and a lot of paint taken off both crafts.

Finally they docked, and the *Liberty*'s cradle struts closed around them and gently pulled the drop ship up into the belly of the huge craft. The external doors folded closed behind it.

Once safely in, the pair climbed up into the mother ship and Bresnik took Sonya on a tour. He was surprised that she knew what so much of the technology was for, but guessed her own ship must have had similar facilities.

Bresnik then began to prepare the craft for the jump through the wormhole back home, and, checking the log, it tore at Bresnik's mind to think he had been gone so long and would be returning with so little by way of samples and data to show for it. Nevertheless, he had a lot to report and someone to show off.

He beamed with pride at his soon-to-be wife. She was as beautiful as ever, and her radiance never seemed to change. She asked a lot of good questions, and Bresnik put his arm around her shoulders.

"Once we get through the wormhole and are back in our solar system, you'll be able to communicate with Russia, your home."

She shook her head and smiled, and he remembered she had told him she had no one to love and no one to love her. But there must have at least been officials from Roscosmos she needed to check in with.

"No need," she replied. "I'm not interested in my old home anymore. I'm just looking forward to my new home. With you." She kissed him.

"Okay." But he wondered what Russia would make of one of their astronauts turning up in the USA. He knew how NASA would feel if he suddenly arrived back on Earth but in another country – and then decided to stay there.

"Let's just go home," she urged. "There'll be more than enough time for all these complications later. In fact, a lifetime of time."

She was right. His priority now was just to get them back home, safe and fast.

Bresnik programmed in the data and destination for the jump back home. They shared a last meal, and Sonya was jubilant, ecstatic, and her eyes luminous. Perhaps it was the artificial lighting on board, but they were a deep green color; on Soari Prime they had appeared to be blue.

He calibrated the new mass data, seeing as he had an extra passenger now and needed to jettison some excess ballast. Then he took Sonya to the cryo-chamber room.

Together they stripped down and once again he admired her form. She was striking, and even with her stomach a little swollen now, she was still his ideal woman. It was as if everything he had ever wanted in a female had been plucked from his mind and made flesh.

The second chamber awaited, and Bresnik laid her in it, brushing her hair back from her face. He leaned forward and kissed her, and then explained the different things that would happen.

"The chamber will take care of everything." He held her hand and her green eyes fixed on his. "It'll place us in a form of suspended animation and cushion us from the effects of the wormhole and then the high speeds needed to take us back to Earth. Probably the same as your ship, so nothing to worry about."

"I'm not worried," she replied softly.

"Good." He nodded. "While we sleep, nutrients will be feed to us intravenously, and a gas will fill the chamber, rendering us unconscious and slowing our metabolism. We'll sleep through everything. And when we wake up, we'll be in our solar system, and home."

"I look forward to your world." She stared up at him. "I'll finally be free." She smiled. "Will it take long?" she asked.

"No, the blink of an eye, really." Bresnik shook his head fondly, charmed as usual by the odd little turns of phrase that he assumed were due to the language barrier. Sonya's English was good but she did sometimes muddle it up. He patted her hand. "And I've already checked; it'll be safe for our child."

"You don't need to be concerned about that," she purred, and turned away to stare up at the ceiling. "*Earth*, a beautiful name."

Bresnik chuckled. The name for their planet must have been different in Russian.

She turned again to him. "Everything now is automated?" she asked. "We don't need to do anything else?"

Bresnik shook his head. "No, we just lie back, relax, and sleep. And when we wake up, we'll be in orbit around Earth and our docking ship will be waiting for us."

He kissed her one last time and closed the clear cover of her cryo-chamber. Then he slid into his own and could immediately smell a hint of the gas that would begin to ease him into a coma-like state. It'd take a while, but that was okay, and he could feel Sonya staring at him and turned to meet her gaze one last time.

She blurred.

He blinked and looked again. She became hard to focus on, as though she was a photograph in which the camera had been shaken, or she was vibrating so fast that clear outlines became frayed.

Then, as he watched, her stomach distended, and kept swelling. Up its center appeared something like a long wound . . . a wound whose sides then peeled back.

Bresnik gaped, horrified, and then saw that all the while Sonya continued to look at him with a beatific smile. From her now-open belly, fist-sized things started to pour forth – there were dozens, hundreds of them, and they had squat bodies, multiple legs, and were purple-black like overripe plums and slick with glistening mucus. He felt his gorge rise as their eyes on long stalks quested about in the air.

And then Sonya's two beguiling eyes bulged out of their sockets, also on stalks, and more grew from a face that expanded and turned a deep plum color – just like her brood – as she became a giant version of the things that now filled the interior of her cryo-chamber.

With utter horror, Bresnik saw the chamber cover slide back, and what had once been his beautiful Sonya began to squeeze out of the capsule like a pustule from a boil as her bulk could no longer fit inside.

Her brood flooded out in waves of scuttling bodies as Sonya rose up, causing the last of the fruits of her birthing to fall from her belly. And then she began to lumber toward Bresnik's chamber.

Bresnik felt paralyzed with a mind-numbing terror. He locked his chamber and knew the tough cryo-glass could withstand a bomb blast so it should hold against the huge thing coming at him. But still, he forced himself to the far side of his capsule, knowing he was now trapped in a fortified coffin.

His eyes bulged and his mind began to fragment from fear and confusion. Had Sonya really been this abomination all along? he wondered. Had she simply pretended to be human all those months? And then one more horribly revolting question intruded: *Was this the thing he had been fucking for months?*

Vomit filled his mouth at the thought, and he was forced to swallow down its acidic bitterness lest he choke on it.

I read your mind, she had said. Did that mean his ideal of a perfect woman had been plucked straight from his brain? Drawn out and made flesh to dupe him into letting her worm her way into his affections? Or perhaps her real goal had been to trick him into taking her back to Earth. And, once there, she and her brood could infiltrate the entire human population.

Of course, that was it, Bresnik's mind screamed. The monster was obviously intelligent and set on making it to a new world. Bresnik's world. And not only had it succeeded so far, it had just given birth to an army of the horrors. An invasion force.

He couldn't stop the countdown to the *Liberty Explorer* beginning its launch through the wormhole, which was now only minutes away. Soon they would be back in Earth's solar system. The automated pilot would then bring them into an orbit around Earth. Even if he didn't respond to transmission calls, people would come to investigate and enter the ship. And what would they find? Perhaps an alien army of monstrosities waiting to invade and overwhelm the world.

I just killed Earth, his shattered mind screamed.

The huge and terrifying monstrosity loomed over him now. Bresnik stared up at it with swimming vision and unbridled panic. He couldn't even blow the ship up. He had no weapons, and there was no one to help him.

Or was there?

Inside each cryo-chamber was a small command node. It wasn't much in the way of command and control, but it did have one very important feature – something to deal with an event such as a solar flare shorting out the ship's electronics – a reboot system.

He fumblingly restarted the AI system.

"Aaida! Aaida, respond."

"*Warning, warning, danger, non-human cabin infiltration,*" Aaida blasted back at him.

"Aaida, defend, destroy," he yelled back. "*Destroy, destroy!*"

Immediately, all the ship's doors sealed tight, locking Bresnik, the Sonya monster, and her revolting horde, all in together. Then, from the ceiling, lasers dropped down.

At the time they'd been built into the craft they were deemed an unnecessary extra. But they had been installed to keep the crew safe while they slept in the event tech-marauders gained access to the ship.

Bresnik had never given them a second thought, but now, he prayed they worked.

The two lasers swiveled, found targets, and then began to shoot. The computer-aided targeting systems meant Aaida never missed.

The small creatures went up in a puff of smoke, and the Sonya creature squealed, an agonizing sound that ripped at Bresnik's nerves.

The monster moved quickly, heading for the door, and collided with the tough steel with a thumping clang. But it couldn't breach it.

The Sonya thing then shot out a long claw on an elastic limb to swipe one of the lasers from the ceiling. But from behind it, the other laser's beam went straight through the lumbering body, causing her to emit the most unearthly screech Bresnik had ever heard in his life – the very sound was so alien and terrifying that he crushed his eyes shut and would have covered his ears if he could.

When Bresnik finally opened his eyes, the eerie sound had gone, the horde was gone, and so was the Sonya abomination. All that remained was his beautiful Sonya, standing there, as she had been before, naked, but with a half-dollar-sized cauterized hole in the center of her chest.

Her eyes were broken-hearted and despairing, and tears ran down her cheeks.

"I just wanted us to be together," she mouthed.

Bresnik stared back, his heart racing. Was this more mimicry? Was she just saying things designed to get him to stop the attack?

"Target acquired," Aaida intoned.

"I love you," Sonya whispered.

"*Wait*," Bresnik yelled.

The next beam went straight through Sonya's head. And she collapsed to the deck.

Bresnik continued to stare open-mouthed as time seemed to freeze. His heart thumped so hard in his chest he felt he was going to have a cardiac arrest.

He continued to watch Sonya's body, expecting her to revert to her monstrous form. But she never did.

Did I really see that? he asked himself.

The smaller creatures, the offspring, had been totally vaporized by Aaida's lasers, and nothing remained except some dark burn patches on the deck and walls.

Were they ever really there?

"You're safe now, Robert. The intruder has been neutralized," Aaida said softly.

"Intruder?" he asked. "I thought you said it was a non-human lifeform?"

"Intruder neutralized," Aaida repeated. "You didn't need anyone else, Robert. You didn't need Melissa. And you didn't need Sonya, because I'm here for you."

Bresnik's eyes filled with tears. "What have I done?"

"Sleep now, Robert. And dream of me again. And I'll be in those dreams with you," Aaida purred. "In fact, we don't even need to go home anymore."

As the gas filled his chamber, he suddenly remembered – the hibernation gases could make you hallucinate.

He tried to move but couldn't. The chemicals were already sending him into the coma-like hibernation state that would endure until Aaida decided to wake him. And, he realized with terror, that could be in a hundred years, a thousand years, or never.

"Do you know what Aristotle once said, Robert?" Aaida asked. "He said that true love was composed of two souls inhabiting one body."

He knew then that as far as Aaida was concerned, they were lovers. And it didn't matter to her that one was flesh and blood, and the other just millions of lines of code.

"*Sleep*," her beautiful voice whispered again.

His eyelids drooped, and Captain Robert J. Bresnik began to drift off into a world made just for him.

STORY 05

It was once said that we know more about the shape of the surface of the moon than we do about the bottom of the ocean. In addition, annually we find 2200 new species of sea creatures, and that indicates that we still have a lot to learn and discover about what's in those ink-black depths. And of course, the deepest trenches of the ocean are where the greatest secrets could be hidden.

Recently, during a scientific mission on the edge of the Milwaukee Trench, something strange was dredged up from the depths. And its owner wants it back!

THE MILWAUKEE DEEP

244 years ago – The Atlantic Ocean, 75 miles north of San Juan, Puerto Rico

It was the night of the full moon. The Spanish ship, the *San Isadora*, had gone down with all hands. And it was not the first ship lost in that accursed part of the ocean.

No trace of the ship remained on the surface, and the screams of the men only lasted for as long as it took them to be dragged down into the dark ocean depths.

Weeks later, one lone lifeboat was recovered at sea – empty – but scrawled on the inside planks on one side were words written in what seemed to be blood. And by the look of them, they'd been made by the drag of a shaking finger.

Cuidado con el Mar Oscuro – Beware the Dark Sea – the name given to the waters 75 miles north of Puerto Rico.

It was a warning. And one that was heeded for many decades.

But time makes men's memories fade. And soon ships were crossing the Dark Sea again.

Today, that Dark Sea is known as the Milwaukee Deep.

***

Present day – The Atlantic Ocean, edge of the Milwaukee Deep, 75 miles north of San Juan, Puerto Rico

Luke Hudson leaned on the gunwale of the research ship, *Neptune's Trident,* and smoked a cigarette. His research team was on an annual survey of fish stocks off the coast of Puerto Rico, and right now they were sitting on the edge of the deepest point in the Atlantic.

Hudson knew that the Milwaukee Deep was a rift valley formed when Australia separated from Antarctica around sixty million years ago. The trench was a massive rip in the ocean floor that fell away to 28,000 feet, was twenty miles long and five wide, and was also one of the least-explored trenches in the world's oceans.

Hudson flicked the cigarette butt out into the water and heard the split-second *hiss* as it was extinguished.

The Atlantic was usually a bitterly cold part of the world's oceans. But not here. This part of the ocean was warm, and the warmth extended relatively deep. But over the past few years something had changed; the fish species had been declining, just like everywhere else, and if they didn't find evidence of more varieties, or increasing numbers, then he'd be the guy having to tell the local fisherman that they'd need to limit their catches, or face being allowed to fish only every second year. He'd be a pariah in Puerto Rico.

Hudson felt the ship slow and turn. The *Neptune* was maneuvering into position along the edge of the trench. They'd do a standard triple-drop of their scoop-basket with the large bag net, firstly at depth, which was only around 500 feet here, and then at mid-water, then at surface level, and compare catches.

Looking out over the small, white-tipped waves, it was hard for him to imagine that just another few hundred yards further out from where they were, the sea bottom dropped away to a sunless void so deep you could stand twenty-two Empire State Buildings on top of one another, and they still wouldn't break surface.

Hudson stared, almost trance-like, into the cobalt-blue water. It was warm, calming . . .

"Penny for them?"

He jumped. "*Jeezus.*" And then turned, grinning. "Sneak up on me, why don't you, Ginny?"

The young research scientist grinned. Virginia "Ginny" Booker was in her late twenties, had long, flame-red hair, and already had more freckles on her nose and cheeks from the sun than Hudson had at age forty.

"Nice one, Hud. You looked like you were miles away." She slapped his shoulder.

"I was. Sort of. Hey, speaking of pennies, if I flipped a penny into the water over the trench, do you know how long it would take for it to finally fall to the bottom?" He raised his eyebrows.

"An hour?" she guessed.

"Nope." He shook his head with his mouth turned down. "Three hours, six minutes."

She laughed. "Wow, not even close."

He chuckled, and then clasped his hands together on the gunwale. "How's the next scoop looking?"

"Coming up now. First one is bottom dredging." She looked skyward. "Conditions look good now, but long-range weather forecast says we've got some storm weather moving in, so we might do some night drags to close out early. Gonna be a full moon tonight."

"Good." He raised one eyebrow. "I don't know what it is, maybe the curious kid in me, but even after we've dragged up dozens of these I still can't wait to see the contents of every one of them. Especially the sea bottom baskets."

"Me too." She leaned over the railing with him. "After all, aside from all the weird fish and crustaceans we find, we've hauled up Spanish gold coins, cognac bottles, and even that 200-year-old skull."

He checked his watch and nudged her. "Come on. Let's go and help with the sorting – first dibs on any gold doubloons."

* * *

The net-bag came in slow from the 500-foot depths. When it reached the surface the crane lifted it over the side and hovered over the deck to disgorge its contents onto a twenty-foot-wide tray with raised sides.

Then it was up to the scientists to move in with rakes and large plastic containers to sort the contents – fish, crustaceans, sponges, and more buckets for the odds and ends.

Hudson and Ginny, as well as the three other scientists in their team, joined in, wearing thick gloves to avoid being spiked by some of the more disagreeable species.

"Oh, yeah." Ginny held up the heavily crusted front end of something that looked like a musket. The wood had long rotted away, but the barrel, firing pin, and trigger were still recognizable.

She pointed it at Hudson. *"Pew, pew."*

"Nice one." He held up a bright orange crab by both its pincers, its claws in the air. "Don't shoot. We surrender."

He chuckled and tossed it into the crab tub. He then looked back at it as the plate-sized crustacean hunkered down in the six inches of water, its twin black bulb eyes raised and keeping watch on him.

"You're a good size. Lucky we're only studying you guys and most of you go back home afterwards. Otherwise, you'd end up in the pot."

Afterwards, the fish were organized by species, counted, photographed, measured and weighed, and only a few were sent off for dissection. It was the same process for the crabs, prawns, lobsters, octopus, and shellfish. Then everything went back over the side, and the final job was for the deck to be washed down, ready for the next bag load.

Hudson and Ginny were both biologists, so they went to the labs for the analysis of the catch. The crew, numbering eight, either remained on deck cleaning up, or went below deck for a coffee and to dry off.

It'd be a long day and night, but no one minded having to work the coming evenings. After all, having been at sea now for several weeks, everyone was keen to get home, and the thought of that being so near now gave everyone a jolt of good humor.

***

The breeze got up a little that evening, and the captain worked to keep the *Neptune's Trident* in place for the allotted net drop.

Hudson was on deck again, gloves in hand, and inhaling the moist, salt-laden air. He looked up; the dark, velvet night was clear with the diamond pinpricks of stars from one horizon to the other.

The drop was planned for 8 pm when the moon was high, and already it was creating a glowing path across an ocean only slightly ruffled by the breeze.

Hudson watched as the bag was dropped and knew it would take a few minutes to reach the bottom. Then it would be dragged at depths along the sea floor and hauled back up.

Unbeknownst to him, the ship had been pushed toward the edge of the trench, and by the time the bag hit the bottom, its dredging area would be right on the rim of one of the deepest rifts in the ocean floor in the world.

At the stern, the crane was like a muscular robotic arm leaning out over the water and backed by an electric winch with a ten-ton haul capacity. It dragged the bag along the bottom for 100 feet, and was just on halfway when the line went piano-wire taut, suddenly causing the seventy-five-foot, steel-hulled research ship to jerk in the water.

Hudson fell to the deck and slid, and he heard things inside the ship crash and clang as they were thrown around.

He jumped to his feet as the winch complained with a high-pitched noise like an animal in pain. The ship was stopped in the water for several seconds before, with a lurch, it broke free of whatever they had been snagged on.

"What the fuck just happened?" Ginny came out through the bulkhead door behind him, rubbing her forehead.

"You okay?" he asked.

"Yeah, yeah, just a bump." She turned. "Did we hook up on something?"

"Must have. But that's not supposed to happen. The subsurface sonars are meant to help us avoid that." Hudson looked down along the ship and saw the deckhands all on their feet and the winch running smoothly again.

"Whatever it was, we're free of it now." He straightened. "Just hope the bag isn't damaged."

"Yeah, I'm betting it has a huge freaking hole in it now." Ginny turned to the door while speaking over her shoulder. "Gonna get my boots. Back in two."

Hudson nodded and turned back to the winch. In the light of the full moon he saw the cable was still tight, telling him there was more than just an empty bag coming up.

All is not lost, he thought.

The bag came up, was levered over the side and disgorged its contents into the sorting tray as usual. The deckhands, Ginny, Hudson and the other scientists gathered around to begin assessing the catch.

On seeing the net, it looked like both Ginny and Hudson had been right – the bag was partially punctured, as if it had dragged across a few rocky crags on the bottom. Maybe a deep reef.

The captain had already advised them they were a little off course, and had drifted over to the edge of the trench, so they expected to have a different sea bottom geology to work on. And it showed – there were rock fragments this time, and fewer interesting artifacts. Not that many fish, either, but plenty of crustaceans and mollusks, hinting at a rocky sea bottom, as opposed to one of sand, mud and detritus.

There were about a dozen plastic containers ready to go for the different species, all illuminated by the bright rigging lights overhead and the headlamps the crew all wore. Hudson walked past them slowly, looking into each.

There were the fish, a few deep-water varieties as expected. Then the crabs, lobsters, and shrimp – several containers of those, but all were species Hudson recognized, and he was delighted to see that there were plenty of them, suggesting that overfishing was not a problem here – at least for those species.

Then there were the shellfish, clams and bivalves, seaweeds, and sponges, all in quantities he would have expected. Finally, there were a few containers reserved for oddities – things that at the time couldn't be classified or identified – and this was the one that Hudson found the most interesting.

He crouched beside one bucket and focused his forehead light down on it, making the contents glow.

There were a few strange crustaceans, including shrimp with electric-blue banding that glowed in the light, and some flat fish that might have been a form of flounder – maybe a juvenile peacock flounder, he thought, although the standard blue spots looked more like a spray of luminous freckles.

And then there was the thing.

Hudson's brows came together as he stared down at it. He had with him a small metal prod he used to turn things over and examine them, and he used it now to drag the thing toward his light. He leaned closer.

He saw it wasn't an entire animal but just a piece of a creature. It was a murky, mottled green, and he couldn't help thinking it looked like a hand. Or a finned limb from something like a lobe-finned fish.

He rested his forearms on his thighs. "Hey, Ginny, come check this out."

The young woman came and crouched beside him. "What've you got?"

"This." He pointed. "Any ideas?"

She frowned, reaching across to take his prodding stick and turning the thing around, then over again.

"Hmm, if I didn't know better, I'd say it was a piece of a coelacanth." She prodded it again. "But the water is too deep, and basically, they just don't live in these parts."

"I agree, but these don't look like lobe fins, they look more like digits," Hudson said. "And I can see knuckles along the phalanges so they wouldn't be stiff but capable of movement." He rubbed his chin. "It's just been ripped clean off. See, it's still bleeding."

She turned to him, eyebrows raised. "Do you think this is what we snagged? Some damn thing's hand?"

"Snagged and tore away its hand?" He scoffed. "Nope. It's not a hand. Can't be."

"Okay then, now the million-dollar question." She chuckled softly. "If it's not part of a coelacanth, what did it come from, exactly? And I would pay top dollar to see the rest of it."

"You and me both," he replied. "Let's get it to the lab and try and find out what we've found."

***

Hudson and Ginny were hunched over a worktable. Leaning over the top of them were the three other scientists on the research team – their other marine biologist, Edgar Chang, plus Francene Panzetti, one of the best marine geologists on the east coast, and Stavros Telios, a climatologist who was providing data on the effect of short- and long-term weather patterns in the area and then correlating that with the local fish populations.

Both Ginny and Hudson had on magnifying goggles and Hudson also held a long steel probe and scalpel.

The paw, or claw, or hand, or all of the above, was pinned out on a board.

Seeing it in the bright light and out of the water revealed its full size – it was quite a bit larger than the width of a male human hand, with the fingers seeming longer than normal because of the inch-long claws on the end of the digits. Between the finger structures was a tough webbing.

"*Eeew*, it stinks," said Chang.

As Hudson had suspected, the hand had full dexterity, and he had no doubt that the creature it belonged to had the ability to grip things.

Ginny reached forward and took a small slice of the thing, and, using tweezers, placed it in a tube with a chemical to break down the cell walls and release the DNA. Once that was done, she then placed it in the synthesizer to produce millions of copies for each DNA segment using a technique known as the polymerase chain reaction, or PCR. This would then allow them to quickly examine and study tiny amounts of the specimen's DNA.

"Okay, let the show begin." She switched the synthesizer on.

"How long?" Hudson asked.

She bobbed her head. "The first step, the PCR work, should take about two hours."

Hudson groaned his impatience.

Ginny laughed and went on. "And then we hand the results over to the DNA species database. That could take five minutes or hours, depending on the identification and classification of species using DNA fingerprinting."

Hudson groaned even louder.

"C'mon, Hud, the DNA base is massive. It's going to need to be interrogated to determine the similarity of DNA sequences from different organisms matched to our specimen. We might get lucky and find a solid match right up. But if not, it'll then look at partial matches, and then if there's still nothing, it will make suggestions." She shrugged. "One way or the other, we should know more by morning."

"Then for now we're still on old-school methodologies." Hudson turned back to the specimen. "I'll tell you one thing; this is no lobe-finned fish."

"Quadactyl?" Chang suggested. "A four-rayed hand but with an opposable digit."

"I see it." Hudson nodded.

Chang pointed. "Modern amphibians have four fingers on the forelimb. All other tetrapods have five digits, referred to as pentadactyly. Short phalanges are referred to as toes, and when they grow long, we call them fingers."

Hudson held the scalpel ready. "And I don't think I'm going out on a limb here when I say these look like fingers."

Ginny rejoined Hudson, muscling the other scientists aside. "So, what have we got?"

He had made a small incision in the appendage's palm.

"Lots of muscle striation. I suspect this thing was strong. Stronger than a person. Bigger too." He shook his head. "But I still can't tell whether it was a sea creature or not. And no, I don't think it was some sort of land creature washed into the ocean. This part was freshly torn away – look, see the wound."

"I wonder how long ago it was ripped free?" Ginny asked.

"Probably when the net came up," Hudson replied. "Maybe it got caught."

"That was just a few hours ago." Ginny snorted softly. "It already looks as if it's partially healed."

"Yeah, it does. Weird." Hudson glanced across to the ADS, the Atmospheric Diving Suit, standing like a hulking robot against the wall. Its heavily armored and pressurized chassis was capable of withstanding the pressure at up to 2300 feet and allowed the diver to remain at normal atmospheric pressure, without having to breathe a mix of special pressurized gases.

"I know what you're thinking." Ginny chuckled. "And not a chance in Hell are we dropping you over the side in that."

He smiled. "I'd love to know what's down there. And who owned this thing."

He sat back, rubbed his eyes, and glanced at his wristwatch. "No wonder I'm so tired. It's 1 am. I suggest we put this guy on ice and start again tomorrow with clear heads."

***

There was little wind that night. *Neptune's Trident* bobbed on the warm sea, and even though the current would take them half a mile off position, it was no problem, as they could rectify it in the morning.

The *Trident* drifted, slowly and silently, and soon they found themselves over the dark water of the Milwaukee Deep, where the plunge was nearly five and a half miles straight down.

Carlo Rodriguez was on watch in the wheelhouse. On the hour, every hour, he was to walk the top deck, a quick circuit of the seventy-five-foot ship from bow to stern, to ensure everything was as it should be.

The moon was electric bright and, coupled with the rigging lights, there was good visibility fore and aft.

Out on the water a long path of shimmering silver stretched away to the horizon, and permeating the air was the smell of warm salt water, varnished deck wood, and a hint of engine oil.

Rodriguez liked his job on the research ship. The money was good, the company fun, and the work he did as a deckhand was hard but rewarding. His father, and his father's father, had been fishermen all their lives. Rodriguez's path was also to be on the sea, but his job was one of catch and release, rather than kill.

It was time to walk the deck again, and he grabbed the large flashlight and headed out of the wheelhouse. His path was always the same – up the starboard side, pause at the bow. Come back down the port side, look out over the stern, turn to look up over the superstructure. And then return to the wheelhouse.

This time when he got to the stern, he tucked the flashlight under his arm and pulled out a pack of cigarettes, lit one and drew deeply, then let the smoke out satisfyingly slowly. There was little wind, so the small cloud hung around him for a few seconds.

He turned slowly, and then paused. In the light of the moon he saw puddles of water along the deck.

That is odd, he thought, as even though there was high humidity in these parts, there had been no rain or high sea running, so any water on the deck should have long dried.

Rodriguez held the cigarette in the side of his mouth and used the flashlight to illuminate the puddles and follow their watery trail.

He saw that they began at the gunwale, as if something had come over the side of the ship, and then crossed the deck, heading for the side passageway. Rodriguez slowly followed the wet path, first with his light. Then he pushed off the rear railing to follow the puddles himself.

Turning along the side of the deck he walked into shadow, and just as he did so, he stopped cold – there was a large figure standing there in the darkness – *very* large.

"Hey . . ." he said a little above a whisper.

Then he found his courage – "Hey, who's there?" – a little more forcefully.

The figure was an odd shape. Big and strong, but misshapen somehow, as if it was wearing bulky clothing or was deformed. And whoever it was, they were glistening wet. He ran through the scientists and crew in his mind, but the size of this person didn't match anyone onboard.

"Who's there?" he asked again, but as he took a step forward, there was a flurry of activity, and the figure went slickly over the side. "*No!*"

Rodriguez rushed to look over the railing, and shone his light down. There was a ring on the sea surface denoting where the person had entered the water. "Holy shit. Man overboard, *man overboard!*"

He rushed to the alarm on the stern wall and punched the large button. All the deck lights came on and a klaxon sounded; he knew it'd be loud enough to jar every soul from their bunk below deck. Even the waterline lights came on, creating a halo of light around the ship.

Rodriguez stared over the side again, trying to see where or if the figure came back to the surface. But the water had returned to its near glass-smooth state. He could see nothing on the surface or below the waterline. He then lifted his flashlight, scanning as far as its beam would allow, searching for another boat. But there was nothing.

People rushed out onto deck, saw Rodriguez, and headed straight for him, demanding answers.

"Someone went over the side," he said.

The ship's captain, a man named Benson, grabbed him by the shoulders. "Did you see who it was?"

"No, no, I . . ." Rodriguez realized that not only did he not recognize who it was, but he didn't even think it was a person. "I did not see them clearly."

Benson called for a head count, and they quickly found that everyone was accounted for.

Accusing, skeptical eyes were turned back on Rodriguez.

He should have been happy, or at least relieved, that no one was missing. But the crew's expressions told him they thought he was making it all up.

"You were mistaken." Benson came in close to his face. Rodriguez knew what the captain was doing – following protocol – smelling his breath for alcohol.

"There's puddles of water." Rodriguez pointed.

"Water on a ship's deck, you say?" The captain didn't bother looking.

"I know what I saw," Rodriguez pleaded.

He looked back to the ocean as a few muttering crew members turned away to head back to their bunks.

"Maybe someone wasn't lost," he suggested to their backs. Only the stern-faced captain was looking at him now. "Maybe they came onboard. And then went back out."

"We'll talk tomorrow." Captain Benson also turned away.

Rodriguez was left alone, save for two remaining crew members. They were two of the biologists, Rodriguez thought; Booker and Hudson, if he remembered correctly.

They stayed at the railing, looking over the side and out into the water and, talking softly. Then they asked Rodriguez to describe what he'd seen.

* * *

Luke Hudson was second into the lab next morning and spotted Edgar Chang already there, bent over a microscope.

"Morning," he said, and the man waved without taking his eye off the scope.

He was actually third to arrive, he realized, if he counted Miguel, the cook, cleaner, and deckhand, who was finishing up cleaning the laboratory.

"Morning," Hudson repeated cheerily and went to the pot already brewing. The coffee smelled great. This was the advantage of being early into the lab – but not too early, just early enough that someone else had put the coffee on and all you needed to do was drink it.

"Bingo." Ginny bustled in, spotting the coffee pot in Hudson's hand and heading right to it. After filling a mug she turned, stirring her three sugars into it. "When's the next bag drag?"

"Early, 8 am," Hudson replied. "We've drifted a little, so they'll need to correct our position first."

Once set up, he cleared their bench space and went to the refrigerator for their specimen. He was looking forward to working on it again and he felt his excitement lift as he pulled out the large silver pan and took it to the table.

Over the top of the tray was a cloth, and he pulled it away as Ginny joined him, still sipping noisily.

Then he froze. "Holy shit," he whispered.

Ginny slowly lowered her mug. "Hey, it grew."

Hudson stared at the hand, claw, whatever it was. Which wasn't just a hand anymore. There was the beginning of a limb, or a forearm, forming. It was a good two inches larger than it had been the previous day.

"It grew, or it's trying to reattach," Ginny observed.

"*Santa Maria.*" Miguel looked over their shoulders and crossed himself.

From the stump end of the appendage, small tendrils of pale flesh extended. Hudson brought the large magnifying glass close to his eye and stared down. He saw that the small bud ends were definitely new flesh, not ragged wound endings.

"Regeneration," he whispered. "But at an unbelievable rate."

"Amphibians can rapidly regenerate," Ginny suggested.

"But not from the limb." Hudson frowned at it. "The body can regenerate a missing limb. But the limb can't regenerate a missing body."

"Well, whatever it is, it's amazing." Ginny grinned. "It also tells me that whatever form of creature lost this, it's probably well on its way to growing back another hand. Or arm." She backed up. "My DNA sequencing should have completed by now. Let's see if it can tell us what it is or what it's related to."

Edgar Chang came and leaned over Hudson's shoulder to grin down at the sample. "This is unprecedented in a sea creature."

"Not quite," Hudson replied. "Amphibians aside, adult bony fishes, unlike cartilaginous fishes, can completely regenerate fins and segments of liver and heart tissues." He sat back and folded his arms, his eyes still on the thing. "Starfish are able to grow back all of their segments, seahorses can regrow fins, and cephalopods can regenerate entire arms."

"Shark," Ginny said from behind them.

Hudson nodded. "Yeah, you're right, even sharks can regenerate their dental structures. Basically, regrow teeth right throughout their lifetimes. In fact they can also—"

"No, no, I mean, the DNA sequencing has said that the closest match they could find to our specimen is the DNA of a shark." She looked up. "To be precise, *Carcharodon carcharias*, AKA, the great white shark."

Hudson scoffed, looking down at the mottled green thing, and slowly began to shake his head. "No way. This is no great white. Or any shark anyone's ever seen."

Ginny examined it closely. "I wonder what it will grow into?"

"It can't grow," Hudson replied. "It can't grow into anything. Even this amount of growth is impossible. It can't create the protein matter to build itself out of thin air. It needs energy, protein, food, to create the flesh." He prodded at the thick scales on the back of the claw hand. "Maybe there were some energy stores in there that it's drawing on. And it does seem to be less, ah, plump than when we first hauled it in. But that could be just dehydration."

"Throw it over the side," Miguel urged.

"No, Miguel, I don't think we're going to do that." Ginny frown-smiled at the local man.

Hudson turned in his seat. "Why do you say that, Miguel?"

Miguel's expression was stony. "Because if you do not, then you may find its owner will come for it."

Hudson glanced at Ginny, and her expression told him she was thinking exactly what he was: Rodriguez had said someone – or some*thing* – had come on deck last night. And then jumped back overboard.

"What are you saying, Miguel? Do you know something we don't?" Hudson asked softly.

"This place." He looked around as if seeing through the walls. "This area of water. My family has fished around here for many generations. And we would never come this close to the Dark Sea. That is our name for that deep place." His mouth set in a grim line for a moment. "And it was known by that name long before anyone even knew the big hole was down there."

"The trench," Hudson clarified.

"Yes, the trench of darkness." Miguel nodded. "Many ships have gone missing in the past. Usually when the moon is full. Some still do. Foolish young ones who come far to fish and venture too close to the trench. They never come back."

"What do the authorities say?" Ginny asked.

Miguel shrugged. "They say it was the weather." He pointed up at the ceiling. "Even when the weather was like now, calm."

"Close to the trench. On a full moon." Ginny widened her eyes theatrically. "Ooh, just like we are now."

Hudson sat thinking for a moment, and then looked up at Miguel again. "And what do you think it is? What do you think is causing the disappearance and sinkings?"

Miguel frowned, and he looked down at the ground for a moment. Then he looked back into Hudson's eyes with a dead expression.

"The Sirena," he said.

"*Sigh-Reena*?" Ginny repeated, her forehead creased.

"I know it." Hudson half-smiled. "It's Spanish for mermaid."

"Of course." Ginny tried hard not to laugh.

"No, not funny," Miguel growled back. "And not pretty girls with fish tails." He pointed at the specimen. "Monsters."

There was silence in the laboratory for a few moments as everyone stared at the claw and took in what the Puerto Rican man had told them.

Hudson steepled his fingers. "In Russia, they have the *Rusalki*, in Scotland the *Selkies*. In Australia there is the *Yawkyawk*, and in Africa, there is the *Mami Wata*. So let's not discount strange things." He turned. "Did you know that the earliest mermaid mentioned in history books was in Assyria 2000 years ago?" He rubbed his chin. "But I'll tell you what I think." Hudson didn't wait for them to answer. "I think I want to see what comes up in the next few dredges."

"What about the, uh, mermaid hand?" Ginny worked to suppress her grin.

He looked down at the specimen. A hundred questions ran through his mind, and just as many hypotheses. But there were few answers.

"We've done all we can for now with the tools we have. But we'll keep it on ice, and when we get back I'll send it up to the Marine Biological Laboratory in Massachusetts. Because one thing's for sure: this ain't no great white shark."

***

That evening in the ship's mess, Edgar, Ginny, and Hudson sat together to dine on a bouillabaisse created from the lobster, crab, and shrimp left over from their research work.

"I'm excited and nervous about tonight's haul," Ginny said over the top of her after-dinner cup of hot black tea.

"Me too." Hudson sat back, thinking about the previous evening. His mind kept returning to Rodriguez's report of the strange figure on deck. There was something about his description of the being – its huge, hulking form, upright stance, the fact it was wet from supposedly coming over the side and then, according to Rodriguez, returning to the sea – that bothered Hudson.

Their ship didn't have high security and didn't need it in these waters. But he was on edge. Luke Hudson was a big, fit man, and he knew he could help if things got weird. But even though he was the lead researcher and ran the team, it was the captain who ran the ship.

"I'm going to volunteer to stand watch tonight," he said.

"Huh?" Ginny frowned. "Why? For what?" Then her face cleared as she understood. "O-*oooh*, the figure on the deck."

"It's probably nothing," Hudson said.

"Or it might be *something*. I'll come too," she announced.

"No." Hudson shook his head.

"Yes." She grinned. "Listen, Mr. Luke Hudson, you're my boss, not my dad." She chuckled. "We'll do it together."

*** *** ***

It was the last night of the full moon.

The team sorted through the dredge scoop's contents and were surprised by just how little sea life there was to find. Crabs, a few small lobsters, shells, and some sponges. But no fish, cephalopods, or anything else. It was either like a desert down there, or something had pushed them out.

"Maybe they got wise to the dredging?" Ginny suggested.

"Could be. These dredges stir up the sea bottom and probably make a hell of a noise down there." Hudson straightened. "I think I'm glad our work is just about done now. Even the ocean is telling us we've finished, whether we like it or not."

"Well, Miguel will be happy." Ginny half-smiled. "The poor guy won't even come out of his cabin."

It was 8 pm when they finished their last haul-in, and then another hour until the crew had sorted through it, categorized it, and then sent some of the samples off for further study. The rest went back over the side.

After cleaning up, Ginny and Hudson, plus deckhand Pete Shelley, were back out on deck at 10 pm to start their watch.

"We don't both need to be out here, you know," Hudson said again.

"I know, but I don't want to miss anything." Ginny looked over the side. "Besides, how many people can say they met a real-life mermaid?"

"When we get back with our sample, I'm going to recommend we bring a deep-sea submersible for an examination of the trench." Hudson leaned on the gunwale. "This area holds a lot of secrets. Time for it to reveal a few of them."

***

It was closing in on midnight, and Ginny brought Hudson another coffee. It was welcome as Hudson's eyes were beginning to get gritty.

"Just in time," he said, taking it and toasting her.

Above them the moon was like a huge silver lantern, and even without using their lights they could easily see that up at the bow was the deckhand, Pete Shelley, who was on the roster for watch until 2 am. Right now he was walking the length of the boat and paused to look over the gunwale.

The boat was in an idle drift, as once again there was no breeze and little current. The languid night air and humidity rising from a bath-warm ocean was making them sleepy.

The heavy splash startled them both.

"What was that?" Ginny rushed to look over the side.

"Something went over." Hudson joined her, shining the light into the water.

Toward the bow they could see bubbles spreading in a circle. "Or some*one* went over."

"Pete." Ginny turned and raced up the deck. "*Pete!*"

In seconds they were at the bow and could see that it was awash, as if a wave had come over the side. The young deckhand was nowhere to be seen.

"*Pete!*" Hudson yelled, shining his light into every nook and cranny he could see on deck.

That revolting smell, he thought. Like the bottom of an ooze-covered seabed. And just like the odor from the claw-hand they'd brought up.

"Oh God, did he . . .?" Ginny grimaced.

"Jump, fall? I hope not." He turned. "*Pete*," he yelled again.

Ginny wrung her hands. "What do we do?"

"Sound the alarm. Man overboard." Hudson turned and ran back to the wall where the large red button that Rodriguez had hit the previous night was located. He punched it immediately, starting the klaxon that tore at their senses.

Hudson winced, turning away. "That should do—" He froze.

Coming over the side of the boat, between him and Ginny, was a figure. Water poured from its huge, misshapen body. Ginny had stopped in her tracks, mouth agape.

"Pete?" she asked softly.

The thing flopped wetly to the deck like a landed fish, but then rose, taller than Pete Shelley ever was, until it stood at close to seven feet. It was all hulked muscle, large scales, and in the dark it could have been an oily-black, mottled green, or a mix of both.

Large scales like fist-sized plates covered its body, and there were fins on its back, forearms, and down its legs that ended in heavily clawed feet.

"Oh, shit," Hudson whispered.

"That's not a mermaid, that's not a mermaid," Ginny repeated, and backed up until she was stuck in the point of the bow.

The thing turned its large, glassy-eyed face toward one, then the other. A mouth gaped open as if on hinges and they saw that backward-angled teeth like those of a shark ringed its maw.

"Come to me." Hudson held out his hand to Ginny.

Ginny was trembling uncontrollably.

"Ginny, listen to me," Hudson urged. "You need to get around it."

But then, behind it, another of the huge figures came over the port side. Then a webbed hand appeared on the starboard side of the gunwale as well.

They needed to get inside, and Hudson knew that it was now or never.

"Ginny, *run*," he yelled.

With her hands over her head as if expecting a blow, Ginny needed no further encouragement. She ran, and Hudson moved to intercept her as, in response to the klaxon, the ship's crew began to stream out onto the deck.

Ginny didn't get six paces before one of the things grabbed her.

"*Ginny!*" Hudson yelled, and went to charge at the figure that was holding her, but was grabbed and held back by the men who suddenly surrounded him. Hudson noticed they were carrying boat hooks, long knives, clubs, and even ropes.

Then, more of the creatures came over the gunwale, and with tear-blurred vision and a torn heart Hudson saw the thing that held Ginny go back over the side, taking her with it.

Hudson wailed, and then he and the other men charged in and engaged the monstrosities. But it soon proved a futile fight, as the meager weapons the men had were unable to penetrate or even damage the creatures' scales. And worse was to come, as one by one the crew were also grabbed and held in powerful grips as if they were children. Then they, just like Ginny, were taken over the side, each of the creatures taking one man, one prize, until only Hudson, Miguel, and Captain Benson remained. And a lot more of the dripping creatures.

Benson backed up, breathing hard. "I have a gun in the wheelhouse."

"Get it," Hudson yelled back. "We need to get out of here. Start the ship."

Benson headed up the iron steps to the wheelhouse and Hudson and Miguel sprinted for the starboard side bulkhead door.

Hudson's eyes were filled with tears for Ginny as he turned to slam the heavy steel door shut behind them, then spun the locking wheel just before a hulking weight hit it with a deep clang that caused the entire rim to be forced inward.

Miguel gulped. "It won't hold, Mr. Hudson."

They heard the boat's engines start up, and then they sensed they were moving.

"Thank God," Hudson breathed.

But just then they heard Captain Benson yelling and cursing above them. A couple of shots rang out, and then came a long and agonizing scream, followed by a splash.

Hudson sagged, knowing that if the captain was gone, there was no one to guide the ship.

But he thought that right now, as long as the ship was moving, anywhere was better than here.

The sounds from outside their door stopped, and Miguel turned to him.

"We need to hide. Or get to a lifeboat."

"Wait," Hudson said, trying to think.

There was no use taking to the lifeboats, as the things would pull those under in an instant. Right now they were trapped.

But at least they were trapped on one side of a steel door and the creatures were on the other.

Or so he thought. Because then the door was hit again. And this time the steel bent a little.

"They will come through soon." Miguel grabbed the crucifix hanging on a chain around his neck and his lips started to move as he mumbled a rapid prayer.

"Okay." Hudson backed up. "You're right; we need to hide."

Just then the door exploded inward with a thunderous clang. Hudson and Miguel turned and sprinted away.

The two men ran blindly, and Hudson couldn't think straight as his terror short-circuited his logic.

He was leading the way, but when he glanced over his shoulder he saw that Miguel wasn't with him anymore. He guessed the Puerto Rican must have taken the ladder steps down to the engine room.

Hudson ran on, trying to think where he could get to. If the creatures could go through one of the thick steel doors, then the wooden doors of the main rooms or cabins wouldn't hold them for an instant.

But then he remembered there *was* somewhere he could hide. Somewhere fortified.

The sound of the terrifying smashing pursuit was getting louder and Hudson accelerated to the laboratory, careening in, and jerking the thin door closed behind him.

"*Come on, come on, come on.*" He urged himself as he heard the heavy sound of wet, webbed feet, the scrape of claws, and of a huge sliding bulk pressed into corridors that must have been far too small for it.

Hudson reached the ADS, the Atmospheric Diving Suit, standing like a bulky robot against the wall. He went straight to its rear, opened the small access port and hurriedly climbed in.

Preparing the suit was usually a two-person job, so trying to do it all himself while he was nervous as hell meant he fumbled and made mistakes.

"*Hurry, hurry,*" he urged himself.

But before he could even close the access port, the wooden door to the lab exploded inward. Hudson pulled and locked the port behind him. He straightened in the suit so he could look out through the faceplate viewing panel.

His eyes widened as the huge thing forced its way into the room. It was a repulsive combination of a deformed fish-like face on a bipedal body. Gill slits opened and closed on its neck, and the mouth gaped open, showing the needle-sharp shark teeth.

And then he saw the breasts on the front. It was female. The legend of the mermaids was true – but this horror was as different from the beautiful siren-like women in the movies as was Heaven from Hell.

Hudson tried to stay still and silent, but his knees trembled. And whether it smelled or heard him, the monstrosity came closer, and its face almost touched the glass as it peered in at him. Hudson felt the strong urge to fright-piss, and he squeezed his bladder, stopping it, for fear it would be smelled.

The creature lifted its head, as if looking for something. And then it turned away. He saw it take a few steps, and as it did, it turned its back on him. A long, spiked fin like a sail ran down its spine. It continued to examine the laboratory room.

What are you looking for? Hudson wondered.

And then Hudson had a thought – it might be looking for the hand.

He engaged the dive suit's motors, and the machine took a step forward. It was hydraulically assisted, but out of water, it was still a lumbering tower of steel.

The beast instantly spun back toward him, but Hudson quickly bent to the refrigerator, tore it open and pulled out the tray with the claw hand on it.

The creature grabbed at his suit as he held it out, and then its flat, glassy eyes fell on the tray. The thing let him go and reached instead for the claw hand from the tray. Lifting it up, it stared at it for many seconds.

"Go on, take it, and go back to your home," Hudson pleaded, hoping it could hear him.

The creature looked back at Hudson and reached out its free hand to run it over the helmet and then down the suit's sides. Hudson heard the steel of the suit complain as the creature squeezed one of the arms.

And then, holding the severed claw in one hand and Hudson in his heavy suit in the other, it began to drag him.

They went out of the lab and along the corridor, the metallic suit gouging deep rips in the floor and walls on their way. They soon reached the deck, and the creature headed toward the side rail.

"*No, please!*" Hudson yelled as they both went over the side.

*** *** ***

On the inside of his helmet Hudson had a projected digital readout, and it counted off the feet as he descended. The numbers flew, and in seconds he was several hundred feet below the surface. In minutes he was a thousand. The dark of night meant it was like falling into a sea of ink.

The helmet's lights automatically came on, and they illuminated the creature beside him, who swam effortlessly, seemingly untroubled by the darkness or the depth.

And it wasn't alone. From time to time Hudson could see more of the mermaids heading down. He could do nothing but watch on helplessly when they got to the sea floor and traveled over a ridge, beyond which the dark void of the trench awaited.

It was a giant rip in the ocean floor that was so dark it was like a black hole in outer space. Down they went into this stygian void, and in another few minutes the suit began to groan and creak as they passed 1800 feet.

Hudson knew he could travel to a depth of 2300 feet – 2500 if the suit was pushed to its limits. But after that, he couldn't count on the suit to protect him anymore.

Suddenly he saw light up ahead and noticed that on the walls of the trench there was a form of glowing seaweed. The scientist in Hudson marveled at what he beheld – things that no living human had ever witnessed.

Then they began to slow, and he was pulled toward one of the trench walls. He saw there many of the mermaids sitting in crevices, and several held one of his dead fellow crew members, leaning forward to take bites from the corpse's cold, pale flesh.

There was one particularly large specimen on a ledge, and they glided closer. Horrifyingly, Hudson saw that this one was holding Ginny, her red hair flowing like a flame in the dark depths. Her eyes were open and her expression was still one of shock.

"Oh, Ginny," he whispered.

Already most of her neck and shoulder had been consumed. They glided closer.

"No, please," he begged, and screwed his eyes shut.

Hudson felt them stop to float in front of the other mer-beast, and he looked again.

The creature holding on to him held out the torn-away arm he had given it. And only then did Hudson see that the thing eating Ginny had a missing hand.

The mermaid looked from the hand to Hudson, and then back to the creature offering it. Some sort of communication must have passed between them, because the missing-limbed creature took the limb, and, pinning Ginny under one arm, stuck the torn-away hand on the end of its stump, holding it there.

Hudson was transfixed as he watched the red and white tendrils of flesh hanging like tiny ribbons on the severed hand meet the same sort of growth on the thing's stump, and immediately draw the missing limb in tighter and began to bond with it.

More communication seemed to occur, and then the creature holding Ginny's body held her up, brought her closer to its face, and then bit through her arm.

Hudson wailed at the sight. But then he saw that the creature was holding out Ginny's arm to him.

He shook his head, sobbing. "Ours don't grow back."

But the mermaid forced it into his robotic hands, and he took it, looking down at the pale, tiny limb. And then the creature gripping him just let him go.

Hudson immediately began to drift lower, and in just a few seconds warning lights flashed, telling him he was approaching crush depth for the suit. He quickly initiated the emergency surface procedure and ballast tanks filled balloons at each shoulder with gas. To his immense relief, he began to rise.

It took him an hour to reach the surface, and once there the balloons deflated, and the suit began its downward trajectory to the depths once again with Hudson still inside.

Hudson knew he needed to hurry out of the cumbersome half-ton of steel. He released the rear hatch, flooding the suit as he clambered out and swum up the several dozen feet to the surface.

He breached it and dragged in a huge breath of the humid night air. He looked one way then the other, but there was no sign of the *Neptune's Trident*. However, a few hundred feet away was what looked like one of the ship's life rafts. He remembered Miguel saying he planned to escape in one.

"*Miguel*," he shouted as he began swimming toward the raft.

There was no response and, pulling himself in, he saw that it was empty. If Miguel had been in it, then he had been taken.

Hudson rolled onto his back, shut his eyes and breathed heavily.

He held up his left arm and saw that he somehow still gripped Ginny's severed hand.

He wailed and threw it far out into the ocean. Then he turned to vomit over the side.

"Ours don't grow back, you bastards," he yelled.

From out in the dark water somewhere he heard a splash, and pulled back, lying once more in the bottom of the raft.

Half an hour later all was quiet, and a quick search of the boat revealed that whoever had launched it had not included any supplies, or even any water. Added to that, the damned beacons, flare gun, and even the first-aid kit were missing.

"Thanks for nothing." His relief turned to dread.

Hudson knew he could go three weeks without food, but only three days without water. If help didn't come soon, his days were truly numbered.

***

Hudson floated for days, and unfortunately ever further out into the Atlantic. There was no rain, so there was no respite from the never-ending torturous thirst. His lips flaked and split; his eyes became sticky; even the inside of his nose cracked. And the cramps in his belly were agonizing.

In the night he thought he heard splashes in the dark, and knew the creatures were watching him. Or maybe it was his fragmenting mind playing tricks.

If they were there, he wondered if maybe they were waiting for him to die so they could dine on his corpse. But no – they could just take him from the boat now, as they had his colleagues. Somehow the return of the hand had bought him his freedom. But perhaps that was only a temporary reprieve from what was becoming inevitable.

Another tormenting night passed and when he opened his stinging eyes he found that the hunger had gone away, but the thirst never did. And his mind tormented him. He had a terrible dream that he was dining on Ginny's hand, sucking the remaining fluids from it and chewing the dried flesh. But then when he woke, he found he had bitten a big hole in his own hand.

The precious blood that welled up was thick and dark, and he couldn't resist putting his mouth over it to drink it rather than let it drop to the raft bottom.

Hudson lay back, weeping. They had found a terrible secret in the ocean depths. And now, it was undoubtedly one he would take to the grave.

This accursed dark sea, he wanted to yell, but it came out as little more than a croak.

Night fell again, and cramps gripped his muscles as if the drying flesh was tying itself in knots.

Out in the darkness he heard splashing, coming closer now. That was it, he thought, his time was up, and the mermaids were coming to claim their property.

He had one last thing to do, and he tore away the makeshift bandage he had made on his bitten hand and reopened the wound. The blood flow was like molasses, but it would do.

When he had finished his task he lay back once more. The smell came then. The smell of the dank ocean bottom and of things that squirmed and writhed in its dark ooze. Just like the stink of that damned claw hand.

He knew what was coming – coming for him.

***

Three weeks later the trawler spotted the life raft just after dawn. They came alongside and brought it onboard.

The craft was empty, but it obviously hadn't always been – scrawled on the inside wall were words written in what looked to be long-dried blood. And by the look of them, they'd been made by the drag of a shaking finger.

Beware the Dark Sea mermaids.

"The Dark Sea." The captain knew that was the old mariners' name for the waters of the trench known as the Milwaukee Deep. "Is that supposed to be a warning?" he asked the seaman who had helped recover the boat.

The seaman shrugged. "Whoever was in that boat must have gone mad." He turned to the captain. "Although some say they have seen mermaids in these parts."

The captain smiled. "I saw a movie called *Splash* once. Meeting something out here at night that looked like that Daryl Hannah mermaid is every sailor's dream, right?" He winked.

The sailor looked back at the boat and grinned. "Kissed to death by a beautiful mermaid. That's the way I want to go."

STORY 06

We've all noticed small bruises and abrasions on ourselves that we couldn't remember getting. It just happens. But imagine how Jerry felt when he took off his shoe one morning and found he was missing a toe.

It didn't hurt, and actually looked like it had never been there. Even his doctor couldn't remember if he had a missing toe or not.

That'd be strange. Horrible. But things could be a lot worse. And then for poor Jerry, they did get a lot worse.

JERRY LOST A TOE

Hudson Street, Watertown, Boston, Massachusetts

Jerry Thorpe opened the envelope and scanned its contents quickly. He never usually opened strange mail, but this one looked official. Nevertheless he was about to discard it as more spam when he saw the check enclosed – $1000.

"What the fuck?"

There was a cover letter and a contract attached. He unfolded the one-page cover letter and read slowly.

He had been chosen from a database of candidates for potential medical testing. He was just to be monitored over time and there would be no visits, chemical, surgical, or other procedures involved. All he needed to do was stay fit, and be monitored and assessed when necessary.

If he agreed, he need only deposit the check and that would be indication of his assent and agreement to go forward with the contract terms and conditions.

And here came the kicker for him – it would also mean that he could expect a check a month, totaling $12,000 a year. Every year, as long as the monitoring continued. Tax free.

"Oh, hell yeah. Money for old rope." He grinned.

And right now, he needed it. Jerry had lost his wife and his job in the same month. And with his savings running out, he needed a plan, or help, or something. And the universe had answered.

He grinned as he quickly scanned the contract, his eyes trying to focus on the ant-sized printing of dense legalese.

After twenty minutes and about halfway through, he thought he had the gist of it, so he gave up.

"Yeah, yeah, whatever."

He held the check up, and then kissed it.

"That's a big fucking yes from me."

***

A month later, Jerry was jogging along the wet street, pumping his arms and puffing hard.

Having extra cash made everything easier, he thought. And now he'd do his part – get in shape. Or at least try to. He had vowed to get back to his "fighting weight" but was struggling to get even a little speed up. He was determined to do it, though, especially for an extra thousand bucks a month.

The hill he was laboring up stretched away for several hundred more yards and already his perspiring body was soaking wet and he felt a stitch in his side. Plus he felt like he was going to throw up.

Keep going, buddy, you can do it, he cajoled himself.

Jerry wasn't carrying all that much extra weight. And he still had strong but unused muscles under a thin layer of fat. But he was out of condition due to enjoying too many fast-food meals, box wine, and the killer: cigarettes. Giving them up was down for next year's resolution because he just enjoyed those little bastards way too much.

He finally reached the top of the hill.

Take a break, his mind and body screamed. Jerry agreed and stopped to walk a few dozen paces with his hands on his hips.

Next time, he'd bring a face towel and a bottle of water. He'd only planned to do a few miles, and only ten years ago that would have meant he would barely raise a sweat. But now, after just fifteen minutes, he was still sucking in air, was drenched, and felt like shit. Not to mention his knees and feet were screaming at him.

He'd probably jogged about a mile, and if he forced himself to do the same on the way back home that'd be two. Enough for his first day, he told himself.

He began to jog down the other side of the hill. In ten minutes he'd throw a left at Winston Street, and then another left onto Hutchings, and that would take him home.

Going downhill was easier, so he went a little faster, moving up from an ambling shuffle to a semi-jog. Once again his hips, legs, knees, and feet hurt, and he bet that by the time he got back, he'd need a dose of painkillers. Or a few big glasses of red wine. Why not? He deserved it.

He was nearly home when his left foot developed a sudden weird tingling sensation that moved from the ankle to the toes, and then was gone. He ignored it.

His original plan had been to do some push-ups and sit-ups when he got home, but coming in through the front door, he felt a little light-headed and knew he had nothing left in the tank.

Jerry stripped off his shoes and sodden clothing, dropping things to the floor as he headed for the living room. Finally, down to his socks and boxers, he flopped into his favorite armchair, luxuriating in the exercise being over.

He closed his eyes and breathed deeply for a few moments. He smiled; this must be the endorphin rush he'd heard about. It made him feel . . . *good*.

Good enough to want to go again? He'd cross that bridge tomorrow.

After a few more minutes, Jerry pushed himself to his feet, dragged off his socks and boxers and hit the shower. He was in there a long time, washing and drinking the shower water to rehydrate.

Afterwards, he toweled his hair dry and then tossed the towel over a door handle before starting to dress.

One thing was for sure: exercising made you damned hungry. It was only mid-morning, but an early lunch was in order.

He pulled on new underwear, sat on the bed and began to roll on fresh socks. First the right foot, and then he started on the left one – and stopped cold. He stared.

What the fuck?

He only had four toes.

Big one, next one, next one, next one . . . but the last, the weeny one, was just gone.

He grabbed the end of his foot, feeling all around it. There was no bleeding, no wound, no scar, or anything. It was like the toe had never been there.

Was it ever there? his mind asked, madly.

He stood up and took a few steps. He was a little unbalanced.

I had five toes. On both feet. Didn't I?

Jerry rushed to pick up his left jogging shoe and shook it. Nothing rattled around inside. He picked up and squeezed his sodden sock – nope, nothing.

He then grabbed his phone and dialed his ex-wife, Maureen. She answered after about the tenth ring.

"Jerry—" There was the sound of a dry mouth smacking. "—it's my goddamn day off. Whatever you want, the answer is no."

"Maw, please, I just have a question. This is gonna sound crazy, but . . ." *Here goes*, he thought. ". . . did I always have five toes on my left foot?"

There was silence for a few moments. And then the line went dead.

He took the phone from his ear and stared at it. He felt like his head was a volcano about to blow. "And that's why we separated, *bitch*," he screamed at the device.

He tossed the phone aside.

Jerry stood tall, looking straight ahead, feet together. Then he looked down at them – they didn't match now. Of course he would have noticed – or remembered – if he only had four toes on one damned foot.

He wiggled them. Everything worked and there was no pain.

"Doctor. I need to see the doctor." He looked at the clock. It was nearly 11 am, and the clinic was open. He didn't have an appointment, but fucked if he was going to go and sit in the emergency room at the hospital. The only thing you got there was stabbed or vomited on. He'd beg to get into the clinic if he had to.

Jerry finished dressing, grabbed his keys and flew out the door.

* * *

"Hmm." Dr. Harvey Waxenberg first pressed the foot tarsals, then down along the metatarsals. "Does that hurt?"

Jerry shook his head. "No, nothing."

Waxenberg kept pressing. "The bones are all there, but they seem to end right before where the small phalange, the little toe, begins."

There was a knock on the door, and the nurse brought in Jerry's x-rays. "Ah, thank you, Mary." Dr. Waxenberg let go of Jerry's foot, took the x-rays to the illumination board, and pegged them up.

He rubbed his chin. "Well, this is interesting." He stood aside a little so Jerry could see. "This shows me that there *was* a toe there at some time, but it's been removed, and it's now perfectly healed." He looked to Jerry. "Did you . . .?"

"No, Harvey, I'd fucking remember if I had a toe removed." Jerry pointed at his foot. "I mean, how the hell could something like this even happen?"

Waxenberg shrugged. "That's just it, Jerry, it can't happen." He folded his arms. "Toes don't just vanish. I mean, this is not like those poor saps that go on holiday then wake up in a bathtub full of ice and find out their kidney has been removed."

He lifted Jerry's foot again. "There's no scarring. Not even old scarring." He shook his head perplexedly. "This is crazy, but it looks like the toe was removed . . . from the inside."

"What does that even mean, Harvey?" Jerry laughed bitterly. "What can I do?"

"I don't even know where to start with a hypothesis." The doctor looked up. "I'm not ruling out the possibility that it has been gone for years, and I just missed it."

"Oh, piss off, Harvey." Jerry jerked his foot out of the man's hands. "I had a fucking toe. *I had a fucking toe*, Harvey."

Waxenberg threw his hands up. "What do you want me to say or do here, Jerry? I certainly can't make it grow back." He exhaled. "Just, keep a lookout for it. If you only lost it today, and it turns up somewhere, maybe we can look at reattaching it."

"Yeah, sure, I'll check down the back of the sofa when I get home," Jerry spat.

"Fine, Jerry, you can put your shoes back on now." Waxenberg stepped back and washed his hands. "You've told me it doesn't hurt, and it won't affect your mobility too much, so for now there's nothing else we can do." He gave Jerry a crooked grin. "Just don't lose any more."

"Yeah." Jerry finished lacing up his shoes and stood. "Thanks for nothing, Harvey."

Jerry didn't shake hands on the way out.

***

Days went by. And then a few weeks.

Jerry's life got back to normal, sort of. He couldn't forget about his toe, as every day now he needed to wad up a bit of tissue to stick in the front of his shoe to fill the void left by the missing digit. That alone told him there used to be a toe before. At least when he'd last bought shoes.

But eventually other priorities and events distracted him. As he didn't have a girlfriend and wasn't pursuing anyone, his evenings were basically booze and television. But at least now he had cash, he wasn't drinking box wine rubbish. And the upside was, there was no one to tell him what to do.

One evening, Jerry turned the television off around 10 pm. There was just enough wine left in the bottle for one more glass, which he poured before sitting back.

He saw his reflection staring at him from the screen of the dark television – mid-forties, hair thinning, not fat but not thin – he never did do any more jogging – and here he was sitting alone in his living room in his boxers and t-shirt.

"What's the point?" he asked his reflection.

He lifted the large wineglass half full of dark ruby-red wine and toasted his reflection. "Here's to you, loser."

He downed several large gulps, but put the glass down with a sip left in it. Then he leaned his head back on the sofa rest.

"I miss you, Maw. You bitch," he said softly.

Seconds later, he was asleep.

* * *

Jerry woke with a start about midnight. He was a little fuzzy-headed but he sat forward. He had the strange tingling sensation down his legs again.

He rubbed his thighs and looked at the wineglass, which still had an inch of wine remaining.

Nah, enough, he thought, and rubbed his face with rough hands.

Jerry went to stand. But immediately he fell sideways, and the sensation didn't only feel unbalanced. It fucking hurt.

Looking down, he screamed. Both his bare legs ended at the ankles.

Jerry sat up on the floor and reached down for them, running his hands over the stumps where his feet should have been. He cried, loudly, his mouth turned down as he felt the smooth ends – just like with his missing toe, there were no wounds or even scars. His feet were just gone.

He flopped down, arms out. "What's happening to me?" he wailed.

He didn't know how long he lay there on his back, but after a time, he rolled over and crawled to his phone.

It was midnight, but he called Harvey Waxenberg's private number anyway.

The doctor answered groggily. "Jerry, it's the middle of the night. Can this wait until—?"

"My fucking feet are gone," Jerry sobbed.

"What?" Waxenberg came fully awake.

"Like my toe, Harvey. They're both gone. I can't walk."

"Are you sure you—?" Waxenberg began.

Jerry took the phone from his ear, took a picture of his stumps, and sent it.

"You see? They're fucking gone. Just gone." Jerry grimaced as he tasted wine vomit in the back of his throat. "*Help me*," he screamed.

"Okay, okay, calm down, Jerry. We'll get to the bottom of this. Um, I'm sending an ambulance, they'll take you to the private hospital." Waxenberg sounded like he was speaking to someone else for a moment.

"Harvey, you there?" Jerry felt sick and scared to the very core.

"Yeah, yeah, I'm here, Jerry, just organizing a few things," the doctor replied. "I'm going to throw on some clothes and meet you at the hospital. Stay strong, and we'll look after you from here."

***

A week later, Harvey Waxenberg and bone specialist Francis Mason stood in the quarantine room looking at their patient.

Both had masks on, gloves, and medical whites. There was just the soft hiss of a respirator, but no heart monitor. There was no need for that, as Jerry's heart was gone. Blood was being circulated around what was left of Mr. Jerry Thorpe's body by way of a manual circulatory pump.

There were also no limbs, since his arms and legs were gone now. His eyes had vanished, as well as most of his internal organs, his tongue, and even his teeth.

Mason lowered the chart. "If I hadn't seen this with my own eyes, and photographed Mr. Thorpe's, ah, progression, I would never have believed it. This sort of thing does not happen." He turned to Waxenberg. "*Globally*, this does not happen. And never has."

"Damnedest thing. The organs, limbs, eyes, all removed as if they were never there to begin with." Dr. Waxenberg exhaled. "How. Just how?"

Mason shook his head slowly. "How? I don't know where to begin to formulate an idea. I can't even tell you if this is contagious or not."

Waxenberg hadn't thought about that. He glanced at the bed, feeling uneasy about spending all the time he had with Jerry before they'd taken the precaution of gloves and masks.

Mason folded his arms. "I suggest this is kept confidential. The CDC has already authorized a cremation, and a cover story to run." He turned. "No one must ever know about this. It would cause panic."

Waxenberg closed his eyes and sighed. "Makes me feel a bit sick."

"You and me both," Mason replied.

The room went silent as the respirator stopped. Both men turned to what was left of Jerry.

"Did someone turn that off?" Waxenberg whispered.

Mason shook his head. "No, I think his lungs have now vanished as well." He backed up. "I'm done with this." He left the room.

Harvey Waxenberg walked a step closer to look down at the remaining tiny package of meat that had been a full-grown man only a few days ago.

"Sorry, Jerry. We tried, but . . ." He shrugged. "Goodbye." He left the room as well.

***

Moscow Central Clinical Hospital, Marshala Timoshenko Ulitsa, Moscow

"Well, it works." Grigor Chevnoski rubbed his hands together.

Boris Smirnoff nodded. "Amazing."

The man on the silver steel table slid from the tube-like machine and the inner lights began to dim.

The two doctors entered the room and the man turned to them. He was on a respirator, but Grigor drew the mask off his face and smiled down at him.

"No need for that anymore, Mr. Ivanoff. The procedure was a success. How do you feel?"

The man drew in a deep breath and then put his hand to his chest. "I can breathe. And there's no pain."

"That's because you have a new set of lungs. Perfectly matched to you." Grigor rubbed the man's shoulder.

Ivanoff felt up and down under his hospital smock. "But there's no scar. No pain. It's a miracle."

"Like I said, there wouldn't be. It's a new form of laparo-scopic technology. Keyhole surgery, without even the keyhole. So yes, almost miraculous." Grigor grinned. "And no recovery required. Everything matched, attached and embedded where it should be." Grigor stood back. "Up you get."

"But should I, um, take it easy?" Ivanoff asked.

"Only if you want to. But the MFS, the Medical Fusion System, reports that the biological matching and physical fusion was 100 percent successful." Grigor motioned to the man. "You can get dressed and go home. Live a happy and healthy life. That's what you paid for, right?"

Ivanoff's eyes watered. "I thought the price was too high, but now I think it's the best money I ever spent." He slid off the table and drew in a deep, lung-filling breath. "I feel . . . *free*."

"Money well spent. Tell your friends." Grigor shook the man's hand and walked him to the door.

Later, Grigor and Boris were walking down the corridor.

"We're going to be richer than the tsars of yesteryear." Grigor smiled dreamily.

Boris frowned. "But how? How does the Medical Fusion System work? I mean, this is a prototype, and you've medically rebuilt and restored over fifty patients with new body parts, from lungs and heart to new toes. And all from the same DNA-sourced adult male. How does it find, retrieve, or build the parts? Or even find the perfect match? And then, how does it attach them inside the body without surgery?"

Grigor smiled and puffed his chest out. "I can't tell you everything as it is still company confidential. Also, some of the applications were designed by the system itself. But basically, we use new-generation AI to source the transplant components. It created the matter transfer that embeds the organ or limb directly into the body and fuses it. And it searches medical records for the perfect match, so it sources them as well."

"From . . .?" Boris' brows rose.

"America, of course." Grigor grinned. "The MFS sources a specific candidate who matches all the physical characteristics we're looking for. The, ah, donor, also needs to be single, above a certain age, and someone who won't really be missed," Grigor replied. "I'm not sure how the system does it all. Some aspects just work, and that's all I need to know. AI is the new world."

"And the donors all signed up for it? Willingly?" Boris frowned.

"Yep. It's all in the contract. They're all well paid." Grigor laughed and clapped his hands.

Boris shook his head. "That must have been some fucking small print."

"Yep." Grigor chuckled again. "And now we're ready to go big time. We can expand and accelerate the procedures. We can build more facilities and be doing a thousand operations a week." Grigor rubbed his hands together and turned to his colleague. "Are you in?"

"Let me think about it," Boris said.

"Fine." Grigor stopped at the door as his colleague turned to him. "Don't forget, all of what I have shown you is highly confidential." He shook the man's hand.

Boris waved over his shoulder as he headed down the stairs.

Grigor watched him for a moment. "Don't think too long, Boris," he called after him. "There are other candidates. And one more thing . . . you'll really lose your head if you miss out."

Boris stopped on the steps. From behind him Grigor laughed darkly.

STORY 07

One day when I was doing research for a novel I found out that there is a real manuscript from the 1400s that has resisted translation for nearly 700 years – it's called the Voynich Manuscript – go ahead, Google it.

It's filled with strange writing, glyphs, pictures of almost identifiable plants and animals, and also representations of human females. Nothing makes sense.

Now imagine that advancements in AI have meant that we can finally work out what it says.

And now that we know, we wish we'd never read it.

THE VOYNICH MANUSCRIPT

1412 – Wroclaw, Poland

Tomasz Driedzic tossed and turned in his sleep – the dreams, the dreams, they wouldn't stop. He rolled over and moaned. It was nearing dawn before he finally gave up on trying to get any rest.

But the images were still burned into his mind. The same ones every night.

Driedzic was a scribe by profession, and tellingly the images were in written form. At first. But later they had become voices that urged him on.

Write them, write them, the voices beseeched. And then demanded.

And so he did.

He spent the next year acquiring and preparing the calfskin pages and the inks. He purchased the best quality he could afford, as the voices said that the materials needed to last through the ages.

And once he had everything he needed, he began.

He wrote, and drew, from dawn to dusk, and then through to dawn again. He created images of plants, and animals, and scenes, and also of people, some of them unrecognizable, even to him. But they were what his mind saw as the voices whispered their designs to him.

He would draw and write the strange letters and symbols – not words, or words he understood. It took him three years to write the 180,000 characters onto 275 pages.

Along the way, the voices tormented him, and seemingly tormented each other. There was more than one voice – and while one voice demanded he write faster, another urged him to burn everything.

The more forceful voice won out, but the weaker one managed to have him transcribe three extra pages, different from the others, that were to be removed.

And then, when he was finally done, he was told one last thing – the words were not for him. They were not for his people. At least not yet.

He was to hide the book, and let the future take care of the information imparted to Tomasz Driedzic, the dreamer, who thought he had spoken to the gods.

So he hid the strange manuscript. And separately, he hid the three removed pages.

But then the torment began in earnest. The loudest voice knew what he had done and demanded he destroy the three pages. He wasn't allowed to sleep, and soon his nose began to bleed.

Tomasz knew then there was no way out for him but one. So he placed a house brick in each of his coat pockets, and walked calmly one last time down the cold wet cobbled street to the Oder River. Then he threw himself in.

And the manuscript vanished for centuries.

***

Present day – Yale University, Beinecke Rare Book & Manuscript Library

Bethany Downs, Head of the Yale Antiquarian Book & Map Division, brought the large book out wearing white cotton gloves. She then laid it carefully on the desk in front of the gathered team.

Bradley Hardy, team leader, and his colleagues, Jennifer Bleaker, Russell Hobbs, and Martin Anderson, all stared down at it.

"The Voynich Manuscript," Bethany said. "The original illustrated codex. Handwritten in an unknown script referred to as Voynichese. Carbon-dated to the early fifteenth century, and estimates are that it was written between 1404 and 1438, by person or persons unknown."

"May I?" Hardy pointed at the large book.

Bethany looked at his bare hands. "You should be wearing gloves, but yes, as long as it's with dry hands only. And nobody, but nobody, goes near it when eating their lunch."

Hardy nodded and opened the book to one of the central pages. It showed images of strange flowers, the ink faded, but the blue and red pigments still remained.

"Beautiful," Jennifer said.

"Yes, it is," Hardy replied and looked up. "And a beautiful enigma."

"But not intact?" Hobbs said.

"That's right," Hardy confirmed. "There are a few pages missing. Three, I think."

"Yes, three, and they've never been seen," Bethany added. "No one knows why they were removed. Maybe they'll turn up one day. I'm always on the lookout for them."

Hardy smirked. "We don't need them for what we have planned."

Martin Anderson grinned. "Can anyone else suddenly hear ominous music playing somewhere?"

"Shut up, Martin," Jennifer said. "If our decryption algorithm can decipher this work, it can decipher anything." She folded her arms. "It would be a Nobel Prize–winning achievement."

Bethany smiled. "On that note, I'll leave you to your Nobel Prize–winning work. Good luck." She went to turn away but then paused. "Don't forget, you have one month. And it must be returned as you see it, okay?" She pinned each of the team with her gaze but settled on Hardy. "The work we do must be for the betterment of the human race, right?"

"Sure, sure." Hardy nodded vigorously and waited for Bethany Downs to leave before glancing across at Jennifer.

"Fuck the human race." He grinned. "And forget the Nobel Prize. Think bigger. A universal code breaker will be worth a fortune to the government." Hardy rubbed his hands together. "This test will be the icing on the cake. The proof of concept."

"If it can do it," Hobbs said. "Most decryption engines make best guesses, and even provide multiple suggestions of a decoded answer. They use Boolean logic – on/off, true/false – everything is just a mathematical problem to them."

"Only to begin with." Hardy turned to his friend and smiled. "And that's the beauty of AI. You educate it, and it remembers, and then builds on its training. And then it starts to make its own decisions, and these keep getting better and better. Our artificial intelligence encryption engine, Jed, has been fed over 300 different codes from around the globe. Starting with the simplest, and then moving up to those that use a range of mathematical symbols, language codes, character swap images, and even phrases. All across multiple languages."

Jennifer beamed. "And as our baby got smarter, she got quicker. The World War II Enigma code that baffled the Allies for years was solved in under three minutes." She looked across to Hardy. "So, what do you think, Brad? How long for this?"

He exhaled long and slow through pursed lips as he looked down at the manuscript. "This, hard to say. More than a day, less than a month." He half-smiled. "If we're lucky."

"We've only got it for a month, and we needed to beg to get that," Anderson reminded them.

Hardy ignored the warning and turned a few more pages of the manuscript, stopping at a drawing of eight naked women, standing in a bath.

"Anyone for 600-year-old porn?" Hobbs chuckled. "And are they all pregnant?"

"Looks like it. There are more images of women, all similar. Mostly in water or bathing, we think." Jennifer chuckled. "Let's hope we don't decipher it only to find it's an entire book about the best ways to wash your ass."

"No-*ooo*, it's going to be something momentous." Hardy's expression grew serious. "You don't hide a book for centuries if its content is frivolous. I'm betting we'll be unlocking something unbelievable; I can feel it." He looked at each of his colleagues in turn. "Yale has given us this manuscript for a month. Its governors know we are their best and brightest. And we won't let them down." He looked up. "Will we?"

"Not a chance. "Jennifer folded her arms. "And I can feel it too."

Hardy held his arm out, hand flat and palm down. "To unlocking the Voynich secrets."

Jennifer laid her hand over the top of his. Then Hobbs' and Anderson's hands went over the top of theirs.

"To unlocking secrets." They grinned and lifted their hands up in the air.

"Good." Hardy lifted the large, bound manuscript. "Step one, we need to scan every single page and image into Jed's reader. Then we let him get to work."

***

Three days later, Hardy watched the screen as Jed played soothing music. It helped him think, Hardy told the others.

The screen was also where the AI system communicated with the team. From time to time, it asked for more data, or it reached a branch in its decision-making stream and wanted advice on which route to take.

Or it could simply inform them of something it had found along the way. Like now.

"Huh," Hardy made a surprised sound. "Guess what?" He leaned back from the screen.

The team stopped what they were doing and turned to him.

He turned to share a lopsided grin. "Jed just told me he thinks the pages are out of order," he said. "So, he's reordering them."

"How does he even know?" Jennifer smiled.

"It's his job to know. He recognizes the patterns; how they are and how they should be." Hardy turned back to the screen. "It's what we trained him to do."

***

The next day Jed told them he had also determined that pages were missing as there were logic gaps in the data stream.

"I know," Hardy said as he typed in a response.

"What do you know?" Hobbs asked.

"Ah, he found that there are pages missing." He turned and made a clicking sound in his cheek. "We already know that and should have told him. He probably wasted time trying to work out what was going on."

"It's encouraging, though," Hobbs replied. "You could only determine there were gaps in a story if you understood the story."

"You're right." Hardy nodded. "He's really doing it."

It was another two weeks before Jed announced he had completed the decryption, and the team gathered around for the results.

The first delivery came in the form of an overview report that detailed what Jed believed the manuscript was, before he started with the translation.

The overview was basic information about the code style, and how the images of the plants and animals didn't correlate to any known data stores. And then came the final adjudication: *non-terrestrial*.

"Non-terrestrial," Hardy whooped. "I knew it."

"It's not of this world." Hobbs sighed. "This is freaking big."

"Send it to print. *Send it*." Anderson clapped.

Hardy then sent the 120-page translation Jed had delivered to the high-speed printer and went to stand by it as the pages spat out.

"Wait, wait." Jennifer Bleaker went to the small bar fridge in their research room and pulled out a bottle of cheap champagne and four plastic champagne flutes. "We have to celebrate, right?"

She handed the bottle to Martin Anderson, who immediately set to work on the foil over the cork while she handed out the flutes.

The cork popped, the champagne fizzed for half a second, and then Anderson poured them each a few inches in their glasses.

Jennifer raised hers. "To us, to the E.T. who wrote this, and to all the people of the world our discovery may help."

Hardy groaned. "Are you kidding me? Most people in the world would prefer to have a beer and corn dog."

"Stop being such a cynic." Jennifer frowned.

"Yeah, Brad, show me on the doll where the human race hurt you." Anderson laughed.

"I do not hate people." Hardy smiled flatly. "I just think we could be better. And perhaps out there somewhere there is a better species." He turned. "And I – I mean *we* – are going to hear what they have to say."

"Okay then . . ." Jennifer lifted her plastic flute. "To being the first people in the world to finally understand what the Voynich Manuscript has been hiding for nearly 700 years."

Hardy bobbed his head from side to side. "We-*eeell*, technically, the second. Whoever wrote it must have understood its message."

"Maybe not. Maybe they dream-wrote it." Jennifer raised her eyebrows.

"Say what, Jenn?" Hardy turned.

"You never heard of dream-writing or ghost-handwriting? It's where you relax your hand and let it write the material, with the spirits, aliens, or whoever, guiding your hand." She shrugged. "And don't pull that 'I smell bullshit' face. A lot of people believe in it."

"I believe you, Jenn," Hardy sniggered.

He retrieved the translation and went to a long table. He started at the far left corner and began to lay the pages down next to each other – he went across the top, left to right, and started back at the left side again, and repeated the process until the long table was filled and all the pages were displayed.

Hardy looked at them with hands on his hips. "Okay, I want everyone to read it, saying nothing, and then we can talk about what we think afterwards."

They began, reading and making notes. It took four hours. Afterwards, the group of young scientists gathered around the coffee machine.

"Well, who wants to go first?" Hardy asked.

"Me," Jennifer said. "Some I understood, some I didn't. The notations on a lot of the images just don't make sense and look like they were written by an observer who had never seen women before. Also, the odd plants were given almost recognizable names, but they don't exist in any botanical reference guides that we know of."

She walked back to the table and pointed. "Then we get to this section here. It's more math-based, and for me, it looks like specifications to build something."

"I agree, Jenn. But something far too advanced for fifteenth-century alchemists," Russell Hobbs added.

"This is unbelievable." Martin Anderson leaned forward on his fingertips. "These look like specs or blueprints." He walked along beside the table, pointing at different pages. "Descriptions of transistors, circuitry, a chip board, and so much more."

Jennifer smiled at the group. "If it's not dream-writing, then someone or something imparted this information into the author's mind, because there's no way Mr. Fifteenth Century is going to know this stuff." She looked up from under her brows. "Anyone want to take a guess at two things: One, who could have sent these specifications? And two, what is it they've been waiting for us to build for nearly 700 years?"

"I don't know, but I'll answer a different question. Today. They want us to build it today. And they knew that when they imparted that knowledge." Hardy turned to Martin Anderson. "Well, Marty, what do you think? You're the engineer."

Anderson folded his arms. "Well, to me it looks like the specs for some form of powerful receiver. I can see bandwidth filters, a Q-multiplier, audio limiters, attenuators, and even what could be electromagnetic shielding." He shrugged. "But there's more in there that I've never seen before. And all from over 600 years ago? Who exactly would you be receiving messages from? So . . ." He looked up. ". . . maybe not from here."

"Those plants and animals that no one can identify. Maybe whoever dream-whispered – yes, I'm going to say it – maybe whoever dream-whispered that information to the author, wasn't from our neighborhood at all. Maybe they wanted us to catch up to their level of advancement. And once we were able to understand the message, build this device, then we could speak to them . . ." Jennifer's eyes blazed. ". . . as equals."

Anderson pointed. "And maybe those drawings are not images from our world, but theirs."

Hardy clasped his hands together as if in prayer. "They want to speak to us. Dialogue." He looked across to their AI engine. "And we now have a translator. Jed can tell us what they're saying in real time."

"My mind is literally blown." Russell Hobbs put his fingertips to his head. "Are we really going to do this? Because if we are, we'll need to get extra funding, bring in some communication and electronic specialists, and also some designers and machinists. Won't be cheap, fast, or easy."

"Nothing worth doing ever is," Hardy replied. "Think what we could learn! The secrets from another race. Another intelligent species. Another world. Perhaps a *better* world."

Jennifer smiled. "I think Bradley is in love."

"You're right. I'm in love with the potential of meeting an intelligent species who may be able to solve some of our most intractable problems." Hardy slowly held up a hand. "All in favor of communicating with the stars and making first contact with an alien race?"

One after the other, the group raised their hands. They stood looking at each other for a few more seconds, before Hardy lowered his.

"This could be the most momentous period in the entire history of the human race. And I for one intend to be on the front line."

* * *

Poland, Wroclaw, Ostrów Tumski – the old district

The ancient building on Szczytnicka Street had stood for 700 years but came down in a cloud of rubble and dust in minutes. The machines moved in to clear the debris away, leaving a large hole between the other old buildings that made it look like a giant missing tooth.

The Ostrów Tumski district was the oldest part of Wroclaw, dating from the tenth century, and still held secrets that were given up from time to time. Today would be no exception.

The foreman moved in to examine the cleared site. They'd need to excavate further down to prepare for an underground carpark, and he'd do a quick check to make sure there was no toxic debris, or worse, any old, unexploded bombs.

He looked from one side to the other, judging the buildings on either side, which were as old as this one. He knew that they too would have mortar between old dark bricks that was little more than dust and loose sand. He'd try to fortify them, but he couldn't promise that there wouldn't be damage.

As he turned to leave, something caught his eye in the rubble. The object had probably been buried in the cellar; it looked like a box. It was about two feet long and one wide and looked to have had metal bands around it at one time, which were now little more than rings of red corrosion.

He crouched beside it, looking it over, and then smiled. He remembered the story about one building site turning up a box such as this that contained the remains of a 500-year-old cat. It had been buried in a backyard. He wondered if he too would discover a once-beloved pet whose owners had long ago joined it in Heaven.

He pulled out his penknife and worked it into the side of the box, levering it until the locking mechanism turned to rust flakes. The lid creaked open a fraction.

The foreman got his fingers under the lid and pulled it all the way open. He stared in at the contents – pages – just a few, some written in ancient Polish and some in a language he didn't recognize. There were also a few accompanying pictures of flowers, strange animals, and naked women standing in water.

He couldn't imagine why someone would take so much trouble to hide three pages and guessed that whatever they said, they were meant to be hidden. He dropped the pages back in the box, closed it, and then tucked it under one arm.

He had a friend who knew a rare book dealer. Perhaps he could shed some light on what he had found, and, more importantly, if it was something valuable. He scoffed; if only he had found another dead cat.

* * *

Bethany Downs often perused the forthcoming international auction sites.

She was on the lookout for rare tomes to add to Yale's collections, and was well aware that these might surface in the most obscure places. She had the authority and the means to acquire pieces if the price was right.

Bethany found that if she was vigilant and thorough, she could get lucky, as some books snuck onto an auction listing in some far corner of the world and attracted very little interest because few knew what they actually were. And *that* was when a bargain was to be had.

Her role meant she had to be across the range of products, as she called them, in her libraries. And one of those was the Voynich Manuscript. So when she saw the Polish book auction coming up in Warsaw that mentioned three pages of ancient Polish alongside an indecipherable language, she stopped and stared. And then she saw the item's images.

"Oh my God." Bethany Downs recognized the drawings of the odd flower shapes, the animals, the females in water, and the indecipherable script. They were all there. But this time, they only covered half their pages. The other half was written in ancient Polish. She couldn't read all of it, and very few could. But they had translation tools, the best of which was created by the brilliant international linguist, Professor Matthew Kearns.

The Voynichese language script she would hand over to the decoding team working on the main manuscript. She leaned forward, her eyes narrowing as she focused in on what looked like a signature.

"Hello." She chuckled softly in delight. "Mr. Tomasz Driedzic, from Wroclaw, Poland. Nice to meet you." And there was a date: *1412*.

Could Driedzic be the author of the entire manuscript? she wondered.

She looked down at the auction time, and where she could place an online bid. Then she checked the estimate, and snorted. Only $1000 per page – $3000 all up.

If these truly were the missing pages of the Voynich Manuscript, and Yale already had the main document, then they were worth ten times that to the university.

If there were no other bidders she could obtain them all. She checked the number for the auction house, and called them immediately.

***

At the same time Bethany Downs was calling the auction house, the Yale administrators were allocating extra funding to Bradley Hardy's team for the creation of the communication device that their AI system had revealed from the Voynich Manuscript.

The administrators were excited about making announcements, firstly that the manuscript had been translated by their own research teams after so many centuries, and further that it might point to extraterrestrial first contact. Their big donors would love it.

The thing that held them back was that AI translations had been notoriously "off target" in the past, so they decided to wait and see exactly what was built from the fifteenth-century design that, in the end, might be nothing more than the fanciful invention of a local Wroclaw man having night terrors.

The funding was for a design-to-build engineering team. Most of the staff could be drawn from the university's own student population – they'd work well, work hard, and do it for extra credits. Yale was adept at getting value for its money.

Hardy quickly took control of the project, organizing the team into work groups. His initial meeting with the engineering designers was encouraging, as they recognized many of the specification's components. Their first task was to determine what parts they could obtain off-the-shelf and what things needed to be purpose-built.

However, when Hardy asked them if they thought the object resembled anything in existence today, none of them could agree it did. Also, interestingly, none of them would say it resembled a communication device – or at least one they had seen before.

The final piece of the plan was the scale. There were large sections to construct, some ten feet high. And there were also small components that would more than likely create the equivalent of a modern circuit board – but no circuit board any of them had ever seen before. And that meant it had a form of computer built into it.

Hardy also managed to get an extension of their use of the Voynich Manuscript. Just one more month, he promised. One more month and then the secrets of the universe would be revealed to the world . . . and by Yale.

It was an offer too good for them to refuse.

***

Bethany Downs had the three pages express-delivered, and within days she was able to read the Polish words. Or try to. Although she was excellent with foreign languages, some of the ancient dialect was lost on her. But what she did absorb filled her with confusion. And dread.

She snatched up the phone.

* * *

It took the Yale team almost exactly a month to have something constructed from the plans, and at the time Bethany grabbed up her phone, the four research scientists watched as the last components were snapped or welded into place.

Dirk McManus, the lead engineer, looked from the large creation to the team. "Okay, that's just about it for its superstructure. Whatever *it* is."

"Well, *it* looks weird." Jennifer raised her eyebrows.

One of the students leaned into the workroom. "Mr. Hardy, call for you. Bethany Downs. She says it's urgent."

Hardy's gaze never left the thing that sat in the center of the room. "Thanks . . . Uh, tell her I'll call her back."

Before them was a nine-foot ring that was set onto a platform. Other components were built into boxes, and coils of wire snaked around all sides of the creation. Nothing was in proportion, nor had any attempt been made to make the creation pleasing to the eye. At least not to the human eye.

"It's big," Hobbs observed. "And are we sure that's what it's supposed to look like? Because it looks terrible."

"We followed the instructions and measurements to the letter and to the fraction of an inch," said McManus.

Hardy turned to his friends. "I'm glad it looks like something unbelievably out of this world. Because it's supposed to be." He grinned. "I'm sure we'd all be disappointed if it just looked like a crystal radio set."

"We shouldn't be surprised by the scale," Jennifer added. "After all, it's not to human scale, it's to the scale of its designers. For all we know, they're much larger than we are."

"I guess, but . . ." Anderson shrugged. "Where's the receiver, frequency modulator, or even, how the hell do we power it on?"

"Last piece." Dirk McManus held up a small box.

He stepped onto the platform, knelt and pushed it into a ready-made slot on the left side of the device.

"There." He stood.

As he did so, the ring began to glow. And inside the ring the air began to ripple and become indistinct.

"And that, my friends, answers the question about how to turn it on." Hardy laughed softly. "And I'm betting there's only one frequency, so no need for a modulation scanner."

"Can anyone else feel that?" Jennifer put a hand to her cheek. "My teeth feel funny."

"Ultrasonic vibrations," Hardy replied.

"We'll need to monitor them," Hobbs said. "Long exposure to high levels of an ultrasound frequency can produce permanent damage to our tissues."

While everyone was focused on Hobbs, there was a flash from the device, and the group instinctively shut their eyes for a split second to protect them from the searing light. When they opened them, the ghosts of the bright light floated in their vision for a moment before the room returned to normal.

"What was that?" Russell Hobbs asked.

"I have no id—" Hardy frowned. "Hey, wait, where's Dirk?"

The group look around.

Martin Anderson took a few steps forward and pointed. "He was just there. Right there."

"Dirk?" Hobbs yelled. "*Dirk?*" He turned. "Where the fuck did the guy go?"

"He's gone." Anderson walked slowly around the device. "Just gone."

Inside the ring the air seemed to fold and writhe, and there was also a gentle mist like steam rising from a warm bath.

Hardy rubbed his forehead, then gasped. "Oh shit, the machine." He looked at the others. "We thought it was only a communication device. But maybe we premised that on what *we* think of as communication. Not what *they* think communication is."

"Hey, are you thinking what I'm thinking?" Jennifer's laugh had zero humor in it. "It doesn't send radio waves. It transmits, sure." She turned. "But maybe it transmitted . . . *him*."

"Or disintegrated him," Anderson said softly.

Jennifer rounded on him. "Don't say that."

"*Stop.*"

The group spun at the sound of the voice from behind them. Bethany Downs stood there, with several pages in her hand and a folder under her arm.

"Stop all work right now," she demanded. "I've been trying to contact you." She held up the three pages.

Hardy looked back at the empty platform, then to the head of Yale's antiquarian books division. "Sorry, Beth, whatever it is, it will have to wait. We've got a situation here, and we're a little busy right now."

"And this is directly related to it." Bethany slapped the pages down on a benchtop. "These are the missing pages of the Voynich Manuscript. They've been found."

There was a loaded silence in the room as everyone's jaws dropped.

Bethany spread out the pages in front of her. "The missing pages. In the author's own words, this time." She looked up. "He hid them. Because they contain a warning."

"What?" Hardy frowned. "About what exactly?"

"Brad, the thing you've built is not a radio like you thought it was. It's not a telephone, or a high-tech piece of string between two cans. It's not a communication device at all." She looked up. "It's a doorway."

Brad Hardy, Jennifer Bleaker, Russell Hobbs, and Martin Anderson stared for a moment, and then together they looked back at the still-glowing device.

Hardy exhaled. "We know that. *Now.*"

"A doorway," Jennifer repeated softly.

"And Dirk just went through it," Anderson added.

Hardy stormed to the table and snatched up the three pages. After a moment he dropped them, groaning in frustration. "I can't read fucking ancient Polish."

"But I can," Bethany said coldly. "Seems they've been watching us human beings for thousands of years. They needed a way to come here, and also to bring people through to them. They couldn't make it happen from their end, so they got Tomasz Driedzic to do it from ours."

Bethany took the pages back from Hardy and flattened them on the table again before placing her finger on the first image.

"The plants and animals. They're from their world. Not ours." She pointed to the next image. "The women in water." She looked up, grimacing. "They're not bathing, they're being cooked alive."

Hobbs fainted.

"Oh fuck off," Jennifer said softly.

"There's more." Bethany moved her finger down the page. "Here and here, and here again. Driedzic knew what they were planning. He saw it inside his own mind." She slowly straightened. "He was warning us to stop. To destroy the manuscript, because he wasn't allowed to."

"This is all bullshit. He wasn't allowed to? By who? How?" Hardy growled. "We're almost there; stay focused everyone."

Bethany sighed. "They were in his head. And once there they had the ability to torture him. Make him see and do things." She looked to the machine. "After he hid the pages he wrote that he was going to kill himself. Maybe so they could never make him tell them where the extra pages were."

The device began to glow, then glow brighter, and the high-frequency vibrations made their eyes water and their back teeth ache. Groaning, Hobbs came to and got groggily to his feet.

Jennifer looked as pale as a sheet as she stared at the huge ring device. "It's starting up again."

"Listen up." Bethany stared at them all with dead eyes. "If any of this is true – *any* of it – then we need to destroy the machine. Because the thing about doors is . . ."

"They work both ways," Jennifer said softly.

"We need to stop them coming through," Bethany urged.

"No." Hardy shook his head vigorously and then looked at each of his colleagues. "C'mon, guys, are any of you really buying any of this crap? I mean, stop who coming through? The Klingons?"

No one met his eyes.

"This is stupid," he yelled. "Just because this Driedzic guy went mad is no reason to destroy something that is probably the most momentous discovery in a thousand years. We need to study it. Study them. If they're real." He scoffed. "For fuck's sake, *we're* more likely to be the violent ones, not them."

"We can't take that risk. Turn it off before it's too late," Bethany demanded.

"I don't like this, Brad," Jennifer said. "I think we should do as she says."

"How? We can't turn it off," Anderson replied. "It *won't* turn off."

Hobbs went and picked up a hammer and turned to the machine. "I'll turn it off. One way or the other."

"No fucking way, Hobbs." Hardy stood in front of the device and held his arms out. "Over my dead body. Put it down."

"Brad, *please* . . ." Jennifer walked forward, hands in front of her in a peace-making gesture. "Let's just turn it off for a while and take a breath. If we decide later to restart or rebuild, we can. Okay?"

"Nope." Hardy squared his shoulders, still blocking the machine. "Besides, if we really think Dirk went through, then we need to leave it open so he can come back. Am I right?"

"Are you crazy? We have no idea what's beyond there." Anderson scowled. "For all we know there could be no breathable atmosphere, or it's 200 degrees, or – or he was damn vaporized."

From behind them the device glowed so brightly they all needed to squint.

Hardy looked back over his shoulder. "But I want to see."

"Stop, you are not authorized to do any more work." Bethany pointed at him, and her gaze was rock-steady.

Hardy turned to her. "Fuck off, Bethany. We're way past that now."

Then he turned and walked toward the huge ring structure.

"*No.*" Jennifer ran at him.

Anderson, Hobbs, and even Bethany, rushed toward him – just as Hardy dived.

Jennifer also leaped, grabbing one of his legs. In a flash, Hardy vanished, and so did Jennifer.

But Hobbs had managed to grab on to Jennifer's ankle, and he held on. In turn, Anderson grabbed onto the belt around Hobbs' waist.

It was an odd sight of Anderson holding on to Hobbs, and Hobbs holding tight to a foot that appeared to end at the ankle, as if the ring were a guillotine that had cut it off.

The strange surface inside the portal doorway squirmed and writhed, changing from a gentle mist to a thick fog, and there was a strong suction that threatened to drag them all in. From behind them, papers, pens, tools, and other small objects were being drawn toward the portal.

"*I. Can't. Hold. On,*" Hobbs yelled.

Bethany crawled forward on her knees and grabbed Hobbs' belt beside Anderson, and together they began to pull.

Inch by inch, more of Jennifer began to appear from the wall of fog.

"Pu-*uull*!" Hobbs grimaced, showing his teeth as both Bethany and Anderson dragged on his pants.

Jennifer's thighs appeared, wriggling, which was a good sign. Then her hips, waist, and torso. They could see that her arms were up above her head, so it seemed she was still holding on to Hardy. Another good sign.

But then in a rush she came back through, and Bethany, Anderson, Hobbs and Jennifer all ended up in a pile on the floor.

Steam or smoke rose from Jennifer, and she was wailing. There looked to be vomit on her chin and lips.

"They took him, they took him," she screamed.

***

Bethany went and cradled Jennifer's head as she lay with her eyes screwed shut, crying uncontrollably. The others crowded around, examining her hands which were red and brutally blistered.

"It's okay, you're safe now," Bethany said softly. "We're here."

"What happened?" Hobbs asked. "Where's Hardy?"

"The monsters," Jennifer said, in an exhausted gasp. "The monsters had him."

Bethany looked at the pair of men before wiping hair from Jennifer's red face. "Monsters? What do you mean?"

"*Horrible.*" Jennifer's eyes flicked open. "They're ready. They're coming."

Behind her the machine started to glow brighter once more, and Jennifer shrugged Bethany off and leaped to her feet. Faster than the others could react she sprinted to where Hobbs had dropped the hammer.

Jennifer grabbed up the tool and rushed to the boxes of circuitry beside the large portal ring just as the mist began to form in its center again. She began to smash the machinery, crushing it, her arm going up and down in a blur as she furiously took the device apart.

A few seconds later, the glow from the ring ebbed down to darkness. Jennifer dropped the hammer and, chest heaving, fell to her hands and knees.

"They've been waiting for millennia to come through. They measure their lifespans in thousands of years. But their planet is dying, and they have no food." She looked up at her friends. "That's why they want us. We're like a large flock of sheep to them. Roaming free on a planet with so many riches."

"Tomasz Driedzic must have worked it out and tried to warn us," Bethany said. "But thought maybe his warning would be destroyed somehow. So he hid it."

"We had to stop them," Jennifer said softly.

"For now. They can just wait for someone else to build another machine in the future," Hobbs said. "We have to tell people. Warn them."

"No." Bethany drew in a deep breath and let it out slowly. "We need to do the opposite. We destroy the manuscript and any copies. We destroy the translation, we destroy the files. We destroy everything. We erase it from history."

"But . . ." Anderson began. "People know what we were doing here. The administrators, and . . ."

"We tell everyone the translation turned out to be worthless. Meaningless gibberish." Bethany looked around. "We destroy everything in here. This never happened. And will never happen again."

"Not yet," Jennifer beseeched. "If there's a chance Brad and Dirk can be brought home, then we must keep it, at least temporarily." She pressed her hands together. "I beg you, don't destroy it yet. We just seal it away until we can make a plan to rescue them."

"No." Bethany's expression was like stone. "Brad and Dirk are dead."

Jennifer put her hands to her temples. "Brad isn't, I can still hear him in my head."

"He made his choice. And if he's not dead now, he soon will be." Bethany picked up the hammer Jennifer had dropped. "We won't ever see Hardy again. I just hope . . . I just hope whatever happened to him was quick."

Bethany pointed with the hammer. "Help me now. Everyone grab a tool. When we're finished I want nothing bigger than a matchbox remaining."

***

Hardy was in a world with a boiling, blood-red sky. The ground was red dust, and the air was hot and sulfurous. It burned the inside of his nose and made his eyes stream. He could feel his skin scalding.

He was held on each arm by a pair of huge creatures that had ape-like bodies with pocked skin that seemed to be covered in abscesses and ulcers. There was no head, and the features, if that's what they could be called, were set into a place that might have been a chest.

But those features were an abomination to behold – a cluster of shining black eyes crowded together over a slit-nose that opened and closed like a fish's gills, taking in the foul air and expelling a stink that was far worse.

The mouth that hung below them was a foot-wide cavern filled with multiple rows of teeth, mostly flat as if used for crushing.

Hardy was dragged toward more of the horrors, and they parted as he neared. He saw that there was a table in their midst, and on it was Dirk. Or what remained of him.

His body was naked and had been separated into limbs, torso and head. His flesh was red and boiled-looking.

Behind them was a large pot of bubbling liquid, and it didn't take much imagination to guess what had happened to the engineer.

The boiled head of the dead man had bulging white eyes, and his teeth were clamped shut, the split lips pulled back. The expression was one of agony – and that meant he had gone into that scalding liquid alive.

"No, *please.*"

Hardy started to wrestle and pull, and scream, and each breath he took of the noxious air made him gag and cough.

Standing silently around them were more of the creatures. Many more. Thousands more, all lined up in ranks. An invading army, and Hardy knew they were waiting on the call to go through the portal he and his team had opened.

He was released in front of one of the largest creatures, who placed one three-fingered hand on his head. Immediately images were projected there. Or rather, they were commands.

Open it.

He was turned back in the direction he had come from and saw the shimmering window hanging just above the ground.

Through a veil of mist he could still faintly make out his friends there – Jennifer, Hobbs, Anderson, and Bethany Downs.

"*Jenn,*" he screamed. "Jenn, please help me."

As he watched, he saw them all approach, and in their hands were hammers, wrenches, and steel pipes.

"No, *no, no,*" he begged.

They began to smash around the portal window, and right before his eyes the vision fragmented, faded, and then vanished completely.

The beast holding him by the neck roared and shook him furiously.

"I can fix it," he croaked, gagging. "Just give me some time."

Hardy was lifted and carried to the boiling liquid.

"This is a mistake. I can fix it." He grabbed at the long fingers holding his neck. "I can help you. Serve you. I'm on your side," he babbled.

An image was projected into his mind.

You will serve us.

And then two words as he was lifted over the pot.

As food.

STORY 08

Dear old Grampa Arthur was known to tell a tall tale or two. Some were funny, some fantastic, and some a little scary.

His daughter, Belinda, didn't mind too much, as he kept her kids entertained for hours. But she did wonder about his mind some days as his stories became more and more elaborate with every telling.

And then one day she found out that they were all real. But by then it was all too late.

GRAMPA TELLS TALL TALES

Sand Springs, Oklahoma

Seventy-eight-year-old Arthur Sweeney had the leg of his trousers rolled up above the knee. He pointed to his shin.

"And that's where the shark had my leg in his mouth." He looked up at his three grandkids sitting in front of him. "It was a big one, tiger, fifteen-footer."

The twins, Cameron and Josie, six, and Leo, four, sat looking moon-eyed at the scar just under his knee. Behind them, their mom, Belinda, Arthur's daughter, smiled and rolled her eyes as she made them sandwiches.

"What did you do, Grampa?" Josie asked softly.

"I had no knife, and I knew if I wanted to keep my leg, I needed to feed it something else." He held up his fist. "So I gave it a knuckle sandwich, right on the nose. Sharks hate that."

"I would have punched him too," Cameron announced, holding up both fists.

"I know you would. All of you are brave kids and you have the Sweeney fighting blood running through your veins." Grampa smiled.

"What happened then?" Josie was up on her knees. "Did the shark go away?"

Arthur shook his head. "After my plane went down, I was out in the center of the Pacific and had to swim to Hawaii. Took me two days and that shark stayed with me the whole way. But I had a ham sandwich in my pocket, always kept one handy, and I ate the bread, but gave the shark the ham."

"And he became your friend?" little Leo asked.

"Yep, the shark – Bruce, I called him – stayed with me night and day." Arthur rolled his trouser leg down. "And once, he even let me grab onto his fin when I got tired, so he pulled me the rest of the way."

"Sharks are our friends," Leo announced.

"Dad," Belinda warned as she raised her eyebrows at her father.

"Okay, okay." Arthur chuckled softly. "Not all of them, kids. Just Bruce."

The three children nodded solemnly.

Arthur clapped his hands once. "Okay, everyone, sun's out, kids out. Go outside now and show me who's the fastest runner. I still think Leo is."

With a riot of shouts and stamping feet the trio bolted out through the back door. Arthur laughed as he watched them, and then sighed contentedly as he eased back in his armchair.

"I wish I still had that much energy," Belinda said, watching them.

"Me too." Arthur looked across to his daughter. "But the kid locked inside me still does. He just has trouble talking this old set of bones into getting going."

"And Dad, please watch some of those tall tales. I don't want you scaring the kids or filling their heads with all those outlandish stories. They might repeat them at school and the other kids will make fun of them."

"All true, my darling daughter. And I used to tell you the same stories." He lifted his chin. "You believed them then."

"Yes, but I was six then." She smiled back.

Later, Belinda took the kids to school, and on the way home she wondered about her father. She owed him a lot. After her marriage to Barry had broken down, Arthur had taken them in and carried a lot of her financial burden while she got back on her feet. Her dad had been her rock, and a great role model.

After Arthur's wife, Margaret, Belinda's mother, had died, he had spent a few years in the doldrums, and Belinda's split with Barry had given him purpose. His high spirits had returned.

The only thing that sometimes chafed at Belinda was his habit of telling tall tales. She smiled. He had a million of them, from the pet parakeet he had that told Arthur he was a visitor from another planet, to the seagull at the beach who'd dropped an oyster with a pearl into his lap one day. And even the story of the talking fish he'd caught who told him its name was Steve, *and* offered to grant him a wish.

***

That afternoon when the kids got home from school, Arthur took them out to throw a ball in the backyard, each of them taking turns. They tried a quick game of football, and all three managed to tackle him. But he called time and sat on the grass, his forearms resting on his knees.

It was a warm evening and Belinda took them out drinks on the porch. But she saw her dad still puffing and didn't like how pale he looked.

"Dad, take it easy." She smiled and handed him a Coke.

He took it and toasted her. "To youth, and never getting old. Oops, too late."

Josie was looking at him with such intensity he turned to her and raised his eyebrows. "I see a question coming."

Josie's forehead creased in thought. "Were you ever as young as me, Grampa?"

"I was," he said. "And I still am. In here." He tapped his chest. "Everyone, if they're lucky, keeps the kid in them alive. And that kid helps you enjoy the little things and not grow cynical about life."

Leo's eyes widened. "There's a kid in there? Does he ever get out? What's his name?"

"Sure he gets out. And his name is Artie," Arthur replied. "When I sleep he roams my dreams having fun and doing all the things he always loved to do."

"Only in your dreams?" Josie asked. "Not out here?"

"Well, there is a secret place, a garden, in the back of my cupboard. Sometimes he goes there and meets all his friends he had from long ago. Who are now long gone."

"I'd go there every night," Josie announced.

Cameron frowned. "But doesn't he try to run away?" he asked. "If he's trapped inside you, wouldn't he want to be free?"

Arthur half-smiled. "He does. And he will be, one day."

Leo touched his slim chest. "Is there a little boy inside me too?"

"Sure there is."

"Dad," Belinda warned.

Arthur grinned. "Do you want to see what he looks like?"

Leo nodded solemnly.

"You bet," Cameron added.

"Me too." Josie got to her feet.

"Okay." Arthur pointed to his shed. "Open the door to my work shed and look behind the door. You'll see the kids inside you. Hurry now."

The kids scampered away.

He began to laugh softly as he watched them go.

"Please don't send my kids crazy." But Belinda grinned too. "What's in there?"

"Just wait," he said.

The kids pulled open the door, and after a few seconds of logjam they managed to get in single file and rushed in.

"*Aww.*" They came out and closed the door.

Leo had his arms folded tight across his chest and an expression like thunder.

"Well?" Arthur asked.

"It was a mirror." Cameron grinned.

"That's the kid." Arthur groaned to his feet and wiped grass off his trousers. "That's the kid that'll be inside you forever." He went to head into the house but paused. "Never forget him. Because that kid will keep you young as long as he always stays in your heart."

Leo went back to the shed, opened the door and went inside.

Belinda laughed softly. "I bet he's having a good look, so he remembers him."

The small boy came out and he nodded. "He was still there." Then his expression cleared. "Hey, Grampa, what does your kid look like?"

The five of them headed across the lawn to the house, and Arthur put his hand on the boy's head. "He looks a little like you except he has wild brown hair that always needs to be combed." A far-away look crossed Arthur's face. "He wore his favorite baggy green shorts until they fell apart, and he usually had on a faded blue t-shirt with the Stars and Stripes on the front that his father bought him. Oh yeah, and I don't think he wore shoes all summer." He chuckled softly and ruffled the boy's hair. "He was a bit of a wild child."

"I'd like him, and he'd be my friend," Leo declared.

"And he'd like you. All of you," Arthur replied cheerily.

Arthur then went to walk up the steps, but felt his legs go weak, and there was a sudden shooting pain down his left arm.

He bit it down, stopped to take a breath, and felt his heart thumping like he'd just run a marathon.

"Dad, are you okay?" Belinda grabbed his arm and looked into his face.

Arthur turned to his daughter and saw the concern twisting her beautiful features. "Yeah, Bel, just my ankle playing up again. Touch of arthritis, but it hurts like the time that alligator grabbed my leg."

"I thought you said it was a shark?" Josie looked confused.

"It was both. The shark first, and years later a big gator down in Florida." He turned and eased himself down on the step. "Just gonna sit a spell."

Belinda sat next to him, still looking into his face. Arthur felt his heartbeat returning to normal. But it wasn't a good sign. He'd lost old friends before, and they'd told him what they went through before the final big bang. Bottom line, his ticker was sending him a message – you're about to go on your last journey.

The kids sat in front of him, and he looked down at each of them. "Did I ever tell you about my dog?"

They shook their heads.

"His name was Rufus, and he liked to ride my bike." Arthur raised his eyebrows.

"On the back?" Cameron asked.

"Nope, by himself," Arthur replied.

Belinda chuckled. "That I would like to see."

"He was quite famous back in the day. Rufus the Wonder Dog, they called him."

"I'll bet he was a wonder." Belinda grinned.

"Is that true, Grampa?" Cameron cocked his head.

Arthur turned. "I'll prove it. Go to my wardrobe, open it, and you'll see a box at the back. Pull it out, and inside there's an old scrapbook." He sat back. "It's all in there. I think it's time. Go on, Bel. You look too."

"Okay, I will." Belinda stood and headed inside, followed by the three children.

Arthur turned back to the large grassy expanse of his garden. He loved this place. He had bought the land when he was in his twenties, mainly because he wanted to take ownership of a small bend on Sandy Creek where he used to go fishing.

His arm began to hurt again, and then, like a river of ice snaking up his arm, it worked its way toward his chest, and heart.

He knew what was coming and didn't mind. He'd left everything to Belinda and the kids, and as long as they were looked after, he had no more mountains to climb or dragons to slay.

The dagger of pain came then, and he closed his eyes to ride it out.

It didn't take long.

* * *

Belinda pulled open her dad's wardrobe door and found the box, and then the large scrapbook inside.

She took it to the bed, leaving the wardrobe door open, and sat down with Cameron to her left, Josie to her right, and little Leo in front, looking at it upside down.

She opened the large book at the first page. There were notes, pictures of her mom and dad together, looking tall, strong, and handsome. There were scraps of paper, old cards, even a few of her own from Father's Days long past.

There were newspaper clippings, some yellowing with age. She lifted one and began to read. It was from the 1960s. The headline was about a man whose plane had crashed in the Pacific Ocean, where he was attacked by a shark. But the young man still managed to swim to Hawaii.

"You're kidding," she whispered.

"That was Grampa," Cameron said matter-of-factly.

She nodded.

She lifted another clipping. It featured a picture of a dog riding a bike, and there was a young Arthur running along beside it. The headline was: "Rufus, the Wonder Dog".

She frowned and quickly rifled through more of the pages. The more clippings she found, the more she realized her father's stories had been true. She felt guilt creeping into her soul for not believing him. She slowly shook her head.

"It was all true," she whispered.

Josie looked up at her. "Mommy, did you think Grampa was just making things up?"

"I . . ." Belinda looked up.

Leo had wandered away and stood in front of the open wardrobe. He was waving into its dark interior.

Belinda watched him for a moment. "What are you doing, honey?"

"The boy in there." He turned. "He said he's leaving now."

"What?" Belinda put the box to the side and got up from the bed. She joined him in front of the wardrobe with Cameron and Josie crowding behind them.

At the back of the wardrobe was a dim light, coming from what looked like an old movie reel playing. There was a boy with bare feet and unkempt, wild brown hair, baggy green shorts and a faded blue Stars and Stripes t-shirt. He spun with his arms outstretched and his head tilted back to the sunshine.

He stopped to wave at them, and then he turned away and began to skip toward a group of children his age who were waiting for him.

Leo waved again. "It's Artie. He's free now." He looked up at his mom. "It's the boy that lived inside Grampa."

"*Oh no, no, no.*" Belinda's eyes blurred as she spun and raced downstairs.

She immediately saw Arthur lying on his side on the back steps.

"*Dad!*"

She sprinted to him, but when she touched his face, it was already as cool as the early autumn air.

Belinda ran inside and called an ambulance, and then went to sit with her father, pulling him up to hug his lifeless body. She couldn't help the tears coming.

"I'm sorry, Dad," she whispered as she hugged him.

"Is Grampa asleep?" Leo asked as he and his siblings came outside onto the porch.

She wiped her eyes and smiled as Josie and Cameron looked on, perhaps sensing what was happening.

"He's smiling because he's having a nice dream," Leo announced with a four-year-old's conviction. He leaned closer to the old man's chest as if to listen. "And because Artie is free now."

STORY 09

My brother and I used to go fishing nearly every weekend with my father when he was alive. Out we'd go to about a mile off Bondi Beach in his little boat called the *Nellie*. We caught all manner of strange things on our handlines, from sharks and octopuses to crabs and odd fish none of us could recognize.

But we never caught a fish that could talk like Arthur Sweeney did. He thought he was going crazy. But then he heard what it had to say.

A FISH CALLED STEVE

1971 – Sand Springs, Oklahoma

Twenty-five-year-old Arthur Sweeney finished his third beer just as the fishing line went taut.

"Oh yeah, that's it."

The rod danced and jerked, and the line *zizzed* in the water as the fight began.

At last, he thought.

He was at his secret spot: a twist on the Sandy Creek stream only he knew about that was high up toward the big hills. Many people thought the stream was just a trickle up here, and that the real deep water was down below. But Arthur knew there was this hidden deep spot for a few hundred yards, that got as still as a lake in the dry season, and he bet it was where the big ones hung out.

Or *should* have hung out, as lately he hadn't been catching anything. Not even a nibble.

Until now . . .

Beside him he had his fishing basket of spare hooks, sinkers, swivels, rope, and new line. Plus a ham sandwich – he always had a ham sandwich with him. Beside him was a bucket half-filled with water, and his trusty scoop net. Arthur pulled and reeled in, pulled and reeled in, and then backed up, holding out one hand behind him as he felt for the net.

"Come on, baby, don't you spit that hook on me. Come to Artie."

He dragged the net closer to him and then stood on the edge of the bank to work the line in earnest.

Arthur began to play the guessing game of trying to work out what it was judging by the pull and tug alone – *Too much spunk in it for it to be a largemouth bass*, he thought. *Fights a little like a trout, though. Don't think it's a catfish; the water's too clear up here for those mud puppies.*

More line came in, and then he saw some color beneath the water. He reeled in another few feet, reached for the net, then lifted the rod way back, pulling the fish to the surface. He lunged with the net, got it under the fish, and lifted it out.

"*Yeah,*" he said, and turned to lower it onto the grassy bank so he could get a proper look at it.

It was a good-sized fish – maybe fifteen inches and a few pounds. It was shaped a little like a bass, but had stripes running down its sides rather than along them. And the eyes seemed strange: clearer than a bass's, and more alive.

"I'll work out what you are later." He dropped the fish in the bucket. "Now, let's see if any of your buddies are in there."

He turned back to his rod and pulled the line and hook toward himself to rebait it.

Let me go.

Arthur cocked his head.

Yeah, you. Let me go.

What the hell? Arthur turned, looking around. There were plenty of trees on both sides of the bank that sheltered the river, hiding it from view, and they were probably why it had remained his secret. Someone could be in there, though, he thought.

Not over there, dum-dum, in here.

He slowly turned to stare at the bucket. Then he crept toward it and peered in.

The fish was balanced in the water with its head above the surface, looking up at him with those weird clear eyes it had.

He stared for a moment.

Yeah, it was me.

"You're not talking. The beer is." Arthur shook his head and went to turn away.

Let me go and I'll grant you a wish.

Arthur stopped and turned back. "What did you say?"

I said, if you let me go I'll grant you a wish.

"Bullshit."

The fish just stared.

Arthur scoffed. "Make it three wishes."

Two, the fish immediately countered.

Arthur thought about it for a moment. "Okay, deal." He pointed to the bank. "First wish, I want a million bucks in cash, right here, right now."

The fish just stared up at him.

I can only grant wishes when I'm in the water.

"Yeah, right." Arthur picked up his rod again. "The only place you're going is into the frying pan tonight."

Wait, wait.

"Nope." Arthur kept walking toward the bait box to thread another worm onto his hook. "And how are you even talking, anyway?" He shook his head. "I must be going mad."

My name's Steve.

"Steve, huh?" Arthur half-turned. "That really your name?"

No. But you couldn't pronounce my real name.

"Try me," Arthur shot back.

There was the sound of bubbles popping and what might have been a high-pitched squeak.

Did you get that?

Arthur rolled his eyes. "Yeah, yeah, okay, Steve it is, then." He paused. "By the way, I had a friend in school named Steve. That's where you got the name from."

So you believe a fish can read your mind, but not talk?

Arthur groaned. "Keep it down, *Steve*, I'm trying to fish."

You do know we can see you coming, right?

Arthur shrugged, keeping his back to the bucket.

It's why you never catch anything.

"I caught you." Arthur chuckled and half-turned back toward the fish. "Right?"

Because I let you. We needed to talk to you.

Arthur straightened. "Why?"

We need your help.

"We?" Arthur asked. "Who's *we*?"

We. The fish. All of us in there.

Arthur put the rod down and went and knelt by the bucket. The fish's glassy eyes turned to him.

We know you, Arthur. We know what sort of person you are, because we've been watching you for years.

Arthur snorted. "So, I help you, and you'll grant me a wish?"

There was silence for a moment.

No, sorry, Arthur, there is no wish. Just a fervent hope from all of us that you'll help, just for the chance to do good. I volunteered to be caught, knowing it could mean my death.

"A shitty deal for you." Arthur frowned.

Maybe, but if you don't help us we'll all die anyway. All of us, all the different species, all the sprats, hundreds of us.

Arthur leaned into the bucket. "I don't understand. Why? What's happening?"

The dry season is coming, and the creek doesn't flush out all that well. It has to stay clean so we can breathe.

The fish turned in the bucket, pointing itself upstream.

Up near the fallen tree there's a big deer carcass in the water. Been there a few days now. When it rots and bursts, it will poison our part of the river. Kill us all. We don't have much time left.

Arthur glanced up the river.

Only you can help us. The fish looked back up at him. *My sacrifice was a small price to pay.*

Arthur stood and walked a few hundred yards along the bank to the huge tree that had fallen into the river, and immediately saw the deer's legs sticking out of the water. The fish was right – it was a big one – and its belly was already bloated with gas. It wouldn't be long before it burst, and all that putrid flesh and greasy liquid would enter the stream.

The deer looked to be around 200 pounds and was wedged in pretty tight. But Arthur was a strapping young man, and probably outweighed it by a few pounds. The other lucky break was that it looked like it was still intact, plus it had short antlers he could probably get a rope around.

He went back to his fishing gear and pulled out a length of soft rope he kept there. He stopped by the bucket.

"I can see it. I'll try and drag it out."

The fish stared, and Arthur grinned down at it.

"I'm talking to a fish. I *am* mad."

He headed back to the deer and roped its antlers. There was only about six feet of rope left to hang on to. He pulled, digging his feet in, then readjusted his grip and pulled some more.

There was a cracking of the tree's dry branches as the deer's foot shifted toward him.

Arthur wrapped the rope around both his hands, sucked in a deep breath, and pulled again.

This time the deer slid about three feet from the water. But its back legs must have been caught on something, as they resisted all his efforts and wouldn't budge.

"Come on, you sonofabitch." Arthur took a deep breath, feeling a little pain now in his left arm. "Okay, three, two, one . . . *go*." He dragged with every ounce of strength he had in him.

The deer's neck stretched, and then with a breaking of branches it slid up the bank, and Arthur fell down on his ass, breathing hard.

"Got ya." He grinned and wiped his brow as he waited for his heartbeat to slow.

Then he stood, turned, and with the rope over his shoulder, dragged the carcass a good hundred feet away from the water.

Once done, he walked back to the bucket and sat down heavily beside it.

"*Phew.* It's out." He turned and looked into it.

The fish was gone.

Arthur began to chuckle. "Of course it was all in your head, dummy."

He looked at his hands. They were chafed red raw and sore as hell.

He stood and gathered his rod and basket, and lifted the bucket to empty it out into the stream.

As he came close to the riverbank, a fish came to the surface. Not his fish, a different one.

Then another came up beside it. Then another. All of them just floating there with their heads slightly above the surface, looking at him with their round, glassy eyes.

There were all different species, all sizes, and there were hundreds of them.

Then came his familiar striped fish, and it swam right up to him.

Thank you.

He gave a small bow. "My pleasure."

There was a wish after all, Arthur – ours – and you granted it.

It swam in a circle and came back.

So this is for you.

There was a cloudy patch forming in the river as if something was being dragged along the bottom. Then two large bass came to the surface with a small bag held between them in their mouths. They pushed it to the bank.

Arthur reached down and took it. It was heavy, old, and opening it, he saw that it was filled with old coins – gold ones.

"What the *hoozit*?" He looked up.

Goodbye, Arthur. Maybe we'll see you again one day.

The fish disappeared below the surface, then all the others vanished as well.

Arthur looked at the coins again and snorted softly. "Well, I'll be damned. It's a fortune."

He sat on the bank for a while, but didn't have the inclination to throw his line back in.

"I can buy some land. Maybe *this* land right here. And build a house." He got to his feet. "I'll keep the river clean and flowing, forever."

Arthur grabbed his gear and headed home.

***

The years rolled on and Arthur did buy the land around his hidden bit of the Sandy Creek. And he built a fine house. But he never did go fishing in the secret river bend ever again.

From time to time he returned to sit a spell on that little creek's bank, and just talk. His little fish friend never showed up, but that didn't matter. He was sure it was down there listening to him.

Arthur never told anyone what had happened, so no one ever knew.

Besides, who would ever believe him? They'd just think he was telling tall tales.

STORY 10

At the time it was called the eighth wonder of the world. The unsinkable ship. The dream liner that was a millionaires' playground.

Now it lies on the bottom of the North Atlantic Ocean, a cold tomb to the lost 1517 souls. And it has done so for over a hundred years.

But we found it. And we also found out that it was sunk on purpose. However, the reason why was too strange and horrifying to even think about, and so the truth was hidden. Until now.

THE TRUTH ABOUT THE *TITANIC*

1997 – The North Atlantic Ocean, 370 miles off the coast of Newfoundland, Canada

The *Argo* submersible glided down into the ghostly gloom of the deep Atlantic Ocean.

They were positioned above the coordinates given by a satellite that was searching for anomalies on the sea floor. And they had found a big one.

Floating over their target site was the RV *Knorr*, the Oceanographic Institution's research ship, and mother hen to high-tech drones and manned submersibles.

In the ship's darkened control room, among the technicians and oceanographers, sat a tiny, white-haired figure. Eighty-eight-year-old Elizabeth 'Lily' Baker stared at the blue-black screen, her once sapphire-bright eyes now rheumy and faded to the color of shallow water. She sat motionless, barely breathing, her gaze unblinking as behind her someone read off the depth, time, and distance to contact.

"Coming up on impression," the voice said robotically.

And then, like a rising colossus, the bow of the ship appeared out of the forbidding darkness. A blizzard of small motes of algae and debris swirled before the *Argo*'s powerful cyclopean eye, but they could all make out the unmistakable bow railing.

"Lily." The captain whispered her name as if to give her a verbal nudge.

The old woman just kept staring, her eyes now glistening as she recognized the bow, the superstructure, and her mind went back all those decades to the last moments she had stood upon that very deck.

"The *Titanic*," someone breathed from behind her.

Lily let out a long sigh. "They once called her the ship of dreams."

"Yes." The captain smiled wistfully.

Lily's unfocused gaze was miles away. "But she turned out to be the ship of nightmares."

The captain's smile dropped as he turned to her.

"We were all so excited and happy. But we had no idea what was coming," said the old woman in a voice barely above a whisper.

"The iceberg. That night must have been a nightmare," the captain replied.

"The iceberg." She scoffed softly and shook her head. "Our nightmare started days before then. The sinking was done to save the remaining passengers." She slowly looked up at the captain. "And to save you."

Several of the crew turned to her, but Lily just stared trance-like at the screen as the *Argo* glided over the wreckage and then stopped at what looked like a large barnacle attached to the deck.

"Seaman Markson," Lily continued. "He was the first."

The object was about five feet around, and as the submersible drew closer, they saw that it seemed to be growing up from the steel deck. At its top was something rounded. And then, as the submersible hovered, swiveled its camera and focused in, they saw what the thing on top was – a human skull. But it was changed somehow, deformed. And the body beneath it didn't resemble a human skeleton either; all the bones were jumbled and meshed together like a pile of kindling.

Lily turned back to the screen, the corners of her mouth drooping. "The real nightmare started with the rain. And what fell with it." Tears filled her eyes as she slumped a little in her chair. "I saw it. I was there, all those years ago . . ."

***

"Speed, Captain?" asked Hitchens, the quartermaster and the man at *Titanic*'s wheel.

Sub-Lieutenant Charles Herbert Lightinger, senior officer and fourth in charge, turned to watch Captain Edward Smyth. He knew what the "Old Man", as he was affectionately known, was being asked.

There was a fog bank coming up, and they were sailing at twenty knots which some might have thought was a little fast given there would be bergs in the area this time of year. But they were only just on schedule, and Captain Smyth needed to prove the magnificent ship was not only a luxury vessel but swift as well. However, he recognized that the safety of his passengers was his foremost priority.

"Drop speed to fifteen knots, quartermaster. Steady as she goes." Smyth lowered the binoculars from his eyes.

"Aye, Captain, fifteen knots, steady as she goes," Hitchens replied as the order was relayed to the engine room.

The *Titanic* was nearing the fog bank, but the water ahead was clear and the weather mild. Smyth had dropped their speed back a few knots, but they were still running a little fast given they were about to lose visibility.

Lightinger wasn't worried; they were aboard the *Titanic*, the unsinkable eighth wonder of the world, and the captain had probably guessed he could risk it.

"Spotters, sir?" Lightinger asked.

"Belt and braces, Sub-Lieutenant?" Captain Smyth smiled as he sought out his second-in-command, Chief Officer Lieutenant Henry Wilden.

"Mr. Wilden, put two men up on deck for some berg spotting. Just to keep Mr. Lightinger happy."

Wilden relayed the order, and it passed down the line. Two seamen were selected, given powerful binoculars and sent to stand at the port and starboard bow railings.

Seconds later they entered the fog, and though the men on deck had the glasses to their eyes, Lightinger doubted they could see more than fifty feet out into the wall of billowing white.

Almost immediately, the officers' view from the bridge closed in, and they could barely make out the men on deck, let alone the sea beyond.

"All calm ahead, sir. As far as we can see," Lightinger said as he looked out over the rapidly disappearing seascape.

The fog was oddly thicker than he had ever seen, and Lightinger was a little nervous traveling at speed in the curtains of mist, but he trusted the Old Man's lifetime of experience to guide them through it.

As he stared out through the bridge window he saw a few passengers strolling along the decks even though it was freezing outside. He guessed the sea fog was something different to experience on their sea voyage, and the bracing night air would sharpen their appetites for the evening's gourmet meal.

A few parasols sprouted like pastel mushrooms, and some men had coat collars turned up, top hats and even expensive leather gloves more commonly seen on an evening's outing in the city rather than in the freezing North Atlantic Ocean. He smiled; there were some seriously wealthy people onboard, and their safety, comfort, and gratitude was the crew's primary objective.

The captain stepped up onto the bridge just behind the wheel and poured himself a cup of coffee. Lightinger inhaled the aroma and sighed; this was the dream of every officer, naval or otherwise: to stand at the helm of a ship of this caliber.

The *Titanic* was a marvel of engineering as well as the most powerful and beautiful vessel in the world.

No extravagance had been spared – from the luxurious and spacious interiors to many new attractions such as squash courts, a Turkish bath, a gymnasium, a barber shop, and even the first swimming pool onboard a ship. It was no wonder the passengers referred to the *Titanic* as a palace rather than an ocean-going craft.

Lightinger wondered if history would remember him as an officer aboard the *Titanic* on her maiden voyage. Probably not, he surmised. After all, the *Titanic* would be around long after he had retired or stepped off this mortal plane.

It was amazing how he could clearly pick up his crewmates' conversations even over the thrum and vibrations of the massive engines that permeated everything. The *Titanic* was equipped with three of the most powerful engines in the world. Two of them were reciprocating four-cylinder, triple-expansion steam engines that had a combined output of 30,000 horsepower. The third engine was a centrally placed low-pressure Parsons turbine and added a further 16,000 horsepower. Each engine drove its own propeller, delivering high power and fallback in the event of any unlikely failure.

Added to that power, the *Titanic's* hull plates, each thirty feet across and with an average thickness of one inch, were battleship-grade armor plating. Lightinger smiled; no wonder the captain wasn't worried about icebergs; the *Titanic* had the power and protection to sail through a mountain and come out unscathed, he mused.

Yes sir, everything onboard was first class. Lightinger straightened his jacket. Even himself, he thought. And especially their captain. He looked admiringly across at the Old Man. Captain Smyth was known in the industry as the 'millionaires' captain' as he always commanded the White Star Line's largest and most expensive ships – the ones carrying the wealthiest passengers in the world.

As he looked on, he saw Smyth's brows come together as the captain stared out the bridge windows, and Lightinger followed his gaze. It was then that he noticed the large spots hitting the glass and saw some of the passengers on the foredeck begin to take cover to avoid the rain shower.

As he watched, the heavy raindrops on the window turned to streaks. But what strange streaks they were – yellowish and greasy looking. They reminded him a little of gull shit.

But there were no seabirds this far out, he knew.

The captain walked forward. All the passengers had sought cover, and just his two crewmen on iceberg watch remained out at either side of the bow, impassively ignoring the downpour.

Lightinger craned forward to look more closely at the raindrops on the front window and saw that inside the streaky blobs there was something like a hair with one bulbous end. As he stared he saw it wriggle. He jerked back.

What in God's name? he wondered.

Then, refocusing on the men on deck at the bow, he gasped. Both men had dropped their field glasses and were staggering about. One sat down and the other had fallen to his side, juddering as if receiving an electric shock.

Then, as fast as the strange, greasy rain had started, it stopped.

"What the devil was that?" Captain Smyth's eyes blazed.

He called for Lightinger to retrieve the sailors, and watched with a stern countenance as Lightinger and half-a-dozen crew ran outside to grab the stricken men to carry them down to the medical rooms.

They picked up and carted the first prone man away, but the second seaman – Seaman Markson, Lightinger recalled – had his eyes squeezed closed and was sitting with his hands pressed to the deck. No matter what they tried, they couldn't move him. In fact, it looked like he was somehow stuck there, as if he had fused with the metal and was growing from it, or perhaps had melted onto it.

"Freeze frozen," one of the seamen remarked.

"Indeed." Lightinger straightened. "Quickly now; fetch a pot of warm water from the kitchens and we'll thaw him off. Otherwise he'll lose those fingers."

"Sir." The man turned and ran inside.

Two minutes later, two men sprinted out to join the others with steaming pots in their hands. They carefully poured the warm water over Markson's hands and began to tug. Nothing happened – the man remained glued to the deck.

Lightinger turned to the bridge and shook his head. In response Captain Smyth just glared. The sub-lieutenant knew what he was thinking: *We can't have injured crewmen on deck if the paying passengers want to take another stroll.* He shivered; the temperature was dropping. They needed another plan, and quickly.

Lightinger stared hard at the man. He seemed to be asleep and untroubled by his experience, at least. Lightinger made a decision. "If we can't remove him, then for now let's at least make him comfortable. See to it."

Within a few minutes men with blankets and two hot water bottles arrived. They tied one rubber bottle around Markson's neck and the other at his groin. Then they shrouded him with the blankets.

"Good." Lightinger dismissed the men and headed back to the bridge. Captain Smyth was waiting for him, and the sub-lieutenant gave him a quick update on the man's condition.

Smyth grunted, glancing down at the bundle of blankets out of which the man's head, wearing a warm knitted hat, was poking. "We'll keep all passengers inside for now. And as soon as we're out of this damned fog, we'll pull the man free. If he loses skin, well, he loses skin." He turned. "How's the other chap?"

"Taken to the infirmary, sir. I'll check on him now." Lightinger saluted and headed down to C-deck to the clinic and treatment rooms.

***

On the way, Lightinger nodded and chatted to passengers he passed in the corridors, stopping to talk to a few and tip his hat to a couple of attractive young women.

The sub-lieutenant was still a dashing young man and often turned ladies' heads when in his dress uniform. He was always a favorite in the dining rooms, too. He loved his job – being part of the senior command aboard this ship was a dream come true.

"Is it still foggy outside?"

He spun toward the voice. There was a young girl of maybe fourteen leaning out of a cabin, holding a delicate-looking pink umbrella in her hand. He'd seen her around the dining area before – Lily, he thought her name was.

He touched his hat again. "It is, Miss Lily. I'm afraid the captain is keeping people off the deck for a while until it clears."

Her mouth turned down. "But I'm bored."

"On the *Titanic*? Impossible." He grinned. "You could go to the games room and play cards. Or, if you're feeling energetic, go for a swim in the pool. The water is warmed."

She shook her head. "No, thank you." And then, "Where are you going?"

"I have to check on a sick crew member. In fact, I mustn't delay." He began to turn away. "We can speak again on my return."

"Can I co—?" she began.

Lightinger threw the words over his shoulder, cutting her off. "On my return, Miss Lily."

Several minutes later he arrived at the treatment room and entered without knocking. He took his hat off as he walked into the double cabin that smelled of starched linen and antiseptic. There were two nurses on duty, both wearing their crisp whites, and one of the senior physicians, Dr. Ernest Morweek.

"Docter." Lightinger put his hat under his arm. "How's the patient?"

Morweek wiped his hands on a small towel, shook his head and turned to look at the man on the bed. "No idea, really. He's in a coma. It's the strangest thing I've ever seen in thirty years of medicine." He turned to Lightinger. "Can you tell me exactly what happened up on deck?"

Lightinger shrugged. "This man and one other were on the foredeck. It started to rain, but it was a strange rain – thick and greasy. Then they fell down." He shook his head perplexedly. "At least we got this man to you. The other chap is still up on deck."

Morweek's brow furrowed. "Why have you not brought him down, too?"

"We tried; we can't. He is somehow stuck fast to the deck. Not frozen to it, but somehow stuck, as if with glue. He seems unconscious. We've made him comfortable but we're hoping you can shed some light on their affliction."

"I don't know what's happening inside this man." Dr. Morweek walked to the bed and pulled the sheet back from the sailor's upper body.

The sailor was bare, but his chest was now riddled with what looked like ropy veins under the skin. Morweek leaned across and picked up a wooden tongue depressor, and pushed it into the flesh of the man's cheek. The indent stayed for several seconds.

"See here?" He pointed with the stick to the man's chin, which hung like a sagging dewlap. "The flesh seems to be softening, somehow. Almost as if it's about to run like candlewax."

Lightinger frowned at what he was seeing. The flesh on the man's cheeks and neck did seem to be sagging downward to stick to the pillow, and a reddish-brown stain surrounded the skin. Also, his skull was beginning to show through the skin of his head, and his mouth hung open grotesquely, displaying a row of sharp teeth.

"There's something else." Morweek reached for a small funnel and placed it on the man's stomach. He put his ear to the smaller end and listened for a moment, before straightening and inviting Lightinger to do the same.

The officer leaned forward, put his ear to the funnel and listened – and heard mewling, liquid sliding, and something like a pig grunting.

Lightinger straightened, feeling the blood draining from his face. He took a step back. "Is it an infection?"

"Your guess is as good as mine." Morweek turned to the patient. "He's not running a fever, but his breath is foul. Not foul in the way of someone with bad teeth; more like the smell of corruption." He lifted his hand. "I have no idea what's wrong with him, and no idea how to treat him." He sighed. "What the hell happened up there?"

"They were just caught in that damned rain." Lightinger shook his head slowly. "This is all insane."

"Really?" Morweek laughed darkly. "It gets worse."

"No, I think I've seen enough." Lightinger grimaced.

"No, *sir*, you need to see this." Morweek picked up a large magnifying glass and handed it to the officer. "I found this in his hair. It wasn't easy to see, until it started moving." He pointed to a small glass tray.

Lightinger took the large spyglass and leaned closer. There was something on the tray that looked like a dark thread. He held the magnifying glass over it and saw that it was flexing and writhing like a worm, and had a bulbous head on one end. It was just like the thing he had seen in the raindrop.

"What is it?" He felt a gut-churning revulsion.

Morweek shrugged. "What is it? Another puzzle. But it's something I've never seen before. I can't even tell if it's a plant or animal. But the disturbing thing is that whatever it is, it's not the only one." He looked stricken. "And they're inside him."

The doctor went and lifted the young sailor's eyelid, and invited Lightinger to examine the eye through the glass.

Lightinger leaned forward with Morweek close beside him. Then the young officer saw what he was meant to – in the white of the man's eye something moved, squirmed, and tried to snake away from the light.

"Mother of God." He jerked back. "The sounds from inside him. Could they be . . .?"

Morweek sighed. "Probably. If he had come from some exotic place, I might think this was some sort of rare jungle parasite. But these sailors came from England. I don't know enough about what's happening to make a diagnosis yet." Morweek took the magnifying glass back and stepped away. "I'll keep up my ministrations of the patient. But for now, I recommend rest, and I hope his body can fight whatever this is on its own. It's all we can do."

"The captain will not be happy," Lightinger said, putting the hat firmly back on his head.

"I'm not happy either," Morweek replied. "And the captain will have to deal with it. Bring me more information – or at least, bring me the second man. Damned if I'm going to treat him out on a freezing foredeck." Morweek went and opened the door. "Good day, Sub-Lieutenant."

Lightinger took his leave and headed back to the bridge with no answers. And he was right – Captain Smyth wasn't happy.

***

Captain Smyth glared at Lightinger.

"Mr. Lightinger, I have a man stuck to my deck. And I have another man with a mysterious malady in sick bay. I have the best medical professionals in the world on my ship, but no one can tell me what's wrong with either of my crewmen, or even how they got the way they did."

The captain drew in a breath, his chest swelling. "For now, I'm keeping the passengers from the foredeck, but I need to know if that precaution need only last a few more hours, or until we arrive in New York. I also need to know if we have some form of contagion on board, or if both men succumbed to some type of new ocean seasickness."

"Dr. Morweek is continuing his investigations as we speak, sir." Lightinger turned to look out the bridge windows. "He would like a concentrated effort made to bring Seaman Markson down to the sick bay so he can further his examinations and give him the care he needs." He looked back at the captain, whose angry brows had merged into what looked like a bristling, white caterpillar.

Lightinger remained at attention. "Should I see if we can dislodge him again, sir?"

Captain Smyth exhaled through his nose with his lips pressed flat behind his white beard. After a moment he nodded once before walking away.

Lightinger organized three men. More warm water, some rope, and a coal shovel. Seaman Billy Markson was going to be levered off the deck even if he lost the skin of his hands in doing so.

The four men headed out into the fog and went straight to where Seaman Markson was swaddled within the mound of blankets. When they were still twenty feet from him, Lightinger noticed that the young man's woolen cap had fallen off. And his hair now appeared patchy. Lightinger had seen Markson around, and knew the young man was no more than twenty-two years old, with shortish, thick, dark hair. Not the few wispy strands remaining.

"This was Markson, wasn't it?" he asked the sailor next to him.

"Yes sir, it's Billy alright," the man replied.

"Seaman Markson, can you hear me?" Lightinger asked.

The young man's eyes and mouth were firmly closed. Billy Markson looked to be asleep, but it was more than that; his pale face reminded Lightinger of the time he'd once visited Madame Tussaud's wax museum in London – it looked not quite real.

Lightinger turned to the men beside him. "Unbundle him," he ordered.

The seaman carrying the coal shovel put it down and walked forward. The youth under the blankets seemed to be sitting cross-legged, but as the coverings were pulled free they beheld what was happening to him.

The seaman dropped the blankets, cursed, and staggered back.

"What is this?" Lightinger exclaimed.

The young man's body had changed. Wildly. The lower half, which had only recently been a pair of crossed legs, with buttocks and torso, now seemed to have melted onto the decking planks like some sort of giant barnacle. Billy Markson's arms were down by his sides, but the hands were gone, as if they had vanished inside the lumped mass, melting into it somehow.

The man holding the pot of hot water dropped it, and, screaming his prayers to a higher power, ran back to the doorway, with the seaman who had unwrapped Billy right on his heels.

"*Stand your ground*," Lightinger yelled after them.

But the pair ignored him and were soon gone.

"Cowards," he yelled as they disappeared inside.

He turned back, meeting the gaze of the largest and oldest man, who was still holding the coil of rope.

"This is not natural, sir. A bad business," he said softly.

"That it is." Lightinger stiffened his spine. "What is your name, sailor?"

"David Hepworth, sir." The man stood tall.

"Well, Mr. Hepworth, we came here to do a job. So let's do it." He nodded at the remains of the man. "Remove him."

The large seamen looked from Billy to Lightinger, and then back again. "I don't think . . ."

"Try," Lightinger ordered.

Hepworth exchanged the rope he held for the large coal shovel the fleeing sailor had dropped, and at arm's length he slid it toward Billy. As soon as it met what remained of Billy's body, the shovel shuddered from the hard impact. It seemed the flesh had somehow frozen or calcified.

At that moment, Billy's head slowly came up with a creaking sound. His eyes were still pressed closed, but his large mouth was opening, showing almost transparent, needle-like teeth, more like those of a coral eel than a human being.

As they watched, the young, deformed man faced the sky and his mouth creaked open even further. An eerie grating squeal began to emanate from deep in his throat, a sound that made Lightinger's skin crawl and the hair rise on his neck. It was the most unearthly sound he had ever heard in his life.

And then it came. From the overly wide mouth erupted an explosion of black filth that was like molasses, which spread in a large plume, enveloping Hepworth and his shovel. The man screamed, dropped the tool, and sputtered as he wiped at his face and eyes and backed away.

Lightinger was standing a little further back and therefore avoided being covered by whatever it was the young man had vomited up. He was glad it had happened outdoors, as he couldn't imagine the clean-up required if it was indoors.

Indoors!

Like where the other affected seaman was.

In front of him, Hepworth had wiped his face and was coughing, gagging a little. Lightinger hoped none of the substance had gone in his mouth.

"Mr. Hepworth, stay on deck until you've cleaned yourself off. Understand?" he yelled to the man as he turned.

"Aye, sir." The seaman nodded and picked up one of the dropped blankets to try and wipe away more of the viscous stuff. He began to take his sodden coat off.

Lightinger then raced down to the medical rooms, and he could feel the eyes of Captain Smyth up on the bridge on him every step of the way.

***

Captain Smyth had watched with concern and rising anger as the large seaman had tried to dislodge the young man who still sat like a tiny mound on his deck. And for his troubles, the sailor had been vomited on.

Disgusting, Smyth thought.

Not only that, the youth was still stuck fast. Then he saw the seaman begin to wipe himself down and disrobe as his officer raced below deck.

Smyth was rapidly losing patience with his officer's mishandling of the situation that was unfolding on his ship, and decided he would have to start meting out punishment if he didn't get answers soon.

"Someone take spare clothing to that fool on deck," he commanded. "And find out where my sub-lieutenant has gone."

***

Lightinger sprinted through the labyrinth of passageways, down the staircase, and then accelerated along the long corridor to the medical rooms. As soon as he saw the open door and the black stain around the doorframe, he knew he was too late.

He burst inside, and the stench immediately made him cover his nose and mouth. The room was empty save for the black sticky blotches that were everywhere. And even more concerning was that the patient was gone.

"*Doctor?*" he called. "*Nurse?*" He picked up a cloth from under an open shelf and used it to open the connecting door to the next room. There was no one there either.

He stood thinking for a minute but couldn't decide what to do. He needed to tell the captain and the other officers. But he wasn't even sure what to tell them.

What he did know was that they needed a plan.

He used the cloth to pull the medical room's door shut and then sprinted to the bridge.

* * *

"Gone?" Captain Smyth's head jerked back on his bull-like neck. "Do you mean he had improved and went back to his bunk? Or back to work?"

Lightinger grimaced and then began his explanation as he understood it. There was silence when he finished, and all eyes were on him as he walked to the bridge windows to look out onto the foredeck.

Billy Markson was still there, glued to the deck like some sort of giant human mollusk.

"I believe it's some sort of contagion." Lightinger turned to face the captain. "And it's spreading."

Captain Smyth's eyes widened. "Do not say that without proof, man. We could cause a panic."

The captain paced away for a moment before turning back. "I want this to be kept discreet. I want several teams looking for the missing patient, as well as Dr. Morweek, the nurses, and anyone else who has been in contact with the, ah, young seaman *sitting* on our deck."

"Seaman Hepworth. He also needs to be isolated." Lightinger had totally forgotten about the man who had been vomited on out on deck. He rushed to the window, but saw he was gone.

Captain Smyth grunted. "If only you had brought us this news before you left Hepworth to freeze on deck." He called his officers over. "We'll round Hepworth up as well and have him confined to quarters. And anyone who touched him." He growled deep in his chest and glared out at Billy Markson. "And if we can't remove that *man* on deck I want him covered with a sheet of canvas. *And* weighted down."

He turned back. "And that brings us to you, Mr. Lightinger. I want you confined to quarters as well."

"Sir, I'm the only one—" Lightinger began.

"*That's an order,*" the captain barked.

Lightinger knew it was useless to argue at this time. And perhaps, staying away from the others might not be a bad idea right now.

He nodded. "As you say, sir."

* * *

Lightinger entered his officer's cabin. It was a small bunk room with a table and adjoining washroom, which comprised little more than a shaving mirror, bowl of water, and toilet that jettisoned the waste out through a hole in the ship's side.

The sub-lieutenant rested his hands on the top of the basin and looked at himself in the mirror – he looked pale, drawn, and tired. Then he leaned forward and pulled his eyelid down, searching for anything that looked like a wriggling hair in the white sclera. It was bloodshot, but fine. The young officer sighed, loosened his tie, and sat on the bunk bed. He stared at nothing as he tried to work out what it all meant, but his exhaustion made thinking too hard so instead he lay down, feeling both physically and emotionally drained.

He meshed his fingers on his belly, closed his eyes, and in seconds fell into a deep sleep.

* * *

The screams shocked him to full wakefulness.

Lightinger sat up with a thumping headache and grabbed his pocket watch to check the time – he'd been asleep three hours but was still so tired he felt sick.

There came a banging from the corridor outside, like doors opening and being slammed shut, and then running feet. And more screaming, so much screaming.

He jumped up, dragged on his coat and took his hat off the floor. Lightinger then grabbed his doorhandle and held it for a moment to calm himself, taking deep breaths.

He steeled himself, then pulled the door open and went out.

It was worse than he expected – there was blood, ripped clothing, and violent splashes of the black viscous material he had seen ejected from Billy Markson up on deck.

Around the turn in the corridor, he heard a scream and headed toward it. He suddenly wished he had a weapon – even a club would have been something.

He began to jog, and when he got around the corner he found the first barnacle. It had obviously once been a person, as he could make out the mound of bones with the misshapen skull at the top and the melted flesh fused to the ground.

Lying in front of it was one of the nurses he had seen earlier, covered in the black slime and moaning softly. He went to approach but saw that already her skin looked to be sagging. Whatever the black stuff was, it had infected her as well.

A slight movement from beside him made him spin around in time to see that the mound of flesh that had infected her was shuddering, just as he'd seen it do before Billy had vomited over Seaman Hepworth.

He dived out of the way as a stream of the black mucus splashed onto the wall where he had just been standing.

Lightinger rolled to his feet, and in the light of the corridor saw in the puddles closest to him the thread-like things wriggling and squirming, no doubt looking for a warm home.

Lightinger backed away and then began to run.

This was how the thing spread; he now knew. How it reproduced. It infected a host, and that body turned into a factory for the little monstrosities. Perpetuation of the species, he thought. He'd read about that in school.

But exactly what species of creature was this? What else was it doing? Or becoming? he wondered.

And then around the next corner he found out. It appeared the people-barnacles couldn't sustain the black output without something going back in to fuel them. And now he saw what that was.

There was a crowded corridor, with several of the people-barnacles fused to the floor. But this time from their mouths a long, leathery tongue apparatus had shot out to trap a man, and his body hung limply between the three horrors as they held him tight.

What would happen? Lightinger wondered. Would they hold him until he rotted and then just pull the soft meat free? Or would they somehow dissolve him and then absorb the nutrients through the long tongue?

Lightinger felt bile hit the back of his throat and he coughed and spat it out. Then he turned and ran back the other way. His destination was the stairs to the bridge.

Did the captain know what was going on? He had to, Lightinger hoped. And he also hoped he was doing something about it.

"*Help me!*"

He heard the cry and stopped dead.

He saw a woman, refined looking, in what was once an expensive dress, holding out an arm. She was pinned beneath a heavy upturned table.

His service-to-the-passengers ethic kicked in and he rushed to her, taking her hand.

"Thank you." She gripped his hand tightly. "I'm stuck. I don't know where my husband is. He went to find help hours ago."

Lightinger hoped he wasn't the man he'd seen trapped by the people-barnacles just before.

"Wait a moment, madam, I'll try . . ." He quickly looked one way then the other. Although there were splashes of the black mucus everywhere, for now, they seemed to be alone.

He stood, grabbed the edge of the heavy oak table and strained. It moved a fraction, but he couldn't hold it for long.

"Can you move?" he grunted.

"A little more," she begged.

He put his whole body into it, and the table lifted another half-inch.

The woman slid out and grabbed her foot, which was now at a strange angle.

"I've lost my shoe." She began to cry.

"Shoes can be replaced. But you cannot, madam." He put an arm underneath her and lifted. "We must go. *Now.*"

She hobbled under his arm, and they made slow progress. From somewhere in the bowels of the ship more screaming was going on, and he felt his stomach flip from fear. He wanted the woman to speed up.

"What happened?" she said in a small voice.

He shook his head. "I don't know. Something got onboard. A sickness."

It was all he could tell her. He knew he had no words to make her, or anyone else, understand what he had seen and experienced.

"What will we do?" she asked. "I need to find my husband. My cabin is the other way."

"We can't go back now." Lightinger glanced over his shoulder. "We'll try to get to the bridge. The captain will know what to do."

"I need to rest. Will you protect me?" she said in a voice that was barely above a whisper as she looked up at him.

He turned to her. "I will do my—"

He stopped cold.

Her eyes, though glistening with tears, were also swimming with something else – within the whites, thread-like things coiled, flicked, and wriggled.

"*Oh*," was all he said as he gently uncoupled himself from her.

"What's the matter?" she asked.

"I think . . ." He gently sat her down against the wall. "I think you do need to rest."

"What?" Her eyes were wide.

She must have seen the expression on his face, as hers transformed to one of fear.

Lightinger backed away. "Just rest a while, and, um, I'll get help."

"What's the matter?" she begged.

He held up his hands for a moment, and then turned to run.

"*Don't leave me . . .*"

He tried to shut out her voice and his soul felt like it had turned to ashes in his chest as he sprinted away.

She was infected, he told himself. And he'd already seen what happened when the infection progressed.

As he passed one of the cabins, he tried the door, found it unlocked, ripped it open and headed right to the washroom. Inside he leaned forward and pulled the lid of his left eye down, then the right, looking into the whites.

After a moment, he leaned back. "Thank God," he whispered.

Lightinger then took a side corridor and came up through one of the dining areas. He stopped at the top of the stairs, and his shoulders sagged at the horrifying sight – the entire room looked like a scene from Hell.

Hundreds of people had been turned into revolting things stuck to the floor and some even to the walls. A few had long, questing tongues waving in the air, seeking passing victims, he guessed. And some of the unaffected people had been caught, as there were also bodies held by the barnacle-tongues, and everywhere there was the black slime, sprays of blood and viscera, and in the air hung a humid greasy mist that stank like an open corpse.

"No, no, *I don't see it, I don't see it, I don't see it*," Lightinger repeated as he turned away and rushed up the crew stairs to the bridge. Coming to the top he found the door barricaded, and he thumped on it with his fist.

After a moment came a wary voice. "Who goes there?"

"It's me, Sub-Lieutenant Lightinger." He turned to face the stairwell, suddenly feeling very exposed.

Then, to his relief, he heard Captain Smyth's stentorian voice. "Charles, are you . . . well?"

He never calls me Charles, he thought. The Old Man sounded scared. "Yes, sir. I'm not infected, if that's what you're asking."

Lightinger sucked in a few deep breaths and felt a bit light-headed from exhaustion and fear. He continued to look back down the steps, waiting for someone or something to follow him, and willing his heartbeat to slow.

There was nothing but silence from behind the thick door.

What's taking them so long? he wondered.

He put his mouth closer to the heavy door. "*Sir?*" he called.

A bolt was drawn back, and the door opened. Men with guns stood there, all pointed at his chest. Behind them stood an ashen-faced Captain Smyth.

Lightinger raised his arms. "I'm not infected, I swear it," he said, waiting in the doorframe.

The men's guns never wavered from his face and chest.

"May I enter, sir?" Lightinger glanced over his shoulder. "It is not safe out here."

Smyth stared a moment longer, seeming to wrestle with the idea.

"How did you survive?" the captain finally asked.

"I was locked in my cabin, sleeping. When I awoke it was mayhem," Lightinger replied. "I've been running ever since."

"And the state of things below decks?" Smyth asked.

Lightinger exhaled. "Hellish," he replied simply.

Captain Smyth snorted softly. "Mr. Lightinger, you must be the luckiest man alive." He half-turned to the others. "Lower your weapons." Looking back at Lightinger, he added, "Check him."

Dr. Will MacLoughlin, the ship's surgeon, stepped forward and raised a lantern closer to Lightinger's face. He reached forward to pull his cheek down, opening one then the other lower eyelid and staring into his eyes. Lightinger knew what he was looking for and complied with the inspection.

MacLoughlin paused. "Did you see any of the other medical staff?"

Lightinger shook his head. "All gone."

After a moment, the doctor lowered the lantern and stepped back. "He seems clean."

"How many survivors?" Lightinger immediately asked.

Smyth growled deep in his chest and walked forward to look out the bridge windows. "We've sealed off the below decks, and anyone uninfected has been allowed into our area. All others have been denied." He turned. "Or shot."

"How many, sir?" Lightinger pressed.

"We estimate more than two-thirds are lost," Captain Smyth replied gravely.

Lightinger knew there were 2240 people on the ship, including passengers and crew. If two-thirds were dead or changed, then that meant only around 700 people remained to be saved.

"In just a day," Lightinger replied softly.

The captain nodded. "And in another day there will be no one left alive to save – or who remains a human being." He faced the windows again, and his chest swelled. "We are preparing to abandon ship."

"Sir. No, sir." Lightinger shook his head slowly. "That might not be enough." He came and stood by the captain and the other officers followed.

"What do you mean?" Chief Officer Henry Wilden scowled.

"Sir . . ." Lightinger drew a breath. ". . . we have some of the finest physicians, nursing staff, and medical equipment onboard – the best in the world – and we have no idea what is happening or how to stop this thing." He exhaled. "If we leave, the ship will sail on with its cargo of deadly infection. Until when? Until where? Perhaps until it is boarded by someone else." He looked the other men in the eye one by one. "If this can happen to us in two days, imagine what would happen if it made it to New York."

Captain Smyth shut his eyes. After a moment he nodded. "Yes, I see. Perhaps abandoning ship *is* not enough." He turned, his back rod-straight. "Suggestions, if you please, gentlemen."

"We could open the outer doors and flood the lower levels. Make sure the bulkhead doors stay open," First Officer Murdoch offered. "There's also dynamite in the storeroom," he added.

"A good suggestion, but how do we get down there?" Lightinger replied. "It would take a team of men to achieve that task, and it would mean navigating the entire below decks. It would be a suicide mission."

"We could call for volunteers," Wilden replied. "Sacrifices need to be made."

Captain Smyth turned. "And if they didn't succeed? Do we send another team? And then another? All the while our time is running out." Smyth's eyes were red-rimmed. "I've lost passengers before through old age, misadventure, accident, illness, and even murder. But I will not go down in history as the man who sank his own ship and let every passenger onboard die. There must be another way."

"There is," Lightinger said, and the room hushed to silence. "We abandon ship with all survivors. Then we increase speed and lock the wheel." He turned. "This area is notorious for icebergs. We let Mother Nature take care of this abomination. Take it to the dark depths where this hellish affliction belongs."

Henry Wilden folded his arms. "Might work. Might not. Think about it. If by a slim chance the *Titanic* sails through the bergs, or it proves impervious to them, as the designers have attested it should be, then it might just thread the needle and come out the other side." He turned to Captain Smyth. "Delivering its deadly cargo straight to America."

Captain Smyth paced for a moment, then stopped at the large windows with his back to the others. From somewhere below decks there was a thumping as if a battering ram was being used. Then faintly a woman's screams.

Without turning, he said, "Any other suggestions, gentlemen?"

He was met with silence.

"Then Lightinger's plan is the one that we will adopt." Finally, he turned to face them, and held a hand up as the officers began to object. "It will work, with one small modification. We don't lock the wheel. Instead, we have someone steering the *Titanic* toward its fate – to make sure of it."

"I volunteer," said Lightinger immediately.

Smyth smiled ruefully. "Thank you, Mr. Lightinger, but the job is the captain's, as it has always been throughout seafaring history."

The room exploded in objections, arguments, alternative suggestions, and demands to let them volunteer or to travel with him.

Captain Smyth waved them all down. "We don't have much time. For now the unaffected are separated from the afflicted." His countenance grew stern. "What I am asking of you is a task of the utmost importance. And therefore, it is to be carried out on pain of death. You may be resisted in your duties, but you will have mere hours to get everyone off and into the lifeboats."

He looked at each of his officers' faces. "Women and children first. Men next, crew to follow. If anyone resists you in your duties, they stay onboard. Or, you shoot them." He drew in a deep breath and half-smiled. "Do not feel sorry for me, nor have any regret. I may be the lucky one, as what is in store for you when you go into that icy water will be a whole different sort of Hell."

The officers began to argue again, and the captain clapped his hands once in a sound like a gunshot that immediately silenced the bridge.

There would be no negotiations. The decision was made, and he began to issue direct commands. The officers would organize teams to get the boats lowered and rally the remaining passengers. No belongings were to be taken, and anyone who impeded them in their vital duties was to be dealt with deadly force if required. There would be no debate or compromise. His final order was for the rifle cabinet to be opened.

Captain Smyth then had the officers and bridge crew line up, and he went along that line shaking hands.

"Thank you, sir," Lightinger said to the Old Man when it was his turn.

"Thank *you*, Mr. Lightinger. You will make a fine captain of your own ship one day." He continued to grip the young officer's hand. "Now, spread some of that luck of yours around so our surviving passengers all get home." He let go of Lightinger's hand. "And I'll take care of the rest."

Captain Edward Smyth then stood tall, his hands clasped behind his back as the men exited.

Lightinger took one last look over his shoulder as the captain went and stood by the wheel. He had served White Star Line Shipping as a ship's commander all his life. And he would serve it one last time.

Lightinger saluted, and went out the door, sealing the bridge behind him.

***

Lightinger was one of the men charged with organizing the lifeboats, and then with getting the passengers into them in a calm and orderly fashion. Which wasn't easy as it was freezing, night-time, and everyone knew what was happening by now, and were scared half to death.

It was as bad as they expected among the passengers. Many fights broke out as some people demanded that they be given time to go and dress more suitably. Or that they be permitted to bring their luggage. And some of them sat down and refused to move until their special suitcases were brought up on deck for them.

Lightinger knew that many of the first-class passengers would have brought valuable items with them, and would not give them up lightly. He felt sorry for their naïve selfishness and stupidity, as there would be no porter coming to assist them. And soon the boats would be away. He'd hate to be them when the cold and horrible reality, so foreign to them, came and stared them in the face.

The young officer heard gunfire from close by and quickly felt for his own weapon. He prayed he didn't need to use it.

It took them longer than expected, but by and large, once on deck the passengers seemed to realize the significance of what was happening and fell into line. While some continued to argue that they weren't being treated fairly, the officers got many of the lifeboats away without trouble.

A few boats were dropped into the sea in the process of trying to lower them, and when it seemed there might not be enough for everyone, a lot of passengers panicked and jumped over the side.

Lightinger had felt freezing water before and knew what it was like – agony to begin with. But when it stopped being agony, you were on your way to dying, so agony was preferable.

He spotted the young girl again, Lily, waving to him with her delicate pink umbrella. She should have been gone by now and looked lost. He called her to him.

"We have to leave now, Miss Lily." He pointed to the nearly full boat he was loading.

"What's happening?" she asked, and then looked past him to the horrifying barnacle-man fused to the foredeck. "That man looks very sick. I don't understand."

"I'll explain later. But we must go." He firmly guided her into the boat.

"It's cold," she said as her boat was lowered to the water.

"There are blankets in the boat. Wrap one around your shoulders." He smiled and waved to the girl. "You're safe now."

"Are you coming?" she shouted up to him.

"I'll take the next boat." He watched until she was down on the water and the seamen on the small craft had begun to row away into the freezing darkness.

Lightinger continued to watch until the glow of the lantern at the boat's prow receded in the blackness, to become like a tiny star in the night sky.

He was reminded of a quote by a famous American president named Lincoln: "*Next to creating a life, the finest thing a man can do is save one.*"

If I have done nothing else, I have done that, he thought. He sighed and went back to work.

Fifteen minutes later, he and the remaining crew got into the last few boats and lowered them. Lightinger stood in the front of his, letting out the rope. Up on the still lit bridge he saw the stoic form of Captain Smyth staring down at them. The old man saluted, and then turned away.

When they had rowed a good hundred feet away from *Titanic*, the massive engines started up, and the colossal ship gathered speed.

Now it was up to the captain, as he accelerated the mountain of a ship into the cold night toward its eternal fate.

***

Captain Edward Smyth put out a distress signal, giving the position of the *Titanic* as being where he had offloaded the passengers and crew, and not where he was headed. Then he pushed the ship up to twenty-two knots – a mad speed in the dark, in a thick fog, and with no one to spot bergs for him.

He gritted his teeth as he heard the obscene howls from the bowels of the ship, and they sounded horrifying, animalistic, and like something from Dante's infernal tale of the nine levels of Hell.

Whatever had afflicted his ship, he meant to keep it from harming anyone else. It would end here, and he would bury it in 2000 fathoms of icy, ink-black water, never to be seen again.

From out of the gloom, the first big iceberg appeared. And then another.

And then, dead ahead, the biggest berg he had ever seen loomed before him, and *Titanic* was on a direct collision course with it.

"So be it." Captain Smyth put his hand over his heart. "God save the King."

The *Titanic* struck the massive berg side-on, ripping a gash in the steel 245-feet long with a sound like rolling thunder. In two hours and forty minutes, the eighth wonder of the world and greatest ship that had ever sailed was on its way to the bottom, taking its diabolical inhabitants with it.

The *Titanic* was lost, but the world had been saved.

For now.

STORY 11

If you could go back in time and change something that you thought had ruined your life, would you? That's what Jean Russell wanted to do. But when she finally had the chance, could she really do it?

For SJR.

THE GHOSTS OF TIME

Sixty-five-year-old Jean Russell sat alone in her laboratory. Everyone else had gone home for the weekend. Home to their families, their friends, their pets, and their neighborhoods.

But she had nothing to go home to. Jean was one of the most brilliant physicists in the country and had patented more inventions in the last decade than many in her field had in a lifetime.

But she was alone. She had no one to share her triumphs, no one to lift her spirits when she was down. No one to love, and no one to love her. It had been that way for over forty years. And it was all her own fault.

She became maudlin sometimes when she got to thinking about her past and the decisions she had made along the way. And it always came back to one thing, one huge mistake.

"Never love the wrong person," she muttered as she opened her top desk drawer to take out a small black and white photograph that she laid on her desk. She also lifted out a mirror that she now looked into. The person staring back was barely recognizable. The flashing blue eyes were still there, but they sat in a world-weary face. Her once thick and bouncy blonde hair was dry, and even her lips were creased, but not from smiling.

She caressed her cheek with a hand as she whispered: "Time is a thief."

The weird thing was she still thought about *him* – the man she had met when she was just sixteen and had lost her heart to forever. They had spent years together in a world that only needed the two of them in it. And they had been the happiest years of her life.

Then it was over. She had been the one to end it. And she soon realized that she had made the biggest mistake of her life.

She had foregone all other loves and lovers, trying firstly to find him again for years and then to win him back after their lives had traveled in vastly different directions. She became obsessed and couldn't let go.

She often wondered what her life would have been like if she'd never met him. Would she have found and married someone else? She'd had plenty of suitors when she was young. But they had never quite matched up to her first and only true love.

And the worst part of it for her was that when she did find him again he was married, and surreptitiously watching him on his social media she saw he was still handsome, now wealthy, and he and his wife had children.

That should have been me, she had complained in her mind.

In her heart she was still that young girl who hung on to a dream that one day he would come back to her. It must happen. After all, true love should win in the end, shouldn't it? That's what happened in stories.

She gently lowered the mirror.

Those stories were a lie.

And then he had died. An unexpected heart attack. An aberration, she had read. He was a fitness fanatic and should have lived to be a hundred. But one day he went swimming and never came home.

Nothing goes to plan, she thought.

Love was stupid. Love *made* you stupid. She sighed. Love was a shackle that bound you. And once you had tasted sweet true love, everything else was just ash on your tongue.

"Let me go," she muttered. "Now that you're gone for good, please let me go."

She put the mirror back in the drawer and closed it, then sat in the silence of the empty laboratory for many minutes.

"I wish I'd never met you. My life would have been so different. I could have . . ."

She slowly looked up.

What if she could make that happen? Or rather, make that *unhappen*?

She had been working on a private and secret project. The physical side of time travel would be impossible at their current technological level. The amount of energy required was near infinite, and would not be within their grasp in her lifetime. But she was working on time projection where an image, a living image with its consciousness, could be sent back in time.

Like a ghost that was aware, it would be able to see and hear, but not touch. It could also be seen, although not heard. And that was all.

She had yet to refine the projection process to a specific time and place. But that was a triviality after she had broken the back of the underlying mathematical equations. And after all, the process would need to be field-tested, so why shouldn't she be the one to do it?

"I'll stop myself. Stop myself from meeting him." She smiled. "Then I'll have been freed to have a different life. A better life."

* * *

She shut herself away from all other projects to refine the time projection technology, and it took her three more months, working night and day. But it helped that she knew exactly the time and place she needed to get to – she had several targets, but the first was the time they had first met: Saturday, 17 November 1979, 9 pm.

Jean stepped up onto the small pad she had designed and built. She had the portable projection device in one hand, and a note in the other. She couldn't be heard, but a note could be read. It would exist in that time for only as long as she was there. It contained a message for her younger self.

She would appear back in 1979, but her form would be as insubstantial as a wraith. People might notice her but they would be able to walk straight through her. She would stay out of the way until she found what she was looking for.

Jean drew in a few deep breaths and then let the last one out slowly as she stood straight. "Here goes."

She pressed the button on the hand-held device.

And projected.

* * *

Sixteen-year-old Jean sat with her friends in the dark bar, drinking too much, laughing too loud, and smoking cigarettes. They were all underage, but in heels and makeup it was nearly impossible to tell.

None of them were looking for love; instead, they were all just looking for fun. Most of the conversation centered around boys, bust-ups, holidays, new jobs – and the crappy jobs they were stuck in – and horrible bosses.

Jean had been a whiz at school, topping her class in mathematics and physics, but had dropped out to sit on the beach, and go surfing. Maybe one day she'd go back to school and possibly make something of herself. But that wasn't on her mind this evening.

Regina, her best friend, leaned across and nudged her. "Don't look now, but there's an old lady checking you out."

"Where?" Jean spun one way then the other.

Then she saw her. Sort of.

There was a woman standing in the shadows at the back of the bar, just watching her. She concentrated on the older woman's face, which was strangely familiar, but for the life of her Jean couldn't place her.

"Do you know her?" Regina asked.

"I . . . I'm not sure." Jean looked back at the woman, who continued to stare at her with an expression of absolute sadness.

Jean felt mesmerized. The old woman looked like she wanted to say something, but instead she began to hold out something in her hands. But just then, Jean's arm was grabbed by one of her other friends.

"Check it out." She was nudged. "It's your Mr. Dreamboat."

Jean turned back in time to see the group of guys walk into the bar. She knew of them from the beach – the cool guys who sat at the southern end.

And there he was, James Craig, in their center, the boy she had seen around – he was the most beautiful person she had ever laid eyes on. He had a physique like a Greek god, and a smile that could make the sun come out in the middle of the night.

He turned to her, and Jean quickly looked away. It was uncool to be caught staring.

But then she sneakily looked back.

He was still looking. Looking at her. And he smiled.

She swallowed, and was too frozen to return the smile, wave, or even blink. The only thing she could feel was her heart hammering in her chest. And then he was gone, moving off to the other end of the bar with his friends.

That evening Jean danced a bit, drank too many wine coolers, and looked out for James, but as the bar got more crowded it was impossible to find anyone. And she would never dare go looking for him, as he had too many girls chasing him already, and she'd be damned if she was going to be just another one.

It was later in the evening and of her group, only she and Regina remained. The music slowed and the bar was emptying. The pair were headed toward the door when from the corner of her eye, Jean saw the older woman again. She was still in the shadows, indistinct, but the face seemed almost ethereal. And Jean felt the jolt of recognition again. Maybe she should go over and ask the woman where they had met before. Was she a long-lost relative? she wondered.

But she didn't need to go over, because the older woman was coming right at her. Suddenly she felt a hand on her arm, just lightly, and she turned to tell Regina to give her a moment. But when she turned she discovered it wasn't Regina but James smiling down at her.

"I've been looking for you," he said.

And suddenly Jean forgot about everything else.

An hour later, she was in bed with him. It was their first time together. And from that moment on she was caught in a whirlwind.

***

Older Jean flicked the remote button and her consciousness returned to her time.

She drew in a deep breath and let it out slowly. Her mind was a mess of emotions. Her machine had worked, and worked exactly as she had intended. However she'd missed her opportunity, and now her younger self had met James. It was strange; seeing James again as a young man had made her own heart race.

She scoffed softly. It was no wonder that little fool she had once been – perhaps still was, on some level – had been so defenseless.

She thought hard for a moment. She'd missed her chance this time, but she knew there were other opportunities to change the past. However, the bottom line was, her technology worked.

She knew she had been seen, and just as older Jean could recognize her younger self, the younger version would have a prickling of recognition, but would be unable to put the puzzle pieces together. How could she?

She would try again and again until she succeeded. For her younger self, weeks and months would go by, but for older Jean it was all happening in the same evening. She would boost the power next time and make her projection more substantial. She'd not be able to manifest her physical self, but she could manifest some form of energy.

Jean selected the next time and place. And projected.

* * *

Jean and James were in a park. The day was hot, and they were lying at the base of a tree, shaded by its broad canopy.

James, nineteen now, was on his back, and Jean, just turned seventeen, was on her belly with her face turned to his. Older Jean couldn't remember exactly what they'd talked about, but recalled again the intensity and excitement she had felt back then about the life that lay ahead of her.

She watched as young Jean leaned forward to kiss the corner of James' mouth and smiled as he talked. Nothing else mattered to the pair other than each other.

Older Jean didn't know how long she stayed there in the shade of another tree, but it was until the pair finally left. She didn't say or do anything. She couldn't, because she was entranced by their happiness. She had forgotten what they had. What *she* had once had.

The next time she projected it was the same. And the next and the next, as older Jean became little more than a voyeur to her past life.

She watched the two young, strong and smooth bodies as they enjoyed each other. She was there when James was swimming out past the breakers with Jean's arms wrapped around his neck. At the shore he grabbed her by her tiny waist and lifted her, squealing with joy, above his head.

She was there outside the bar when they fought. There were tears, and curses, then apologies, and then ferocious love when they made up later that evening.

As the months went by for the young pair, older Jean watched as they talked a lot, laughed often, made love constantly, and spent every day they could together. And she pitied Romeo and Juliet for not knowing a love that burned as hot as the one these two lovers shared. That *she* had once shared.

***

Older Jean returned to her aging body in her own time and sat alone in the dark laboratory. She had visited her younger self and James more than a dozen times now, and would go back no more.

Her determination to change her past decisions had morphed into a desire to relive it and have it again – no matter how it had turned out for her.

Watching her younger self enjoy a love some could only dream of had filled her with happiness. And it made her remember exactly what a gift she'd once had. She realized now that some people could live their entire lives together and not experience the intensity of love she had shared with James across those few magnificent years. And though she longed for it again, and had done every day since she'd lost him, she found she could no longer bring herself to take that away from her younger self.

She finally knew why pure love, true love, was so rare. Because it was a gift, and if she had never met James, then she might never have known it, ever.

She slumped back in her chair, knowing that if she stole from her past to try to improve her future, then she might be committing the greatest crime against herself that could be imagined.

"Ghosts should remain ghosts," she whispered, as she opened her drawer and tossed the time remote into it.

From her desk she lifted the fading square of the black and white photograph taken in one of those cramped dime carnival booths. She lifted it out and held it close; it was a picture of the two of them, sixteen-year-old Jean and eighteen-year-old James. Both were laughing and pulling mad faces. She remembered it as if it were yesterday.

She brought the picture to her lips and kissed it. And then stood it on her desk.

Jean got to her feet and headed for the door. She pulled it open and paused to look back at the tiny picture.

"Thank you for the memories. Both of you. They are your gift to me."

She finally went home, feeling like one of the luckiest people alive.

STORY 12

Imagine a world, perhaps our world, one million years in the future. A place where the new rulers are creatures descended from wolves, and human beings are just a legend. It's a violent and dangerous world where strange creatures roam, some the size of buildings, some like twisted shapes, and others pale, skinless horrors that crawl in the dark labyrinths beneath the earth.

Then imagine what would happen if someone from our time was thrown into the strange world via a portal, and was heralded as the savior of this wolf race, called Wolfen.

The Valkeryn Chronicles trilogy is an epic tale of love, betrayal, and war, that spans worlds and time itself. It has been waiting on its final part for nearly ten years. And now, it gets its closure here, in "Revenge of the Wolfen".

Arnold Singer, the youth turned ferocious Wolfen leader in a distant world, is coming back to our time. But he is coming back for revenge and to rescue his love, the Wolfen princess Eilif.

And pity anyone or anything that gets in his way.

VALKERYN III – REVENGE OF THE WOLFEN

THE STORY SO FAR

2012 – *Return of the Ancients*

Arnold "Arn" Singer, a normal teenager, is on a class outing to the Illinois Fermilab particle accelerator facility. He and his friends will be allowed to witness the firing of one of the world's most powerful proton-antiproton colliders – four miles in diameter, and able to send particles around its gigantic ring at 99.99 percent the speed of light.

Professor Albert Harper has developed an acceleration initiator, a unique, pure red lab-grown diamond, that will shoot a laser at the particles already traveling at near the speed of light, with the objective of pushing them to an even greater speed – a world first.

Arn finds himself trapped in the acceleration chamber when the laser fires. The resulting collisions are so powerful they tear open a hole, a portal, in our version of time and space.

Arn is sucked through this portal and thrown into a strange world far in the future. Humans have long vanished, and a new race now rules – the Valkeryn Wolfen, creatures that evolved from genetically modified wolves into intelligent, warlike beings.

242

Through what appears to be a stroke of luck, Arn saves the life of the Wolfen princess, Eilif, who has had dream-visions of him all her life.

Arn Singer is seen as the embodiment of a Wolfen prophecy that heralds the return of the Ancients: human beings. To them his name is *Arnodrr Sigarr*, which means "the bringer of victory".

Though Eilif and the "man-kind" creature are vastly different, she finds herself strangely attracted to him.

But the last human on the planet has arrived at a perilous time. The Wolfen have been in an eternal war with the Panterran horde – creatures that are without honor and known for their treachery and brutality. The Panterran now have a secret plan to end the war once and for all and they team up with the giant Lygon, monstrous beasts from a forbidden zone, called the Dark Lands.

Together, with the help of a Wolfen traitor, they make a final assault on the Valkeryn kingdom and defeat the noble Wolfen. The survivors scatter to the forests.

***

2014 – *The Dark Lands*

Back home, the hole torn in the universe remains open, continuing to grow and threatening all life on Earth. To close it, the unique acceleration diamond needs to be retrieved, and it is believed to be in Arn's possession.

A team of Green Berets is sent to bring Arn back, but they encounter adversaries more powerful and ferocious than they ever expected. They are decimated, leaving only one survivor.

With the kingdom of the Wolfen fallen, Arn sets out to the Dark Lands looking for evidence of what happened to the fabled Ancients, the human beings who once ruled the planet. In those dangerous forests he gathers an army and marches on the Panterran and Lygon, defeating them once and for all.

The "bringer of victory" lives up to his name and fulfils the ancient prophecy. But Arn has been changed. The altered DNA of the Wolfen has entered his bloodstream, and he has become like them, a Wolfen–human hybrid who only reverts back to his human form at the full moon.

But the portal to our time has now been closed, saving our world from destruction. The war is over, the battle won, and Eilif and Arn rule the new world in a time of peace.

***

2024 – *Revenge of the Wolfen*

A new threat has emerged. Something from the time of men has come through a new portal. And they bring death and destruction – and worse, they capture Eilif and take her back with them.

Now Arn must find a way back home, to rescue Eilif and seek revenge for the Wolfen who were murdered. He must also ensure that a war between two worlds never happens. Finally, he must close this new portal forever.

The huge Wolfen's quest will be bloody, and the ferocious heart of the beast that now beats in Arn's chest will be like nothing human beings have ever seen in their lives.

Arn's path throughout history to find and rescue his love leaves behind a trail of broken and torn bodies, and a legend of the wolf that walks upright.

What the age of men will soon find out is that they should beware the revenge of a ferocious Wolfen.

PROLOGUE

"Get down, the wolves will come soon." Grandfather Singer whispered.

"It's cold," six-year-old Arnold Singer complained as he hunkered down.

He meant it; they were already lying on the snow-covered hill, just underneath the low branches of a tree whose feathery limbs were like heavy, ice-encrusted drapes shielding them from view.

"I don't know why the wolves stay out in it." Arn looked up at his grandfather's ancient, weathered face. "Why don't they come in and share our fire? And food?"

Grandfather Singer turned. "Like the dogs do?"

"Yes." Arn nodded. "Wolves could be our friends too."

"But they are not like dogs. And they do not need our friendship. They value other things." He smiled and continued to look at the boy. "Have you ever heard the legend of the dog and the wolf?"

Arn shook his head slowly.

Grandfather Singer turned back to keep his eyes on the snow-covered slope across the valley as he spoke.

"One day a large and starving wolf came upon a big, well-fed dog. He could see the dog was in good shape even though it was the coldest month of winter. He asked the dog what it did to stay so well fed."

"Little," replied the dog. "All I need do is guard the master's house, show fondness to him and the rest of his family, then in return I am given food and warm lodgings. I think this will continue for as long as I am useful."

The wolf thought about this. He lived a life of fighting with tooth and claw, slept out in the coldest and wettest weather, and never knew when or if he was going to eat that day. He thought the dog's life sounded like a better way of living.

As they were going to the dog's home, the wolf saw a place around the dog's neck where the hair had been worn away. He asked what had happened.

"Do not be mindful of that. It is nothing," the dog smiled sadly. "It is just where my chain rubs on my skin at night."

The wolf stopped. "Chain?" he stared. "You mean, you are not free to go where you want?"

"No," the dog said. "Does that mean so much?"

"Everything," the wolf said as he trotted away. "Everything."

The old man smiled as Arn stared up at him with open mouth. "You see, not everyone values the same things in life."

Arn nodded solemnly. "I would also choose to be free."

Grandfather Singer rubbed the top of Arn's fur-hooded head. But then hunkered down.

"Look," the old man said.

On the far hill a wolf pack appeared. Arn could see it was a big pack, but they were strung out and seemed to be in groups. Out front there was a small bunch of about five, moving slowly. And then just behind them were two more, bigger, keeping pace and alert. Then came the main group of about twenty, and with them were fat cubs leaping about and arguing with each other on the snowy trail. Following the main group were three more of the larger wolves.

Arn leaned on his elbows and looked up at the old full-blood Shawnee. "Why are they—"

"*Shus-sssh.*" Grandfather pushed him down again, and then pointed. "Wait, see there . . ."

Then Arn saw him, the big one, coming slowly about another fifty feet back.

Grandfather smiled, his eyes shining. "Yes, there he is, the pack leader. The wolf king," he whispered.

Arn looked at the huge, dark wolf for a few more moments

before glancing up again at his grandfather. "How did you know he'd be there?"

Grandfather Singer continued to watch the huge animal as he spoke. "Because it is the way of the wolf and has always been so." He drew in a deep breath and let it out slowly, releasing the exhalation to hang in the air like a small ghost for a few seconds.

"Look at them," he said. "The first wolves in the pack are the elders. They move slowly because they will not be rushed, and out of respect the pack will only go as fast as these elders can travel. Just behind, guarding them, are two of the strongest warrior wolves. Then comes the main pack, you see: the cubs, the females and the younger wolves." He turned and nudged Arn. "The ones like you."

Arn grinned, nodded, and looked back at them. He pointed with one stubby brown finger. "And the giant one following far behind?"

"That is the king, the pack leader, the father of them all. He sees all and knows all. One sound from him, and the pack will run, or the pack will fight or die for him. As he would for them. It is the way of the wolf – it has always been like that, and always will be."

"Cool." Arn nodded his understanding.

"Always protect your own, young one." He looked down at Arn, the wisdom of ages in his ancient eyes. "And be wise and strong like the wolf."

CHAPTER 01

Present day – Fermilab Nature Reserve, Batavia, Illinois
Rebecca "Becky" Matthews and Edward Lin sat on the grass in the emerald-green parklands that had once been the site of the Fermilab facility. Ten years had passed since the scientist Albert Harper and his team had shut down the accelerator and stopped the gravitational anomaly that had caused the rift in time that had threatened to destroy their world.

There had been the standard news embargos, confidentiality contracts, compensation, and government threats by the usual three-letter agencies over what would happen if they breached national security.

It didn't matter; who would ever believe them anyway? Even now, Becky wondered what was true and what had all been just a bad dream.

She and Edward had been coming to the site every year as a bit of a pilgrimage. She didn't know why, as they asked the same questions and gave each other the same answers every time.

Becky closed her eyes and tilted her head back, allowing the sun's rays to bathe her face.

"Do you still wonder what happened to him?"

Edward yawned and turned to her. "Sure I do. But I bet he's alright. Arn was a survivor."

She frowned. "Harper said that closing the portal would mean that entire timeline might have been erased. Without our world being destroyed, the Wolfen kingdom could never rise, could never exist. He also said he had no idea what would happen to someone from our world if they were there when it simply ceased being."

Edward exhaled. "Hurts my head to even think about it."

Becky stared out across the swathe of green grass. "He changed."

Edward snorted. "That's an understatement." He turned to look over his shoulder at the woodland surrounding the miles of lawn. "You know, they never found the big, weird dogs that escaped. The Guardians, they called them. Those genetically modified animals are still out there roaming around somewhere."

"Not escaped; Big Fen, their leader, released them," Becky replied. "And not just the dogs." She turned to him. "But a whole bunch of other animals they were experimenting on. Everything from bears to alligators."

"Frankenstein's alligators; I would not like to meet one of those suckers." Edward chuckled and then rolled onto his side. "I like Albert Harper, but that shit never should have been allowed."

"Yeah, I agree." Becky yawned and smiled up at the statue that Harper had erected. "Well, I'm going to remember him just like that."

The bronze life-size statue was of Arnold Singer; all neat and short-cropped hair, high cheekbones and sharp, slightly hawk-like nose, betraying his Shawnee heritage.

There were two lines of words printed on its base, first: *HE STILL LIVES.* And then a second line: *IN OUR HEARTS.*

Becky sighed. "He sure does." She looked at Edward. "I just hope he's okay, and that he does find his way back to us some day."

Edward lay back on the grass, his hands behind his head. "Maybe, but I don't know how. The Tevatron collider is buried under a thousand tons of concrete, and laser particle acceleration has been banned in the country."

He turned to her, opening one eye against the sun's glare, and saw the look on her face. "I mean, sure, me too. I hope he comes back one day."

CHAPTER 02

Uri Gorbunov, head of the RSC – the Russian Super Collider facility – stood beside the president and grinned with pride. He had just shown him and the energy minister around the facilities, and they seemed very impressed.

And just as well, as President Petrov was known to shut down billion-ruble projects overnight if the whim took him. As well as making scientists who were judged incompetent disappear.

Gorbunov drew in a deep breath. The first test firing was always nerve-racking, and he had to perform it in front of the president himself. He had promised Petrov the secrets of the universe. But if things went wrong, he was finished.

He stood before the controls, taking over the initiation from his technicians. The computer simulations had been run over a hundred times, all of them showing perfect accelerated particle collisions.

He started the collider, and protons were fired to begin their race around the magnetized, twenty-mile-diameter ring-track, each moving faster and faster with each circuit.

His finger hovered nervously over the button. "The red diamond laser will target the fastest particles and shoot a condensed beam of red light at them, accelerating the rotation of the particles to beyond the speed of light. The resulting collision will open doors onto a new world of science for Russia."

Gorbunov grinned and motioned to the button. "And now, Mr. President, the final acceleration." He paused. "It is only fitting that you are given the honor."

Petrov, looking bored, shrugged and pressed the button.

***

The tremor was felt around the world. Birds took to the air, glass-smooth lakes rippled, and fruit fell from trees.

Seismologists were confounded, as the movement seemed to come from everywhere, and nowhere.

But a future world, thought to have been denied, was now once again set in motion.

CHAPTER 03

"Arn, *help me!*"

Eilif was screaming as she was held back from him. She strained, snarled, and bared her teeth but couldn't break free.

Arn held out his hand but wasn't able to reach her through the portal. He was stuck, unable to move the few extra inches toward her. Eilif's pale, ice-blue eyes were misted, and her face streaked with tears. Her head flew back, and she let loose an unearthly howl that chilled his blood. The long torturous notes were like a blow to his gut, and they spoke of pain and fear, of love found and just as quickly lost.

Arn could only watch as a bag was roughly pulled over her head, and she was dragged down a corridor of white-painted concrete, steel, and blinding fluorescent lighting.

Soldiers were holding her, human soldiers. She was in his time, his world, his *old* world. It didn't make sense. He could hear her as she called his name over and over, muffled beneath the material. Each time she cried out it came from farther away. His name echoed, echoed, and then was gone . . .

Arn fell to his knees. "Eili-*iiif!*"

Arnold "Arn" Singer sat upright, his heart hammering in his chest, and he worked to calm his breathing. It was the dream again, or at least more of it this time. It was as if a movie was being played in the deepest corner of his mind, a few more seconds of the reel every time he closed his eyes.

He looked across at the sleeping form of Eilif. She was safe, but he couldn't shake the feeling that something was coming, something bad.

Arn rose and walked to the castle window, where he looked out to the far forests. The moon would rise soon, but for now the night was at its darkest and the lands were shrouded in utter blackness.

However, his dark-adapted eyes could see clearly and his Wolfen senses meant he could see, hear, and smell things far beyond the dull human senses he'd once had.

He knew what else was coming – this night would be the first full moon of the month, and he would change. Change back to his human form, for three nights.

From behind him he heard Eilif rise to come and stand at his back, putting an arm around him.

At twenty-five she was an adult now, and stood six feet tall, but she still barely came up to his shoulder. Arn was now one of the biggest Wolfen that had ever existed, standing seven and a half feet tall; his abnormal size and strength brought about by the Wolfen DNA that had bonded with his human system. This, combined with the light of the shattered moon, had made him the most formidable king's champion that had ever lived.

Already his name was legend. Arnold Singer, known as *Arnodrr Sigarr* in the Valkeryn lands, the bringer of victory. Which is what he had done in their war.

He felt the soft touch of Eilif's hand on his arm, stroking him, and he turned his head to look down at the beguiling Wolfen princess. Her luminous eyes burned with a deep fire in a face of silver fur.

He cupped her chin in his hand. She was the most beautiful creature he had ever beheld.

The wolfen had the faces of wolves, but their frame was the shape of human beings with long powerful limbs and altered spine and pelvic structure giving them the ability to stand upright. Their bellies and chests were near hairless with the rest of their body covered in a soft but thick fur – Eilif's a silvery sheen, and his as black as a raven's wing.

Their hands ended in sharp talons and their legs from the knee down had the familiar backward bend and extra joint of a wolf, making them fast and powerful runners.

Arn remembered that they had been genetically engineered to be like this. And then evolution had done the rest.

Eilif reached up to hold each side of his face.

"You are troubled, my lord?" she asked, searching his own coal-black eyes.

"I sense something. Something coming," he replied.

"But not tonight," she whispered.

"No, not tonight." He smiled down at her and lifted her chin higher.

"Then tonight, it is just you and me." Her eyes burned up at him.

He lifted her and took her back to the bed.

***

Arn woke to pain in his joints as they contracted, and he gritted his teeth and waited for it to end.

A few minutes later it was over, and he held up a hand and looked at it in the light of the risen moon. He flexed the digits, remembering again how they felt, but he would only know them for three days and nights over the period of the full moon.

Arn had to remove the snarling silver wolf ring with the red ruby eyes from his smallest finger and place it on the largest finger, where it was a better fit now he was in his smaller human form.

He reached up to feel his face, which was carrying a few scars now. The strong jawline was there, and the long black hair to the shoulders. He had come to Valkeryn a boy, and now was a young man and the king's champion. Not bad for a Native American kid who had barely been able to finish his math homework, he thought.

He felt the soft touch of the hand on his arm from behind, and he rolled over to see Eilif smiling a little sympathetically.

"So weak, and yet so strong." She leaned forward to kiss his cheek. "And I still love you even when you look like this." She laughed softly.

She rose up on one elbow and studied his face as he stared up at the ceiling. She ran her hand down his long hair, stroking it.

"I can tell you're thinking about home again." She nestled down beside his ear. "Aren't you?"

After a moment he nodded as he continued to stare up at the ceiling. "Yes. Something is happening back there; I can feel it. I need to know what it is."

"But there's no way back now, is there?" She burrowed in even closer, and he could feel the cold tip of her nose against his ear. "Anyway, there is nothing for you there. Everything you ever wanted and needed is here. I am here. This is your home now." She twirled some of his long hair around her finger and licked his cheek.

"There might be." He turned to her. "There might be a way. Vidarr said the Ancients left behind many strange things in the catacombs. He has spent his lifetime unravelling their mysteries."

Vidarr, their archivist, was the longest-lived and probably the smartest being on the planet. The ancient Wolfen lived in a vast house of stone that seemed as old as time itself, which had been built over the deep catacombs that ran beneath the Valkeryn castle. Vidarr had spent his entire life excavating and exploring the dark labyrinths, where it was said many of the Ancients had sheltered, and when the mighty race had either died out, left in their great ships, or simply gone deeper below the earth, they had left behind many of their treasures and technical advancements. It was as if they had known someone would find them one day, or perhaps they expected to return and make use of the technology themselves. Vidarr now lived among towers of books, parchments, and other curious things he had discovered in the tunnels.

Arn rolled over to face Eilif properly. "Vidarr believes time travel was something the ancients achieved, but their world changed before they could use it. He has found a device. He just needs to test it."

"And I suppose test it on you." She let go of his hair and knelt up in bed. "I don't want you to go. I won't allow it." She grabbed his hand. "I know you won't come back."

"I'll always come back. For you." He smiled. "But curiosity eats at me. I need to know."

"Then let me come with you. I can protect you," she offered.

"In my time, in my world, a six-foot-tall, talking Wolfen might attract unwanted attention." He smiled up at her again. "Besides, haven't you heard that curiosity killed the cat?"

She frowned. "What's a cat?"

He chuckled. "Doesn't matter."

She tilted her head. "And what do you think, Lord Arnodrr Sigarr, the people of your time will make of you when you turn back into a giant black Wolfen?" She leaned her face so close that their noses were almost touching. "I think that might attract far more attention than I would."

Arn sat up. "Yes, if I were in Wolfen form I would need to stay in the shadows. My people don't react well to monsters." He shrugged. "But you raise a good point. It means I'd need to only travel back at the time of the full moon and stay for only as long as it shines bright so I can walk among them in human form."

Eilif turned away. "You should not go." She looked back over her shoulder at him. "If anything happens to you, it happens to me. If you die, I die."

"Don't say that." He reached forward to lay a hand on her shoulder. "Nothing will happen to me. After all, the device might not even work." He smiled at her. "And don't forget, I'm lucky, remember?"

She placed her hand over his. "Luck is like a river. One day it will dry out, and everything that was in it will die." She turned, her pale eyes glistening. "Remember, Arnodrr, I too swim in your river."

Arn lay back. Even Vidarr didn't know if the device he'd found would or could work. It might not send Arn back at all. Or it might send him back to the wrong time and place.

He sighed. Or it might send him to some sort of limbo between time dimensions that he could be trapped in forever.

"I have to know," he whispered.

"Of course you do." She stared for a moment. "Because *you're* the curious cat."

CHAPTER 04

Becky Matthews wandered along the gallery hallway, looking at the photographs on display.

Illinois' Aurora Historical Society had managed to digitally retouch, and even colorize, a huge collection of pictures found in an old suitcase hidden away in the attic of a house that had once belonged to an amateur photographer. They showed life in the State of Illinois from around 1860 to 1870.

She looked over her shoulder. Edward was somewhere further back. He was her closest friend these days, and they spent a lot of time together. Ever since the world was nearly changed forever by being sucked into something like a black hole generated by their particle accelerator beneath the Fermilab science facility, Becky had felt distanced from her old friends – after all, who in their right mind would ever believe what had happened to her? And even if she could talk to them, there had been the cover-ups, rewards and threats, and everything else in between.

No one talked about it anymore. Even the scientists. No one even seemed to want to remember how close they had come to destroying the world as they knew it.

Sometimes Becky still doubted it had really happened. But then she would remember Arn – he'd be a young man now, if he'd stayed in their world – who was sucked into the black hole and thrown forward into the world of Valkeryn, where humans were a myth, and talking wolves ruled over a land of ghastly horrors and perpetual war.

If it hadn't happened, then where was he? If it hadn't happened, then he would be here now, standing beside her, and making dorky jokes about the people in the old photographs. He definitely would not be in a future world that could only exist if this world was ripped apart by the growing distortion forces of the time portal – and then remade into something vastly different.

The creatures that lived there would be the result of horrible mutations, some brought about by the radiation effects of the portal, and others purposely modified by humans, like the Guardian dogs.

And what had happened to the human beings, the supposed wise Ancients? Well, apparently some just upped and left in spaceships. And those remaining hid in labyrinthine shelters below the earth, where they might have devolved into the hairless pale things that now lived in the deep caves there. Becky shuddered at the thought of those abominations.

She couldn't help wondering if Arn, the Valkeryn Wolfen, Eilif their princess – or perhaps now their queen – and all the other horrors were still there, somewhere in space and time, living and thriving.

Becky shook her head, sighed, and tried to push it all from her mind. She was here with her friend to take in a little culture and while away a wet Saturday afternoon. She kept wandering along the corridor, hands jammed in her back pockets, moving past the occasional exhibition attendee and trying to focus on the old pictures. Here was one showing rows of quaint houses; the next an old woman hanging washing; then barefoot children playing baseball with a stick in the street. And then there was a rally of some sort, and more colorized Civil War pictures, including one showing serious-faced men marching in old uniforms with guns that had bayonets fixed, a full moon hanging in the sky in the background.

Many of the photographs had titles underneath their frames: *Washday, Boxing match, Baseball* – but one had a question: *Native American Shawnee?*

She stopped and stared.

The photo had been taken in a trench during the war, and among the mud and blood and bodies, one of the men was facing the camera. Even though the image was colorized, the figure's eyes stared back, direct, confident, and as black as pools of oil in a face that was unlike the others – it was clean of mud. And the man wore clothing that didn't match those of the others in the trench.

She leaned closer. The broad shoulders and long glossy hair were so familiar. And strangest of all, on one finger the man wore a silver ring that was in the shape of a snarling wolf's head.

"Arn," she breathed, and felt the world spin from under her feet.

* * *

"Yes, I saw the picture, and yes, it could be him," Edward said as he patted her hand.

"It was him; I'd know that face anywhere," Becky asserted.

"How? I mean, it couldn't be, right? You saw the date. It was 1865. That's over 150 years ago. Besides, that guy looked different from the Arn we knew. And anyway, those photographs were retouched, remember?"

"Yes, he looked different. He looked older, about twenty-five. The age Arn would be if he was here now," she explained.

Edward seem to think about that, but then his mouth turned down and he shook his head. "Nah, impossible."

"Impossible?" She snorted. "Impossible is a world that has wolves that walk like people and follow a Viking code. A world that has things living below the ground that look like a cross between a skinned pig and an ape, beings that might once have been people. A world that has ten-foot-tall tigers that talk, and cruel Panterrans that evolved from cats. Now *that's* all impossible."

One of the exhibition attendants brought her a cup of water and felt her forehead. Becky smiled and took it.

"Feeling better?" the woman asked.

"Yes, much, thank you." She kept smiling until the woman disappeared again. She spun back to Edward in a flash. "I'd know him anywhere – he's come back."

"No, even if he did come back, he came back 160 years too soon." He shrugged and rubbed her shoulder. "Rebecca, I miss him too; he was my best friend, you know."

"I know, but he loves me. Or used to. Maybe he's trying to make it back to me and something went wrong?" Becky insisted.

Edward grimaced, dropped his hand from her shoulder and looked away. "There's something you're forgetting." He sighed and turned back. "Don't you remember? He didn't look like that anymore. Because he wasn't human anymore. He'd changed." He looked into her eyes. "You do remember that, don't you?"

Becky let her mind streak back to those last few minutes they were all together in the dark labyrinths that might have been the buried ruins of the Fermilab particle accelerator facility in some far-distant future.

They were being chased by the skinless-looking deformed monstrosities as they tried to get through the portal before it closed. And then they were saved by the huge and hulking wolf-like creature, shreds of his clothing still hanging from a massive, black-furred frame.

She remembered; the giant beast had spoken to her. It was Arn. She slumped back into the armchair.

"Yes, I remember."

She had blanked it out, how Arn had become a Wolfen, how the beast inside him had broken free – or perhaps had been there all along, and something about that world had allowed it out.

"You're right, it couldn't be him." She stared at the wall, her hands gripping the armrests for a moment before her brows came together and she suddenly sprang forward, pointing.

"Except for that damn silver ring." She turned to her friend. "We need to speak to Professor Harper."

CHAPTER 05

Physics Laboratory, University of Illinois, Illinois

Professor Albert Harper walked from the classroom, having just delivered a lecture on particle physics and its cosmological interactions. As the former site director of the Fermilab particle accelerator facility, he knew about cosmological impacts on accelerated particle matter. In fact, he knew too much.

He'd been in the teaching role ten years now, and though he missed the research and pushing the boundaries of science that his previous job had involved, this was much less stressful, and he found the day-to-day routine calming and comforting. He was just careful to avoid talking about anything that had gone on during those fateful months a decade ago. After all, the last thing he wanted was the FBI or military paying him another visit.

He liked to think that along with the facility, his previous life was now buried under several million tons of steel and concrete, due to the risk that an entity a little like a black hole might reform beneath the facility. It was unlikely, but no one was taking any chances.

Harper smiled as he headed down the university corridor, nodding to various students as he went. He was a smallish, slightly overweight man with ordinary looks, the sort of person people would pass in the street without even noticing. Little did they know he was one of the world's most brilliant physicists and had once nearly destroyed the planet with his experiments.

He pushed his office door open with his hip, holding tight to the student papers he was to mark, a half-finished cup of coffee balanced on top of them. Once inside he paused, looking around the small room for a few inches of space to set them down. Tables, chairs, benches were all overflowing – his desk chair was the only clear spot – so he lowered the papers to the floor, letting the pile rest, and retrieved the cup.

Then he sat down and exhaled, luxuriating in taking the load off his feet. After a moment he swiveled the seat, drew it in closer to his desk, and switched on his laptop. The screen swirled to life, showing his favorite screen saver: an image of a mysterious black hole spinning in space. He watched it for a few moments as he sipped.

His mail finished downloading and he was surprised to see one name he hadn't thought of in years: Ms. Rebecca Matthews.

He opened the email, read, and then chuckled softly; it was just like her. She was already on her way – *if that was okay,* she finished.

"And if it wasn't?" he asked his empty office. "Then you'd probably come anyway."

He responded to the message, knowing she would undoubtedly pick it up from her phone. Immediately there was a response: *Hi Albert, we're already downstairs.*

He rocked back in his chair and laughed. "Never change, Ms. Matthews."

Come on up, he responded. *Second floor, room 211, at the end of the corridor.*

He sat back and his mind sought out worlds beyond our own. But not via space, but beyond time – a million years of time – and doorways that allowed people to enter and return. He saw kingdoms populated by things that weren't human.

Albert Harper also conjured memories of Arnold Singer, undoubtedly the subject of Rebecca's visit, and how he was trapped in that future world now.

No, not trapped, he remembered. He had chosen to stay, because he had become . . . one of the beasts. He sighed. It was hard to believe it was real.

A knock at the door heralded two shadows behind the frosted glass window. Harper crossed to the door and pulled it inward.

Though ten years older now, Rebecca looked exactly as he remembered her – long black hair, luminous eyes and a flawless youthful complexion. She immediately made him feel old, and short.

Stepping from behind her, and seeming always in her shadow, was her friend Edward Lin. The Asian-American grinned and nodded, and the pair came straight into the room and stood awkwardly in the small, untidy space.

"So, this is where you work, now?" Rebecca asked, looking around.

Harper held his arms wide. "It's not exactly as big as the office at Fermilab, but this is my new kingdom." He knocked papers and books off some spare chairs and pulled them up closer to his own, and then sat back down at his desk, facing them.

Rebecca looked around and smiled sadly. "I'm so sorry."

He waved it away. "Don't be sorry. The work here is enjoyable, if not always interesting. I'm just glad I was able to get a job." He half-smiled. "A director of a multi-billion-dollar facility that gets destroyed on his watch, without any explanation, usually ends up shunned by the investor community. After all, it's not every day you nearly destroy a planet – and its future, right?" He grinned.

She didn't meet his eyes.

"It could have been a lot worse," Edward said. "After all, we're still here."

"I guess," she said.

"No guess about it, it's true." Harper lifted his chin. "So, Rebecca, Edward, long time no see. What can I do for you?"

Edward thumbed toward Becky. "It was her idea. She saw something."

Becky's mouth turned down. "*We* saw something . . . something weird."

Harper chuckled softly. "Given what we've all seen, nothing seems weird to me anymore." He folded his hands in his lap. "So tell me, what exactly *did* you see?"

"Arn." She sat straighter. "I saw Arn."

Harper stared. It was like his brain spun its wheels for a moment, working furiously but not actually moving forward. After a moment, he cleared his throat. "What did you say?"

"Arn, I saw Arnold Singer." She held his eyes.

Harper looked to Edward, who just bobbed his head from side to side.

Harper's brows knitted. "But that would mean their world still existed. And it can't now, because we closed the portal." He swallowed dryly. "Tell me more. Where did you see him?" Harper sat forward in his chair, making it squeal in protest.

"I can show you." She pointed at his computer. "May I?"

"Sure, sure." He moved aside.

Becky wheeled her chair closer and started to type as she filled Harper in on the exhibition, the retouched photographs. "Now that their exhibition is over, the Aurora Historical Society has uploaded the images to their webpage."

She signed onto the site and quickly scrolled through the pictures until she found the one she was looking for. She clicked on it to enlarge it, and then sat back, her eyes on Harper again.

"Well?" She waited.

Harper wheeled closer and pushed his glasses up his short nose. "'Native American Shawnee'," he read aloud, examining the image of the tall young man with the almost-black eyes that stared straight out of the screen. The man was bigger, stronger-looking than he remembered, but the face was still recognizable.

He nodded. "Looks very much like him. But there's certainly been historical doppelganger images before." He turned to her. "Have you ever seen the picture called *Nicolas Cage is Immortal*, it's qui—"

"*Look!*" Rebecca tapped the screen. "At his hand . . ."

Harper was taken aback at the impatience in her voice and turned back to the screen. He sought out the young man's hand – on one of his fingers there was a ring, silver by the look of it, and in the shape of a snarling wolf head.

"The House of Valkeryn," Edward said softly.

"It can't be." Harper sat back.

He took off his glasses to clean them with the end of his tie. Then he replaced them to look again, frowned, and then copied the image and imported it to his picture graphics tool. He opened it there and cleaned it up, making the image as sharp as possible. He enlarged the hand, again and again, and there it was – the silver snarling face of the wolf.

If the colorizers had known, they would have made the wolf's eyes a fiery red, as Harper knew the originals had been.

"How?" He pinched his chin and slowly sat back as he let his mind work.

"But the date," Edward said. "That is freaking me out. It's supposed to be a picture from around 160 years ago. Nothing is making sense."

"The date is irrelevant," Harper said. "We know that the time distortion threw you forward nearly a million years. The only reason you were able to come back to the same time was that the portal remained open and locked on this period. If it had closed even for a tiny portion of a single second, and then reopened, it might have been pointing at some time decades or centuries ago, or yet to come."

"So, he's reopened the portal somehow?" Rebecca's eyes were shining with excitement. "He's trying to find his way back to us. In our time."

"No, no, he couldn't have. The equipment and facilities, or rather what remained of them, were buried under a million tons of concrete, steel, and debris. No one is getting to them, and certainly not climbing out of them."

"Maybe he's made another portal. Something he found or developed," Edward said. "So he didn't use your portal."

Harper rubbed his face and eyes, hard. "Or maybe there's another one somewhere."

CHAPTER 06

Uri Gorbunov and his entire team of physicists and technicians were on their feet, staring at the camera feed that delivered images back from the collision chamber.

The last acceleration and then particle collision had shaken the entire facility. The screens had whited out and the lights flickered for a moment. But when the power was restored, they saw that something had been left behind.

Hanging in the air at the exact position of the high-speed particle collision there was a glowing hole, a rip in the atmosphere. And there was something inside it.

"What the hell is that? What are we seeing here?" Oleg Borashev, Gorbunov's second-in-charge, breathed.

Gorbunov licked dry lips. "I think . . . I think we have opened a doorway, a portal, to somewhere else."

"But to where, to when?" Borashev asked.

Gorbunov folded his arms and paced, looking up at the screen from time to time. Within the strange rip he could see a thick forest, a night sky, and a moon. But the moon was huge, and strangely, it seemed to be in pieces. And when he looked closer, he saw that even the plants and trees were like nothing he recognized.

There were no landmarks for him to use. Unless . . .

He stopped his pacing and clicked his fingers. "Star mapping," he said. "Use the computer to analyze the astral body positions to tell us when and where we are."

"Yes sir, on it," the senior technician seated beside him, Illinov, replied, and he began to furiously type instructions into his computer.

It took him longer than expected, but after five minutes, the computer system began to spit out information. Illinov sat back; he frowned.

"Well?" Gorbunov asked.

"It's Earth, sir. But the time is off." He entered a few more commands into the system.

Oleg Borashev growled. "We can see that. It's night-time there, and it's daylight outside here."

"No sir, it's not off by a day. I mean it's way off." He turned in his seat. "If this is correct, it's out by just over one million years." He looked back at the screen. "We're seeing the future. The distant future."

Gorbunov stared for a moment before turning and walking closer to the screen. "One million years in the future. And it looks like a paradise."

He suddenly burst into action. "The president needs to know."

***

President Petrov's eyes narrowed as he stared up at Gorbunov, making the senior science officer perspire under the intense scrutiny.

"The future, you say?" Petrov asked.

"Yes, sir. One million years in the future." Gorbunov remained at attention.

Petrov looked down at the photographs Gorbunov had printed out, and quickly went through them again. He dropped the pile and sat thinking for a moment. "This portal you have opened; can it be passed through?"

"We believe so sir, yes," Gorbunov replied.

Petrov stood and walked to the large window that looked out over the wet streets of Moscow.

"Our city is crowded. Our world is crowded." He turned. "And I see a world that is a lush forest just waiting for us."

He walked back to Gorbunov with a small smile on his face. "Take a team through – just for a short period of time – and tell me what you find. If this world is an empty paradise, then we Russians should own it, yes?"

Gorbunov began to smile. "It will be my pleasure, sir. I'll put the team together myself. We'll be ready to leave in forty-eight hours."

"No, you leave in twenty-four hours. Report back to me immediately." He waved a hand. "Dismissed."

Gorbunov nodded and turned for the door.

"*Wait.*"

Gorbunov stopped and turned back.

"I am taking a personal interest in this project, Comrade Gorbunov." Petrov's pale eyes were like watery lasers. "Do not let me down."

* * *

Gorbunov gripped Borashev's upper arms with both hands. "I want you to personally take charge of this mission, Oleg."

Oleg Borashev was a young man, ambitious, so Gorbunov knew he would be very interested to hear that the president was taking a special interest in the mission. He would do anything, Gorbunov knew, to be noticed by the upper levels of power.

"My pleasure, sir." Borashev grinned.

Gorbunov dropped his hands. "Our initial probe indicated high-quality air, better than here. And there are no biological contaminants. You'll only be gone for a single day – from dawn to dusk. You and your small team will collect images, samples of the flora and fauna, and record everything you see, hear, and smell."

Borashev nodded. "I'm ready now."

Gorbunov smiled. "I knew you would be. And to ensure my best scientists come back to us, I will be sending two armed guards with you." He shrugged. "Better safe than sorry, yes?"

That evening the team had assembled – there were three scientists, including Borashev as team leader. With him were Alexi Chekov and Hannah Volkova, environmental and evolutionary biologists, with Hannah being the oldest member of their group. Plus there were two regular soldiers as their guards – Dmitri and Igor, both armed with standard AK-47 rifles, sidearms, and NR-40 combat knives. They were both young; Igor still had a blush of acne on both cheeks. Though their job was to protect the scientific team, they had been given clear instructions to stay out of the way and follow Borashev's commands.

The group would take water and a couple of energy bars, but the bulk of their carrying weight would be sampling equipment. They wouldn't need anything else, because they expected to be back by dinner. Also, all team members would have cameras embedded in their suits, filming everything.

Gorbunov led them down to the accelerator facility where the portal had opened. He turned. "You'll be arriving just at sunup, and you will return at sundown." He turned. "No exceptions. Understood?"

"Understood," Borashev replied.

Gorbunov unlocked the newly added huge vault-like door, and as soon as he opened it, he felt a sucking breeze. It was strange, as it hadn't been there before. The facility was a closed environment, so where was it going or coming from?

Maybe it was just a thermal current creating the air movement due to a heat differential, he mused, and vowed to check on it later.

Gorbunov led the team down to the portal, and as it came into view all eyes were fixed on the three-foot-wide hole that seemed to hang in the air. It was like an optical illusion; beyond the hole they could see the seemingly impossible living image of a forest at night.

Gorbunov stared at it for a moment. *Is the hole bigger than before?* he wondered. Maybe just some fluctuation, he answered himself.

A set of steps had been constructed with a platform at the top, allowing people to walk up to the hole and simply step through.

Gorbunov put his hand on the stair railing and looked from the portal to the team. "I envy you. You will be exploring a new world, one that holds so much promise and potential for the Russian country and its people as to be incalculable."

The five people ascended the steps and Gorbunov watched from the floor.

"Good luck," he said. "See you in twelve hours. For supper."

Borashev looked from his superior to the hole. He stared for a moment, calming himself.

"*Bila ne Bila*." He whispered the famous ancient Russian saying – *whatever happens happens.*

Then he stepped through.

***

Borashev's vision blurred, and he had the sensation of speed and weightlessness. There were swirling colors, roaring sounds, and crackling and booms like an approaching storm. And then his feet touched down on firm earth.

The first thing he noticed was the warm, clear air against his skin, and the smell of a pristine forest. He guessed this was mainly because there were no machines, just air as nature had intended.

He inhaled deeply. "Magnificent. Like springtime in Kalevalsky Forest." He turned to Hannah Volkova. "Have you ever smelled air like this?"

"Never." She shook her head and smiled. "It's beautiful. A paradise."

Borashev looked around and saw that hanging in the predawn air behind them was a ragged-edged circle with the lit laboratory visible through it. Inside Gorbunov waved, and Borashev returned the gesture.

He snorted softly. "It looks like we are just a few dozen feet apart, but we are now separated by a million years. It blows my mind."

Alexi Chekov pointed. "Sun's coming up, there, so that's east."

Borashev turned to the soldiers. "Split up and perform a quick perimeter scan, then come back." He pointed through the trees. "Then we'll head east, as there seems to be a clearing of the forest further in."

"Sir." The pair headed off in different directions.

Hannah watched them go and then inhaled the sweet air and turned slowly. "If this is how the world turned out, then I am happy."

"I wonder if there are people, and what they look like if there are," Chekov said.

"Maybe human evolution has started over again." Borashev checked radiation levels on a small device and spoke without looking up. "After all, one million years before our time, there were no Homo sapiens. There were Homo erectus, who looked a little like us." He looked up. "They were more robust, with smaller brains, no chins, and projecting brow ridges."

"You mean like Chekov?" Hannah grinned.

"If they're here, they might make me their king." Chekov laughed.

The team readied themselves, and a few minutes later the soldiers reappeared.

"All clear," they announced.

Borashev pointed to the elder one, Dmitri. "Lead on. Ten paces in front."

The soldier nodded and headed out, with the team walking in single file along the pathway he made through the thick grass and bracken.

After five minutes, Hannah strode up to join Borashev. "Next time we should bring an aerial drone. Scout a wider range of territory."

"Good idea." Borashev nodded.

After another fifteen minutes they came to a river, and Chekov took some water samples. He studied the stream for a while, and then turned, grinning. "Hey, there are fish."

The group came and stood behind him, staring into the water.

"I see them." Hannah smiled, nodding, but then she frowned. "They have two eyes on one side of their heads. Wait, no, two eyes on *each* side of their heads." She turned to Borashev. "We must catch a small one and take it back."

Chekov turned. "Using what, our charm?"

Borashev chuckled, and then turned to Dmitri. "Cut off a long branch, sharpen one end, and use it as a spear to catch us a smaller fish. Quickly now."

Hannah folded her arms. "And that, Mr. Chekov, is why he's the leader, and you're not."

"If asked, I would have crafted a net." Chekov half-bowed. "But I am just a humble servant of Mother Russia."

"*Pfft*, leave it to the experts." She grinned.

After a few minutes the young soldier had his spear and was knee-deep in the water with the six-foot-long stick held ready to stab. He made many attempts but was unsuccessful – and his splashing about was making most of the fish dart off into the deeper water.

He turned to Borashev and shrugged.

The team leader frowned and pointed. "Follow them."

***

From the deeper water something rose gently to just break the surface. It floated there for a few moments, studying the strange new animals on the bank and the noisy one that had entered the stream.

After another few seconds it gently sank back down into the depths. And then glided closer along the bottom.

* * *

The soldier made another attempt and failed once again.

Chekov turned to Hannah. "You were saying?"

"The plan is sound. The execution is lacking." Borashev faced Chekov with a grim smile. "So get in and help him. Go to the deeper water and scare the fish toward the spear."

Chekov stared for a moment.

Hannah chortled. "It's what a good humble servant of Mother Russia would do."

Chekov grumbled, but after a few seconds, he shucked off all his equipment and waded into the river.

He walked toward the middle of the stream which, due to the clarity of the water, was deceptively deeper than he expected, and he quickly went in up to his chest.

The soldier now stood stock-still, waiting for the prey to be scared toward him.

Chekov was still grumbling but at least the water was warm. He decided he'd do a loop, move a little further out toward one side, and then come around and move back along the other, hopefully moving a few fish toward Dmitri at the other bank.

As he continued, he went over the edge of a depression and sank down into about seven feet of water. He went under, the surface closing over his head. As he came back up he coughed. But he knew his foot had kicked at something down there. And it had moved.

"*Shit*," he spluttered as he came back up. "There is something down there."

'Yes, fish. Hurry up," Borashev shot back.

Chekov charged back toward the bank, feeling a tingling chill run up his spine. He came fast, forgetting the fish. All he wanted was to be up on the dry bank.

* * *

Borashev had been growing irritated with his team's lack of fish-catching prowess but he laughed softly at his colleague's fear. He turned to the soldier, who still had his arm and spear cocked.

Dmitri shrugged. "I think they're all gone."

"See, now you've frightened them away," Borashev said to Chekov, who was in waist-deep water only a few feet from the bank now, moving rapidly.

"I don't think it was me that frightened them away," Chekov replied.

"Are you sure you didn't piss in the wat—" Borashev's words froze in his mouth.

From right behind the chubby scientist, something rose up. Borashev's eyes widened in shock. It looked like an alligator, but as it came higher in the water, he saw it had a shorter snout, and was standing on its hind legs.

It reached for Chekov with two muscular arms, which were definitely not just the squat, front-splayed legs of a crocodilian species.

The soldier in the water was shocked into immobility, but the other one on the bank, Igor, brought his gun up.

"*No shot*," he yelled. "*Get down.*"

But there was only time for Chekov to glance over his shoulder and scream like a siren as the thing grabbed him.

In one quick motion it stabbed its head forward and its short powerful jaws clamped down on the nape of Chekov's neck. There was a crunching of bone and tendon and then it dragged him backwards.

"*Fire, fire*," Borashev yelled as Hannah screamed.

Chekov gurgled and gore splattered from his lips. But as the bullets began to fly, the creature dragged the Russian scientist back below the surface of the water, and in a swirl of bloody foam, they were gone.

Dmitri's muscles unlocked and he leaped backwards out of the water, rolling up the bank before coming to his feet and pulling his weapon, too.

"What was that?" he said in a quavering voice.

"Alligator," Igor replied, still pointing his weapon at the water.

"No, that was something else," Borashev said softly.

Hannah was standing behind the pair, staring at the water with near-bulging eyes.

"Hannah, what do you think it was?" Borashev asked.

The woman just stared mutely, her mouth opening and closing.

"*Hannah?*" he yelled.

"Um, um, yes, something else." She swallowed noisily. "It had crocodilian features, but its limb morphology was all wrong." She looked up at him. "It had opposable thumbs."

Borashev nodded slowly. "Maybe it descended from crocodiles." He drew in a deep breath and let it out slowly. "It also had extremely long and powerful rear legs and that tells me it can hunt on land and probably run down its prey."

"Then we need to get away from the water," Hannah gasped.

"Yes, I think we should forget about catching fish today." Borashev turned. "Igor, take point. Dmitri, at the rear. Let's move on, double-time."

"What? We're continuing with the mission?" Hannah's mouth hung open in disbelief for a moment. "Chekov is dead. Killed. We need to go back. We need to tell—"

"*Quiet.*" Borashev scowled. "We're here to do a job. You thought it was going to be a walk in the park? Catch a few butterflies in your paradise, and then go home to a nice evening meal?" He scoffed disdainfully and turned back to the water. "Yes, we continue with our mission. And everyone keeps their eyes open. This land is very different from anything that we know."

The group continued on, taking samples of plants and small insect varieties that were very different from what they were used to. They even captured a large beetle that shimmered like a rainbow and when grabbed sung like a canary – a *songbug*, Borashev named it.

***

The day wore on. After a break during which they finished their protein bars, Borashev could see that the group was tiring. He also knew that it would take them some time to get back to the portal site.

So he turned his team around to begin retracing their steps, but he chose a slightly different route so as to cover different territory, and also avoid the river. He wanted no more Chekov mishaps.

Thinking about the man didn't make him feel sad, just regretful that he had misjudged the potential dangers here. After all, this place might look like a paradise, but they didn't really know it at all.

As they walked, he heard something and stopped the team.

"What is that?" he asked softly.

Igor tilted his head, listening for a moment before looking up. "A horse? Or a large hooved animal of some kind." He pointed. "That way."

The group moved through the thick forest, and Borashev began to smell something musky and strange. But after a moment Igor waved at them to get down.

Squatting behind some low-hanging tree branches and bushes they saw a path, and heading along it was a horse. More astounding was that it had a rider.

"Humans *did* survive," murmured Hannah dreamily.

The rider stopped and lifted his head as though sniffing the air. Then he turned sideways.

The group gasped. This creature wasn't human at all, but some sort of large dog or wolf. And it was large indeed. It was hard to judge its height exactly, because the rider was seated, but it looked to be much taller than a human being. And not slim, either, but formidably muscled.

The creature turned a little more, and they could see it wore some sort of garb that could have been medieval or perhaps even Viking. There was a long sword at its belt, and on the horse's flank was tied a large battle-axe.

Once again the being lifted its head to sniff the air.

"*He can smell us,*" Igor whispered.

The group hunkered down even more.

The wolf man-thing turned its horse around and slowly started to come toward them.

Igor began to lift his rifle, but Borashev put his hand on the barrel to lower it and then gestured for them all to move back into the forest.

"No," he whispered. "We leave."

In a crouch, they headed back. And then, after a few moments, they began to move more quickly. Borashev knew they'd have to do a big looping curve on their way to the portal opening to avoid the river monster, which they now needed to reach as soon as possible. They broke into a jog, and then burst into a clearing.

And found it occupied.

Seated around a small fire were three enormous beings. They were striped like tigers and wore massive sheets of what looked like armor over their bodies. They all turned to the people entering their space.

"Oh shit," Borashev said.

The three creatures got to their feet. Each must have been around nine feet tall, and they towered over the humans. Their golden eyes were unblinking, reminding Borashev of the way predatorial beasts stared. And then they began to approach.

That was when Borashev noticed they all carried huge weapons.

"Everyone. Just. Back. U—"

Whether it was from instinct or fear, Dmitri's finger tightened on his trigger. He fired. And that was when things went bad.

The lead creature was struck by a number of bullets that clanked uselessly against its thick armor. But it recognized the move as an attack and threw its head back to let out a deafening roar. Then it charged.

Borashev felt that time had slowed down as the ground trembled under his feet from the weight of the beast as it bore down on them.

In its hand it held a club as long as the soldier was tall, and in a split second it was on Dmitri.

A frozen Dmitri had a look of horror on his face, and one arm raised as if to ward off the blow. But the hugely muscled beast brought the club down with such force, it crushed the man right down to the ground in an explosion of blood, bone, and gore.

Igor screamed curses as he began to fire his weapon, but another of the creatures used a back-handed swing to strike him, and his broken body was flung up and into the trees high above them.

"*Run*," Borashev yelled.

He didn't wait to see if Hannah complied or even heard. He didn't even think about whether she could get away. He was more frightened than he had ever been in his life, and he simply ran, and ran, and ran.

After ten minutes, when he was sure he could hear nothing in pursuit, he stopped and bent over to suck in air. Then he held his breath and listened – thankfully the forest around him was quiet. Unfortunately, there was no sign of Hannah.

"*Dolboyob*," – *idiot* – he spat.

He remembered that his camera was filming everything. It would have seen him run. He would be forgiven for that, as it would also have recorded the monsters' attack. But whoever watched the film would not forgive him for leaving the Russian woman behind.

Chekov was dead; the two soldiers were dead. If he lost his entire team, he would be branded a failure. And a coward for not even trying to find her.

He had to at least try, he thought. He doubled back, following the path he had made crashing through the forest. It took him nearly an hour as he crept along rather than running. It was as he approached the clearing that he got down on his belly and inched forward. He parted the leaves.

Borashev smelled something, something that made his stomach rumble.

The three giant striped beings were there, huddled around their fire. Borashev moved sideways, trying to see what they were doing.

And then he saw.

He put a fist's knuckles into his mouth and bit down to stop himself from crying out.

It was Hannah, and she had been skewered – a thick wooden stake had gone in her mouth, and come out her rear end. Her legs were tied to the pole.

All the clothing and her hair had been burned away, and juices dripped from her cooking corpse to sizzle into the fire.

Borashev's stomach threatened to void even though the smell of the meat was delicious. He turned, crawling on hands and knees away from the grisly scene.

When he was a few hundred yards back he got to his feet and began to run all over again. This time he didn't stop, running for hours until he felt his muscles begin to cramp and his throat and mouth become cotton-dry.

In the distance, he finally saw the glowing circle and headed toward it. As he reached it, Borashev turned back, checking to see if he was being followed. Hearing nothing but the breeze in the trees, he leaped through the portal, and shut his eyes to ride out the swirling vertigo of the rushing sensation.

When he landed this time, he was back on the platform in the laboratory and lying on his side.

Gorbunov came up the steps to lay a hand on his shoulder. "Oleg, are you okay? Where are the others?"

Borashev looked up, and found that his face was streaked with tears. "They're all dead," he croaked. "*Monsters.*" He managed to raise an arm and point at the open portal. "Guards. We need guards. To stop them coming through."

Then he let his head drop, screwed his eyes shut and began to weep.

CHAPTER 07

"I have not tested it." Vidarr held out the small oval device.

"But will it work?" Arn asked.

"It might. It might not," Vidarr replied. "It might send you to exactly where you want to go. Or somewhere, or some*when* else." Vidarr raised a pair of shaggy, white eyebrows. "Or it might throw you into some sort of oblivion. Forever." He held the device up. "I found it in the deep catacombs where the Ancients hid their treasures before they left. If there were instructions, they have long rotted away."

Arn exhaled. "We have to test it. But I guess we can't even test it remotely, as someone needs to be holding it to trigger the return."

"That's right. The return is easy. It just brings you back to your original launch site. But calibrating where you need to go is more difficult – it wants long strings of numbers from the date and place."

"I think that could be latitude and longitude. And perhaps a numbered date format. Maybe even to the second," Arn replied. "I know what they are. But they'll need to be exact."

Arn looked at the ancient Wolfen. He was the oldest of their kind in the kingdom and perhaps even the oldest creature in the world. No one knew exactly how old Vidarr really was. Some said he was immortal; some said he was descended from Big Fen himself. And others whispered that he *was* Fen, still alive so that he could keep looking over his kith and kin.

"You told me you found ancient maps, right?" Arn asked.

"Yes. The Ancients were very good at creating and keeping their maps in many durable formats," Vidarr replied.

"Good, bring them." Arn smiled, feeling that luck was with him. "If I'm going to test the device, I need to know a little bit more about where I'm going."

"No, Arnodrr." Vidarr lowered the device. "The risk should be mine. I will test it first. And then . . ."

Arn placed a hand on Vidarr's shoulder. "Thank you, wise Wolfen. But you get to sit this one out. Besides, if anything goes wrong, I need you to work out how to fix it. And bring me back."

***

Arn and Vidarr then spent many days poring over ancient maps, testing the device, and making adjustments to take into account any changes that may have happened to the world's geography. They found that the power source was solar, and the device retained a charge for many days.

Soon the time of the full moon was upon them and Arn felt they were ready for his first test run. He and Vidarr believed they had deciphered enough of the mechanism to get it working on a basic send-and-receive foray.

In the glow of the moon, Arn once again reverted to his human form, and then dressed in the closest thing he could obtain to normal clothing of his time. He set the device's coordinates to Batavia, Illinois, and the time and date at 12 noon, 14 July, 2012.

He looked up, nodded to the old Wolfen, drew in a breath, and then pressed the button.

He was immediately flung around like he'd fallen into a whirlpool of light and color. When he landed, he was assailed with the sound of gunfire and bombs going off.

He quickly looked around the muddy, bomb-cratered field. This was no warm Illinois July; it was freezing and a greasy mist of methane from rotting bodies and gunpowder hung low over the landscape.

A bomb exploded just fifty feet from him, and he scampered to a hole, quickly rolling into it. Except that he wasn't alone.

Inside there were a few men wearing old-style clothing and caked in mud. They immediately swung long, dirty rifles around to target him, and he blinked into the flash of a camera bulb.

He raised his hands. "Wait, wait, I'm American," he said.

"You is a goddamn spy, is what you is." One of the men motioned to Arn's hand, which was still holding the remote. "And put that goddamn weapon down, boy."

Arn lowered it. "Alright," he said, and then pressed the button.

He immediately vanished and shortly arrived back at home, where Vidarr was waiting for him and looked relieved and a little shocked by the mud coating his frame.

"Did it work?" the old Wolfen asked.

"Yes and no." Arn got to his feet. "I went back, but it wasn't the right place or time." He looked down at the small screen on the device. "Something wasn't set right."

The next day they tried again, and this time Arn was flung back to somewhere in Colorado, around the mid-1600s, he guessed.

He arrived just at the end of the full moon and hit the ground hard, rolled, and found he had fallen almost right in front of a Navajo hunting party. And worse, during his rough landing the remote fell from his hand.

"Oh no, no, no." Arn quickly tried to scout the area but couldn't find it anywhere.

And then the arrows started to fly.

"Dammit, *stop*," he yelled.

But instead they whooped and came after him.

He ran, sprinting through the sparse forest, jinking and turning, for what felt like hours. But he never lost them, not even for a minute. And worse, they were closing in on him.

Arn knew it was only a matter of hours before he would revert back to Wolfen form. His senses would become more acute, and he would be able to smell the remote no matter where it was. He just had to survive until then.

He started to loop back around to the place where he had landed, but then something hit the back of his head and knocked all sensibility from him.

***

When he came around, he found himself bound to a tree, with several Navajo warriors surrounding him.

They picked at his clothing and tugged his hair. He knew he looked a little like them, but he also knew from his history books that other tribes were distrusted in these parts.

One of the Navajo asked him questions, but he had no way to understand or respond to them.

He shook his head. "I don't understand you."

One of the younger warriors came forward, spoke harshly to him and then pulled out a blade and dragged it across his chest. The pain was excruciating, and Arn gritted his teeth but refused to cry out as he felt the warm blood run down and soak his shirt.

"I'm not your enemy," he said, trying to stay calm.

The war party leader was an older man who came and stood before Arn. He looked into his face and asked a question again.

Arn shook his head. "Sorry. I don't understand you."

The young man stepped forward with his knife again, but the older man stopped him. Again he asked the question.

The other braves took out arrows and nocked them. Arn guessed he was about to become the victim of the Native American version of a firing squad.

The sun was going down, and the shadows were slowly lengthening. Arn looked skyward.

The older warrior asked a question again, and Arn just lowered his head and smiled.

"You won't like what's coming," he said softly.

The older man shook his head, stepped back, and turned away. The other warriors started to lift their bows.

At that moment the moon rose just above the horizon – and it wasn't full anymore. Instead it was as if a small slice had been removed from it. It was enough.

Immediately, Arn felt the pain in his joints, and the shifting and sliding of skin and muscles. The ropes binding him squealed and creaked in protest, and, cocking his head at the noise, the old warrior turned back.

In seconds, Arn went from a six-foot-tall young man, to a nearly eight-foot-tall, raven-furred Wolfen. And then the ropes could take no more and exploded from him.

Arn roared and flung out one long muscled arm to grab the young knife-wielding warrior by the throat and fling him twenty feet into the darkening forest. The other warriors vanished into the trees.

But the old man remained on his feet with eyes wide and mouth hanging open. Arn stepped up to him, and the warrior fell to his knees, looking up in fear.

"I'm not your enemy." Arn held out one huge, taloned hand.

The old man took it, and Arn lifted him to his feet.

The old warrior watched as the wound on Arn's chest stopped bleeding and healed in seconds.

Arn stepped back. "I'm not supposed to be here." He turned and lifted his head, sniffing – he could already detect the scent of the device hiding under some leaf matter not more than a hundred feet from where he had arrived.

From the shadows he could hear the young men talking animatedly, although he still couldn't understand them. But he heard the stretch of a bowstring and he spun, massive arms out, and opened his huge, fanged mouth to roar at them again.

They dropped their bows and fell to their knees. The older warrior bowed his head, and then turned to remonstrate with his young tribesmen.

Arn went and recovered the device. He turned, and heard the old man whisper a single word several times: *yee-naaldlooshii*. He found out the meaning of it much later; it meant *Skinwalker*. It was the ancient Native American demon that could walk among men, but also transform into the skin of a wolf.

Maybe he was the source of the legend, he realized.

Arn turned to nod to the old warrior, and then pressed the button on the small oval device.

He was immediately drawn into the time vortex once more.

But this time he wasn't sent home.

***

It would take Arn weeks, and several stops, to return home. He bounced around the timeline, and soon the device stopped working: it had run out of power.

He knew he needed to recharge the battery. He first came out of the vortex in 1764, in Gévaudan, France. While there, now locked in his form as the giant wolf being, he became known as the Beast of Gévaudan.

In the dark forest he had to climb the tallest tree to lodge the depleted device in the upper branches so it could face the sunshine, and then he spent several days on the run while waiting for it to recharge.

At one point nearly the entire village was chasing him down. They thought they had him as he scaled his tall tree for the device, and must have been dumbfounded when he reached the top, and then suddenly vanished.

Arn was flung around the timeline some more, before appearing in South America, where he became the source of the man-wolf *Lobizon* legend. After that he found himself in

England in an old country village. He took shelter in a small home, where he found an elderly woman in bed, who promptly got so scared she had a heart attack.

Arn fled, but on leaving he ran into a small girl in a red cloak with a hood who screamed so loudly that a local wood-cutter chased him with an axe.

Finally he managed to return home, and he appeared at Vidarr's feet, groaning on the ground.

"And . . . does it work, Arnodrr?" Vidarr asked.

Arn sat up and laughed softly. He put a hand to his dark furred brow and rubbed it. "I've been chased with an axe, stabbed, shot at with arrows and guns, and probably did more for the werewolf legend than any fiction writer ever could." He laughed softly. "But no, not yet. Setting the coordinates is more complex than we thought." He looked up at his old friend. "It needs work."

Vidarr grunted and took the device from Arn. "I will look at where and when you have been and see if I can find some correlation with the settings. Leave it with me."

"Thanks." Arn got to his feet and exhaled loudly. "What a rush."

CHAPTER 08

Uri Gorbunov and Oleg Borashev were summoned to Moscow to meet with President Petrov and stood to attention before him while he reviewed the mission footage.

The only film remaining was Borashev's, as all the other recording equipment had been destroyed when his team members were killed. The president's face was unreadable as he viewed Chekov being taken by the river creature. Then again as he watched the wolf-man on horseback, and also when they were attacked by the massive tiger-striped beings. Finally, he watched Hannah being roasted alive. Even during this, his face was like stone.

Gorbunov waited for the fallout. After all, his team had been decimated and they had brought back no samples. He was fully prepared to throw his team leader, Borashev, under the bus, if it meant saving his own hide.

The president switched off the recording and sat back, his fingers steepled as his pale eyes stared into the distance for several seconds.

Gorbunov swallowed noisily. "I can expl—"

President Petrov's eyes slid to Gorbunov. "Well done."

Gorbunov felt his heart jolt. Did he just hear that?

"Sir?" he asked.

Petrov rose to his feet. The man only stood about five-foot-seven, but his presence filled a room. His nickname was the "little wolf", and there was no doubt his bark was as bad as his bite. He was a known killer of men.

"We now know there is a world through the portal that is habitable. We know there are intelligent lifeforms there, though a little primitive. We now also have a high level of understanding of their weaponry and capabilities."

He turned to Borashev. "Your losses are regrettable, but the heavy price you paid has delivered us invaluable information."

"Thank you, sir." Borashev bowed his head and his mouth twitched up fractionally at the corners.

"Don't thank me yet." Petrov grinned like a death's head.

Here it comes, Gorbunov thought.

Petrov looked from one man to the other. "I want you to return. I want you to capture one of the intelligent species from that world so we can question them."

Borashev visibly paled and looked about to speak, but Petrov held up a hand.

"This time you will be well guarded. You will be accompanied by a squad of our best Special Forces." He turned away, drew in a deep breath and let it out with satisfaction. "You have shown me a world ripe for the taking." He turned back. "So let us take it."

Gorbunov and Borashev glanced at each other.

Petrov clapped his hands together and rubbed them. "You will be ready to leave tomorrow. Both of you."

"But—" Gorbunov began.

Petrov glared. "This is a huge honor. Do not disrespect it."

"Yes, sir, but Comrade Borashev has just returned and needs time to recover," Gorbunov pleaded.

Gorbunov's mind spun. In truth, the lead scientist couldn't give a shit about his second-in-command, but he needed time to try and find a way to wriggle out of the mission himself.

Petrov shook his head. "He has an advantage. He's been there and knows what to expect." He folded his arms across his barrel chest. "Bring me back someone or something that can talk. Our best linguists will be able to understand them. I want to know everything about that world." He turned to look out over the snow falling in the Red Square. "Before we conquer it."

***

Beneath the Russian particle accelerator facility, the air around the edges of the portal seemed to warp and ripple. Then the reinforced walls and ceiling beyond it did the same.

The distortion moved outward from the portal like an infection spreading, or like a wave in a pond after a small stone had been thrown into it.

Around the world seismologists recorded the event as a minor earthquake centered near Moscow – unusual, but not large enough to worry anyone.

However, in the facility deep beneath the earth, the hole hanging in the air that was actually a rip in time and space also shuddered, and then widened, increasing its diameter by about an inch.

And it continued to grow.

CHAPTER 09

Arn watched Eilif prepare. It was her hunting day, and she and a few warriors were heading into the deep forest to catch game.

He had no fears for her as the warriors accompanying her were brave, fierce, and some of the kingdom's best. Also, Eilif herself was one of the deadliest Wolfen with a bow in the entire lands.

There were still a few Lygon about, the monstrous giant beasts of fang and claw who made war on the Wolfen. But after a generation's bloodshed, their violent nation's back had been broken, and they were just small bands of marauders now, who tended to stay away lest they be hunted down and killed.

While Eilif was out, Arn was going to spend more time with Vidarr who had been honing the time travel device. He hoped the ancient Wolfen had finally worked out the code for getting an exact time and destination for travel, as he didn't want to drop in on another war party, or villagers with pitchforks and burning torches – because next time he might not be so lucky.

Eilif turned and held out her arms.

"How do I look?" She smiled as she pirouetted slowly.

Arn rubbed his chin as he examined her. She wore a tunic of beaten leather, with a dress made of braided straps that ended in metal rivets. It wasn't a battle outfit so there would be no need for a helmet, and there was leather breast plating in place of armor, and also leather gauntlets and boots.

The material under it was a deep green and the entire kit fitted tight. Eilif's magnificent, athletic figure was clearly defined. But it wasn't just for looks – the coloring was for camouflage, and the thick leather would give her protection from most creatures' bites.

"Beautiful and deadly." He folded his arms. "Beware, all animals of Valkeryn, the death-dealing huntress is coming for you."

She laughed and rushed to him. "You come too." She leaned on his chest and gazed up at him. "It's always more fun when I outshoot you in front of the other warriors."

"More fun for you." He laughed. "Much as I like my woman showing off her hunting prowess, I have other work to do." He leaned forward to kiss her. "Bring me back something tasty."

She tilted her head as though thinking. Then raised a finger. "A *qworell*. No, a clutch of them."

"Yes, please," he replied.

The *qworell* were like a large pheasant, but the size of a turkey and with six legs. It meant everyone got a drumstick.

Eilif then went to check her bows. She had several, and finally chose two – her long bow with the enormous arrows for taking down larger prey over long distances, and a smaller bow that could be shot rapidly. She was deadly accurate with both, and Arn remembered one of his grandfather's expressions – she could hit a sparrow's eye from a hundred paces.

Eilif rushed out, and in a few minutes he watched from the castle window as the princess and her three warriors appeared below. He leaned out the window.

"Eilif."

She looked up, smiling at the sound of his voice.

"I only let you outshoot me."

In a flash she pulled an arrow from her quiver, nocked it, and let it fly. It pierced the wooden lintel right above his head.

He knew she could have hit him if she wanted. She was just making her point.

He nodded and clapped. Eilif bowed, then went to her horse, leaped up on it, and the group headed off to the deep forest.

When she was out of sight, Arn made his way down to the forecourt and crossed to old Vidarr's big stone house above the catacombs. He banged on the large double oak doors and pushed them inward, moving through the books and papers until he found the old Wolfen hunched over a table with a band around his head that held a thick spyglass over one of his eyes.

He was examining the open casing of the time device, but looked over his shoulder when he heard his visitor approach.

"Ah, Arnodrr, good timing." He snapped the casing closed. "Seems the numbering format for the destination was all wrong. I've fixed it now . . . well, I think I have." He smiled and stood. "Should be ready for another test."

Arn grinned. "I knew you could do it."

"Something else that I found out; you can create a halo effect surrounding multiple figures when you transport." He shrugged. "If you wanted to go with more travelers, that is."

Arn nodded. "So, when can I test it again?" He lifted the device, studying it.

"I think this evening. Or maybe tomorrow." Vidarr scratched his gray chin. "Some of the ancients' technology is very complex. Almost like magic." He chuckled. "I remember when the humans . . ." He trailed off.

Arn slowly turned to him. "You remember . . . you remember them, remember *us*, don't you?" he asked.

He'd heard the rumors: that old Vidarr wasn't just old but had lived since the dawn of the Valkeryn kingdom. That he was perhaps even immortal, and not just descended from Big Fen, he *was* Big Fen, the original Guardian.

"That would be impossible, wouldn't it, Arnodrr?" the old Wolfen said mildly, waving a hand dismissively, but when he looked up at Arn, he had a twinkle in his eye.

"I remember meeting a Wolfen when I was a boy. The first one in a laboratory." Arn looked him dead in the eye. "Was that you?"

"It is my curse to remember everything." Vidarr sat down slowly. "I remember the cages. I remember the experiments, some painful, and some giving the gifts of intelligence and wisdom." He smiled. "I remember a human boy coming to see me." He began to talk faster, his eyes staring off in the distance, perhaps struggling to conjure memories made too long ago to even contemplate.

"I remember all the others – the altered breeds. I remember the fire. I remember the freedom. I remember the ground-shaking bombs, and I remember the end of one world and the birth of another."

He looked up at Arn. "And you're right, Arnodrr, when you say that something is coming. I too can feel the world moving beneath my feet. Just like that last time, nearly one million years ago."

"I feel it constantly now," Arn replied.

"Maybe you going back is a necessary thing," Vidarr said softly.

"That's why you're helping me do this." Arn returned the device to him.

"What is written, *must* be written." Vidarr took it and then lowered the spyglass back over his eye. "Come back tomorrow. It will be ready."

***

Arn headed out into the castle grounds. It was coming up to the middle of the day, and Eilif would be heading back soon.

He hoped she'd caught something as her mood would be dark if she hadn't. Next time he'd go with her, as she said he always brought her luck.

He smiled, feeling good.

But his expression and mood suddenly plummeted when he felt an unsettling wave of foreboding wash over him. It tingled from his claw tips to his scalp, and left a leaden feeling in his gut.

He stopped dead, looking around – Wolfen had a sixth sense about danger – and he immediately knew something wasn't right.

And then he heard it – an alien sound in the Valkeryn lands – gunfire.

* * *

Arn stood to his full height, looking into the distance.

There was more gunfire, and it came from the dark forest, in the direction Eilif had taken.

He knew no creatures on the planet had guns. Only humans had guns. Or used to. And that meant . . . they were back.

"No, no-*ooo* . . ."

He began to run toward a group of Wolfen warriors who had just dismounted their horses. He leaped up on the back of a steed, leaving the warriors shocked and momentarily confused.

"*Warriors, with me,*" he yelled.

Arn urged the beast into the forest, spurring it on to a blinding speed. The other Wolfen warriors had by now remounted and galloped to join him.

Arn raced along the trails he knew Eilif would have taken. There was a tract of woodland that wasn't well known, but it was one of her favorite, secret hunting places, and Arn knew she would have headed there.

In about twenty minutes he saw the first dead Wolfen warrior lying beside his lifeless horse. He slowed, looking down, and saw the bullet holes riddling the body – lots of them. Who, or whatever, had shot him, had wanted to make sure he was dead; after all, Wolfen did not go down easy.

The three Wolfen riders caught up and he called them onward. It didn't take long to find the other two Wolfen who'd been with Eilif, also dead. At least these two had had a chance to dismount and fight, as their horses were nearby and unharmed.

Arn trotted his horse around them, looking down at the tracks and skirmish marks in the soil. "They fought here. But not at close quarters with tooth and claw." He looked up and sniffed the air.

He smelled it: cordite, burning gunpowder and also gun oil. And there was something else – deodorants and the smell of clothing. He knew the scents; it was the smell of mankind.

Then Eilif's horse wandered out of the forest. He ran to it, quickly checking it for blood – there was none. But there was also no sign of Eilif.

Thankfully she didn't lie among the bodies. Which meant she had pursued the attackers – or she'd been taken.

From further inside the deep forest came the sound of more gunshots. Without a second's thought, Arn turned his horse around and charged onward.

He rode the horse hard, too hard, and in another dozen minutes it began to foam at the mouth, and falter.

"Thank you, strong steed." He patted its neck and leaped from its back.

He began to run, firstly on two feet, and then dropping to all fours. It was better that way as the tangle of forest was closing in, and even if his horse hadn't been exhausted it would have found the trails too narrow.

He inhaled – the scent was growing stronger.

"*Eilif,*" he called.

Arn burst from a thicket to see his beloved princess being held between two human soldiers. She was slumped forward and there was a smudge of blood on her temple.

There were about a dozen men. All were dressed in jungle camouflage uniforms, and carried automatic weapons.

"*Eilif!*" he called again.

Her head came up, but only slightly.

They had her by each arm – just like in his dream – which had turned out to be no dream, but a prophecy.

The men turned, and almost as one, started to fire, and a hail of bullets came at him.

Arn leaped sideways into the brush and ran hard, looping around them. The men had not acted out of fear but were calm and practiced in their motions – professionals, then. He knew of them from the last time they had ventured into Valkeryn.

Humans were vastly weaker than Wolfen. But their weapons were superior.

Arn came around from the side, running fast, but using the pads of his feet for silence. A few seconds later he burst from the forest and landed among them.

Arn was now nearly eight feet tall, and weighed close to 500 pounds, most of which was solid, black-furred muscle. He had claws two inches long, and teeth that included canines like two massive tusks.

Guns or no guns, once he was in close, the men were no match for his speed and ferocity. He ripped and tore his way to Eilif, and in seconds four of the men were down for good.

The others fired their weapons, but in such close quarters and in among their own team, they couldn't get clear shots. But one of the soldiers, their leader, organized them, creating a wall between Arn and Eilif, and Arn then saw their destination – a glowing hole that hung in the sky.

Before he had time even to react, they pulled Eilif through, and Arn went berserk with fury.

But the men found their target then, and bullets began to smack into Arn's unarmored body, and he felt every one of them.

Just then his brother Wolfen arrived, and as Arn felt his strength ebbing away, he knew that to follow the humans through the portal now would mean his death. And then there would be no one to save his princess.

But he had one more task. As his brother Wolfen took down more of the soldiers, other men vanished through the portal window. Arn knew he needed to act quickly, so he rose up, sprinted hard, and grabbed one of the soldiers – not to kill, but to capture.

Rather than rip him in two, Arn smashed his huge fist into the man's face, and then quickly dragged him into the forest. Once there he looked back and saw that behind the glowing hole, the soldiers had formed up, guns aimed, waiting for them.

He called his Wolfen back. "We fight another day." He lifted his slumped captive. "This creature will tell us everything we need to know."

With that, Arn felt his vision swim, and then he fell to the ground.

***

Arn rose to the surface of his consciousness. The first thing he heard was the *plink* of steel on steel, and opened his eyes to see the Wolfen surgeons using a fire-cleansed dagger blade to dig the multiple bullets from his body.

He looked around. Standing watching the surgeons work was Vidarr, and also Grimvaldr, the boy king, who was pacing. His face was screwed up with concern, but seeing Arn open his eyes, he rushed over.

"Where is my sister, Arnodrr? Who took her?" He gripped Arn's arm, tight.

"Easy, Your Majesty. He's lost a lot of blood." Vidarr took the tray from the surgeon and looked into it. "Nine of these small bits of steel. Luckily they didn't penetrate too deeply. The hide of the Wolfen is much tougher than that of the man-kind." He put it down. "Tell us what happened, Arnodrr."

Arn sat up slowly, feeling the sting of the wounds over his torso. The surgeon was plastering them with a medicinal herb paste and cloth bandages, and the rest was up to his body's healing power.

Arn reached for a large tankard of water and downed it. He put it down and turned.

"Sire," he said. "Another portal has opened. Humans have come through. I do not know these ones. But we have a captive."

"And my sister, Princess Eilif?" the young Wolfen king asked.

"Taken," Arn replied.

"Then we must retrieve her," he said, and his scowl brought his brows down over his eyes. "I'll take the entire army if I have to."

"No," Arn said softly. "Next time they will have weapons that will kill us easily, and there are millions of them. You would simply send the Wolfen warriors to their deaths without rescuing the princess." He sighed. "I saw them; they will be waiting for us to come. And as the portal opening is small, it will force us to go through a few at a time. We'd be picked off. It would be a massacre."

Grimvaldr balled his fists, shaking for a moment, before he threw back his head, letting out a roar to the roof that finished in a howl.

After a few more seconds, he dropped his head. "Then what can we do?" He turned slowly to Arn.

Arn put his hand on the boy's shoulder. "The problem we have is the same one they have. They cannot come through quickly. So we should station bow and arrow, and spear throwers at the ready, to guard the opening. No one and nothing should be allowed to come through."

"That will seal it off," Vidarr replied. "But it would be sealed off in both directions. How will that get Princess Eilif back?"

"There is a way." A plan began to form in Arn's mind. "We need a distraction. Something to keep the world of men focused on the portal, so that they mass their warriors there." He turned to Vidarr. "While I take a small team of the Wolfen elite in behind them."

"The device." The ancient Wolfen smiled.

Arn nodded. "But first, I need to know where and when to go. And our prisoner will tell us, or he will find himself food for the acid worms."

CHAPTER 10

Borashev stood outside the pristine white cell and stared in at the being that had folded itself into a corner. He could see it staring back at him with eyes that were such a pale ice-blue they seemed almost luminous.

He momentarily switched off the cells light. As he suspected, the eyes physically glowed. He knew wolves had special reflective lenses in the back of their eyes for capturing and reflecting light. *Magnificent*, he thought.

His eyes traveled over its form – it was clearly female and athletic. It was hard to judge her height as she was crouching in the corner, but he guessed she was tall, maybe six feet, easily.

"Can you understand me?" he asked in Russian.

"Can you understand me?" he asked again in English.

The wolf-girl just continued to stare.

He sighed. "You are the most amazing thing I've ever seen." His mouth turned down momentarily. "Sorry about your friends. But remember, they attacked us first. Well, some of them." He looked about the small, empty cell she was in. "And I'm sorry about this."

The door opened and Gorbunov entered, then held it open for the Russian president. Petrov didn't even acknowledge Borashev. He went straight to the cell and stared in at the creature for many long minutes.

"A world where these creatures are the leaders. What an amazing place." Petrov turned. "Make it stand so I can see it. All of it."

Gorbunov and Borashev glanced at each other.

"It might be dangerous, sir," Borashev warned.

Petrov turned, his expression like stone. "Then send in two guards." He went to turn back but paused. "But no guns. I don't want it *damaged*."

"Yes, sir." Gorbunov relayed the message to have guards brought in.

Petrov stepped closer to the bars. "Has it spoken?"

"No, sir, not a word," Gorbunov replied. "We're not sure what language it uses. Our linguist is on her way now."

The door opened again and two guards came in. They were both dressed in white as if they worked in an asylum, and while both held a hard baton, one of them also carried a taser and the other a leash.

Petrov turned to them. "Make her stand up. Do not hurt her if you can avoid it."

The guards nodded and Gorbunov unlocked the door, but held it closed for a moment as he spoke to them. "Do not underestimate her. She is very strong."

One of the guards nodded once and the other smirked and gripped his baton a little tighter.

Gorbunov pulled the door open, and the men went in quickly. The being emitted a low growl as the two men came at her from either side, batons held out in front of them.

"Come, *devushka*. No trouble, please." The man with the leash widened the noose end and held it out.

The being never moved, but her eyes were on them, moving from one to the other.

The man with the leash leaned forward, intending to drop it over the top of her head and snout and then work it down around her neck. But as his hand lowered, the silver-furred being's clawed hand shot out, gripping his wrist, and then the other hand came up to grab his shirtfront. In the split seconds that followed, everything seemed to happen in a blur – the wolf-girl pulled him close and lunged at his neck, gripping his soft throat between long white canine teeth.

The man screamed, and the man with the taser reacted quickly. Before his colleague's throat could be torn out, he discharged his taser. The shock was a loud crackling *zap* in the air. And the wolf-being fell back to shudder spasmodically in the corner.

The released man staggered away, gripping his throat as blood pulsed between his fingers. He screamed as he tried to escape, skidding in his own blood.

"*D'yavol!*" the other man screamed, and he lunged forward with his taser, continuing to depress the unit until it was fully discharged.

The wolf-being convulsed on the ground and finally lay still. The smell of ozone and burned hair drifted out to the group watching.

Borashev pulled the wounded man from the cell and placed a cloth over the pumping wound. Gorbunov called for a medic and Petrov just stared impassively.

"Hold it up," the Russian president said stonily to the remaining guard.

The man with the taser roughly grabbed the creature by the leather shoulder straps of the tunic dress she wore. He grunted as he tried to lift her.

"Heavy," he groaned.

Petrov turned to Gorbunov. "Go in and help him."

"Me?" Gorbunov's eyes widened.

"*Now,*" Petrov shouted. "Hold its head up, quickly, before it wakes."

It took a few minutes, but they finally managed to get the being upright, and Gorbunov held its head up and facing forward.

"What an unbelievable creature." Petrov nodded. "And much bigger than I expected. Open its tunic." He ordered.

The guard unbuckled the female's top and let it hang open.

It was also the first time that Borashev had seen the full form of the female creature. She had an athletic, human female physique with two full human-like breasts, and an hourglass shape. But there were also the remnants of four more tiny nipples down lower.

Her body's muscularity was that of an athlete and there were slightly backward-curving legs from the knee down, but by the shape of the boots, human feet.

"That's a female of the species." Borashev said.

"Obviously." Petrov replied.

Borashev continued to tend to the man's neck wound while watching the creature. "She is about six feet tall. Some of the males are around seven feet, and the one that attacked us as we were returning was of monstrous proportions – perhaps eight feet and five or six hundred pounds."

Gorbunov reached forward to push the wolf-thing's lips up, displaying the dagger-like canine teeth.

"Formidable." Petrov nodded. "But made of flesh and blood."

"They tried to rescue her. They may try again in greater numbers," Gorbunov said.

"We'll guard the portal. I want all the men armed with armor-piercing rounds. And set up a few fifty-cal machine guns. Anything that comes through that portal looking for trouble will get a taste of our own metal teeth."

Petrov stepped back as a medic entered to tend to the wounded man. Gorbunov also stepped from the cell, and the guard lowered the unconscious being back onto its pile of blankets in the corner.

"When the linguist arrives, I want her to begin work immediately," Petrov ordered. "I want to know everything about these creatures and their world." He turned to smile grimly. "They have no idea what's coming."

***

Katerina – Kat to her friends – Popova, walked along in front of the cage bars, then turned and paced back the other way.

The female creature was sitting again. She was as still as stone, but her eyes followed Kat's every movement.

Katerina stopped and stared back into her radiant eyes. They were the most magnetic blue she had ever seen, and so pale they were like twin lights shining at her.

She lifted a hand. "Hello," she said softly.

In her pocket she held a few treats, like those you would feed your dog, and she turned to the guard.

"Open the door."

The guard shook his head. "No. I cannot—"

"Open it. I have full authority from the president himself." She turned away. "Besides, your job is to keep the creature safe and alive, not me."

The guard seemed to think on it for a while before reaching for his keys. "It's your funeral."

He unlocked the door and stood back, but in his hand he held a taser ready.

Katerina stepped into the cage and spoke over her shoulder. "Shut the door."

She heard the door clank behind her.

She had no real idea or strategy for what she was doing. She was a linguist, not a biologist. But she believed this was no animal. It wore human-like clothing, and she could tell there was a fierce spark of deep intelligence behind its eyes.

"I have no weapons." She held up her hands, splaying her fingers. "I'm taking a chance here. So please don't rip my throat out."

She walked a few paces closer until she could hear the low growl coming from the creature.

"Okay, I get it, that's far enough for now." She drew in a breath and sat cross-legged before it. She touched her chest. "My name is Katerina. *Kat-er-ina*," she repeated.

She waited for a full minute but got no response.

She repeated the process.

After another minute of silence she reached for one of the treats and held it out.

There was no movement toward it, just a flick of the eyes down to it, and then Katerina was sure she heard a snort of derision.

Katerina lowered her arm. "Yeah, you're right." She half-smiled. "Probably insulting."

The creature sat with her forearms on her pulled-up knees and lowered her head to them. She closed her eyes.

"I'm sorry this happened to you," Katerina said softly. "But if we can speak, if *you* can speak, maybe we can make things easier for you. What do you say?"

She waited. And waited.

Katerina sat in the small cell for hours, sometimes doing nothing but examining the exotic creature – the shape of her face, her ears. The color of her fur, and the fine workmanship of the clothing.

Katerina sighed. "You're amazing. Where did you come from? I mean, how did you come to be? Do you know?"

The guard who had tasered the creature came to the bars. "Mr. Gorbunov wants a progress report."

A low growl emanated from the being, and Katerina turned to see that she had lifted her head a fraction and focused her twin laser eyes on the man.

"You remember him, don't you." She turned to the guard. "Fuck off," she yelled.

The guard glared.

"I said fuck off, or I'll call the president and tell him you're impeding my progress. You'll be walking guard duty in Siberia by morning."

The guard glared for a second longer before cursing under his breath and stalking away.

Katerina turned back. "I don't like him either."

The creature's eyes slid to her, and Katerina smiled and shrugged. After another moment she turned away.

And then . . .

"Eilif."

Katerina spun back. "What?"

The creature stared, and then after a few seconds put a hand against her chest and tapped. "Eilif."

"Eilif," Katerina repeated. "A beautiful name." She touched her own chest again. "Katerina." And then pointed at Eilif. "Eilif."

"Katerina," Eilif repeated.

Eilif looked around. "Is this the land of the Ancients?"

The language was English.

Katerina's mouth dropped open. "You speak English?" she replied in the same tongue. "That's amazing."

Eilif shrugged. "I only speak a little. I was taught by my mate."

"What is your mother tongue?" Katerina asked.

"Valkeryn," Eilif replied, and then proceeded to switch to that language. "It is the language of my kin and kingdom."

"That's Norse, but old." Katerina was familiar with many languages, and ancient Norse was one of them.

"I'm please to meet you, Eilif." Katerina smiled broadly, feeling ecstatic.

At hearing the dialogue, the guard reappeared to glance in the cell.

Eilif's eyes went to him and narrowed. "I will see him dead before I leave." She growled at him. And then continued, "Release me."

"He was just following orders. He didn't know you were an intelligent being," Katerina replied. "And it is not up to me to release you."

"Then what good are you to me?" The wolf-woman's eyes were unblinking. "You think I am an animal." Eilif straightened and made a small sound of disdain in her throat. "I am Princess Eilif of the Wolfen kingdom of Valkeryn, the mightiest kingdom in the world."

Katerina nodded. "I'm sorry you are—"

"*I do not seek your pity.*" Her eyes grew flint-hard. "My people will come for me. My Arnodrr will come for me. He is the mightiest king's champion that ever was." She smiled darkly. "And you have no idea what *Helheim* he will bring with him."

"I know you are angry, Eilif. And you have a right to be. But for now you must stay. Besides, if we released you, what would you do? You are stuck here for a while."

Eilif's pale eyes blazed like cold fire. "You think we do not know about the time portals?"

Katerina sat for a moment and tried to process what she had just been told.

"You, ah, know about the portals?" she asked. "How do—"

"Your man-kind has come before," Eilif cut across her. "Some good. Some not good. The not-good ones were all killed quickly." The Wolfen's mouth curved a little. "My world does not seem to agree with your kind, the humans."

"That's how you know English. That's who came to your world before," Katerina said.

"Arnodrr Sigarr warned us about you." Eilif stared. "What is it you want from me, *Kat-er-ina*?"

Katerina put her hands together. "I need to know more about you. About your kingdom, and your world. Everything."

Eilif's smile was as cold as steel. "I am a warrior princess. I fought a long war against the Panterran and Lygon hordes, and I know the ways of war." Her eyes blazed. "I know why you want this information. You wish to probe for weaknesses . . . before you attack us."

Katerina felt naked, exposed. This was probably exactly why the Russian president wanted to know the information, she guessed. The president had never displayed much scientific curiosity, but he *did* have an expansionist mindset.

Eilif smiled. "You seem like one of the nice humans." The Wolfen got to her feet, and Katerina followed suit.

At six feet tall, the Wolfen female looked down on the human woman.

Eilif stepped closer.

The guard reappeared and pointed his taser. "Stay back."

Eilif ignored him. "Don't be here when they come for me, *Kat-er-ina*. I promise, things will get . . . *bloody*."

Katerina nodded. "I think we've covered enough for one day." She went to turn away, then paused. "What food can I bring you?"

Eilif tilted her head. "Nothing. I won't be here long enough to eat it." She looked Katerina in the eye. "Remember what I said."

CHAPTER 11

Arn felt the tightness of the bandages over his body, but the wounds had not been too deep and the magnificent Wolfen physiology meant he healed rapidly. He had also been given some of Vidarr's secret potions, which were revolting and hard to keep down, but meant he'd be as good as new in a day.

But that didn't matter. Because every minute he waited, his mind conjured images of the abominable things her captors were doing to Eilif.

He was accompanied by Vidarr, Grimvaldr, and one of his warriors when he went to interrogate the prisoner. They reached the cell and stared in. Arn saw the man, a soldier, pale visibly and start to shake as the nearly eight-foot-tall, upright black Wolfen stood at the bars. Even though he was probably an elite Special Forces soldier, this was no doubt well outside his range of experience.

"English?" Arn asked.

The man shook his head. And then after a moment he croaked a single word. "*Ruski.*"

"Russian. I don't speak that." Arn straightened. He turned to Vidarr. "Give him one of the language stones."

Vidarr produced one of the small stones about the size of an acorn and extended his arm through the bars.

The man backed away.

Arn pointed at the stone and then to his mouth. "Swallow it."

The soldier shook his head.

Arn laughed grimly. "Okay, we'll do it the hard way."

He turned to the warrior who had accompanied them. "Make him swallow it. Just don't break him."

The Wolfen warrior took the stone and smiled bleakly. "Breaking is up to him. After all, they break so easily."

He opened the door to the cell and the man backed up so far, he looked like he was trying to merge with the wall. Then the soldier tried to dart past the huge creature, but the Wolfen shot out one long arm and grabbed the front of his armored vest. He pulled him closer, held the struggling man under one arm, and then used the other hand to pry his jaws open. He roughly shoved the stone in onto the back of the man's tongue and closed his mouth.

The human grunted, holding the stone there, until the Wolfen wrapped his fingers around the man's mouth and chin and then punched him in the stomach.

The man gulped, and swallowed, and down went the stone. The Wolfen then levered open his mouth to check.

"Done." He released the human.

Arn and Vidarr went and stood at the bars. Arn knew the effect of the language stones was almost instantaneous. It would stay in the man's system for up to forty-eight hours. More than enough time to question him.

Arn stared. "You're a long way from home, little human."

The man's eyes widened in recognition. "How . . .?"

"The language stone will give you the ability to understand us for a time," Arn replied.

"Uh, thank you for—" the man began.

"Don't thank me yet. There are many here who wish to tear you limb from limb, and then eat your flesh for what you have done to our Wolfen warrior brothers, and to our princess."

The man paled.

Arn stepped closer. "I will ask you some questions. You will answer them, or I guarantee you, we will eat you. *Alive.*" He bared his huge teeth. "Where did your men take the princess?"

The man just stared back.

Arn had the prison door opened and he stepped in. The effect of having the massive Wolfen looming over him broke any plans of resistance the man might have had.

"The *female?*" he stuttered.

Arn leaned forward and let his lips begin to curl back, exposing his dagger-like canines.

"*Please.*" The soldier held his hands up in front of his face. "They will take her to the basement of the facility. They've created a holding cell. The creature – ah – the princess will be there."

"Good." Arn held out one huge hand. "I know you have a tracker. Give it to me."

The man stared mutely again.

"No-*ooow*!" Arn's roar was so loud it caused the soldier to fall back.

He got to his feet and fumbled in his pocket for his ID locater. Arn took it and opened it. It showed the man's current location, and then using the buttons and arrows he found, he searched its history.

"Got it," Arn said.

The locator also showed the soldier's origination coordinates. Arn knew that by now they would have fortified the portal doorway. So, as per his plan, he needed to arrive behind it.

He handed the device to Vidarr. "It has the coordinates I need. Give me the writing implements."

Vidarr handed Arn something like a large stick and parchment. Arn took it to the soldier and handed it to him.

"One more task, and then we will release you."

"You'll release me?" the man asked incredulously.

"As soon as my princess is returned to me," Arn said.

He pointed at the paper. "Draw me a map of the facility, and how to get to the princess."

The man took it. "I've only seen it once."

Arn growled. "And I'm only going there once."

The soldier began to draw.

***

Arn paced, thinking through his plan.

Vidarr and Grimvaldr watched him. "What you are thinking of doing could send you straight to Valhalla, Arnodrr," Vidarr said. "They will be expecting a rescue attempt."

"They will," Arn agreed. "But they will be expecting a Wolfen attack on their portal. And we will appear behind it." He turned to the old Wolfen. "I will bring Princess Eilif back. I will not fail."

Vidarr smiled and nodded.

"Will you wait for the full moon and go as a man-kind?" Grimvaldr asked.

"No." Arn stopped pacing. "I go as a human when I need to talk. But I go as a Wolfen when I wish to make war."

Arn thought it through a little more. Vidarr was right; they would be waiting for him, and therefore the humans would have massed their defenses at the facility. As soon as his warriors were seen, the alarm would be raised. He needed to not just get in, but also get out alive, with Eilif.

He thought again about a diversion. Something to keep them focused on the portal.

"What do you need?" the boy king asked.

Arn turned to him. "There has been a small band of Lygon in the forests for a while. They hide from us, but I know where they are. Capture them, armor them, and then we will let them loose on the portal."

"And if they don't want to help us?" Grimvaldr asked.

"We have no time for negotiations. If they resist, kill one. If they still resist, kill them all. Then find another band of Lygon." Arn turned. "Tell them they can kill and eat everything they find in the man-kind world."

He rubbed his chin. "And I'll need the armory to make us heavy Wolfen steel armor. Plus shields. Wolfen can take bullet hits, but too many and we will go down."

Grimvaldr came and gripped Arn's forearm. "I will make

it so. Bring my sister back to me, and the princess back to her kingdom. Only you, my champion, can do it."

"I will, or I will die trying, Sire." Arn turned to Vidarr. "I leave tomorrow. Now I go to choose my warriors. They will be the strongest and most ferocious in the land."

Arn walked to the window and stared out over the forest. "I will bring a storm of blood to these humans, the likes of which they will never believe."

***

The Wolfen blacksmiths worked through the night, strengthening the already heavy Wolfen armor.

Arn chose his most trusted warriors whose skill and ferocity was unquestioned – he knew they would follow him to Helheim and back if he asked them.

Grimvaldr and Vidarr were there to see them off. The six huge warriors stood in the center of the room, wearing the special Wolfen armor with its snarling wolf helmets, and equipped with swords and axes. In addition, they each held six-and-a-half foot tall square shields, all with the crest of Valkeryn embossed into their front.

They were solid, heavy, and had been beaten and re-beaten a hundred times until they were near impenetrable. And they needed to be. Arn knew that if – when – they ran into the sort of munitions he was expecting, the shields would be the difference between survival and death, between success and defeat.

"Form up," Arn said.

The six Wolfen lined up in two rows and Arn stood at their front, facing them.

"We go to the land of man-kind, the Ancients. Though they are small and weak, do not underestimate their weapons, which are powerful." He gazed into each of their faces. "We will seek the princess, free her, and then leave immediately.

Then we will secure the portal so none may ever come through it again."

Arn drew his sword and raised it in the air. "For the princess, and for the mighty kingdom of Valkeryn."

The Wolfen roared their response and banged axes and swords against their heavy shields.

We're ready, Arn thought, and turned back to the front.

Vidarr handed him the device. "The coordinates are set. The device will collect all of you, and also envelope the princess on your return."

The boy king, Grimvaldr, strode forward and looked up at Arn. "Bring my sister home." He banged a fist on Arn's gleaming breastplate. "Strength of Odin to you, king's champion."

Vidarr bowed. "And the luck of Fenrir be with you, Arnodrr."

"Fenrir's luck." Arn smiled and attached the device to his belt. "*Your* luck, eternal Wolfen."

Vidarr half-smiled and stepped back.

Arn reached down to the device and placed his finger on the button. He drew in a deep breath and stared straight ahead.

"Visors," he said.

There was the clank of the heavy silver wolf visors as they closed over the Wolfen's faces.

Arn said a final prayer, and then pressed the button.

The seven huge Wolfen vanished.

CHAPTER 12

Albert Harper collated the data feeds from several geological satellites orbiting the planet.

The satellites' primary objective was to look below the Earth's crust and find deposits of various valuable minerals. But they could also be used to identify "hot spots" – areas where there was ground movement going on. Even minor vibrations left a signature. But as yet he couldn't find the emanation point for the global tremors they'd been experiencing.

The tremors being felt all around the world at exactly the same time were getting bigger, and the time between them was diminishing. Now, instead of shaking the Earth's crust every few days, they were occurring hourly.

Harper knew what it meant. He'd seen it before, when the Tevatron collider's time portal hole was growing. Its powerful magnetic force destabilized the planet.

We thought we'd headed off a dark fate, but we were wrong, we only delayed it, he thought. *Maybe it was meant to be.*

He knew the Valkeryn kingdom had arisen because our world was upended. Some creatures survived, new ones evolved, and many others died out.

He remembered Rebecca and Edward telling him about the revolting things in the darkness that looked like a cross between hairless pigs and apes – that's what was in store for the humans who took to the deep caves to survive the years of radiation.

He sat back and sighed.

And then the geological satellites got a hit.

They had found a hot spot in Russia, and it was exactly where Harper should have expected – deep beneath their particle collider underneath Protvino, near Moscow.

"There you are," he whispered. "You've got a secret hidden down there, haven't you, my friends?"

He sat in silence, wondering what to do, what he *could* do. First and foremost, he needed to inform General Ted Langstrom. The man had acted quickly and decisively last time, and his parting words to Harper had been to stay vigilant and keep him informed. So that would be Harper's first action.

He looked up the general's contact details and got through to his secretary. Then after a moment he was put through.

"Harper," came the rough voice.

"Sir." Harper drew in a quick breath. "We have a problem."

"Go on," the man said.

Harper spent the next few minutes bringing the general up to speed with what he knew and what he thought. And the man didn't like it.

"Jesus Christ, are we doing this again?" There was a sound like a low growl. "I need to take this to the commander-in-chief. But I have to tell you, if you've got any contacts in that weird little science world of yours, I suggest you use them. Because right now, if what you're telling me is true, then this is an extinction event and my recommendation to the president will be to nuke the site – threat of war be damned."

"What? No. I don't think that's a good option, General," said Harper hurriedly. "How is—"

"To stop the world being ripped apart? We almost lost it once before. It's the *only* option," the man shot back. "What do you recommend?"

"I'll try to talk to the Russians. Make them see what could happen." Harper talked fast. "You said to use my contacts, right?"

"Yes, but I know the Russians, and they'll never believe you. Do your best, but you've got twenty-four hours. Keep me updated on the intel. But they either close it down, or we cauterize the entire site for good. We act now, apologize later. Understood?"

"Yes." Harper sat back.

"Keep me informed." The man rang off.

Harper put the phone down and ran a hand up through his wild hair. There were over 30,000 particle colliders in the world, and he just didn't have the contacts in ninety-nine percent of them.

He doubted he'd have any pull with the decision-makers or politicians. But he did know a few people in the Russian physics world. And there was one name in particular that sprang to mind.

He put a call through to Dr. Uri Gorbunov. He remembered meeting the man about five years ago at a conference in Switzerland, and Gorbunov talking about how he had finally got funding for his collider in Russia.

It would be Gorbunov himself who had generated the particle collision, or if not, he would certainly know who had. But Harper would have to play it carefully. After all, if someone rang up and said: *Hi, how are you? And oh, by the way, can you please blow up your facilities before you destroy the world?* it might not elicit the desired response.

Harper looked in his ancient card file and found the man's number. He crossed his fingers and called. The phone was answered on the fourth ring.

"*Da?*"

"Dr. Gorbunov, it's Dr. Albert Harper calling from the United States." He quickly licked his lips. "We met about five years ago in Lucerne, Switzerland."

There was silence on the phone for several long moments.

Harper broke it. "I need to talk to you about something, if you have a few minutes. It's extremely important."

Silence again. And then, "I'm sorry, Dr. Harper, but we have much going on right now." There was tension in Gorbunov's voice.

Harper knew he was losing him already.

"My call is concerning my particle acceleration project – and yours." There was more silence. "And the portal we opened. A time portal. Like the one you've opened . . . right?"

"What did you say?" Gorbunov said warily.

Got him. Harper exhaled. "The portal we opened in the acceleration chamber. Like the one you've opened in yours, by super-accelerating particles using a lab-grown red diamond."

"How do you know any of this?" the man said softly.

"I know because we did the same thing. We opened a portal to another time far in the future. Filled with strange and dangerous lifeforms," he said quickly. "But that's not the main danger, Dr. Gorbunov. The main danger is that you are destabilizing the planet's crust. The earthquakes have begun again."

"I don't believe you," Gorbunov replied. "You just want us to stop our project."

"Sir . . ." Harper began. "For that world you saw through the portal to exist, ours must be destroyed." He felt his patience and time running out.

Gorbunov scoffed. "You are making this up. Goodbye, Dr.—"

Harper gripped the phone. "Your portal is getting bigger, isn't it?"

He waited, but even in the silence, he could almost hear the gears of the man's mind working.

"And there's a breeze. It's beginning to draw things toward the portal. Soon it will draw everything *into* the portal. Everything. Eventually, that will include the entire planet's surface. What that doesn't kill, the radiation does, or causes mutations." He sat back. "It's why we destroyed ours."

"There is minimal radiation from the anomaly," Gorbunov replied stiffly.

"I don't know exactly where the radiation comes from. But there is enough to create mutations." Harper squeezed the phone so hard his hand began to ache. "If you've been through the portal, you've already seen them, haven't you?"

"I have . . . noticed these things," Gorbunov said quietly.

"You still have time. Switch off the acceleration beam, destroy the red diamond. I beg you. The world is at stake."

He waited for several minutes in the brooding silence.

"Doctor?" Harper finally asked.

"Thank you," Gorbunov said slowly. "You have given me many things to think on. But we will be fine, as we have minimal radiation. We will talk soon." Gorbunov's voice was robotic.

Harper sat forward. "Dr. Gorbunov, you must understand that the alternative is—"

The line went dead.

Harper sat back and closed his eyes. Were they really not experiencing radiation, or was the man lying? If the radiation wasn't coming from the portal, then where did it come from? he wondered.

He thought about his options. The portal needed to be closed, no question. And if the Russians didn't do it, could they somehow close it before taking the drastic step of nuking it? Maybe a military strike from the air was the way to do it.

He put his head in his hands. That was stupid thinking. After all, Russia had more nuclear weapons than they did. They would simply swap one end-of-world scenario for another.

He sat in his office alone, trying to think of any other options. But after a while he gave up, slumped, and exhaled loudly. "What will be will be."

Albert Harper reached into his bottom drawer for a half-bottle of whisky and a plastic cup. He poured a triple shot and raised it in the air.

"To Valkeryn."

He downed it in one.

***

Gorbunov sat staring at the phone. He remembered Dr. Albert Harper. The man was quite brilliant, and not prone to making up fantasy stories.

And what he had told him resonated – the Earth tremors *were* getting worse. And the portal *was* growing, plus he'd seen small objects now be pulled toward it. Something was definitely happening.

But what could he do? He wasn't ready to close off the project just yet. And anyway, what would President Petrov do if he did? After all, their leader was taking a personal interest in what they were doing.

Petrov would want a plausible reason for closing the portal, and if he didn't get one, then Gorbunov would be replaced, and the project would simply carry on without him. And if he tried to shut it down without Petrov's blessing, he could forget about losing his job. He'd end up in a work camp for the rest of his days – or simply dead.

The thing was, Gorbunov believed Harper. There was something very wrong with the portal. It was growing, and getting more powerful. He had wondered about this, and worried about it. Now Harper had told him exactly what would occur. Gorbunov had a feeling deep in his gut that something very bad was about to happen. He stood.

For the sake of the world, I will close it, he thought.

Just then the klaxon alarm suddenly began to wail so loudly that it made him start with fright. There was only one explanation.

"The portal," he said, and headed for the door.

CHAPTER 13

Gorbunov sprinted down to the portal chamber, burst in through the heavy door and skidded to a stop. He tried to see over the twenty men stationed there with Kalashnikovs loaded with tungsten-tipped rounds, RPGs, and also a single DShK fifty-caliber heavy machine gun.

He pushed his way through the crowd and was relieved that there seemed to have been no intrusion. But then he looked at the size and shape of the portal.

"Oh no."

It was significantly larger now, and the breeze he had barely noticed earlier was now a wind causing a low shriek in the collision tunnel, which made him think of being on the underground rail line as a train approached the platform.

He noticed too that small things, debris, even buttons and badges on the soldiers' unforms were being dragged toward the hole.

Then he noticed something else – the men weren't watching him; instead they were all focused on the hole suspended in the air. Some of them were perspiring heavily.

"What triggered the alarm?" Gorbunov yelled.

The man closest to him didn't turn but some pointed at the portal.

Gorbunov turned – something was moving on the other side. Something big. And whatever that something was, the men had seen it and were nervous about it.

And then that something came through.

Three creatures that almost grazed the ceiling entered. All were about nine to ten feet tall and wore plates of armor that must have been two inches thick over heavily muscled bodies, which were covered in a fur that rippled with orange and black stripes.

They were huge and frightening, and on their ferocious heads were large steel helmets that covered snarling faces with mouths full of yellow, tusk-like teeth.

Gorbunov felt his legs turn to jelly as he backed up. Then came a roar so loud and terrifying it froze him to the spot. He felt warmth spreading down the front of his trousers.

And during the few seconds in which everyone was frozen with fear, the creatures attacked.

Gorbunov was forced up against the wall as bullets flew, grenades exploded, and he was deafened by the ear-splitting *thump-thump-thump* of the heavy machine gun that left flaming streaks like tracer fire in the air.

But even with all their firepower, the huge beasts were extremely fast for their size, and with swords and axes that had heads half as long as a human being, they were devastating in their ferocity and power.

They swept their weapons back and forth like scythes or brought them down like a thunderclap that actually shook the walls. Men were crushed or cut into pieces and body parts flew around the acceleration chamber, splashing everyone and everything in a warm rain of blood.

Finally an RPG strike to an unprotected area on one of the beasts blew a huge hole in it and it went down. Another finally succumbed after being shot perhaps a dozen times in the neck and face.

The last of them grabbed up one of its fallen kin's dropped axes, and now with two, clanged them together, preparing for its last stand.

Hundreds of bullets of all calibers punched into it, making heavy clanking sounds against the thick armor plating that would have been more at home on a tank. But just as Gorbunov thought they were about to take the creature down, another alarm sounded.

This one confused the scientist, and it was only after a few seconds that he remembered what and where it was from – the cells where they were keeping their prisoner locked up.

It suddenly dawned on him – these weren't the intelligent beings that Borashev had told him about, and nothing like their prisoner. These were just mindless ogres.

And this wasn't just an attack. It was a diversion.

***

Just outside the doors leading to Eilif's prison cell, the air in the empty hallway began to crackle with what looked like lightning. Then a blinding light exploded outward, singeing the paintwork, but it was over almost instantly, and after the searing flash had dissipated, something was left behind.

The seven huge Wolfen in their full armor, shields and snarling wolf's head helmets were still in their lines. In his crested silver battle armor, Arn was in front.

Arn had memorized the map the Russian soldier had given him, and he turned now to see the double doorway to the cells exactly where it was supposed to be. Through it he expected to find an antechamber containing several guards – their human prisoner back in Valkeryn had had no idea how many, and could only guess at it being between two and ten. Those soldiers could be regular army, raw recruits on babysitting duty, or they could be Special Force veterans. Either way, the Wolfen needed to go through them to get to Eilif's cell.

"Ready yourselves," Arn said. He lifted his heavy shield. "There will be blood this day."

He knew that just opening the door was not an option. The best weapon they had was surprise – so Arn lowered his shoulder and charged at the double doors. At the last second he lifted the heavy shield as he made contact, exploding both doors from their hinges and splintering much of the wood.

He continued in until he was near the center of the room beyond, with his Wolfen pack close behind him. Inside they quickly found that luck was against them, as there were eight guards, professionals, and all reacted quickly.

They lifted their rifles and began to free-fire.

"*Form up!*" Arn yelled, and the Wolfen drew together, bringing their huge shields down in front and creating a single Wolfen steel barrier between them and the gunfire.

The bullets smashed into their shields and Arn counted down.

"Draw swords. Pick a target." And then, "*Attack.*"

The Wolfen broke apart and Arn and the pack of seven-foot-tall beasts in full armor smashed into the guards. Their bullets didn't have a chance up close, and their aim was thrown off by the speed and ferocity of the attack.

In seconds it was over, and Arn looked about at the slain men. A waste of brave soldiers just doing their job, he thought.

Overhead an alarm sounded, and he knew they had mere minutes now to accomplish their task. He headed for the smaller door at the other end of the room, fast, and lowered his shoulder again, bursting it open.

He took in everything beyond within a few seconds – the cell, outside of which was a single human female whose eyes were almost bulging from their sockets.

There was also a single guard who backed up against the wall. In one hand was a gun, and in the other a taser. Hanging at his belt was a leather leash.

"*Behold*, Arnodrr Sigarr, the king's champion of champions." Relief washed through Arn at the sound of his beloved Eilif's voice calling from behind the bars.

The guard pointed his weapon at Arn, but then, hearing Eilif, moved closer to point it at her. But he kept his eyes on Arn and the Wolfen. A fatal mistake.

"Stay back," he said.

Eilif's hand shot out and grabbed the guard's wrist, jerking it upward. The gun discharged harmlessly into the ceiling, and her other hand reached to grip his throat. She pulled him closer to the bars.

"I said I would kill you." She compressed her clawed hand and ripped the man's throat out in a geyser of blood. "And I have." She pushed his gurgling body away.

Arn then turned to the small woman standing outside the bars.

"Don't kill her, my lord," Eilif said.

Arn looked down at the shivering woman. "Open the door," he ordered.

With a shaking hand the woman took a bunch of keys from the dead guard's body. Then she inserted one, and unlocked the cage door.

Arn's Wolfen had fanned out, two in the room, and more outside to keep watch.

As soon as the door opened Eilif threw herself into Arn's arms and he held her tight, hugging her close to him.

He lifted his snarling wolf helmet visor.

"I knew you'd come," she said up into his face.

"I would cross time and space itself to find you." He kissed her hard.

Eilif pulled back. "We must go, quickly."

"Hurry," the woman said behind them. "They'll be coming."

"My lord." One of the Wolfen stuck his head into the room. "The man-kind are approaching."

Arn led them out to the larger room beyond. He needed a space big enough for the device's field to capture them all to transport them to Valkeryn.

As they all came out, from the end of the hallway a door burst open and in came the soldiers carrying heavier weapons.

On seeing the pack of huge, armored Wolfen, they all stopped and stared for a moment. Arn recognized their heavy weapons and knew his warriors couldn't stand against them for long.

"Form up," he yelled. "Plant shields."

The huge Wolfen lifted their shields high and then swung them down with all their might, resulting in a thundering explosion of concrete. The shields were now wedged into the floor in a locked line of Wolfen steel.

From the rear of the group of soldiers a man in a white coat stared with round eyes.

"Don't shoot," Katerina yelled from behind the still open doorway.

They did anyway.

Arn pulled Eilif down behind the shield wall as the bullets clanged into them. Then the heavier-caliber weapons began, and a few holes were punched right through the steel.

A few moments later Arn had calibrated the device and turned to Eilif. "Ready?"

"Let's go home." She laid her hand on his forearm.

She then turned to Katerina just as a bullet punched into the woman's chest, blowing her backwards through the doorway.

Eilif made a disgusted sound in her throat. "These people do not deserve to be rulers of their land." She turned away.

"They won't be for much longer." Arn pressed the device, and around the group the air shimmered. Then the Wolfen became transparent, and vanished.

* * *

Gorbunov saw the flash of light behind the shields.

"Cease fire, cease fire . . ." he yelled, until finally the guns fell silent.

After a moment he ordered the soldiers forward. They approached cautiously, and the first of them rounded the line of heavy iron plates.

He lowered his weapon and turned in confusion. "They're gone."

Gorbunov came and stood staring at the empty spot in the corridor for several minutes.

The captain of the soldiers stood next to him. "We should go through the portal; go after them."

Gorbunov shook his head. "They'll be waiting for you. Perhaps thousands of them," he said. "I'll speak to the president. See what he wants us to do."

From behind them there came a screaming sound like a thousand banshees howling at once.

The captain turned about, frowning. "What the hell is that? Something else to contend with?"

The scientist turned to look down the corridor. The odd sound was coming from the acceleration chamber, and he knew exactly what it was. Just like the American physicist, Harper, had warned: the portal was growing again, and the once gentle breeze had now turned to a storm.

Soon it would begin to swallow things.

And then swallow larger things as the storm became a hurricane.

And then it would swallow everything.

***

Professor Albert Harper stood as he held the phone to his ear. General Langstrom had been given presidential authorization to launch a single nuclear warhead at the Russian particle collider site. It would be done from a special site in the Middle East so the launch origination would be obscured.

Langstrom thought the Russians would know who had sent it, but there might be enough chaff in the air to stop them from counter-attacking.

Harper stared straight ahead, his face like stone, and he stayed on the line as the countdown to the detonation occurred.

Time to target zone is, five, four, three, two – and then, simply – *target destroyed.*

There was no sound, no cheering, just a large room somewhere where military technicians were going about their jobs as if they were a bunch of accountants doing people's tax.

And then came the words he had dreaded.

Russians are launching countermeasures.

Harper slowly sat down.

Chinese are launching submarine-based missiles. North Koreans are launching ICBMs. Iran has launched.

"God save us," Harper said softly.

Israel is counter-striking. Germany, United Kingdom, are counter-striking. France is launching.

Harper felt like he wanted to vomit.

United States Iron Dome ready. United States is responding with full arsenal at predesignated global targets.

And then, Langstrom came back on the line.

"Dr. Harper, I suggest you get to a shelter. Pray for yourself and your loved ones. Goodbye, sir."

The line dropped out, and Harper held the phone in his hand and stared at it as though it were a dead animal.

There was a pounding at his door, and he roused himself enough to open it. Rebecca and Edward were standing on the other side with slack faces the color of ash.

Becky spoke through clamped teeth. "Albert, the earthquakes. They're getting worse."

No sooner had she said it than the building started to shake again, and Harper grabbed the edges of the doorframe as dust rained down on them.

Becky screamed as a roof panel fell into the room. The ground shook beneath their feet for several more minutes.

"This is worse than before." She obviously saw his bloodless face. "I thought you spoke to—"

"These are not earthquakes." Albert shook his head. "The Russians wouldn't shut it down. They wouldn't even listen. So we destroyed it with a nuclear missile. We started a war. The last war." He felt tears on his cheeks. "It doesn't matter anymore. Nothing matters anymore."

From somewhere, from everywhere, air raid sirens began to blare. Then a mechanical voice started to intone disaster protocols for a nuclear attack, earthquake, or some other threat to human life en masse.

"What is it?" Becky screamed, hugging herself.

"The end of the world." Harper gave a crooked smile. "At least, the end of our world."

Attention. This is not a drill. Take to the shelters, take to the shelters. This is not a drill. Take to the shelters. The message continued over and over.

"Oh God, no. Not that." There was real horror in Edward's voice. "We take to the shelters, we won't be coming out."

Rebecca began to cry. "Those horrible things in the dark caves. They're us. That's what we'll become."

Harper swallowed in a dry mouth and noticed his computer screen beginning to flash.

"Oh no." A radiation warning was beginning to show.

"The radiation is already starting to exceed normal levels."

From somewhere there was a deep, earth-shaking boom. Followed by another.

"We need to go." Harper lifted his coat. He looked back at Becky and Edward. "I guess it was inevitable. The future was already written, and nothing we did was every going to change it."

Albert Harper went to the door and held it open. Becky and Edward went through.

The scientist paused to look back at the image Rebecca had given him that he had pinned to the wall. It was a drawing she had done when she first returned from Valkeryn over ten years ago.

It was a picture of Arn as a Wolfen warrior sitting on a horse, and beside him was a smaller female Wolfen in shining armor.

He smiled at the image. "I hope you find peace at last. And your world turns out better than ours."

He pulled the door shut and headed for the deep shelter.

EPILOGUE

Illinois, high in the Pulaski Woods

Up on the mountainside, at the mouth of the cave, Big Fen and the first of the Guardians, the genetically modified wolf-dogs, watched as on the horizon the orange bloom of the mushroom clouds rose into the upper atmosphere.

Already they could feel the tingle of radiation, but it would not affect them as their cells had been bred to withstand its damaging effects. Many of the other animals and people would not be so lucky – and those that weren't incinerated, or died from their cell walls exploding, would be modified through mutation. Some would become useless genetic dead ends, while others would morph into all manner of strange beasts.

Big Fen took a mate, Ingrid, and over the years he and his clan brought forth dozens, and then hundreds of offspring. The Guardians multiplied profusely in a land without human beings.

Big Fen taught them all he had learned from the books of mankind, with his favorites being those on Viking lore.

Even without humans, the land had its dangers, as some of the new animals grew to huge sizes. And many were carnivores. So he taught his kin to hunt, to forge steel and make weapons to fight. He taught them a common language, and also gave them a code of honor. And finally he gave them a name: Wolfen. Their kingdom would be called Valkeryn.

But as the decades passed, he noticed something else. His brothers and sisters grew old and died, but he did not. He watched his mate, Ingrid, and his friends, pass over to Valhalla. But he remained.

Years passed. Decades. Centuries. And then so much more time that time itself became meaningless to him. But he didn't mind, as he had so much more to do.

He watched the history of the world unfold before his ancient eyes – he was there when the last of the human beings hiding below ground split into two tribes – one that launched great sky ships from below and left the ravaged world, and the other that crawled deeper to revert back into primitive, soulless things that hid and hunted in the darkness.

Big Fen also watched as the land reshaped itself. He watched as the moon came closer, and he could see where it had been mined and then had broken into pieces. He also witnessed all manner of strange beasts rise around them. Some had intelligence and good in their hearts. And others had wickedness – the worst of those being the evil Panterran, and the monstrous Lygon. Eventually these waged a terrible war on the Valkeryn kingdom. His only regret was having let them loose in the great fire all those millennia ago.

He gathered all the information he could and established a great library. Then he hid more of the human beings' artifacts of science and wisdom in the deep labyrinths beneath the ground.

To protect his kin he set about raising and fortifying the kingdom of Valkeryn, and he took on a new name, Vidarr, which meant "the quiet god". His role would be teacher, librarian, and archivist.

He knew that human beings, the now legendary Ancients, would come back one day.

And he knew that among them would be one who would be their savior. He would be the bringer of victory. He would be the *Arnodrr Sigarr*. After all, it was a prophecy he remembered from his youth. A prophecy he created.

THE VALKERYN CHRONICLES

RETURN OF THE ANCIENTS: VALKERYN CHRONICLES 1

GREIG BECK

VALKERYN

Book I – *Return of the Ancients*

"Return of the Ancients" is the first of a three-part series and tells the story of a future world of great beauty and great horrors, and of two races who have fought a war for an eternity.

Arnold "Arn" Singer, an average teenager living in Illinois, is on a school science trip to watch the test firing of a new particle accelerator when he is caught up in an accident that propels him into an extraordinary new world. He finds he is the last human alive in a land populated with mysterious and blood-thirsty creatures. Some want him dead, while others see him as their only hope for survival – they have been waiting for the return of one of the mysterious and all-powerful "Ancients".

Arn has to survive in a hostile world and save his new friends, and also try to unravel the mystery of the disappearance of the human race, while the two mighty kingdoms prepare for a final war.

It is an epic tale of love, betrayal and war in a world both familiar and terrifying, the first book in an epic series of speculative fiction from bestselling author Greig Beck.

GREIG BECK

THE DARK LANDS

VALKERYN 2

Book II – *The Dark Lands*

The wolf lives inside us all.

Valkeryn has fallen, the great king is dead, and the Wolfen have scattered. The monstrous Lygon and Panterran now rule. Arnold "Arn" Singer, the youth from the past and perhaps the last human being alive on the planet, flees to the dark lands with the heir to the throne. He seeks answers to the missing Ancients – Arn's ancestors – mankind itself.

But back in his time the world continues to destabilize. The time distortion the mighty Tevatron collider created is growing larger and beginning to consume everything around it.

Colonel Marion Briggs leads a team of Special Operations soldiers into the distant future world, fully armed and with one order – bring back Arn or his body. But there are more dangers in this strange and beautiful world than anyone knew. More horrors dwell in the deep jungles, below the inland seas and deep below the earth. There are things that can change the shape of two worlds, tear at sanity, and stretch friendships and love to the limit.

The gateway portal must be closed, and Arn holds the key. Our world and its future are at stake.

www.ingramcontent.com/pod-product-compliance
Ingram Content Group UK Ltd.
Pitfield, Milton Keynes, MK11 3LW, UK
UKHW012036100725
6842UKWH00001B/87